THE THRILLVILLE PULP FICTION COLLECTION VOLUME ONE

A MERMAID DROWNS IN THE MIDNIGHT LOUNGE

PLUS! FREAKS THAT CARRY YOUR LUGGAGE UP TO THE ROOM

WILL VIHARO

DOUBLE LIFE

Cover art by Mike Fyles
mikefyles.co.uk
Design by Dyer Wilk

All persons in this book are fictitious and any resemblance that may seem to exist to actual persons, living or undead, is purely coincidental. This is a work of gonzo pulp madness and is brought to you by Evil Dr. Will and the fine freaks at Double Life Press. You're welcome.

First Printing

ISBN-13: 978-0692417256

Published by Double Life Press

www.doublelifepress.wordpress.com

Printed in the United States of America

CONTENTS

FOREWORD TO VOLUME ONE
by Craig T. McNeely

Will and I met because of a deranged, psychopathic, hypersexual dwarf. Actually, that came a little later. Let me start again.

I have said many times over that we are living in a Golden Age of Independent Publishing. Guys and gals are doing this book thing like almost no one has before. I say 'almost' because before them all there was Will Viharo.

I met Will because I had been looking for him. I didn't know it but I was. "No boundaries" has always been my literary philosophy (more like a war cry) ever since I started the not-so-little magazine *Dark Corners* with my wife Emily and our friend Steve. There really are so many good books and good writers, now more than ever. However, I was looking for the truly great ones -- the ones that defy genre and common sense. To do that, to make truly great works of art, you've gotta reach deep down and pull your guts out through your mouth and see what's there even though it's damn ugly and it hurts.

That's what I needed. That's what I got. Enter Will Viharo.

The things you'll be reading here and in other volumes of The Thrillville Pulp Fiction Collection are truly unlike anything you've ever read before or will ever read again, even when you read other things by Will himself. His bibliography belongs in a museum, a perfect distillation of pop culture filtered through the mind of a mad scientist. It's not in a museum, though, it's in your hands and your hearts and your minds and there it will live forever.

Onward Will Viharo and, as he would say, "Cheers."

INTRODUCTION TO VOLUME ONE
by Will Viharo

I began writing *A Mermaid Drowns in the Midnight Lounge* (after a dozen or so other novels, mostly unpublished) back in 1997, right around the time my first (and extremely brief) marriage collapsed, concurrent with the opening of the Parkway Speakeasy Theater in Oakland, CA. I completed about 35 pages and abruptly quit once I was hired by Speakeasy's owners to create, produce, program, and host my own weekly (Saturdays) midnight movie show, which I initially called "The Midnight Lounge," re-dubbed "Thrillville" when it moved to Thursday evenings back in 1999, with live bands and burlesque added to the film bills. The original idea was to concoct a public persona, which I called "Will the Thrill," that could locally promote my 1995 novel *Love Stories Are Too Violent For Me* (much later optioned for a film by Christian Slater), since the folks who founded Speakeasy Theaters had briefly dabbled in publishing with their startup company Wild Card Press which is now, like Speakeasy Theaters itself, long defunct. *Love Stories* was their first and only effort in this field, since The Parkway—the first movie theater in California to offer beer, wine and a full food menu as patrons reclined on sofas in front of the big screen—quickly became a local institution, and I became an integral part of its success, since shortly after the debut of The Midnight Lounge, I was hired as The Parkway's full time-programmer/publicist, and I left my fruitless fiction career behind forever. Or so I thought until Speakeasy's spectacular implosion in 2009, which abruptly ended my tenure as a film programmer/impresario, a fate to which I had reluctantly resigned myself. However, since I had a well established reputation as a fez-wearing B movie "lounge lizard" by that point, I did take my "cult movie cabaret" on the road around the Bay and beyond, including a monthly movie night at Forbidden Island Tiki Lounge in Alameda, CA, called "Forbidden Thrills" (now home of the original cocktail, the "Vic Valentine," named for my private eye protagonist.)

But I also returned to my first and only true love: writing fiction (though I'd never stopped producing freelance articles on pop culture). "Thrillville" morphed from being headquarters for a roving cult movie/burlesque show to a virtual promotional platform for my own pulp fiction. I relaunched my writing career by going back and completing *Mermaid*.

Soon after I resumed work on the book, our beloved male cat Bubba was suddenly diagnosed with terminal cancer. My agonizing sadness during this period permeates *Mermaid*. Bubba was only given two months to live, but he lasted for eight more. His death still haunts me, but his precious memory lives in the pages of this deeply personal novel. But there's much more to it than resonant grief.

What began as a relatively routine romantic crime drama somehow turned into a hallucinogenic cheap thrill ride, with copious amounts of gratuitous violence, extremely graphic (and kinky) sex, zombies, Elvis, gangsters, bikers, monster men and other denizens of retro-fringe cinema populating a multi-dimensional fever dream. It was the literary equivalent of all the movies I'd shown, combined with my many strange and dramatic real life experiences during (and before) The Parkway era.

My dark world's single bright spot was and always has been my marriage to Monica Cortes, by then locally known as my onstage lovely assistant, "The Tiki Goddess." We'd first met at my Midnight Lounge screening of *Jailhouse Rock* on May 31, 1997. We were wed in a Rat Pack/Elvis/mariachi theme ceremony at the Cal-Neva Resort Lodge in North Lake Tahoe (Sinatra's old joint) on May 31, 2001, followed by a honeymoon in Hawaii.

Shortly after Bubba passed away, on the same day my very first novel *Chumpy Walnut* was published via Lulu (now featured in Volume Three of this series), we adopted a wonderful male kitten, named Googie, who helped my mournful heart heal, along with our young and beautiful female cat, Tiki. Our home felt whole again, though Bubba's lingering presence will always be felt in our lives, even here in Seattle.

After a tumultuous, often traumatizing youth, my personal life was finally fulfilling. But my lifelong dream of becoming a successful novelist still eluded me.

I've had several "near misses" over the

decades, ever since completing *Chumpy Walnut* back in 1982, at age 19. I had a New York agent for many years, and celebrity editor Judith Regan expressed interest in my work, but nothing ever paid off or worked out. Given this disappointing history with the mainstream publishing world, along with the fact that *Mermaid* was so outlandish, surrealistic and extreme, therefore not easily pigeon-holed or immediately commercial, I decided to go the self-publishing route, via Lulu and Amazon. This meant I had to digitally retype all of my old manuscripts, which had been composed on a typewriter, except for *Mermaid.* The times they had a-changed, and so had I.

The original cover for that first edition of *Mermaid* was an image I found online, while searching for visual inspiration, by Canadian artist/photographer Mike Lewis. I contacted him and purchased the rights to the startlingly sensuous graphic, which ironically depicted the book's many bizarre elements, from *noir* to horror to eroticism. Basically, *Mermaid* was a sensuous nightmare, similar in some ways to the films of David Lynch, which provided only a small part of the inspiration. I dubbed it "neo-pulp fiction fantasia" since I wasn't sure how else to categorize it, at the time completely ignorant of the fact that "pulp fiction" was already a thriving rebooted genre and subculture in indie publishing circles. I was totally out of the loop, and truthfully, I still feel that way.

To make this ambitious indie project even more unique and special, I offered a companion

CD featuring an original "book soundtrack" I called *Music For a Drowning Mermaid.* This came about when a musician named Rafiq Gulamani—AKA "Actual Rafiq"—who appeared at a couple of my Thrillville road shows wrote an original instrumental track for me which he called "One Way Ticket To Thrillville," to use any way I chose. He had no idea that there was a story within the story of *Mermaid* that had that exact same title! Given this amazing bit of Kismet, and the fact his music just happened to capture the exact mood of the piece I was working on at the very time he gave it to me, I asked Rafiq if he'd compose a few more tracks to complement the novel. He obliged with three additional original instrumentals, all ethereally evocative in an appropriately Angelo Badalamenti sort of way, which I titled "Porno Noir," "Lunar Lounge Lizard," and "Elvis Zombie." Rafiq even designed the album cover! The Lulu-generated CD is no longer available, but you can find all four tracks for free on Soundcloud, highly recommended even if you haven't read the book, though they're magically matched.

Fortunately, I also knew a lot of great Bay Area artists including Rich Black, Rick Lucey, and Miles Goodrich who had created many of my Thrillville event posters, and graciously agreed to design covers for my novels, too. I'll discuss my other self-published books in the introductions to the remaining volumes, but I still consider *Mermaid* my finest achievement as an author. To me, it sums up my demented, delirious, dreamy inner world—"Thrillville"—perfectly.

And *Freaks That Carry Your Luggage Up to the Room* is actually the ideal companion piece. It was written while I was concurrently writing a much longer sci-fi novel called *It Came From Hangar 18*, which was commissioned by Scott Fulks, whom I met while working as a bouncer (and band booker) at Forbidden Island Tiki Lounge, post-Parkway. Scott is a brilliant amateur scientist and wanted to incorporate his original ideas and theories and complex formulas into a pulpy context, and after reading several of my novels, decided I was his man. He gave me a three page outline and I gave him back a 500 page epic since hey, he was paying by the word!

Meantime, I was still struggling to survive financially, I'd lost several close friends to untimely deaths within a brief time span, I was closing in on 50, and my future felt like a blank slate. Since a lot of these morose feelings surface when I'm writing, I needed an outlet, and *Hangar 18*, with all of its crazy monsters and wild sex, was not the proper context for my personal angst. *Freaks* became the side vessel for my darker thoughts, and the result is even more harrowing, disturbing and outrageous than *Mermaid*, basically distilling all the pornographic horrors from that work into a much shorter but more intense piece. I was so disturbed by it myself I almost didn't publish it. While working on it, it literally kept me awake some nights. Initially published with a fantastic cover by filmmaker/artist Christopher Sorrenti, who edited the original book trailer for "The Thrillville Pulp Collection," and in fact accompanied by another animated book trailer created by Oakland filmmaker Vincent Cortez, it's turned out to be one of my most well-received works, oddly beloved by complete strangers. Go figure.

The admittedly strange title *Freaks That Carry Your Luggage Up to the Room* is a quote lifted directly from an obscure but infamous bootleg recording of a rambling onstage rant by Elvis Presley in the early 1970s, while he was obviously delirious from drugs. Google it. It has to be heard to be believed. Only one other thing will pop up in that particular Internet search—*my book*! Being a lifelong fan of The King, that is a source of great personal pride.

Creative influences for both of these novels derive heavily from the lurid horror comic magazines I grew up with in New Jersey back in the 1970s, like *Vampirella, Creepy, Eerie*, and *Tales of the Zombie.* The setting of *Freaks* was somewhat inspired by my gig as a desk clerk at The French Hotel in Berkeley, CA, circa 1989-91. And like Nick in *Mermaid*, I really did live in a sleazy residential hotel over a strip joint, the Hotel Europa in North Beach, where I also worked as a desk clerk on the graveyard shift, circa 1985-86, when I first moved to San Francisco from Los Angeles at age 22.

But these are only superficial sources of inspiration. The bulk of these books are obviously the products of a severely damaged imagination. Together they make an ideal "grindhouse double bill." I'm very proud of this "definitive" edition. I hope you enjoy them both. Cheers.

Will Viharo
Seattle, WA
March, 2015

A MERMAID DROWNS IN THE MIDNIGHT LOUNGE

Neo-Pulp Fiction Fantasia
by Will Viharo

For My Tiki Goddess, Who Saved Me

Chapter One

A man without a future met a woman with a past…

Blood glistened on Dolores's gown. But she wasn't in any pain. It wasn't her blood.

After the initial panic settled, which really only amounted to seconds slowed down to bits of eternity, Dolores realized she wasn't injured. One of the band members was the sax player, Buddy. He was still breathing, though, crouched down on the stage, his saxophone by his side, screaming as he held his hand over his neck, still gushing a veritable geyser of blood. He had been playing close behind Dolores when the gun went off, eyeballing the shapely ass he coveted so intensely.

While leaning over to get a better look at Dolores, tottering drunkenly on his stool, Nick's gun had slipped out of his jacket and dropped to the floor and exploded. The music stopped.

It was very much a freak accident: the gun had bounced off the base of Nick's stool, inadvertently pointing the gun upward and sideways; otherwise it would have simply shot aimlessly across the floor, probably hitting nothing, since no one was dancing or even walking around at that moment. Otherwise didn't cut it, though. Not in the real world, anyway. Wherever that is.

This situation wasn't anywhere near what Nick had in mind for the evening. It wasn't on Dolores's agenda, either. Nor was it in the plans of the sax player, now lying on his back, trembling as the life drained out of him. He didn't even have the energy to scream anymore.

Nick's charm alarm had been ringing before the shot had rung out, as he'd sat there figuring out a way to approach Dolores after the set. He was staring in a drunken stupor at the vintage pin-up calendar behind the bar, adding to the timeless decor of the tiki bar, especially since the calendar was fifty years old. Nick used to consult his watch when trying to remember his last sexual encounter. Now it was a calendar. But he'd had it in the past fifty years, he knew that, especially since he was only forty or so, hadn't even reached birth when that calendar came out, much less puberty, so the calendar was of no use to him. He turned his gaze towards Dolores and *bang.*

Now it was all a mess. He couldn't switch mental gears fast enough to accommodate the sudden chaos. He collided head-on with sheer madness. Before he fully realized that he'd actually wounded someone, Nick was buried beneath the crushing weight of the bouncer, Domino, a former semi-pro wrestler. Domino was normally of a gentle disposition. He was half black, half Korean, built like a brick shithouse. But very friendly. Until it was time to go to work.

Nick was repelled by the smell of Domino's sweat drenching him like dank dew. He reacted in the only way he could under the pressure of his predicament. He grabbed the gun, which had fallen on the floor nearby, within his reach, and fired again.

The second shot was as aimless as the first, though deliberately set off. It only hit a bottle of gin behind the counter, shattering it, splashing liquid and glass all over Miles, who was cowering behind the bar. Miles had witnessed the whole thing, including the gun falling accidentally from Nick's sharkskin coat. He liked Nick, and didn't want to press charges if he didn't have to. He knew Nick was innocent of any real foul play, except possibly concealing a weapon, but he knew Nick didn't have any violent intent. Miles had often encouraged Nick to visit The Midnight Lounge, and was glad to see him. None of this made any sense, Nick blowing off like a postal worker with a vendetta. It had to be an accident. But then there was that second shot, aimed right at Miles?

The third shot sent Domino jumping off of Nick, since the bullet grazed his ear, hitting the whirling fan and chipping a blade before burrowing into the ceiling. That had been Nick's desire anyway, to be free. Then Nick jumped to his feet, his gun in his hand, and everyone held their collective breath, fearful the maniac would open fire at random once more. Domino just stood still, heaving, glaring at Nick, who was surprisingly calm under the circumstances. Then Nick felt a presence behind him. He spun around to face his aggressor.

It was Dolores, there to talk him down to size, save the day.

"What can I do to convince you not to go through with this?" she asked.

"Sleep with me," Nick said simply.

"There's a way out through my dressing room," Dolores whispered after a nervous pause. "We can go to my place." All this excitement made her wet in all the right places.

"Let's go," Nick said, holding the gun to her head as if she were the hostage, not him. He felt more pride than shame. His dick was as hard-boiled as they come.

Sirens wailed in the background. Nick thought about his dream, the one where he turns into a monster. Ironically, it seemed like his only real escape route now.

Chapter Two

Nick woke and wondered where the hell he was. He looked at the empty space beside him, expecting to find someone.

There was no one. Only the sound of the Theremin, as usual, faint and distinct. Or what sounded like a Theremin, the sound in his skull that had plagued him since he was a child, which reminded him of the '50s B science fiction flicks he grew up loving on TV reruns. His head felt heavy, his eyes swollen. He stumbled over to his computer and looked at what he had written:

"*A man without a future met a woman with a past.*"

That's all it said, but he thought he remembered more. That's right: There *had* been more. Much more. But he didn't write it down. He just thought about it. Then he fell asleep and dreamed the rest. Where the border was, he couldn't determine. All he had to show for his imaginative labor was that single line.

He squinted at the clock. Noonish. In around twelve hours he was due at The Oasis Theater down the street to host his weekly midnight show. Tonight's epic: the original *Invaders From Mars*. Unless the idiot distributor screwed up again and sent him the awful 80's remake. He wondered if Dolores, the waitress at The Moonlight Lounge, would come by tonight. He always caught her "act." Maybe finally she'd catch his. He sometimes thought of leaving a little invitation next to his empty glass. He wondered what she was like, outside of his vivid imagination, his desperate yearning, his incessant horniness.

Nick lived over a strip joint, and he had dated some of

the strippers, but he never fell in love with any of them. They fell for him sometimes, since he was so strange and intense and mysterious to them, but he routinely rejected them when it got to the emotional level. The strip joint downstairs was called Zombieville. The strippers all wore ghastly makeup so they looked liked dancing, naked corpses. It was insanely popular. Nick liked to fuck them only when they had the makeup on, and nothing else. He wondered if he suffered from necrophilia. This is partly why he aspired for something purer, even if it was an unattainable vision, so he could vanquish his own demons.

His obsession with Dolores the waitress was purely literary. In a way, he didn't want to get to know her. The truth might be too disappointing. As a muse, she was much more inspiring as a character in his fiction than as a person in his life.

Nick made coffee, petted his beloved cat, a male tuxedo dubbed Buddy whom Nick had found a few years ago abandoned in the alley next to the theater, and sat back down at the typewriter. It was his day off from his day job, at least. If he could get this thing published, maybe he'd finally be able to quit. If not, there was always crime.

He put on an old LP, the soundtrack to the old '50s Lee Marvin P.I. show *M Squad*, and sat back down at his computer. After a while he couldn't hear the Theremin, at least not enough to bother him. He went back to the beginning, and started over, transcribing the entire dream...

Chapter Three

A man without a future met a woman with a past. It happened at a run down tiki bar next to an old movie palace in a small town on the outskirts of a big town. The woman sang forgotten torch songs in the tiki bar. The man MC'd forgotten midnight movies in the movie theater, where he sometimes worked in the booth taking tickets. The woman just sang and waited tables and tried to stay sober, attending as many AA meetings as she could. Sometimes she drank anyway. After all, she sang in a bar. Sometimes she even went home with a drunken customer, who would call himself a fan. She wanted to believe she had fans. Maybe then she wouldn't drink so much, she told herself. That was her disease talking, though. She knew that. But sometimes her disease was all she had to listen to.

Then the alcoholic singer met the lonely midnight movie host one night, and everything changed.

His name was Nick Winters, and he called himself the Lunar Lounge Lizard for his "act," which really wasn't much of an act. He didn't sing or dance. He simply spun the Wheel of Fortune and asked trivia questions and gave away prizes. His typical outfit consisted of an old red fez hat he picked up for a song in a vintage clothing store, a shiny green smoking jacket, a neatly pressed white shirt with French cuffs and shiny cuff links, black slacks, shiny black shoes, Ray-Bans, and an affected attitude. He acted like the ultimate ladies' man, but no one knew he went home and cried most nights. Alone.

Her name was Dolores Summers. Everyone knew how lonely Dolores was, except for Dolores. She sang sad songs with acute awareness of their melodic melancholia. She had lived the lyrics, and continued to. Her pain was on vivid display. It was part of her act. Nick worked at the Omega Theater for two months before he even went into The Midnight Lounge, which was called that because it was always dark inside, except for the glow of the jukebox and a strand of blinking Christmas lights lining the top of the bar. Several tiki statues remained in place from when it was an authentic tiki bar back in the '50s, called Zombieville. The new owner changed the name and updated the menu when he took it over in the '90s, but he didn't touch the faux-exotic décor or the selections on the jukebox, which still played scratchy old Exotica 45s. When she sang, Dolores worked off a small stage in the back that was dimly lit at best, once graced by burlesque dancers. The atmosphere was more forlorn than festive, more sullen than seductive, with a fake, seedy, tropical tint. Yet it had an undeniable appeal to those that fell under its accidental, incidental retro-spell. Nick felt it right away, and wondered why he had never ventured here before.

It was like where he lived, in a small studio apartment over a strip joint. He lived there for three years before he even went into the strip joint. Then he became a regular, before he had an affair with one of the strippers, who turned out to be a hooker as well. When he found that out, he wanted to dump her. But he couldn't. She had to leave him, eventually. She had a kid, too. Somewhere. He saw the kids' picture, which she kept in a purse, a boy with ice cream smeared on his fearful face. Eventually she moved away, with her pimp. Nick never went into the strip joint again after that.

He still had the stripper's picture hanging on his wall in a cheap frame when he met Dolores.

Nick was in his forties. Dolores was in her thirties. They were too young for the previous century, too old for the next. They were stuck in between the Millennium, but ultimately it didn't matter. Time was over-taking everyone, it seemed. It was racing by so fast that for some, it simply stood still. This is how it was for Nick and Dolores, at least before they met. They remained frozen in a time before their lifetime, in a romantic dream of an era they knew only from music and the movies. They yearned for the time when people dreamed of the future. Now that they were in the future, all they dreamed of was the past. It was a fantasy anyway. A dream.

Dolores wasn't even on stage yet when Nick walked in and sat at the bar.

Nick wasn't a heavy drinker. At one time he had thought of himself as a writer, until he came to the painful realization that he wasn't an alcoholic. To him, all great authors were on one big literary bender. This one night he ordered a Mai Tai, since he wanted to somehow merge with the pseudo-Polynesian ambience of his surroundings. A few trendy types were at the bar near him, a good-looking slicked-up stud with two model-perfect female companions, giggling at his every gesture. Nick wondered what this guy did to deserve such unadulterated appreciation.

Nick still wasn't over the stripper. He'd come in to drink away his memories of her, or at least get drunk enough to fall asleep, even though he'd then be tortured by dreams about her. Sometimes they were so real he woke up in a sweat. Other times he just woke up wet. He hadn't experienced nocturnal emissions like that since he was an adolescent sex addict. But the stripper—Gloria, from Georgia, a tasty peach of a woman—was very voluptuous, and Nick had experienced memorable sexual acrobatics with her. He even thought he loved her, for a few minutes. She knew the difference, though. She liked Nick, and even talked about having his child, even though she couldn't take care of the one she ostensibly already had. But her profession was dangerous, and she didn't really want to be bringing anyone else into this nightmare world. She told him she was a prostitute in order to turn him off. It worked, in a way, but he was still obsessed. He still pursued her, even when he would come home and find she was using his place for a fuckpad. He forgave her. He just didn't want to be alone. Ever. So she left him, moved away, and didn't give him her address. Last he heard she was pregnant. Not by him, it was too late. Someone else, her pimp, maybe.

He felt haunted. Every morning he woke up feeling empty and sad. It was the weather that did it, really. The grayness and constant rain made him melancholy and romantic, and reminded him of her. This was the time of year he had been with her the most, cuddling in their sanctuary, making love with the sound of the rain beating gently outside the window. They were in their own little private paradise. Or so Nick had thought until he learned the truth. It's always that way. You enjoy yourself until you learn the truth, and then it's all ruined.

He loved listening to music, particularly his favorite genre, "crime jazz." He called it the soundtrack to his soul. It was as true as it was corny. It was truth that didn't bring pain for once, because it wasn't real truth, it was romantic truth. It brought enlightenment and emancipation, or at least facsimiles he could live with. His favorite movie was *Sweet Smell of Success*, one scent he had never sniffed, that was for sure. He loved the cynicism and the Elmer Bernstein theme. His favorite novelists were Raymond Chandler, James Cain, Jim Thompson, and

David Goodis. He read almost nothing except vintage crime novels. He could relate to them, even though he'd never actually committed a crime. But that night in The Midnight Lounge, crime was exactly what he was thinking about. He had a pistol concealed beneath his roomy, broad-shouldered, slightly worn, seam-torn thrift-store bought sharkskin jacket, its pockets full of bullets. His hope was to get drunk enough to hold up the place. He didn't expect to get away with it, of course. He just didn't know what else to do with his life, or the evening in particular. It was something to do, something unusual, unpredictable, unprecedented.

True to form, the jukebox was playing old "exotica" music. It was stocked with nothing but Martin Denny, Arthur Lyman, Les Baxter, and the like, just as it had been since it was first founded as Zombieville in 1957. The same guy who owned and programmed the Omega Theater also owned the bar. The only reason Nick even got a job at the Omega was because he was incidentally acquainted with the owner, Miles, an old, fat Greek Jew who wore glasses and sweated a lot.

Dolores was in the back room, resting for the show. Her favorite singers were June Christy, Sarah Vaughan, Nina Simone, Billie Holiday, and Ella Fitzgerald; her favorite songs to sing in public, and to listen to privately, were "At Last" by Etta James, "Cry Me A River" by Julie London, and "Stormy Weather" by Lena Horne. She was lying on the cot in the dark listening to old records to inspire her. Miles didn't make her wait tables on the nights she sang. She had just returned from a meeting, and felt relatively good, but tired. And she still had the urge to drink. A *lot.* She'd been sober for almost a month now—for the fifth or so time since entering the program—and she only blamed herself for her slips. She didn't have a sponsor and didn't really work the Steps as rigorously as she once had, and knew she still should. Something inside of her had given up hope a long time ago. She really just wanted to be drunk, then dead. That was her heart's desire. But she fought it, because something inside of her told her there was a God and a purpose for her lonely little life. But if that purpose didn't manifest itself soon, that was it. She was resigned to drinking herself to death.

Her mood swings were less violent than they once had been, but they still haunted her, and anyone close to her. She'd never been officially diagnosed manic-depressive, but she knew that's what she was: a manic-depressive alcoholic with dreams of being a famous singer. But her dreams were as out-dated as her material. Even after the late century lounge revival, she didn't feel like she could cut it. A record, that is. After her divorce the previous year, she'd gone on a sex binge, reverting to her wild days of youthful abandon. It made her feel sick inside, but she kept doing it, because she didn't turn to her Higher Power anymore. She wanted to be higher than her own Higher Power.

She sometimes billed herself "The Moody Swinger," but nobody got it, because no one knew her that well enough to get it. Sometimes on stage she'd just start laughing after she said it, and people just thought she was drunk again. Sometimes they were right.

Out at the bar, Nick was still contemplating the wisdom of holding up his own boss. His general plan was to disappear, maybe go on a vague search for Gloria. Find her pimp, kick the crap out of him. Kidnap her and the baby, run away to an island. Or sail away. Whatever. Something. His life was too stagnant, too boring and repetitious. He had to live his dreams, and sometimes his dreams were very dark.

He might have been dreaming now. He wasn't sure anymore. The lines between fantasy and reality were blurring, and had been for months, maybe even years. He wasn't sure if he actually pulled his gun out and stood on the bar and demanded all the cash in the register he wouldn't just wake up. Maybe his fantasy of living in a crime novel or B movie had finally materialized, or his dreams had become disturbingly realistic and lifelike. The consequences of a dream, however, didn't last. They would evaporate with the light of day. But in the real world, the one he despised and felt trapped in, the consequences could cost him his life, which would mean all sleeping and no dreaming, no escape from the darkness inside of him and all around him as well.

If this weren't a dream, then he'd get into a shoot-out with the bartender, an ex-cop named Stewart, who kept a sawed-off shotgun behind the bar. Or so Nick surmised. Then Nick would die in a hail of bullets and crawl out into the rain and die in the gutter, right beneath the marquee where his name was up in lights. The Lunar Lounge Lizard would become a legend.

And if he was only dreaming, so what? Anything could happen. He might even win the shoot-out, and the girl, for a change.

That was when Dolores walked out onto the stage, and Nick's world changed forever. Or his dream world. Whichever. It didn't matter before. Now he just wanted to stay in the world he was in, because she was in it, too. Nick fell in love with Dolores, just like that; as soon as he saw her come out onto the stage in her glittering crimson dress, form fitting her voluptuous figure. She thought she was fat, or, politely, *zaftig*, in a Marilyn Monroe kind of way, but with a Bettie Page face and hair. Nick thought she was just right.

Sometimes when Dolores sang, she imagined herself a mermaid, singing to a bunch of sailors. Only since they're underwater, all the sailors are dead. Zombies. It filled her with ghoulish glee to imagine this. Sunken treasure and zombie sailors surrounded her as she sang. She didn't know exactly why she imagined this scenario. It just made her feel good. Well, not exactly *good.* Nothing really made her feel good except booze. But the idea of a mermaid singing to zombie sailors underwater just suited her mood, her perspective, made it seem more real, the whole experience, even though that scenario was impossible. Or was it? Maybe she was a mermaid, and she was underwater, and everyone in the bar was dead. Somehow, believing this made her sing better, because she felt all alone.

She burst out with "At Last" in between sips of her martini. She liked drinking harder stuff, but Miles said she had to drink something "classy" while performing, or nothing at all. No belts from the bottle in between belting out. Reluctantly she complied. She felt sad for drinking tonight anyway. She'd just returned from a meeting, feeling refreshed and rejuvenated. What the hell was wrong with her, anyway? She knew AA worked. She knew personally so many people whose lives had been saved by working the Steps. But that was it. She wasn't working the Steps, really. She went to meetings now for comfort, for companionship if not Fellowship. But then nobody wanted to go drinking with her afterwards. So she had to come back here, and pretend she was a mermaid, the only living thing in this sea of cadavers, alone with the sunken treasure, which was all hers. She was a mermaid in her world. She could never drown.

Not as long as she stayed drunk, anyway. Submerged.

Nick remained transfixed by her presence. So did a lot

of people in the bar. Dolores' gown was low cut and her creamy cleavage was glowing sadly in the seedy spotlight, beckoning with lusty desire each time she breathed a note. Her long, dark, thick hair cascaded sensually over her heart-shaped face as she gently twisted her head with the tempo of the tune. But Nick felt more than lust, he told himself. He felt kinship. Or something. If this was a dream, it had to last. He was forgetting all about Gloria now. Gloria, in the real world somewhere, lost. Nick was in here now, with his new dream girl. He just couldn't allow himself to wake up. Ever.

A shot rang out suddenly, and everyone froze, and then moved again, in slow motion. As if everything was in a dream. Or underwater.

Chapter Four

Dolores wondered when The Oasis Theater would play something she actually *liked*.

Invaders From Mars? When was he going to show something with class? Like a true cult classic. *Shaft. One Flew Over the Cuckoo's Nest.* Even *Saturday Night Fever.* That "Lunar Lounge Lizard," as he so pretentiously called himself, was stuck in the '50s. Which would be fine, if he would play something like a Marilyn Monroe movie, or *All About Eve*, which had Marilyn in it, even it wasn't exactly a Marilyn Monroe movie. Too bad. She wanted something to do after work. It wasn't like she just went out and got drunk with a stranger every night. Not any more. Those days were gone. Now she wanted to settle down and be happy. But she didn't want to just go home, either, to her cable TV and empty apartment. She wanted a life. She didn't want to die just another ordinary person, an anonymous remnant of a defunct millennium.

She was sick of her job. All the people who frequented The Moonlight Lounge were assholes, it seemed. Especially the cops who hung out there while off-duty, the chief in particular, who was always harassing her. She complained to Miles but he always shrugged it off, since the chief was a ubiquitous presence, a locally powerful figure in an impotent community, and Miles didn't want to offend him. So she put up with it. It seemed she either hated or simply tolerated most of the people she came in contact with in this town, and she'd never ventured beyond its borders, so this was the only world she knew. The only person who never bothered her was the Lunar Lounge Lizard. There was something sweetly shy about him, but he never talked to her. He was always too busy typing in his laptop. She caught him looking at her a few times, however, with an intensity that both scared and intrigued her.

Dolores decided to go for a walk around the neighborhood, to find something to live for. In her head she pretended she was in New York in the 1960s, a struggling young stage actress with a penchant for musical theater. She sometimes fancied herself a Beat poetess type, dressed in black, sipping espresso, having affairs with foreign painters in their shabby studios, driving around town in a Vespa, taking in live jazz at smoky Village nightclubs and cafes. "Cristo Redentor" by Donald Byrd often accompanied this reverie. She considered the era she had grown up in to be so drab, so lacking in color and character. She felt lost in time, homeless in the scheme of things.

The midnight movie host guy seemed to be her kind of people, a fellow outsider, but she couldn't be certain because of the distance he maintained. His aloofness was an obstacle for both of them.

As Dolores cruised around on foot, soaking in the sights of a cool, breezy day, she wondered about all the dead people that had appreciated the same views, and pondered what they were looking at now. It seemed unfair that she was able to walk and talk and think and see and feel, and dead people couldn't, at least not on her level of understanding, of sentient experience, whatever that truly was. But then another thought cheered her: it wasn't that long ago that she actually envied dead people and their desensitized state. Dolores admired the old buildings in the Hopperesque downtown area that would have looked exactly the way they did when all the dead people were alive, and walking the same streets. Except many of the buildings probably weren't boarded up back then. So things actually looked better, not just the same. Dolores began to envy the dead once again.

Then she saw Nick through a window, sitting in the Day Dream Cafe, the same one she had planned on wasting some time in. Typically, he was hunched over his laptop, like he always was in The Moonlight Lounge. She tried to avoid his glance as she entered and went to the counter, but he looked up and they made eye contact. "His Latest Flame" by Elvis Presley was playing on the sound system. She was trapped by his presence, and he felt mesmerized by hers. The time had come to meet, face to face, in the real world, or the one they both assumed was real.

Chapter Five

Oblivious to the chaos in their wake and the precarious nature of their new futures, suddenly merged in a maelstrom of mayhem, Dolores showed Nick around her small studio apartment as sirens wailed around the neighborhood, searching for the gunman who had shot a sax player at The Midnight Lounge. The apartment was dimly lit, painted in pastels and very simply furnished, with a lava lamp, a potted palm tree and a stark poster of Billie Holiday on the wall, tacked up hastily, to cover up blank space.

"I used to have it more decorated," she said. "But then I got depressed and burned everything."

"I've done that," Nick said, nodding his head thoughtfully.

She made two Screwdrivers without asking him his preference and they got cozy on the sofa.

"Life is like a movie to me," he said. "I guess I got carried away."

"Really? To me it's a dream," Dolores said sadly. "A dream where I'm drowning,"

"I'm in a movie where I'm being chased all the time, for something I didn't do, or don't remember doing," Nick said.

"Tell me about it," she said.

"My life, my movie, feels like one long flashback," Nick said, staring into space. "But I'm tired of metaphors already. I'm a metaphor whore. I make up metaphors to colorize the black and white blandness of it all. I'm so fuckin' bored I could scream, even now, no offense. I just don't know what I'm doin', that's all. We're all just wingin' it, I guess."

"What's a metaphor, exactly?"

Suddenly he felt superior to her, but only for a second. "Know what an allusion is?"

"An illusion?" Dolores smiled. "Shit, I thought it was *all* an illusion. A dream."

He shrugged, and let the literary lesson go. "Or a movie. Movies are like dreams."

"Whatever," she sighed boozily. "Want to know my story?"

"Sure," Nick said. "I want to know everything. Even if it's made up. Tell me all about your dream. From the beginning."

"I'll tell you what I can remember," Dolores said. "The rest I'll make up."

"So what? If it's all a dream anyway. It's all unreal. And you can always wake up from a dream."

"You can walk out of a movie," Dolores said.

"Not if you're in it," Nick said.

"I can't make myself wake up from my own dream. I've tried. So I just try to make myself dream something nice. Like you."

Nick grinned, but it faded fast.

"The story of my life is simple," Dolores began. "I was born, then I was bored. My parents were both assholes. I'm a drunk and a whore, and I sing for shit in a dive. That's pretty much it."

"Don't say that," Nick said. "There has to be more to you than that." The sirens seemed to be retreating in the distance, giving him a temporary sense of sanctuary. He liked the distraction of her voice, if not her story.

"It's not all bad, I've had my fun," Dolores said, stroking Nick's forehead gently, trying to focus her vision. "Did you know I could come from drinkin' alone? That's a fact. Makes me feel like I just had an orgasm, all nice 'n' wet."

They moved closer, but didn't touch.

"Then when I feel *really* good," she continued in a near whisper, "I have sex to make someone *else* feel good, too, so we can feel good together. My pussy is like a scorpion bowl. There's enough for everybody to take a sip. I *love* sex, I really do, men *or* women, sometimes, even, if they're good company, and they like to drink, too. After a few drinks, hell, I'll screw *anything*."

Their faces were very close when Nick said, "Anything? Anyone? Any time?"

She sat back. "I just get horny when I drink, that's all, more so than when I don't." She looked at her screwdriver pensively. "Shouldn't be doing this. It's not your fault, though."

"Nothing's my fault, and yet I'm always in trouble, it seems."

"I know the feeling," she said sleepily.

"How come you're all alone now?" Nick asked. "You're so beautiful, but so sad. I can tell you're lonely, no matter how many people you take to bed. Like me."

She almost cried when he said that. "I was in love a few times," Dolores admitted. "Or thought I was. Never worked out. Know why? 'Cause love is like booze—after a few sips you think you'll stay drunk forever. You get stoned and sloppy, and then suddenly it's all gone, the bottle's empty, and then whaddya do? You go out and get yourself another bottle, so you don't get stuck to the empty one ya got. So I just kept getting *un*stuck, looking for another bottle to suck on. Just like my father…" Her voice trailed off with her thoughts. Then she said. "Anyway, now here we are."

Nick sat back, suddenly tired, scared, but still

stubbornly horny. "Yup," he said.

Dolores sensed his uneasiness and said, "I don't wanna bore you with the sordid details of my sex life any more, let's forget all that. Hey, wanna hear some music?" She pointed to her old Hi Fi system, charmingly antiquated.

"Sure," Nick said passively. *Maybe it would keep me awake*, he thought, long enough to score, anyway. He set down his drink, half finished, and suppressed a belch that almost turned into a fart, a no-no in the Book of Casanova. His stomach burned.

June Christy permeated the warm, stuffy air with "Something Cool" as Dolores sat back down and said, "I'm not just a slut, you know. I'm also a singer. I *love* to sing."

Nick agreed. "Yes, you're a very good singer. That's something to be proud of."

She smiled. "I am. I really enjoy it, too. It's the only thing that comes close to drinkin' and is even better 'n' sex. It's one long orgasm, hittin' those notes and holdin' 'em, slidin' my tonsils up and down that scale, like I'm givin' the song head and it's comin' right down my throat. And gettin' me higher than booze. Only reason booze is better: it's easier, and there's more of it to come by, so to speak, and you don't need no one's approval to get it. Seems like I'm always suckin' on somethin', like it's a snorkel, and I'm underwater, drownin'. I always seem to have my something stuck in my mouth, whether it's a bottle, a microphone, or a *cock.* Hey, you gonna finish your drink or not?"

"No," Nick said. "I've had enough. I don't drink, really. I did tonight, and look what happened."

Dolores just grabbed his glass and swallowed the rest in two gulps. "Don't want it to go waste," she said. Her gaze was wet, her words slurred.

"Booze makes me fall asleep," Nick said. "I don't want to sleep yet. I'm afraid I'll wake up, and this will all have been a dream."

"A wet dream," she said, noticing his bulging crotch, the spot pooling through the fabric.

"Yea, soaked with blood," he said quietly. There was a good chance he'd wake up in a jail cell. Best to deal with his boner before then.

"Wanna go to bed now?" Dolores abruptly asked, bored with this verbal foreplay, suddenly feeling the fatalistic urgency of their shared predicament.

"Okay," said Nick, and they both rose from the couch and she led him into her bedroom by the hand. June Christy was singing "The Midnight Sun."

Chapter Six

Dolores ordered a cafe latte to go, then tentatively walked toward Nick's table in the window, while he just kept typing obliviously. Now the Day Dream Café's sound system was playing "Atlantic City" by Bruce Springsteen. Nick was lost in the alternate world he was creating, and he didn't want her to suspect she was in it. The real Dolores and his fantasy Dolores couldn't co-exist in the same dimension; he had to keep them separate, or one may cancel out the other. She approached his table, but he refused to acknowledge her. If he did, then it would be over. He'd get no writing done at all. It was bad enough he'd had to leave his little studio apartment, his sanctuary, to write in this café, because of all the racket bubbling up from that strip club, Zombieville. He couldn't allow too much reality to intrude on his carefully woven little fictive universe, where he was in control.

"What are you writing?" Dolores asked. She sensed he was writing about her, but required affirmation, as all aspiring performers do. "I see you in The Moonlight Lounge all the time. I wait tables there. My name's Dolores, by the way."

Reluctantly Nick looked up at her and shook her hand, then looked back down at his computer screen. "I know. My name's Nick," he said, avoiding her gaze.

"Oh, so you *do* have a real name. I only know you as the 'Lunar Lounge Lizard', which is a really fucked up kind of name for a person to go by, if I may say so."

"'With all due respect', as the saying goes? Like you can say anything you want if sprinkle some respect on it, like sugar on shit?" Nick said dryly as he shook his head shyly, slightly blushing. The Theremin grew louder inside his brain.

Dolores didn't understand why Nick suddenly seemed so bitter. "Just making conversation," she said.

"I just want to be alone now, sorry," Nick explained half-heartedly.

"Suit yourself," Dolores said, rising from the table. "That's what I get for being friendly. See ya around, I guess."

"You gonna come to my show tonight?" he blurted out with spontaneous insecurity. Suddenly, he didn't want to let her go.

Dolores mused on the possibility. "What's playing?"

"*'Invaders From Mars.'* The first one, from Fifty-three."

"Hm, haven't seen that one. *Or* the other one. Maybe I'll get off in time to catch it. Usually that's the problem. I get off too late."

"Beats not getting off at all," Nick said boldly.

"Or just beating off, right?" Dolores leaned in closer to him and whispered, "It's like you only want to see me at the theater or in the lounge. I know you watch me from afar, but it's like I only exist in your story. Out in the real world, you're so damn shy, it hurts both of us."

"There is no real world," he said, obviously caught off guard. "Just the one we make up. And you're being way too presumptuous, I might add."

"Like I said, suit yourself." Dolores stood back and sighed nonchalantly. "Maybe I'll see you tonight, maybe I won't." She suddenly had this strange compulsion to tell Nick all of her secrets. If only she could remember what they were.

After she was gone, Nick wrote a scene about making love to her.

Chapter Seven

Lying in bed, moonlight pouring through the half open blinds, Nick and Dolores continued sharing stories and secrets.

"I've never been married," Nick said, as Dolores lay in his arms, both slick with sudden release and redolent of impetuous passion. "Almost, kinda, but not really. She was a stripper. *She* liked to fuck, that was for sure. We'd spend days fuckin' the shit out of each other...this botherin' you?"

"No," Dolores said sleepily, relaxed and softly spinning. Later it might bother her, when she had her usual morning headache and hated everything.

"I thought it was love, but I guess it was just lust," Nick went on. "Just lust. Just lust must rust."

Dolores giggled and kissed his neck. "You a poet now?"

"I used to be," Nick said. "Kinda. Now I'd rather be anything but. Even a stick-up guy, if not a stand-up guy. Stand-up comedian. Stick-up comedian. Whatever."

"You a gangster, sugar? A thief?"

"I thought so. Knocked over a liquor store once."

Dolores sat up slightly, intrigued and titillated. "Really?"

He slyly raised an eyebrow. "Like me better now you think I'm a bad ass?"

"No. I don't think I could like you better," she said sincerely.

"Good. All I got away with was a plastic bottle of vodka and a comb."

She giggled girlishly. "You're still a pretty cool

customer, Nick."

"You mean I'm not just another guy to you, out of the many? I mean, is it me, or the booze, Dolores?"

Dolores lay back down with a sigh. "I wish I could tell. But I liked you from the first moment I noticed you in the lounge. I felt a *connection*."

"Really?"

"Yes," she said.

"I only went in there to see you," he said. "And maybe rob the place. I was just so unhappy, I didn't know what to do with myself."

After a pause, she asked, "So are you happy now?"

"As happy as I get," Nick said truthfully.

"Really?" said Dolores sadly. "I don't get very happy. *Ever*."

"Not even now?" Nick asked.

"No," she told the ceiling.

"You *seem* happy, happy enough, anyway," Nick said.

"Just content," she said with an ambivalent sigh.

Nick kissed Dolores tenderly. "Is that as good as you ever feel?"

"Yes. It doesn't last, though."

He eyed her sore nipples, still pert and tender from his voracious suckling. "Let's just enjoy it while we can, then."

There was a pounding on the door. Nick got up and looked out the window and saw flashing red lights. He pulled out his gun, silently praying to anyone within celestial earshot that none of this was real, yet at the same time, hoping it was. He didn't want Dolores to disappear from his dream.

Chapter Eight

Nick's skin began to itch all over. He attributed it to nervousness, caused by his brief but intense cafe encounter with Dolores. He was prone to nervous rashes, anyway, ever since he was a kid. As a child, he'd also suffered from chronic migraine headaches, including the visual aberration, scintillating scotoma, but eventually, and mercifully, they were replaced by the persistent Theremin. He'd had tests done, but nobody could find anything wrong with him; it was all just a gift from Motherfuckin' Nature. But this was an all-new sensation. He could feel himself tingling on the *inside.*

He went to the mirror and for a second, he thought his flesh had turned a ghastly shade of *green*. He switched the bathroom light off and on, hoping it had something to do with the dim bulb. He really freaked out when he went into the kitchen and his cat, Buddy, hissed, screeched, and ran under the living room couch, apparently terrified by his presence. And the Theremin seemed louder and more intense than ever. Only in Dolores's presence did it suddenly stop. But he figured this was because she temporarily distracted him from his own morbid self-absorption.

He was tired of writing, or *not* writing, as the case may be. To unwind, so he could creatively reload, he watched a B movie on DVD, *The Hideous Sun Demon,* about a guy who turns into a lizard-like monster when exposed to the rays of the sun. Nick wanted to show it at his show, but so far couldn't track down a print of it. He even tried to contact its star, Robert Clarke, but found out he had passed away. Then someone else in the exhibition biz told him a guy named Wade Williams owned the rights to it, and to request a 35mm print from him. But so far Nick couldn't get a response from Wade Williams. So in the meantime, he just dreamed. Watching the movie, his rash got worse. He wondered if he'd have to cancel the show altogether. He was ready to quit, anyway, and find a real job, but first, he had to finish writing his story, the one he could control.

Dolores was likewise experiencing strange sensations. Her legs were stiff, and when she woke up from her afternoon nap, she could've sworn they were *stuck together.* In the shower, while shaving her shapely legs, she thought her hair was unusually rough, almost *scaly*. And after her shower, she got the uncustomary urge to take a bath, and submerge herself under the water. To her surprise, it seemed she kept her head under for a full five minutes. But it probably wasn't that long, she told herself. She, too, chalked up these unusual symptoms to hypochondria induced by dread. She already regretted her encounter with Nick in the cafe. Now she felt obligated to visit him at the movie theater.

Because of her nap and extra long bath, she was a little late for work. Miles had been on her case recently for tardiness, and made his customary threat to fire her if she continued this trend. Under these circumstances, she was afraid to ask him if she could get off a bit earlier than usual this evening, so she could catch Nick's show next door. So she told Miles her legs hurt, and she didn't want to work a full shift. Miles reluctantly relented. He knew she was lying, but because of his lust for her, he allowed her to occasionally indulge this casual vice. Also, Dolores wanted to avoid that creepy old cop who would sometimes come in and harass her after his shift ended, engaging her in conversation as if she was supposed to know or care who the hell he was, but she couldn't place him at all, outside of The Moonlight Lounge, and she wanted to keep it that way. She wanted the whole world to go to hell, except for Nick. She felt a deep connection with him she had to explore and discover, like an island she could then claim all for herself.

Chapter Nine

The cops had Nick and Dolores closed in.

"This is a nightmare," Dolores said, with only a sheet around her, cowering beside Nick, wearing only boxers, who peeked out the curtains at the three squad cars and swarm of cops, fully dressed, guns drawn. "I mean, like, *literally*. Right?"

The pounding on the door increased. Nick was frozen with indecision.

"*Open up. Police*," shouted an authoritative voice.

"*Fuck off!*" Nick yelled. "*I've got a hostage*!"

Dolores smiled slyly. She liked that idea.

There was a long, heavy pause.

"*You all right in there, lady*?" boomed the outside voice.

"*Leave us alone, or he'll kill me*!" she screamed with a smile.

Another tense pause. Nick and Dolores tried not to laugh audibly and blow their cover.

The anonymous cop outside said: "*The guy he shot is dead, lady. Be careful. You're in danger, no matter what he tells you. We'll stand by. Get him to talk to us. We can work this out.*"

Nick choked back vomit. "My god, I'm actually a killer now," he whispered as the reality dawned then fell on him at once. He collapsed onto the sofa, shaking, feeling very weak. "Maybe I should give myself up. It's no use. I don't want to go to jail, though. I'd just be going to a prison within a prison. It was an accident, for God's sake. *You* were there, maybe you can tell them, testify on my behalf."

Dolores sat next to him and tenderly tried to console him. The urge to laugh had gone away, maybe for good. Everything felt dreamy and surreal and sickening. They wanted to wake up, to escape. But there was no exit. Unless he shot their way out.

Nick checked the chamber of his gun. He had many bullets left, in the gun as well as in his pocket, but not enough to kill all those cops, or even wound them, if it got that far. He was already a killer, so what were a few more bodies on his conscience? There was only one viable way out of this shit: he'd have to use Dolores as a shield.

"Would you mind?" he asked her politely.

"Not at all," she said, tingling with the excitement of it all.

"Good. Get dressed. We're leaving."

"Where're we going?" she asked.

"I'm not sure. Where do you want to go?" Nick asked. "Anyplace special?"

"Not really. Someplace tropical, maybe."

He smirked. "You mean like The Midnight Lounge?"

"Yea," she smiled wanly. "But better. *Real.* And real far away, too. From everything. Just you and me."

Nick smiled at first, but then he suddenly looked haunted, forlorn, and said, "Y'know...you don't have to do this. You could just let me leave. Got a back way out?"

"*No,*" said Dolores. "Look, I'm in this with you, all the way, no matter how it turns out. This is *it*. For both of us. Do or die. And I don't want to die, or for you to go to jail. I just want us both to live, *free*."

The phone rang, momentarily breaking the spell.

"Answer it," Nick said. "But no negotiating right now. We—*I*—gotta figure this out. I don't know what the right thing to do is yet. I never do."

"Promise you just won't give up, Nick."

"*Answer it.*"

Dolores picked up the phone tentatively. "Y-yes?"

It was Miles, from The Midnight Lounge. She was almost relieved.

"Dolores, you okay? This is Miles. Did Nick hurt you?"

"No, no of course not, Miles. I'm fine. But he *might.*" Dolores was trying to stall while Nick gestured with his face and hands what to tell Miles. "Right now we're just talking. He still has his gun, though."

"Well, what the hell does he want?" Miles asked irritably. "You know, Buddy didn't make it. He's dead. But I saw the gun slip out of his pocket, out of Nick's pocket. I told the cops that. But they still want to talk to him. Shall I give you the Chief?"

"I don't know," Dolores said nervously, looking for a signal from Miles. Then: "No! No, not now. I have to go, Miles."

"Dolores, *wait,* you didn't tell him about us, about our little X-rated movie project, did you, Dolores? *Dolores*?"

Dolores felt queasy. "No, never," and she hung up.

"What's the matter?" Nick asked.

"I'm scared," Dolores whispered. "I'm mixed up. I need a drink."

"Good. Me too."

"Really?" Dolores felt more turned on than tuned in to their situation.

"Yea, really. Put on some fuckin' music. *Loud.* And let's fuck some more. Okay?"

"Okay," Dolores said, fixing a gin and tonic for both of them. "Whatever you say, Nick. You're my man. I'll go anywhere with you."

Nick just looked at her and smiled. He wanted the world to stop and freeze in this moment forever, with no memories of the past, or fears of the future to spoil the moment.

"You all right in there, lady?" said a cop's voice outside the window, interrupting his trance.

"*Fuck off or he'll kill me*!" she screamed, then she went to take a shower.

"*Fuckin' A I will!*" Nick added.

While Dolores let the water cascade over her naked body, singing a medley of sad songs as fluids cleansed fluids from her flesh, Nick sipped his drink, browsing through Dolores' massive LP collection, looking for some crime jazz to perfectly complement the cinematic mood. He happily settled on Henry Mancini's *Peter Gunn* soundtrack, and played it loudly, tuning out the sirens, the voices, and the mayhem in his own mind.

Chapter Ten

Nick's mystery rash seemed to subside a bit by the time he got to the theater that evening to host the original *Invaders From Mars*, delivered on time and without a screw-up for once. There was a relatively small crowd milling about the lobby, and Miles was on hand to give Nick crap about it, as usual.

"Nick, no one wants to see this old rubber monster shit anymore, everything's CGI nowadays," Miles was saying. "The kids don't dig where you're comin' from, which is Mars, apparently, and they're the ones with the disposable income. See, the thing of it is, Nick, I got a business to run here. You wanna wallow in nostalgia, how about we show '70s porn? I liked how dirty the chicks seemed back then, like they never took a bath. The guys were all hairy and ugly. That's something real people can appreciate and relate to, instead of this time-travelin' freak show you got goin' on."

"But The Moonlight Lounge is a time warp itself, Miles," Nick said, ignoring the porn suggestion. "It's a tiki bar, for Chrissake. You run one of the last original tiki bars left on the planet, and you say *I'm* out of touch? You like all this old stuff as much as I do."

"Yea, but I'm not peddling memories," Miles said. "Next door, the decor may be old, the music is old—because I'm too cheap to upgrade anything, that's the truth—but the *booze* is all *new*. See, people go there to *forget*, not to reminisce. The music and décor are incidental to them. Here, they come for the movies. You have to keep up with the times, Nick. Nostalgia is bad for the bottom line. We may have to start experimenting with a new format soon. My landlord ain't too happy about the fact I have so much trouble making the rent, month in, month out. And every single one of our vendors is out for my blood, too. I don't make money, they don't make money, *you* don't make money. See how it works?"

Nick sighed and relented. He could never win this argument. "Yea, yea, I know all about your prize-winning theory of economics, Miles, but right now I got a show to do, we'll talk about this later, okay? Like we always do." Nick was already sick of this silly gig, anyway. He felt like a clown on stage. But at least he *looked* cool. He was wearing his usual outfit: fez hat, smoking jacket, white shirt with French cuffs, thin black tie, and shades. He didn't want eye contact with anybody. He was the Lunar Lounge Lizard now, a swingin' visitor from outer space, an alien hipster. It was his doppelganger, his alter ego, his escape persona. His only other avenue of release was via his imagination, his work. But nobody ever saw that. There was no spotlight on his haunted brain.

The Oasis basically thrived on its screenings of second run features, shown for a paltry admission fee. Plus the theater was very comfortable, with couches and love seats, and the menu featured pizza, hot dogs, pretzels and other food items, since he had a kitchen built into the premises when he took it over. Miles allowed and even encouraged his Moonlight Lounge patrons to bring their hard drinks into the theater, even though he wasn't licensed for that. But the cops turned a blind eye to this practice, since some of his patrons *were* cops, and they had a vested interest in both places. Other than Zombieville, where the cops also hung out on a regular basis, there wasn't any other entertainment in this isolated town. Miles never bothered to get a cabaret license for the theater, either, since he didn't have to worry about anyone turning him in, so sometimes a jazz combo or traveling burlesque group would perform at Nick's show, but since the weekly midnight show didn't turn much of a profit, the budget didn't allow for this very often. Miles really was considering porn at this point.

Lately, there'd been an escalating tension between Nick and Miles, and both felt their partnership was coming to an end. Nick just wasn't bringing in the business with his archaic programming, and Miles as losing his patience, as well as his business.

"Okay, we'll talk later," Miles said, on his way out, "but first, tell me this: why the hell you keep itchin' yourself? You okay? Got poison ivy or somethin'? Crabs? I don't want you infectin' my patrons with no god damn diseases."

"I'm okay," Nick said, trying to reassure himself as much as Miles. "But hey, now that you mention it, does my complexion look a little *green* to you though?"

"I *wish* you'd turn god damn *green*, as in *profit*," Miles laughed. "Remember, dude, you're not a *real* lizard, just a *lounge* lizard. A *fake* one at that. Anyway, I gotta get back over to the lounge. Dolores is waitin' tables by herself, and she's been flaky lately."

"She's a nice girl," Nick said casually.

Miles grinned. "What, you fallin' for that crazy broad, Nick?"

"She's crazy?" Nick said, then, "And, no, I'm not," he lied.

Miles laughed and slapped Nick's shoulder. "Whatever you say, but they're *all* crazy, Nick. Y'know, Dolores even has this nutty idea of bein' an entertainer. She wants to sing in the lounge, like a, whaddyacallit, chanteuse."

"She can sing, too?"

"She thinks so, anyway," Miles said. "But I ain't runnin' no nightclub. Maybe she should come over and sing at *your* show. Or better yet, do a live sex act. *There's* an idea."

Nick shrugged and said as if it didn't matter, "Whatever works."

Picturing Dolores going down on him with the audience cheering, Miles momentarily forgot all about his tirade concerning Nick's choice of movies for his show, gave him a friendly slap on the shoulder, and split. They were friends again. At least until the following week, when Nick would present to his dozens of followers *From Hell It Came*, a 1957 movie about a possessed killer tree, a rare 16mm print he proudly obtained from some crazy collector in a catalogue. No one would show up for that one either. It was time for a change. He just didn't know what that would be.

Minutes before he was about to go on stage, the Theremin made a comeback in Nick's head, like his old migraines. He never told anyone about the Theremin, even though it had been plaguing him since he was a child. He was too afraid to know what it was. It continued even after the migraines, which were officially diagnosed, finally stopped. He was attached to the Theremin now, didn't want it cured, despite the fact it often threatened to drive him crazy, or may eventually prove fatal. At least it kept him company. It was, by default, his oldest, most loyal friend.

Right before his theme music, Henry Mancini's "Theme from *Peter Gunn*," was cued for the projectionist in the booth to play, Nick went into the men's room and checked his complexion. It was fine for now, and the itching had almost vanished. Maybe it was all in his mind after all. Just like the Theremin. Perhaps he was already insane. He hoped so. That prognosis would excuse him from dealing with this world. He was ready to retire from reality.

Meantime, next door in The Moonlight Lounge, Dolores was in the ladies' room, worriedly checking her legs out in the mirror. They felt better, but every now and then, she suffered the sensation that they were *heavier*. Maybe she was gaining weight. She'd always thought her thighs were too fat. But she also felt a disorienting sense of claustrophobia, and her breath was short, like she couldn't process oxygen anymore. She chalked it up to a suppressed panic attack.

"Where you been?" Miles said to her when she came out. "People are pissed, they want their drinks. *Now*."

She glanced up at the clock on the wall. It was twenty minutes before midnight. "Voodoo Dreams" by Les Baxter was on the juke.

"Miles, I have to go. I don't feel well."

"What, you throwin' up in there?" he asked, brow wrinkled.

"No, but, I feel *strange*. Dizzy, sort of. I need to go."

"Where? Home?" He eyed her suspiciously.

"Well, yes, where else?"

"How the hell do I know what goes in that pretty little head of yours?" he said with slight exasperation. "You're actin' so weird lately. All right, Dolores, just finish up the last few orders and I'll get Domino to do the rest."

"Thanks, Miles. I'll feel better by tomorrow."

"Now I can't go next door and watch the movie," Miles said with phony regret.

"Oh! Where you *planning* on it?" Dolores said with phony concern.

"*Not*. I seen it already, anyway, thousand fuckin' times, late at night on t.v. with my hands down my underwear, drinkin' beer and belchin', the way it should be." Dolores ignored his typical crudeness. He looked into her eyes for a trace of mendacity. "Hey, *you're* not cuttin' out to catch the flick, are you, Dolores?"

"Me? Not my cup of crap, Miles, you know that."

"Hope not," he said. "I'd be disappointed if it was. Just checkin'. Don't be late tomorrow. Get some rest."

"Okay, thanks, Miles."

He gave her a lascivious wink and said, "You owe me now. And remind me—I might have a business opportunity for you."

"Miles, you mean singing?" she said excitedly.

"Something like that. We'll talk later. After all, you don't feel well, right?"

"Right. Later." Dolores slopped a few more exotic drinks on the tables and checked herself out in the ladies' room once more before hurrying next door to The Oasis.

When Nick saw Dolores rush in and take a love seat alone in the rear of the theater, he took that as his cue to start his opening spiel. It was finally show time.

Chapter Eleven

The goddamn phone fucking rang again, and Nick answered it with unconcealed exasperation. He was lying nude in bed with the equally bare Dolores, both reeking of nasty sex. Torn clothes lay at the foot of the bed, collateral damage of their unbridled passion. Dawn's pastels streamed through the blinds, blended with the flashing lights of police cars, creating an unsettling, yet eerily beautiful, disco ball-like collage of colors.

"Hello, Nick? It's me, Miles."

"Fuck you, Miles," Nick said wearily. "What the fuck you want now?"

"Uh, ah, well, I was gonna ask you the same thing, Nick. The cops are hot to nail your ass, but I keep intervening on your behalf. Not sure why, since you closed my joint with this insanity."

"Yea, well, fuck you, fuck the bar, and fuck *everybody*," Nick said. Dolores began to stir, but Nick patted her head and told her "sssh."

"Well, okay, take that attitude, but that guy, Buddy, the sax player, that you 'accidentally' shot, he 's dead, y'know," Miles said. "So *you're* the one who's fucked, my friend."

"*Accidentally*, right," Nick said. "So you know that already. They must know that too. So what's the problem?"

Miles sighed and laughed softly. "The *problem*, Nick, is that you won't give yourself up for questioning, like you have something to hide. And then you went and kidnapped Dolores and probably *raped* her."

"Kidnapped? *Raped*? I didn't kidnap and rape

anybody, man. You're just jealous, you dirty old fuck. I know you got the hots for her, but then who doesn't?"

"I know Buddy was in love with her, and you killed him," Miles said, sidestepping his own feelings for Dolores. "Maybe it was a jealous rage."

"That's just plain crazy," Nick said. "The bottom line is I may be a killer, by *accident*, but I ain't no kidnapper and I definitely ain't no rapist. Dolores is here of her own free will."

"So, so, so, why the hell does she keep telling the cops you're holding her hostage? If it's all okay, c'mon out, Nick."

"Go fuck yourself," Nick said adamantly.

Miles suddenly grew irate, yelling into the phone. "You know what? Fuck this. I ain't negotiating for you no more, you sick bastard, you *killer,* you goddamn *rapist.* You ruined my business. You ruined my *life*! *Fuck you*!" Miles slammed down the phone.

Nick just hung up, feeling oddly relaxed

"Who was that on the phone?" Dolores asked sleepily.

"Nobody, just Miles," Nick said. "Go back to sleep." Nick walked toward the blinds to peek out and see if the cops were still out there. Just then the windows shattered, and tear gas canisters detonated within the room, instantly permeating the apartment with suffocating fumes. There were the sounds of tired, angry expletives along with the explosions; of rifles being readied for a barrage of bullets should the occasion call for it. There were foggy lights and confusion and chaos and tears. And when the smoke cleared, there was a sickening stillness, and the cops, guns drawn, surrounded Nick, who was standing in the center of the bedroom with Dolores, both stark, shivering naked, tears streaming down their grimacing faces. Nick had a gun to her head. This was getting to be a routine, his new act. This was so much more fun and fulfilling than hosting bullshit B movies. Better to *live* one. Dolores was going to let out a phony scream, but she just yawned instead. She'd just woken up, and yet, looking around at the misty mayhem, she still felt like she was only dreaming.

Chapter Twelve

Dolores' presence in The Oasis Theater made Nick even more nervous than usual, but he tried to professionally rise above his anxiety. He had an audience to entertain, for which he was paid, however slightly. Besides, he wanted to impress Dolores, however slightly. This was all he had, and that made him sad.

Dolores herself felt uneasy, not fully understanding her purpose for being there. It wasn't to watch the stupid movie, that was for damn sure. And she didn't want to witness Nick bombing in front of the whole audience, either. She could sense his tension as their eyes met, so she sat in the back, in the dark, to avoid him, give him space to perform, without the visible stress cue.

Nick decided he'd keep his opening monologue relatively brief and cut to the chase, in order to minimize the opportunity for disaster. "Aloha, suckers, I'm the Lunar Lounge Lizard *(he never paused for applause, to save himself the embarrassment of silent response)*, and tonight we have another cult classic from my voodoo vaults, the original '*Invaders From Mars*,' from Nineteen-Fifty-Three. And for the black and white blind, the history impaired, the visually challenged, it's in bee-yootiful three strip Technicolor, so *relax*. It's directed by the guy who did the set design for 'Gone With the Wind,' I forget his name and you wouldn't recognize it anyway, I think he did an Arabian Nights flick in the Forties, too, also in color, but who cares, we're here to meet the Martians, my *favorite* Martians, incidentally, and this one is way better than Tobe Hooper's Eighty-six remake, which shoulda been eighty-sixed from the get-go, let me tell you. Okay, okay, so, I got stuff to give away, some ultra cool prizes, direct from my closet, as usual, and as usual I need a lovely assistant from the audience, a volunteer, or I just pick a victim, volunteer or victim, it's up to you, folks, let me see who we got here tonight..."

People loved getting up on stage to spin the Wheel, reveling in their fifteen seconds of fame, however pathetic the context, and Nick always chose the loveliest female in the group, which was normally a relative choice, and often the one chosen was not particularly attractive, but Nick didn't care; he enjoyed giving the ladies a charge, whether he woke up with a bra and panties strewn across his floor or not.

Leaving the stage as he surveyed his minions, Nick ignored all the soft sweaty hands going up in the air as well as the shouts and cries and pleas for his attention, and he zeroed in on the lone woman in the back of the theater, who shook her head "*no, no, no*" but was pulled up physically by Nick from her chair and almost literally dragged back to the stage. Smiling politely, Dolores bowed for the audience who at first moaned their displeasure at being passed over but then burst into sporadic applause for the evening's "lovely assistant."

"Thank you, young lady, for joining us and helping out with the Big Wheel tonight," Nick said, acting casual, nonchalant, debonair, pretending Dolores was just another broad he might've just banged in the bathroom. Dolores went along with the act, for the sake of her own dignity, if not his, inwardly seething with resentment, for his putting her on the spot, and in the spotlight, this way. But if he patted her on the ass, she'd deck him, no two ways about it, and the next time he came into The Moonlight Lounge and ordered a drink, she'd serve it in his lap.

Nick instinctively knew all this, but he felt if she was up on stage with him, rather than smug and snug in the audience, he'd feel more in control, and he'd be sharing the humiliation if things went south.

Both of them began to itch, all over, but Dolores felt it most in her legs, while Nick again experienced that dreaded tingling sensation all over his face. He still felt *green.* They both thought it was stage fright, combined with the proximity of one to the other in a public situation, their mutual insecurities exposed in the limelight.

"*I regret coming here already,*" Dolores said lowly through clenched teeth, scratching her gams with as much aplomb as she could muster.

"*The night's young, sugar, maybe you'll get something out of it,*" Nick said under his breath, trying to stay in character and keep his cool.

"*You sure won't,*" Dolores shot back.

Nick scratched his face self-consciously as he continued. "All right, the young doll has informed me that her moniker is Dolores, and she works next door, at The Moonlight Lounge, so you probably know her already. "

"I'm not a doll," Dolores announced to the audience, and they all laughed. Nick didn't feel green anymore. He felt red.

"If I'm a guy, you're a doll, *doll,*" Nick said suavely. "That's what the song says, anyway."

"I should know, I've sung it," she said.

"So sing for us, sugar!" Nick said obnoxiously. "That's a good idea! Belt it out, baby! Anything ya want. I'm tired. The audience needs some real entertainment for a change."

"*Just show the movie*!" some slacker in a zombie t-shirt yelled from the audience. Others vocally concurred. Nick ignored them, as usual. Dolores, unaccustomed to public humiliation, was livid.

"I need some accompaniment," Dolores said simply.

"How about I just give you a tray with drinks on it?" Scattered snickers.

"Try it, and you'll be sending your smoking jacket to the cleaners tomorrow," Dolores shot back. The audience roared.

"My jacket may smoke, but can you carry a torch song, baby?" Nick said, and the audience shouted approval.

"Well, any requests?" Dolores said confidently, sublimating her ire.

"'*Freebird*!'" shouted another wise guy.

"Don't know it," she said. "How about 'Bye Bye Blackbird'?"

Nobody recognized that one. Except Nick. He shot a finger at her and said, "Hit it."

Dolores sang the number a cappella. Her voice was a little shaky at first, but as the audience expressed its appreciation, she found her confidence, and when she finished, she was greeted with a standing ovation. Nick just stood back in utter awe of this sad, sexy songbird. She had struck his life like lightening out of the blue, and now she was stealing his thunder, too.

Chapter Thirteen

Saxophones shrieked in Nick's head as he led the naked Dolores out of the room full of drooling cops, guns still erect and ready to shoot. Dolores was shaking violently from cold embarrassment, though she wasn't scared, just titillated. Nick ordered her to slip on a dress and some shoes, no time for under-garments. Nick himself grabbed some clothes with his free hand, but he kept his gun fixated on Dolores, who dressed in a hurry, sobbing delicately for effect. *I should've been an actress*, she thought to herself.

"You won't get away with this, asshole," admonished the squad leader. "You're making this a lot worse than it needs to be. You can choose another life for yourself, right this minute."

"None of us make that choice," Nick said as he stuck the gun back to Dolores's head and made her march out in front of him. "We just choose our reactions to our circumstances, not the circumstances themselves. This whole situation is my reaction to my whole goddamn miserable life, so deal with it." The cops didn't say anything, just kept their guns trained on the perversely compelling couple. Dolores's car keys were lying on the table in the living room. "Grab 'em," Nick ordered. She did.

Then they got into her 1960 Impala and sped off, cops in hot pursuit.

"Where are we going?" Dolores asked Nick.

"I don't know," Nick said. He leaned over and kissed her. "Does it matter?"

"Not any more, thank God. I feel free at last."

They drove till dawn, stopping at a roadside diner somewhere out in the sticks. No cops were on their trail now, none that they could see, anyway. They had outrun them in their four-wheeled retro-rocket, but now what? No place to go. They ate quietly and then drove some more. The song "Ever After" by The Lost Patrol played on the car radio, in a loop, on every station, but that was okay, because they liked it. Finally they stopped rented a room in a cheap motel called The Capri, unchanged from the '40s, and slept all day, into the early evening.

"What do you want to do?" Nick asked when they woke up.

"I don't know," Dolores said. "How about a movie?"

Nick laughed. "What movie could possibly be as good as this?"

Chapter Fourteen

"You're *fired,* bitch!" Miles yelled from the back of the theater, ruining the moment. Then he turned and walked out, stunned silence in his wake.

Nick looked at Dolores and shook his head. "He's full of it. You're not fired. He doesn't have anybody else to take your place."

"I don't feel like singing anymore," Dolores said sadly, and she walked off the stage and out of the theater, then ran outside, trying to catch up with Miles.

"*Movie*!" people began to chant.

Nick signaled for the projectionist to roll it without further fanfare. He felt depressed and sat in his customary seat and tried to enjoy the flick. When he decided this was impossible, he left the theater and went next door to The Moonlight Lounge.

Dolores was there, working as if nothing has happened. "Chant of the Moon" by Robert Drasnin was playing on the juke.

"I told you he was bluffing," Nick said.

Dolores looked horrified.

"What's the matter?" Nick asked.

"Your face…what hap…it's…does it *hurt*?"

"Huh? What are you talkin' about?" Nick touched his face, which felt rough and suddenly itchy. He ran into the bathroom, flipped on the light, tossed off his fez hat, and saw that his face had assumed reptilian features, though his identity was still intact. It was simply an amphibious variation on his customary human appearance, like Bruce Bennett mid-transformation in *The Alligator People*. He clawed at his scaly flesh until blood trickled down his throat, staining his French-cuff shirt and smoking jacket.

Chapter Fifteen

Nick lay awake in the cheap motel called The Capri fantasizing about being a working novelist, like one of his literary heroes. It seemed like such a physically safe, if not financially secure, occupation. The problem was he didn't know how to write anything more complex than a grocery list. Plus there was no money in writing novels, since nobody read anymore. What's the point of even writing a grocery list if you can't afford the groceries? To hell with it.

"What are you thinking about?" Dolores asked him softly. She'd been watching him think for some time now. The violent events of the previous evening seemed as distant as a dream. She could hear the faucet dripping in the bathroom, like Chinese water torture, but was too sleepy to get up and turn it off, so she just lazily settled for the remotely induced torment.

"Another life," he said, as if transfixed by his secret thoughts.

"Whose?"

"I don't know. Mine, I guess." He felt like smoking, though he didn't smoke.

"Any regrets?" she asked coyly.

He thought about it. "I don't know yet. I'm glad I'm here with you, so I guess whatever lead me here was a good thing. I guess."

"This can't end well," Dolores said in a suggestive monotone, rolling away from him. "It feels so real, yet unreal. Like I'm real, but the world around me isn't."

He put his hand on her bare, warm shoulder, and then kissed it. "If this is a dream, it'll happen any way we want it to," he whispered with a tone of uncertain reassurance.

Dolores got up and opened the blinds. Moonlight steamed in and she felt like she'd turn to dust. Outside it was quiet except for some crickets chirping. She turned on the TV and flipped channels. Some bright, peppy design reality show beamed innocuously and obliviously into the dark little room, like postcards from the world she'd just left behind. Normally this type of program would be interesting to Dolores, appealing to her fashion fetish, but now it was simply depressing, considering the ugly hopelessness of their current precarious circumstances. She was in no mood for irony. Flip. News about the world. Depressing. Flip. Infomercial. Flip. Sports. Yawn. Flip. An old Esther Williams movie, *Pagan Love Song*. Freeze.

Suddenly someone pounded on the door, and they froze some more. If they kept freezing, pretty soon they'd be frozen in time.

Nick got his gun and went to the door and waited. The pounding resumed. He motioned for Dolores to remain quiet. They heard disgruntled, muffled voices. Then more pounding. Nick tensely cocked his piece in anticipation of confrontation. He felt like they were repeatedly surrounded and besieged by zombies wherever they went, trapped in a little room that rotated through space, basking in post-coital bliss but with the ghouls constantly trying to break in and eat them alive. *Corpsus interruptus. Dena voodoo.* They were living inside some zombie holocaust nightmare, and no place was safe from the ever-encroaching undead hordes.

An irritatingly familiar voice boomed from outside, "Nick, open up, it's Miles!"

Nick recognized Miles, but not the other voices murmuring in the background. "Who's that with you, Miles?" Nick finally asked.

"Cops."

Nick's stomach flipped.

"*Fuck you, Miles*!" Dolores shouted.

"Just kidding!" Miles said. "I'm with friends. No kidding now. They helped me track you down without any cops. Now open up."

"Bullshit!" Nick yelled through the door. "You don't have any fuckin' friends, man! Except for me! I got a gun aimed right at you, Miles, back off!"

"Open the goddamn door, Nick, we don't have any guns. Just here to help. I know you're a good guy, Miles. You *are* my friend. That's why I'm here. I can help you get away. Both of you. What other chance do you have?"

After an affirmative nod from an obviously panicked Dolores, Nick reluctantly opened the door. He said, "How'd you find us?" when he saw Miles' unsmiling face, then he felt a blinding sense of sharp pain in his shoulder. As he fell backward, he saw the knife slowly slip out of his flesh, the blade dripping blood all the way down the handle and onto Miles' hairy hand. He heard Dolores screaming as he lay on the floor, smelled her sensuous perfume as she bent over him, sobbing, and then the scene began to slowly fade to black.

"I said I didn't have a gun," Nick thought he heard Miles say, before he slipped heavily into the murkiness of his own mind, or somebody's.

Chapter Sixteen

It's one thing to be a B movie impresario, Nick thought—it's another thing to be a B movie *impression*. Stuff like this was only supposed to happen in fiction, in *his* fiction, not in the real world, not in *his* world. This was not the plan for his life. Not *his* plan, that is.

"Maybe it's impetigo?" Dolores suggested without conviction as she dampened his scaly skin with a towel in The Moonlight Lounge restroom.

"*Green* impetigo?" Nick whined. "Man, I gotta go the hospital, I guess. I *hate* the fuckin' hospital."

"Maybe it'll go away," Dolores said, barely hiding her horror.

"Got some kinda cream or somethin'?" Nick asked as his initial shock gave way to panic.

"Just the stuff I've been using on my legs," she said.

"What's wrong with your legs?" Nick said, his gaze in the mirror undistracted as she pulled up her dress to reveal isolated islands of emerging scales on her upper thighs. Green scales. She hadn't noticed this degree of manifestation before, beyond the itching and stiffness, and she freaked out.

"I really, really do hope this is impetigo," she said, voice quivering, eyes welling with tears.

"We haven't even fooled around," Nick observed. "But, did you give this to me somehow? I mean, this just started since we met."

Dolores was too terrified to be insulted. "Did you give it to *me*?"

They wanted to embrace for mutual consolation, but were constricted by fear of further cross-contamination.

"We're turning into monsters," Nick whispered pensively. "We didn't do anything to deserve this."

"Sometimes shit happens to innocent people," Dolores said sadly.

"This is really, really fucked up," Nick agreed. "I'm not sure what to do."

"Want to come over to my house?" she said. "I can put that cream on you."

"I have to finish my show."

"Even *now*? Are you *nuts?*"

He looked at himself in the mirror again, and felt a curious mixture of fascination and repulsion. In a way, this was pretty fucking cool. "You're right. Most of the audience is either asleep or gone by now anyway. I'd just scare 'em. Let's get outta here."

As Nick opened the door for her, Dolores tripped and fell in front of him.

"Are you okay?" he asked, helping her up.

"Dizzy, I guess…it also felt like…my legs felt stuck together or something."

"Must be perspiration. Let's go to my place, it's just down the block," Nick said.

"All right," she said, barely but bravely regaining her composure. "I'll tell Miles."

"Fuck him, he fired you anyway, remember?"

"Not really, and my shift isn't over."

"Neither is mine," he reminded her. "Let's hurry, I don't want anyone to see me like this."

"It's funny," she said, wiping away teary mascara from her cheek. "Now that I've met you, I don't want to die anymore, and yet, I feel like I'm dying."

"Nobody's dying," he said nervously and without conviction. They hurried out the door without anyone seeing them, and down the dark, misty street dimly lit by a single flickering lamppost, two fugitive shadows running from reality, or toward it.

Chapter Seventeen

Hello there. Allow me to introduce myself. I'm the *real* "Nick Winters." You may be confused by now. Welcome to my fucking world. I'm a filmmaker. Exploitation is my racket. I'm making a movie, and you just might be in it.

At this point, I may have lost all credibility with you. For all you know, this first person interjection is simply another ruse to light my muse's fuse. You see what I'm saying? I'm just showing you my hand, at least one of them. The other one is busy, sorry.

I feel haunted by memories of the East. Humid, amber, cold, warm, wet, stark, green, white, blue, brown, sad, yearning, lost. I just thought you should know that.

Anyway, forget this temporary distraction. I'll be back later to check in with you. Promise.

Roll the cameras…and…*Action.*

Chapter Eighteen

Nick felt haunted by memories of the East.

He was thinking about his childhood, which became increasingly idyllic when recalled through the gauze of time, as he lay on the bed at the Motel Capri, Dolores stroking his head, feeling dead. The song “All By Myself” by Eric Carmen played in his hazy, nostalgic brain, mashed-up with Paul Dunlap’s moody score for *I Was a Teenage Werewolf*, a favorite of his while growing up. He wondered how he got from there to here so quickly, and worried that he’d go from here to someplace worse even quicker. “Sometimes I feel like someone is making this shit up, and I’m just going through the motions,” he mumbled, mostly to himself.

“I know the feeling,” she said sweetly, then gently reminded him, “Miles is here….”

“Sorry I had to stab you, man,” Miles’ voice said from somewhere in the room. “I had to take proactive action, though.”

“I don’t get it,” Nick said. “Why the hell did you do that? I thought you wanted to help?”

“I do,” Miles said simply. “I want to help myself. I’m just here for Dolores. You can go to hell, Nick.”

Nick moaned and tried to sit up but his arm felt numb and sore and heavy, and he leaned back down into the pillows Dolores had propped up for him. “What the fuck’s going on?” he said groggily.

“That’s my question, too,” Dolores said, looking up fearfully at Miles.

“I’m afraid,” Nick said as Dolores held him. “Afraid to die before…”

“Before what?” Dolores said, choking back a sob.

“Before I have a chance to show *Invasion of the Saucer Men*. That’s my dream.”

Dolores stared off into space.

“Is that the one where the little big-headed aliens kill Frank Gorshin with booze in their claws?’ Miles asked.

“Yea,” Nick said.

“Well, I’m glad I stabbed you then,” Miles said. “Let’s go, Dolores.”

“Who are these guys with you?” Nick asked as his vision became less blurry, and the ominous humanoid shadows flanking Miles came into sharper focus without revealing their actual identities.

“Hey, what’s the name of the movie they’re watching in *The Blob* when the Blob attacks the audience?” one of the strangers asked Nick.

“*Daughter of Horror*,” Nick said. The stranger nodded, but with a quizzical, unsatisfied expression on his face. Nick then asked him directly, “Who the fuck are you?”

“This is a biker gang that hangs out at the bar,” Miles answered for the stranger. “They’re called Heaven’s Devils.” There were six of them, two bearded, one bald, one wearing a bandana, bare-chested with a leather vest, one wearing a black *lucha libre* mask, all white trash, all well muscled but most with flabby guts, all tattooed, all quietly seething with morose animosity. “I’m gonna make a porn flick starring Dolores. They’re gonna gang-bang her on film while I watch. I’m gonna show it at the theater and make some *real* money. Fuck you and your rubber monster bullshit. I gotta make a living, Nick. I’d film it here so you could watch too, but this is too nice a place. I need someplace really sleazy and disgusting to get the vibe I’m going for. This place is too much like one of your old movies. Let’s go, Dolores.”

Nick sat up again and once again was held back, but it wasn't pain. He just realized he was tied down with ropes binding him to the headboard. Blood had coagulated on the sheets next to him, so it was sticky and gross.

Dolores got up to leave with Miles and the bikers. "Dolores, where you are going?" Nick asked in bewilderment.

"I've done this before, Nick," Dolores said. "I didn't tell you my *whole* story."

"You've done *porn*?" Nick said.

"Not exactly. At least, I've never been filmed before. Don't worry, I know these guys. Goodbye, Nick." She went to the bedside table, picked up her purse, and gave him a kiss.

Nick struggled against the ropes and felt the flesh on his wrists burn. But there was nothing he could do. Dolores walked stoically out the door with Miles and the bikers, leaving Nick there to bleed to death, soon passing out and dreaming of being a pulp fiction writer who literally turns into a lounge lizard. Nick woke up in the middle of the night, screaming, but nobody heard him, nobody but the self-reflection in his mental mirror.

Chapter Nineteen

"This is impossible," Nick said to Dolores as she rubbed the soothing cream into his hideous, leathery face. "This is like one of my goddamn movies, only worse." Dolores, though still quite concerned about her scaly thighs, was singing the song "Wild is the Wind."

"You do have a nice voice," Nick said. "I like both the Nina Simone and David Bowie versions of that song. Johnny Mathis's, meh. Yours is my new favorite."

"I'm glad," she smiled. "Any requests?"

"Something soothing," he said.

"In the shower. Maybe we both need one." Dolores finished applying the cream, even though it would wash off in the water and she'd have to reapply it later, and then she led Nick by the hand to his own bathroom. The booming but muffled sound of techno music beat up against the floorboards, emanating from the strip joint, Zombieville, below. Dolores gingerly and maternally removed Nick's clothes, then hers, as he watched. She was even more beautiful than he had imagined.

After testing the temperature, she stepped into the shower and let the warm water cascade down her curvaceous body. The scales on her legs began to peel off, revealing fresh skin, untainted beneath the mysterious, shedding disease. She then coaxed Nick inside the shower with her, and the scales on his face began to wash away as well, leaving no trace of its existence. It was a miracle. Dolores hummed a tune Nick didn't recognize.

"What's that you're singing?" he asked. "I like it."

"I wrote it myself," she said, happily rinsing the scales from her thighs. They collected by the drain and clogged the water so that it began to fill up the tub. "I call it 'One-Way Ticket to Thrillville.'"

Nick shot straight up. "Holy *shit*! That's the name of the story I'm writing!"

"You're kidding?' Dolores said. "What an incredible coincidence."

"We must be on the same wavelength," he said, his mind completely blown.

"I know," she said incredulously. "That's really amazing. I guess I'm singing the theme to your story, without even realizing it."

"I sometimes write about you, too," he said. "That's what makes it even stranger."

"I know."

"How do you know?"

She shrugged. "I can just feel it. I mean literally. I can *feel* it."

"I guess we really are in sync," Nick said. "Wow. What a weird world we live in."

They both got out of the shower, sans scales, and dried each other off with Nick's slightly skanky bachelor pad towels. Dolores collected then flushed their discarded scales down the toilet.

"I guess we're not monsters, after all," Nick said as he sat on his sofa bed, wearing his silk robe, enjoying this tangible reverie. "What a relief." She was wearing nothing but a towel. "Care for something to drink?" he asked her.

"Coffee?" she said.

"Comin' right up." Nick went into his tiny kitchen and brewed some coffee on the ancient coffee maker, then served some to Dolores in an old-fashioned cup and saucer that had little pinecones painted on them. Dolores smiled in appreciation. Nick went over to his stereo and put on some Miles Davis. "Moon Dreams" filled the air.

He turned it up so as to drown out the strip club techno music below.

"It's like hell down there," he said. "Literally."

"The demons can't get in here, at least," Dolores said. "We're safe."

Nick nodded. "I always figure, since they're down there and I'm up here, this must be heaven. All it was missing was an angel."

They seized the moment, and kissed. The sounds of Miles Davis, the techno music, and even the Theremin in his skull faded away, and all he could hear was her delicate breathing in his ear as they embraced, and her rapid heartbeat, his new favorite sound, the sound of his salvation. He couldn't have imagined it any better. It was all so poetic and pure, like the reflection of the full moon shimmering on the surface of the sea, even while far beneath the placid beauty of the scene, savage sharks tore viciously at their helpless prey.

Chapter Twenty

Dolores came multiple times in a row, sucked into a whirlpool of sexual rapture despite the nausea eating away at her gut. She couldn't look at the drooling, ugly, scarred and pockmarked faces of the bikers, "Heaven's Devils," even when they thrust their tongues into her mouth and licked her face and neck, but she wasn't immune to the sheer animal sensation of hungry, brutal lust. The cocks ruthlessly and mercilessly penetrating her vagina and anus abruptly exploded with semen, flooding her insides and dripping onto her outer skin, injecting her loins with hot, invasive, pervasive fluids that could carry and transmit both life and death into the supple vessel of her trembling body. Miles sat in the corner masturbating. He had already come three times and his cock was very sore, but he still felt good. As the two bikers who just finished withdrew their sated members, one of the other bikers thrust his huge veined cock in her mouth as she lay sprawled across the cot, semen leaking from both her lower orifices onto her sweaty thighs and the dank sheets, mingling with the semen that had already dried there, remnants from the previous orgiastic hours of hedonistic revelry. Another biker sucked on Dolores's toes and hungrily licked the soles of her feet, masturbating as she sucked the other's cock, pretending it was a microphone, and his semen was the song that needed to gush from his instrument. The biker whose cock she was sucking suddenly came down her throat, spilling juices along her jaw, which dripped down her throat and onto her breasts. It was musical, an erotic jazz improvisation, or so she pretended. This was Performance Art. The biker sucking her toes shot his wad and sprayed her torso with even more semen. She was dripping wet inside and out with liquid lust. Heaven's Devils owned her body, which quivered with revulsion and pleasure. Her mind was in the clouds. Her heart was still back at the Motel Capri. Her soul screamed out silently for liberation, even as her body enjoyed, and suffered, undeniable release. Miles was playing Alan Price's version of "I Put a Spell On You" on a portable CD player for background mood music.

"*Cut*!" Miles said to the young slacker video operator, who was also masturbating, then turning off the music. "Let's do this *again*. Dolores, take a shower and clean up. Guys, take a break, you got more work to do tonight. We gotta get as much footage as possible. This has to be a goddamn erotic masterpiece if I'm gonna have a prayer of stayin' in business."

They were in the back room of The Midnight Lounge, which was now closed to the public, still considered a crime scene. The back room was where Miles often slept and dreamed of Dolores. There was only a cot, a pool table, a sink and a shower. The walls were decorated with Playboy centerfolds from the 1960s, Vargas and Elvgren pinups, and the fetishistic photos of Elmer Batters, all haphazardly tacked to the walls. Miles hung them up because they reminded him of Dolores, and he could jerk off to them.

"If you really cared about me, you'd make them wear condoms at least," Dolores said petulantly as she limped to the shower, which didn't even have a curtain, so she washed off all of the semen, old and new, in full view of her violators, who ironically used the scene to reanimate their drug-fueled libidos. *"Condoms are like rubber monsters: bad for business! And these guys are all clean, I told you!"* Miles shouted after Dolores as she turned on the shower and drowned him out. Dolores despised herself as well as the bikers, and yet, she didn't even desire an escape attempt. In some ways, she felt like she was really dominating *them.* The power of her feminine sexuality reduced these grown men to a band of slobbering apes, and she was in total control of their senses, not just hers. She was a malevolent mermaid, a sensuous siren of the sea, and they were merely hapless seamen lured to her lair, seduced, and then…devoured. She was a Black Widow spider, mating, then murdering, her hapless suitors. These were her thoughts as she showered away the slime. She loved the feeling of semen washing off of her flesh and down into the drain, gone without a trace. But then she remembered all the semen still sloshing around inside of her, and she wanted to piss it out, so she did, right down the same drain.

"Can I get another drink, at least?" she called out as she finished up. Miles grunted and went out to the bar and fixed her a Zombie and then brought it to her as she sat on the edge of the creaky cot, smoking a cigarette one of the biker's lit for her, slathering her legs, arm and neck with fresh perfume, the towel draped around the rest of her body, to hide it from the leering eyes of those who had already desecrated it, and were ready to do so again. Only when she was ready, though. She put on her spiked snakeskin high heels, and nothing else.

"All right," she said matter-of-factly, downing the drink, dropping the towel, tossing the cigarette butt and laying back on the cot, nude and spread-eagle. "Let's wrap this up, boys. I'm getting tired." Miles turned "I Put a Spell On You" back on, but this time it was Screamin' Jay Hawkins' version, for variety's sake. Dolores was soon sucked back into the sensual quicksand, trying not to drown in all the fluids engulfing her.

Chapter Twenty-One

Hey there, it's me again. Nick. The *real* Nick. Your humble filmmaker. I just want to give the people what they want, what they *really* want, even if they don't want to admit it. Even if *you* don't want to admit it. It's all just a meaningless distraction, anyway. Sex, love, loneliness, politics, religion, life, death. It's all reduced to the memory of a dream in our collective consciousness. Movies are like that: memories of dreams, captured on film, outlasting the dreamers themselves. May as well make the dream as entertaining as possible. It'll be over soon enough, anyway. I should know. I can see things that you can't from my unique vantage point behind the camera.

Action.

Chapter Twenty-Two

"My cat has been dying of cancer for two years," Nick sadly told Dolores as they cuddled on his sofa bed, with a purring Buddy curled up at the base. "He's all I got. If he dies, *I'll* die of loneliness. I can't live without him. So in a way, I'm dying, too."

Dolores wanted to cry, but wasn't sure why because of her many conflicted emotions. She stroked his face. They had been kissing, but she didn't feel aroused, just nurturing. "That's sweet. He seems pretty healthy."

"Yea, against all odds," Nick said. "I don't know what keeps him going. I can't afford the chemo. He just takes some other pills, I don't know what they are, but they're cheap. And they seem to work."

"Maybe he lives on love," Dolores said. "*Your* love."

"I hope so. That I got limitless supplies of. I know his love keeps *me* alive, so maybe it's a symbiotic relationship." The Miles Davis CD had ended so Nick got up to replace it with some Dave Brubeck. "Take Five" filled the air of the small studio apartment. The techno music downstairs had stopped, since the club was now closed. They finally had the world to themselves.

"I hope Miles doesn't fire me," Dolores said as Nick sat back down next to her, breaking the mood with a reality check. "Or you."

"Fuck him," Nick said again. "Who needs this lousy gig? I got better things to do."

"Like what? Be a Paperback Writer, like the Beatles song?"

"I guess so," Nick sighed. "I don't know, though. No

money in just making things up anymore. It's all one big reality show these days, even if there's nothing realistic about any of 'em. And even if you make the cut, you can still get voted off the goddamn island. I just write to keep myself interested."

"In what?" she asked.

"Life," he said. "It reminds me I'm still awake and safe. Sometimes I have dreams I'm on the run, because I accidentally killed someone, somebody I don't even know. That's how I feel when I'm awake, like I'm on the lam and the cops are gonna bust the door down any second and drag me away."

Dolores smiled at him. "Maybe you'll let me read your stuff someday? I bet it's really good."

He shrugged off her show of support, since he couldn't match her confidence in himself. "Maybe you should wait for the movie. I guess I shouldn't quit the day job till then, huh? Or my night job."

"I know how you feel," she said. "The kind of things I like to sing, nobody wants to hear anymore. Not enough to make a living at it, anyway. That's why I need this job. Miles really saved my life. I couldn't hold down a steady job anywhere else. I owe him, and I feel like I'm letting him down."

Nick abruptly said his secret thought out loud. "Does Miles have a thing for you, or what?"

"I think so," Dolores said simply. "That's my only chance of keeping my job."

"Aw c'mon!" Nick said. "You can't play into that creep's fantasies just to make a living. That would make you, uh..."

"A *whore?*" she said, wide-eyed.

"*No*!" Nick didn't like the trajectory of this conversation. "Just, I mean, Miles is a good guy and all, he gave me my break, but he *is* a little creepy, you gotta admit."

"Just old," she said. "I've dated old guys before. But not *him*. Don't worry. Are you jealous?"

Nick blushed and turned away, but she took his face into her hands, and kissed him. "Don't be," she whispered. Then her towel fell away, and he took off his robe, and he kissed her all over her body, though she wouldn't let him enter her. "I'm not ready yet," she whispered as she massaged his member until he finished. Then they fell asleep in each other's arms, Buddy still resting comfortably at the base of the sofa bed, somewhat disgusted by this display of human passion.

Dolores lay awake for a time as Nick slept. She was beginning to remember things from her past, her childhood, that she had willfully suppressed. Finally, in the dark, engulfed by her own sad, horrible memories, she wept herself to sleep.

A pounding at the door awakened them both. It was dawn. "Open up, Nick. It's Miles," said a mysterious voice from outside. Nick and Dolores looked at each other, then he got up and opened the door.

Chapter Twenty-Three

Still wearing her snakeskin heels, Dolores threw on Miles' discarded trench coat to go with them, but no panties or bra, since they had been ripped off and torn in the initial foreplay of the evening. The men were all asleep on the floor, even Miles and the video operator, exhausted from spent passions. The various versions of "I Put a Spell On You" had stopped. She didn't take another shower. She didn't have time. She had to go rescue Nick, driven by the urgent hope he was still alive.

She lit one last cigarette for the road, and she was still puffing on it when she removed Nick's gun from her purse, which she had been hiding since they left the Motel Capri, and walked up to each man, lying drunk, drugged, groggy and semi-conscious across the floor, and shot them all in or around the head, except for the young video operator, whom she let escape with a flesh wound to the leg. He wouldn't tell anybody, she had scared the shit out of him, and she knew where he lived. She took the video out of the recorder, threw it on the ground, stomped it to pieces, put the gun in her purse, and walked out. All the men were dead, lying in pools of their own blood, brains, sweat, and semen. Or at least, they *seemed* dead. Dead enough. In any case, she'd made her point. When the orgy was finally finished, to her own satisfaction, *she* had discarded *them*. Initially, she didn't realize when she had refilled Nick's gun with the bullets from his pocket that she was in fact preparing for this very scenario. She never planned anything in advance, because things changed too often. She liked to be prepared, just in case, for whatever circumstances she found herself in. She let Life happen, and reacted to it accordingly, armed with the appropriate ammunition.

She drove to the Motel Capri in her 1960 Impala, since Miles had made her drive it back to The Midnight Lounge. She wasn't even sure how long it had been since she'd been gone. It was all a bruised blur of sex and violence, murky mental images awash in cum, blood, sweat, booze and tears. So many fluids. So little air to breath.

When she got to The Capri, there were cop cars everywhere, and the place was strung with yellow tape. She kept going, sobbing, directionless.

She didn't know how long she'd been driving through seemingly endless rural wasteland under darkening gray skies when she saw a hitchhiker on the side of the road. Feeling lost and lonesome, she picked him up with impetuous abandon. The car tilted as he got in. He was around six feet tall, probably close to 240 lbs., with gray hair combed into a perfect pompadour, and he was wearing a jogging suit, leather loafers and a gold medallion, goombah-style.

After he got in, the stranger removed his big gold sunglasses, extended a cheaply bejeweled hand, and said, "Hey there darlin', my name's Jesse, thanks for the lift. Thank you very much."

Chapter Twenty-Four

"The joint burned down," Miles said, tears streaming down his face, as he brushed past Nick and plopped down on the sofa bed beside Dolores, who was beside herself.

"You're kiddin'," Nick said, realizing that was a stupid thing to say, but he didn't have a sensible response handy. "I mean *shit*. How the hell did *that* happen? You mean it's totally, like *gone*?"

"I don't know really, fire trucks are still there. I had to get out of there, too much smoke. I'll fill out the papers later. Apparently some guy was smoking in the back of the theater, fell asleep, and the old couch went up like a pile of tinder wood and spread like crazy, nobody caught him till it was too late. He's dead, I think, I don't know, cops are looking into it, wouldn't let me back in. I was next door at the bar, which is okay…where the hell were *you*?"

"I, uh, just got home a little while ago."

"Bullshit," Miles said without any discernible emotion beyond grief mixed with an odd sense of relief. "I'm wiped out, I mean financially, and I'm beat too. Mind if I crash here for a little while?"

"I'm leaving," Dolores said, as if hypnotized, rising deliberately from the sofa bed. All she could think of was the secret that had risen to the surface of her muddled mind.

"Stay put," Nick said, and she sat back down. "Miles, I can't believe what you're telling me."

"Believe it," Miles said. "Got a drink for me?"

Nick went to the little vintage bar in the corner and poured Miles some Scotch neat and handed it to him. "Cheers," Miles said, downing the drink in a gulp then extending it for a refill, which Nick obliged.

"Let's go out into the hall and talk," Nick said to Miles. "Bring your drink. Dolores, we'll be right back."

"Where am I gonna go?" Dolores said. "I'm so sorry, Miles. I'm glad the bar is okay, at least."

He shot her a look of mysterious disdain as he walked out, Nick following and shutting the door behind them. Dolores felt chilled.

In the dimly lit hallway, Nick said to Miles, "C'mon, Miles, this can't be true. The theater just burned down to the god damn ground, just like that?"

Miles stared at him coldly. "Why the fuck would I lie about something like that? Where'd you go, anyway? If you were there like you were supposed to be, maybe this wouldn't have happened."

"Oh, so you're blaming me now?" Nick said. "Let's go down there, I want to see this for myself."

"Fine, let's go," Miles said.

"Let me get Dolores."

"To hell with her," Miles said. "She pissed me off."

"Why?" Nick asked.

"She left the bar without saying anything, and I find her here with you? What the hell kinda shit is that?"

Nick sighed. "Yea, whatever, man, we'll talk about that later, you got bigger problems right now."

"Agreed. But I *will* deal with her later."

Nick opened the door and called Dolores's name. No answer. He went inside the apartment. There was no trace of her, not in the bathroom, the kitchen or the main room. He ran to the window and checked the fire escape. His studio was on the second story. There was no sign of her in the street.

"Dolores is gone," he said as he ran past Nick, and outside to look for her.

Chapter Twenty-Five

"I'm lookin' for my twin brother," the man who called himself Jesse told Dolores as they continued to drive down the dark road toward no place special.

"Where do you think he is? Is he in trouble?" Dolores asked, her face streaked with mascara and tears, yet trying her best to be distracted by the mysterious yet oddly charming stranger. She felt cold and vulnerable, forgetting she had nothing on beneath the trench coat. Fortunately it was a rather balmy night. But had she remembered her underlying nakedness, she may not have picked up the stranger. Now it was too late. She kept an eye on the gun in her purse, safely tucked in the seat between them. She had one bullet left in the chamber, just in case. She had told him hardly anything about herself, just that she was mourning a loved one, so please excuse her appearance and composure. He was doing most of the talking, and she didn't like what she was hearing so far.

"Oh, he's dead, my brother's stone cold dead," Jesse continued. "Been dead for years. I'm doin' my best to carry on in his name. I've been doin' that for years, workin' little gigs here and there around the country. Then I got word somebody spotted my brother somewhere, um, eating."

"I thought you said he was dead."

"Oh, he's definitely dead. No question about it. But he's still walking around, and apparently, he's traded in peanut butter and bananas for human flesh."

Dolores slammed on the breaks and came to a sharp halt on the side of the desolate road. The night was black and starless, like a beckoning void. "Look, you seem like a nice guy and I could use the company, but..."

Jesse laughed. "Whoa, whoa, *whoa*, ease up, lil' sister, I didn't mean to freak you out or anything."

"Look, you're obviously an Elvis impersonator, and now you're telling me he's actually your brother who's now some kind of fuckin' *zombie.*"

"So?"

"Get out!' she screamed. "*Now*!"

"Hey, hey, hey," Jesse stammered. "Now hold on a second there. You picked me up and now you're just gonna abandon me in the middle of nowhere, in the middle of the night? What kinda gal are you? Ain't I been nice 'n' polite to you?"

"But you're talking crazy."

"Hey, I'm just tellin' you the truth, darlin'. I tell *every*body the truth. But nobody wants to hear it. They all think I'm crazy, but bein' crazy don't mean you're necessarily a liar, too. This ain't even the first time I been kicked out of a car *tonight.* Fact, I was booted out just before you came along, and I didn't even tell the other dude about my brother. You seemed different, all lonesome and sad, but open-minded. My mistake. I promise to shut up if you can just drop me off at the next motel or diner or somethin'. Deal?"

Dolores pulled herself together, then reached for the gun in her purse and aimed it at the stranger's forehead. "Okay, but if you don't, I'll shoot you. I mean it. I'm in no mood for anybody's bullshit. I told you, I'm in mourning."

"Okay, okay, lil' sister, you got it," Jesse said.

She started the car and they drove in heavy silence for a few minutes until she asked him, "Where's your stuff?"

"What stuff?"

"*Any* stuff!" she said impatiently. "Suitcase? Clothes? *Guitar*?"

"I left it behind, I had to leave where I was in a hurry. My car, too, that's why I was hitchin'."

"Where were you?" she asked.

"Motel," he said.

"Which one?" Dolores said, suddenly getting suspicious.

"Why? It's called The Capri."

Dolores slammed on the brakes again, and the Impala remained still and vulnerable in the center of the road. "I was just fucking *there*!"

"Before or *after* the cops showed up?" he asked.

"*Both,*" she said.

"So you pretty much know why I left then," Jesse said, wary of the gun in her purse.

"No, I only know why *I* left," she said.

"Maybe it's the same reason," Jesse said. "You first."

"My boyfriend was there, somebody stabbed him."

Jesse raised his bushy eyebrows. "And you split on him?"

"I *had* to, long story. What does any of that have to do with you?

"Nothin'," Jesse said simply. "Just a strange coincidence."

"So why'd *you* leave, with all your stuff still back there?" she asked.

"The cops are after me," he said simply. "I thought they were there for *me*, not your boyfriend. I'm kinda relieved, but sorry for your loss. You sure he's dead?"

"I don't know, really, but if the police have him, he might as well be," Dolores said. "He was running from the cops too, for accidentally shooting someone."

"Funny, they're after me for shooting someone, too," Jesse said. "But it wasn't no accident."

"Who'd you shoot?" Dolores asked.

"I'm afraid to tell you. You may shoot *me*. Then the cops would be after *you*."

"I promise not to shoot you, unless you raped a little kid or something," Dolores said.

"I ain't no perv, lil' sister," Jesse said. "You've shot people before, haven't you?"

"Just recently, in fact," Dolores boasted.

"I can tell, you're way too confident with that thing."

"Why are you running? *Tell me*."

Jesse contemplated his options, let out a sigh, and then said, "I shot somebody my brother bit. He was already dead when I shot him. But he was trying to bite me too, so I shot him in the head. Nobody believes me when I tell 'em the poor sucker was already dead when I blew his brains out, so the cops want to talk to me. The feelin' ain't mutual."

Dolores didn't respond. They kept driving in silence for a while until they came to a diner.

"Let's eat," she said. "I'm hungry."

"Me, too. I'm always hungry, though. Are you asking me to join you?"

"Yes, but I'm bringing my purse, if you know what I mean."

"Check," Jesse said, and then they both went into the diner.

Chapter Twenty-Six

"Look at it this way," Nick said to Miles as they stood together on the street corner, staring at the smoldering remnants of The Oasis Theater. Rain began to fall, dousing the embers. "Maybe in another world, another life, your theater is still around, risen from the ashes like a sphinx."

"You mean a *phoenix*, dumbfuck," Miles said, puffing on a cigarette, even though the idea of it made him sick now. "And maybe in another life, another world, *I'm* the one who's dead. Maybe in some other place, it was *me* sittin' in the back of the theater, smokin', and now I'm just a fried corpse. I feel that way right here, right now. But instead I'm still sufferin' with the rest of the walkin' stiffs. Fuck *me*."

Nick sighed helplessly, but was weary of pretending he gave a shit about The Oasis. "I have to look for Dolores now. Sorry, Miles." They had already been to her apartment, the first place they'd looked for her, but nobody was there and the landlady said she hadn't seen Dolores all night.

"You don't seem too concerned," Miles said. "About the theater, I mean. You lost your livelihood, too, y'know."

"That wasn't much of a livelihood, man," Nick said. "You were gonna can me soon, anyway, let's face it. And you still got the tiki bar, at least. See ya around, maybe"

"Hey Nick," Miles called after him. "Let me know if you need anything. And tell Dolores her job is still waiting for her."

Nick shot his forefinger at Miles, then resumed his

search for his missing muse.

As he walked aimlessly, searching streets and alleyways, his skin began to itch again, and the Theremin increased its sonic torment. He felt like he was either going to lose his mind, or lose himself *in* his mind.

Chapter Twenty-Seven

The thought of the Elvis zombie wandering around somewhere out in the world attacking and eating people creeped Dolores out. She'd always been a fan of Elvis, but never zombies. Obviously this strange old guy Jesse was a raving lunatic as well as an imposter, not just an impersonator, but something about him drew her into his company. In an odd way, she could relate to him. They both concocted alternate universes to escape into, justifying the sins and crimes of their tangible worlds by blindly believing in the veracity of their imagined parallel worlds instead. This is how Dolores saw it, and for her sake, she hoped Jesse saw it that way, too. Otherwise she was risking her life with this maniac. Meantime, she'd found a kindred spirit to keep her company on an otherwise solitary sojourn.

"I feel like I'm running away from something, just like you," Dolores said to Jesse as they sat across from each other in a booth at the Day Dream Diner, sipping coffee and idly nibbling on eggs and pie. Their stomachs weren't as empty and famished as their souls.

Jesse nodded. He seemed very tired.

"Admit it," she said coaxingly. "You're not *really* Elvis's twin brother. You may *look* like him, or at least how he might look now, I'll give you that—but his *twin*? I mean, didn't he die at birth? Stillborn, they call it? His twin brother, I mean. Jesse isn't even your real name, is it? C'mon, you can tell me."

Jesse shook his head and laughed softly. "Darlin', I keep tellin' you, my name is Jesse, Jesse Mancini, Elvis

Presley was my brother, and now he's back, eating people. I don't tell everybody that, but that's the way it is. Take it or leave it."

Dolores pounded her fist on the table, startling the few other patrons in the diner, which hadn't changed in sixty years, except for the prices. "C'mon, man! That doesn't make any sense! I guess that means *you're* a zombie, too?"

"You gotta die first to be one of those," Jesse said simply. "I didn't die at birth, as has been widely and falsely reported in the mainstream media. That thing buried in a shoebox in a grave in Tupelo ain't *me*. Obviously."

"Obviously," Dolores said dryly. "Because that's the *real* Jesse. Jesse Garon."

"Then who am I?" Jesse said sarcastically.

"You tell me."

"I keep trying to," Jesse said, flustered. "That whole story is a myth. Truth is, I was given away, because the Presleys couldn't afford to have two mouths to feed. They were too ashamed to admit it. They buried a poor puppy named Shep in that grave. I think he got run over by a truck or somethin'. Anyway, I was adopted by another family of eye-talian immigrants that moved away from Tupelo not long after I was born. I was raised in Georgia, and later New Jersey. But I never left my roots." Jesse finished his pie and signaled the bee-hived waitress wearing too much makeup for another slice. When she got close anyone could see that the waitress was hiding a terrible complexion with her gaudy cosmetics. "I was in touch with my brother after he got famous, and we kept in touch, secretly, for years. Till he died. Now that he's back from the dead, I gotta get in touch with him again. Maybe he'll listen to me. Only I understand what it's like to be undead, meaning everyone thinks you're dead, but you really ain't. Plus I'm his own flesh and blood, so maybe he won't eat me. That'd be cannibalism."

Dolores sat back in a daze, staring out the window into the darkness. It seemed like it had been night for days now.

Chapter Twenty-Eight

It was raining like liquid Armageddon, and Dolores was nowhere to be found.

Nick tried not to panic. It's not like she could just vanish into heavy, wet air. What worried him most was the *reason* she was missing. Why had she suddenly decided to disappear on him? Was she hiding something other than herself?

The Theremin was racking his brain as he went into a gas station convenience store rest room to check out his itchy face. The green scales were making a rapid comeback. Now he *had* to panic. He had no choice. It was a natural reaction to his circumstances. But panic wouldn't change things. He was changing enough as it was.

Keeping his face down, Nick ran home to his apartment building and up the stairs past a couple of off-duty zombie strippers who tried to stop him for some idle flirtation. One must've caught a glimpse of him before he went inside, since he heard her let out a little scream as he brushed by her. He locked the door behind him and stared at his reflection in the bathroom mirror with horror. At least his hair still looked good.

The phone rang, and rang. Nick was going to ignore it until he realized it could be Dolores. It wasn't.

"Nick, it's Miles, where are you?"

"Fuck," Nick said under his breath. "Whaddya need, Miles?"

"Can you come down to the lounge? I need to talk to you."

"Not now, man, I told you, I gotta find Dolores," Nick said as he fearfully felt his face.

"Well, that's what this is about. The cops found a body in the lake. They think it might be her."

Nick slammed down the phone and ran to his door, then stopped. He wanted to leave but couldn't expose himself like this. He didn't know what to do. Ice flowed through his reptilian veins. He went back into the bathroom to look at himself in the mirror one more time. Even his eyes were turning yellowish, his pupils contracting into narrow cat-like slits. The transformation was accelerating.

Fuck it, he had to go. He went back downstairs and stared directly at one of the loitering strippers, who let out a louder scream this time, but he kept moving.

When Nick got to The Moonlight Lounge, still smoky from the previous night's fatal fire next door, some cops were standing out front. When they saw Nick, they tentatively placed their hands on their guns, but weren't sure whether to draw their weapons, since Nick was committing no crime, other than bizarre, abject, otherworldly ugliness.

Nick ran past the confused cops into the lounge and saw Miles talking to some more cops by the bar. "It can't be Dolores!" Nick shouted, interrupting their somber conference.

"Nick?" Miles said, recognizing the voice, but not the face. "What the fuck happened to you?"

"Yea, I got a nervous rash or somethin', must be all this stress," Nick said with shocking nonchalance. "What about this body you found?"

"Did you know Dolores Summers?" one of the cops asked Nick warily.

"Yes."

"Can you come down to the morgue and identify the body?"

"I hope not," Nick said. "Lead the way." But the cops had no intention of taking him to the morgue, not in his seriously fucked up condition. Unless he died on the way downtown. That would sure be a shame.

Chapter Twenty-Nine

It's me again, Nick, the exploitation filmmaker. Thought I'd check in to see how you're doing so far. If none of this seems real to you, something you can relate to in your own life, consider this: your memory of the moment that just passed, how tangible is it now?

And now…and now…and now…may as well be a movie you can't touch, only envision. And at least a movie, frozen in space, doesn't change over time. Your memories will. Dreams and memories eventually merge in the imagination, and since both are equally intangible, both are equally real, or unreal, relative to the touch of the present moment, which is fleeting, blending with our dreams of the future and memories of the past before we can capture and hold onto any of them—it all just slips through our grasp like so much sea mist.

Action.

Chapter Thirty

Jesse and Dolores left the diner and drove deep into the dark, seemingly endless night.

"What time is it?" Dolores asked Jesse.

"I don't know anymore," Jesse said. "And I don't care. Where we goin'?"

"I don't know, and I don't care," Dolores said with a slightly uneasy laugh.

Just then some sort of large animal jumped directly in front of the Impala, collided with the bumper and rolled up onto the hood and smashed into the windshield. Then it rolled back off the hood onto the road and Dolores drove right over it with a turbulent *bump* before screeching to a violent halt.

After they stopped, both noticed blood dripping from crescent-shaped gashes in their foreheads, carved into their flesh by the force of their faces slamming against the dashboard upon impact with the animal. Jesse's cheap, fake gold sunglasses were shattered.

Dazed, they got out of the car and warily walked towards the animal, or what was left of it. But they found nothing but bloody footprints leading off to the side of the road. Bloody, biped footprints.

They couldn't see anything, but they heard what sounded like an anguished howl in the near distance, somewhere off the murky roadside. They looked at each other tentatively, then staggered back into the car and sped off, fleeing from the scene of their latest crime against humanity, or something.

Chapter Thirty-One

Nick was getting the third degree even as the scales on his flesh were being wrongly diagnosed by the local quack as third degree burns from an alleged act of arson he didn't commit.

Nick worried about his cat, Buddy. He wondered if he'd left enough dry food out for him. Plus Buddy needed his daily Prednisone pill. The cops didn't care about Nick's sick cat.

Nick recalled a recurring dream wherein Buddy is swimming alongside of him in a pool for a while, and when they reach the end, Nick lifts Buddy out of the water and sets him down poolside. To Nick, this dream always seemed like a metaphor for their journey through life together. He didn't want that odyssey to end. The song "My Buddy" as sung by Mel Torme always reminded Nick of his cat. Tears poured out of Nick's yellow eyes but he couldn't feel them on his dry, scaly cheeks. He feared he'd never see Buddy again, that he'd reach the end of the pool and climb out without Nick to help him and see him off.

"Did you start that fire and then flee the scene?" the police chief asked Nick one more time. "You know, a man burned to death in there."

"*No*!' Nick cried. "You gotta let me go, I have to feed my cat, man, he needs his medicine or he'll *die*!"

"Did you then drown Dolores Summers?" asked another cop. "You were with her after the fire, she was in your apartment, and now she's *gone*."

"*Hell no!* Are you even sure she's *dead*?" Nick couldn't remember the last time he'd been in so much pain, both internally and externally. The scales felt heavy and cloying, like the unbearable weight on his heart. Dolores just couldn't be dead. It was too soon, not her time. "Do you really even have a body? I thought you wanted me to identify."

"Not any more," the police chief said bluntly. Nick's vision was blurred due to the transformation, and he had trouble focusing on their faces. He just felt surrounded by hostile voices. "We fished her out of the lake earlier today, completely unconscious, apparently deceased but then she…well, we don't know what happened. She's just *gone*."

"What? I thought you said she was in the morgue?" Nick said.

"She was," said the chief.

"This doesn't make any sense."

"Tell us about it," said the chief. "Tell us *all* about it. Then we're going to have someone give you a further examination. Both physically and mentally."

Another cop jumped in and demanded, "Did you first drown then kidnap and molest the corpse of Dolores Summers?"

"What?"

Nick pondered the story he'd been writing, about the mixed-up would–be outlaw who accidentally kills a sax player, then goes on the lam with the mysteriously seductive torch singer of his dreams. That was one alternative lifestyle he could really embrace right about now.

Chapter Thirty-Two

"I Was a Teenage Werewolf," Jesse said to Dolores after they'd been driving in silence for some time after the "accident." It was still dark outside.

"Huh?" Dolores said, interrupted from her stupor. "What crazy shit are you sayin' *now*, old man?"

"That wasn't a confession, I was just thinkin' of this movie I saw when I was a kid," Jesse said. "With Michael Landon. You know the one."

"Yea, saw it on TV eons ago, you probably saw it at the drive-in, you old coot—what about it?" Dolores reached for a cigarette in her purse, and Jesse flinched. "Don't worry, I'm not gonna shoot you, I'm too used to you already," Dolores said as she took out a smoke and Jesse lit it for her with the dashboard lighter.

"Was that a werewolf we hit?" Jesse asked rhetorically.

"Elvis zombies are one thing," Dolores said. "I draw the line at werewolves, teenage or otherwise, sorry. Hope you're not tryin' to tell me Michael Landon is still alive, too, and he's your long lost cousin or some shit. Probably we just ran into a bear, or a deer."

Jesse just laughed.

"My front end is banged up pretty bad, though, whatever the hell that thing was," Dolores continued. "Not to mention this fucked up windshield. Not sure how much longer it's gonna hold together." The windshield was badly cracked, but still barely intact. Bits of broken glass were trickling inside the car.

"Could've been worse," Jesse said. "These old cars are built like dang rocket ships. I'm more worried about that cut in your head, lil' sister."

Dolores felt the dried blood in her scalp and on her face and grimaced at Jesse. "You too. We're a mess, Jess. We should stop someplace and get cleaned up, whaddya say?"

"Haven't seen no place for miles, like we're driving through a black hole or somethin'," Jesse said." Dang, this feels like '*The Outer Limits*' meets '*Route 66.*' My brother and I used to watch those shows together. I loved that Corvette those two guys drove around in. If you have to get lost, might as well do it in style." Dolores nodded in acknowledgement without actually responding. They drove a bit further in silence before Jesse said, "Y'know, those tracks in the road weren't hooves or paws, and deer don't walk on two legs, neither do bears."

"That's enough."

"Okey-doke."

They kept driving for a short while longer until they finally saw a neon motel sign flickering in the distance. Dolores sped up, but then slowed down as the sign became clearer.

It said *Motel Capri*.

"What the hell?" Dolores said, "You mean we've been driving in a fuckin' *circle* all god damn night?"

"Looks that way," Jesse said, perplexed but resigned to fate. "Should we keep going?"

"No, fuck it," Dolores said, taking a desperate drag on her cigarette. "No signs of any cops, at least. Maybe the coast is clear now. Let's stop and take a break. Maybe this is a *different* Capri motel."

"Yea, and maybe I'm the King of Rock 'n' Roll," Jesse said snidely. Dolores shot him a look, and he then said, "Hey just kiddin'. That's my twin brother, not me. And hey, maybe this is The Capri's twin, too?"

"Fat chance on both counts," Dolores said as they

pulled into the parking lot of The Capri. Though it looked exactly the same as the "other" Motel Capri, it appeared to be deserted, no other cars in the lot, though the sign still shone in the perpetual blackness like a deceptively benign beacon with an ulterior motive. And no sign of any yellow police tape.

"Watch who you're callin' fat," Jesse said as they stopped and got out of the wrecked Impala and approached the office. One small light shone eerily inside.

Dolores tried the door, and it was locked, so she knocked. When there was no response, she began to bang on the door, and then yell for assistance.

"This is creeping me out, man," Jesse said.

"Hold it," Dolores said. "Somebody's comin'. And it's not Norman Bates."

"That's a relief," Jesse said. "I can't take any more rude surprises."

"Sing it, brother," Dolores said.

Chapter Thirty-Three

With The Oasis Theater in ruins, along with his life in general, Nick was somewhat worried about what he would do for money once he got out of jail, *if* he got out of jail. Ironically, inspired by his surroundings, as well as his own story, he considered turning to crime. He'd always been chronically unemployable. As a general rule he didn't respect people, much less people with authority over him, and as soon as he was reluctantly hired for some shit job, the clock counting down to his inevitable termination began ticking immediately, and typically, it was a stopwatch.

As Nick sat in his cell, illegally but helplessly held on trumped up charges of remotely suspected kidnapping, alleged murder and, most outrageously, necrophilia, awaiting bail Miles half-heartedly promised to arrange, Nick also considered the irony of his new lizard skin. It was his *human* skin he was shedding in favor of this rough, intimidating, but ultimately powerful new exterior. Maybe this was his true self after all. A new career could await him in a circus sideshow. He wondered if such things still existed. He'd always felt like a social misfit, an outcast banished to the outskirts of polite society, so he supposed it was about time he began to actually look like one.

Nick thought of Dolores, and he began to cry. He got a hard-on and his scaly hands reached down for his prickly prick. He began to masturbate thinking of Dolores being gang-banged by a bunch of bikers, like in his story. His leathery skin was still sexually sensitive, and he shot a wad of yellow lizard cum onto the cell wall.

"*Hey*!" a passing cop blurted, beating on the bars. "What the fuck are you doing, you fuckin' freak! *Stop that*!"

"Lick it up," Nick said defiantly as he rolled over on his cot, his back to the exasperated cop.

"*You* lick it up, creep," the cop said.

Nick's tongue instinctively shot out of his mouth and lapped up some of his own cum, surprising and amusing himself, but absolutely traumatizing the horrified cop.

"They're gonna bury you, freak," the cop finally said, spitting for punctuation before walking off in disgusted awe.

Nick didn't care anymore, growing comfortable in his new skin, joyfully discovering his newfound abilities. As long as he kept his hair intact, he'd find a way to adjust to this otherwise ungodly transformation. He needed to embrace his true self, and that didn't just mean masturbation. He needed to devise an escape if he wasn't released soon. Miles had promised to go feed Buddy, but he knew Buddy missed him. Cats need love to live, just like people. Or lizards. Or lizard-people.

Or mermaids.

He felt guilty for masturbating to such a degrading, decadent scenario, but now that it was out of his system, Nick thought of Dolores in a more sacred light, and he began to leak more liquid, this time from his yellow eyes. His world was shattered without her healing presence. But his mind felt muddled and increasingly warped. He was losing control. The reptilian half of him was beginning to consume the remaining vestiges of his humanity.

Nick knew the cops were fucking with him, singling him out as a suspect based primarily on his incidentally menacing, mysteriously alien appearance. They were much more scared of him than he was of them. He had to use their fear to his advantage. Masturbation, then manipulation. He had to escape these narrow-minded confines and liberate Dolores from whatever predicament she was in, even if it was Death itself. The cops had no body, so they had no murder, no proof of her abrupt absence from this world, no crime to pin on Nick, other than accidental grotesqueness. This was all contrived bullshit for the sake of willful ignorance. First Nick needed his freedom, and then he'd find the truth.

Nick internally vowed that, once he was free and had found Dolores, he would finish his story about the *other* Nick and Dolores, the ones who lived in his head. Or maybe he lived in their heads. It didn't matter any more. He liked their story better, anyway, simply because he could control it.

The Theremin swelled in his brain, and Nick crouched into a fetal position on the cot, licking his own cum from his leathery lizard lips, trying to drown out his secret sonic pain with his own blood-curdling screams.

Chapter Thirty-Four

Dolores's insistent pounding on the office door had obviously awakened the desk clerk at the Motel Capri from either a deep slumber or a drunken stupor. He was dressed in black from head to toe, including his boots, which were caked with mud and what appeared to be blood; even his sunken eyes and thick, wavy hair were black, jet black, so he was black all over, like the endless night outside, or the ghost of Johnny Cash. He walked with a limp.

"Kinda looks like my brother when he got messed up on prescription drugs," Jesse whispered to Dolores, but when she shot him a disapproving look, he quickly added, "But it ain't. This fella is still alive, for one thing."

"Where is everybody?" Dolores asked the desk clerk, nervously tightening her trench coat, which thinly veiled her voluptuous, violated nakedness. She felt a chill that had nothing to do with the temperature in the room. The somewhat sleazy clerk sleepily sized her up, from her snakeskin high heels to her tousled bedroom hair, licking his lips with predatory appreciation. He was middle-aged and craggy-faced, vaguely handsome, but haggard, like his best days were behind him, and out of sheer bitterness, he wanted everyone else's to be, too.

"Everyone beat it after the incident," the desk clerk said.

"What incident?" Dolores asked with forced innocence. She thought of the gun in her purse, and how quickly she'd be able to access it.

"The one where the guy got killed, or died, or somethin', I don't know," the clerk said. "Didn't you hear about it? I guess you're not from around here. It was all over the news. I had to shut it off, haven't turned on the TV. since."

Dolores felt paralyzed with shock. "What guy?" she whispered.

"Don't know, wasn't my shift," the clerk said. "I work the night shift. This didn't happen on my watch. Cops are always botherin' the wrong people, ever notice that? Innocent folks get harassed all the time. You get pulled over for doin' five per over the speed limit, then right after you get your ticket, some joker speeds by doing *fifty* over the speed limit. And the cop that nailed you is long gone. The system just ain't fair."

Jesse shrugged off the clerk's non-sequitur diatribe. He shared a disturbing sense of dread and disorientation with Dolores. "Hey, what time of day did this so-called incident happen?" he asked the clerk.

"This morning," the clerk said.

"That seems like so long ago," Dolores whispered despondently. She sank into an Eames chair behind her, feeling numb. Jesse sat beside her and tried to console her, though he wasn't sure what for.

"Do you know who the person was who died?" Dolores asked the clerk.

"Nope, nobody knows nothin' about him," the clerk said dispassionately. "Police didn't release any details, and like I said, I wasn't even here. But all the commotion scared off the customers, I know that much. Now the place is as deserted as a ghost town. Can I get you two lovers a room?"

"We ain't lovers," Jesse said gallantly. "We'll take two rooms."

"No," Dolores said. "One room will be fine." Jesse raised his eyebrows, but didn't protest.

"Suit yourselves," the clerk said, removing what

looked like a toothpick from his pocket, and idly chewing on it as he opened the registry book. “Names? Cash or credit? I’m Eugene, by the way. Need anything, just ring. I got nothin’ but time and you got the run of the place just now.”

When Dolores stood up to sign her name, she noticed the clerk was not sucking on a toothpick. It was a bone—the bone of what appeared to be a human finger.

Chapter Thirty-Five

Nick fell asleep and dreamed more of his story, the one he wished he were at home transcribing right now, Buddy at his feet, Dolores on the sofa bed, reading chapters admiringly as he completed them. When he woke up, he was temporarily disoriented. Then after a groggy scan of his surroundings the grim, bizarre reality of his situation came back to him, and all he wanted to do was go back to sleep. He felt his face. Still scaly. He felt his hair. Still there. That was something, at least.

Soon after Nick shook off the mental remnants of his deeply disturbed dreams, Miles showed up with a cop. He was posting bail for Nick. It wasn't really bail money, though, since Nick wasn't being officially held on any specific charges. It was bribe money.

"I fed your cat, too," Miles said. "All this and my theater just burned down. I'd say I'm a stand-up fucking guy, wouldn't you?"

"You're a goddamn saint," Nick said in a raspy tone. "Thanks."

The cop by Miles' side just looked down at the ground, avoiding eye contact with the yellow-pupils of the ex-prisoner. He mumbled a malediction under his breath.

"Now we gotta get you to a hospital to check out that rash," Miles said.

"Gotta find Dolores," Nick said by rote.

"She's gone, Nick, let her go."

"But not dead. She can't be. The lousy stupid cops even said they have no body, this is all bullshit because of my fucked-up face. I scare 'em and they don't know what to do about it."

"Let's talk about that later," Miles said, forking over

the check and signing the release papers. Nick had to be back in court next week, though the cops had yet to file any official charges against him. Meantime, he wasn't allowed to leave town limits. "You gotta take care of yourself, first."

"Did you give Buddy his pill?" Nick asked worriedly.

"*Yes,*" Miles hissed. "He's fine. You're not. It'll take more than a fuckin' pill to cure whatever's ailin' you. And button your fly, for Chrissakes." Nick had forgotten to buckle back up after depleting his dirty daydreams.

"Stay off the streets, creep," a cop's voice said hauntingly as Miles led Nick into the gloomy daylight, contemptuously followed by "Fuckin' freak."

"Man, I'll miss this place," Nick said.

Chapter Thirty-Six

In their small but swanky-seedy room at the Motel Capri, Dolores turned on the television while Jesse showered, and immediately wished she hadn't. Rampant reports of ravenous, randomly reviving human corpses attacking then devouring their (temporarily) living counterparts were all over the news, on all the local broadcasts as well as the national cable networks. Apparently, while they were out driving around aimlessly and running over werewolves, an all-out zombie apocalypse had begun. Dolores was so tired she just didn't care anymore. She kept flipping channels, desperately trying to ascertain whether this was an epic hoax or the real thing, even though that was virtually impossible. In any case, vividly ubiquitous images of chaotic violence, cannibalistic carnage and fiery, apocalyptic horror ruled the tube, and not just on the news networks. Finally Dolores found an old Esther Williams movie, *On An Island With You*, co-starring Jimmy Durante, Peter Lawford, Ricardo Montalban, and Xavier Cugat, and settled back on the bed to relax and enjoy the vintage visions of aquatic Technicolor splendor. From the shower she heard Jesse singing "Heartbreak Hotel." He *did* sound a lot like Elvis, she thought.

"Anything good on?" Jesse asked as he came out of the bathroom, wearing a robe and slippers, drying then running his hands through his thick, graying hair, letting his pouting pompadour droop over the wound on his forehead.

"No, just this movie," Dolores said. "My turn." She then got up and went into the bathroom, locking the door behind her. She'd let Jesse take his shower first since he had to take a dump, and she knew he'd stink up the place, so he might as well just finish himself off while he was locked up in there. There was a faint odor of old man fecal matter, but the steam of the shower had dissipated much of it. Dolores was too relieved to really notice. Finally she'd be able to wash off the caked blood and semen from the porno-biker massacre at The Midnight Lounge. Hopefully the widely televised zombie apocalypse, real or imaginary, had pre-empted any official reporting of that now relatively minor incident. The whole world had gone mad since then, even if the currently peripheral and superfluous zombie apocalypse was a massive stunt, a globally organized, simultaneous flash-mob reenactment of the old Michael Jackson "Thriller" video grossly misinterpreted and blown out of proportion by ratings-hungry mass media, as she optimistically surmised. She had nothing to worry about, or so she convinced herself as the stains of her sins disappeared down the drain. The bruise on her forehead from the collision would hopefully heal in time as well.

"I'm hungry," Jesse called to her. "Mind if I order a pizza?"

"Go ahead," Dolores called back, not wishing to inform him that the alleged zombie apocalypse may have meant home delivery was no longer being offered.

Chapter Thirty-Seven

The reason I chose to make exploitation films is because they can be done cheaply for a relatively substantial profit. I intentionally appeal to the basest instincts of my potential audience. Gratuitous violence, graphic sex, impossible romance and fantastical creatures freely co-exist in my Creation. I reveal then revel in the basic common denominators of humanity, reduced to their very essence. My world on this side of the lens is a different story. I'll tell you more about it later. Much more.

Action.

Chapter Thirty-Eight

Nick couldn't tell if he was on the outside looking in, or the inside looking out. Too much was happening too suddenly, without rational, every-day explanation, so his lizard-like appearance seemed to be a naturally contextual affliction, given the unprecedented, unpredictable course of recent events, stranger than his own fiction.

At the hospital, the doctors and nurses examined Nick with curiosity, care and caution, drawing blood, checking his pulse, and scraping a small scale-sample off his face for a biopsy and other tests. Nick couldn't afford health insurance, mandatory or not, but this one was on the house. He wasn't merely a patient, but an object of intense scientific study. The doctors wondered optimistically if Nick was the sole harbinger of a brand new plague that could put their town on the map and their careers in the books.

Nick felt safely detached from both his surroundings and his situation. It was amazing how quickly one can learn to adjust to extraordinary circumstances when basic survival is at stake. He let the doctors and especially the cute nurses poke and prod his body while he mentally fantasized about running away with Dolores to a tropical island paradise, or maybe a desert oasis. Or even a snow-covered mountain hideaway. Anywhere but here. Let the professionals do their business, and then he was gone. That was one possible plan, anyway.

Meantime, he was tapping his eternal internal reservoir of lonely sadness to stay alert and in touch with his natural state of being, his true feelings, which remained unaffected and undaunted. The truth was, his external metamorphosis notwithstanding, he was aching for Dolores's healing touch. This was all he cared about, his only goal, his solitary quest. She could wash away all of the ugliness in the world with the mere presence of her ethereal yet accessible beauty. It was like when he wrote about his fictive counterparts. Turning inward forced him to confront dark things in dark places he typically avoided and pretended weren't even there. But acknowledging truth carried its own rewards, however painful.

Then he thought of Buddy, and began to cry.

"What's wrong?" asked the maternally sexy nurse, swabbing the area where the scale-sample had been delicately removed. "Does it hurt?"

"No, I just miss my cat," Nick said simply.

"I'm so sorry, is she dead?" asked the nurse with what sounded like genuine concern. Her substantial cleavage subtlety heaved as she bent over him, momentarily distracting Nick from his self-pitying preoccupation.

"Not as far as I know, and it's a he," Nick said, wondering why people always assumed cats were female, like a self-propagating species.

"Don't you have anyone to take care of him?" the nurse asked.

"No. No one. I'm all alone. And so is he. And he's sick."

The nurse felt a spasm of sympathy. "We should be letting you go shortly, once the tests are in."

"Do I have to wait for the results?" Nick asked, noticing the red hair beneath her cap, the soft freckles on her ivory skin, the depth of her green eyes liberally lined with mascara, the pink painted nails, the sweet but slyly seductive scent of her expensive department store perfume. In a way, she reminded him of Dolores, only older. Nick guessed she was in her late forties, not much older than him. And yet she seemed so much more mature than he was. For one thing, she had a real profession. And she hadn't suddenly transformed into a living B movie monster. He suddenly felt like a life-sized action figure. "I really need to get out of here. I was in jail before this, for no good reason. I haven't been home in a while now."

"Well, my name is Myrna," said the nurse. "I'll see what I can do to make sure you can go home and take care of your sick pussy soon," she added with a wink.

Nick wasn't sure whether she was kidding, but he just nodded in sincere appreciation and said, "Thanks, Myrna."

"I'm the *head* nurse, by the way," she said as she left the room to go check with the doctor in charge of Nick's chart. A zaftig woman, she was stuffed into that tight nurse's uniform like a python into a pillowcase. That's one hot NILF, Nick thought to himself.

Chapter Thirty-Nine

The undead revolution was being televised.

Jesse kept flipping channels, not because he wanted to ignore the unbelievable horrors engulfing them, but because he was hungry for more information, specifically regarding his undead twin brother, whom he was positive had started this whole mess.

"Can't we go back to the Esther Williams movie?" Dolores asked petulantly, sitting with her arms and legs crossed in a slightly worn Womb chair in the corner of the room. She was wearing the other robe available in the motel bathroom. Both were made of pink terrycloth and had the words *Motel Capri* stitched in cursive on the left breast. She pondered how she could acquire a new wardrobe to replace that trench coat hanging in the closet.

"I gotta get to the bottom of this, maybe this will help me find my brother," Jesse said, glued to the tube. "*Now* do you believe me?" he then said, looking over at her for confirmation.

"I don't believe any of this shit," Dolores said. "You're *all* a bunch of crazy assholes, the whole damn world has gone totally insane."

"Aw, you just got low blood sugar, lil' sister," Jesse said dismissively as a horde of zombies ripped apart a milkman in a continuous loop from footage secretly filmed by a by-stander, Rodney King-style. "My brother had quite a temper when he got hungry. Looks like he's pretty hungry, and pretty pissed off, too. Pizza should be here soon enough, so just sit tight."

"You really think anybody is gonna deliver us pizza

with all this insanity going on?" Dolores said.

"I thought you said you didn't even believe it was really happening?" Jesse said triumphantly.

"*Some*thing is going on," Dolores admitted. "I just doubt flesh-eating zombies are the real issue here."

"Hey, they *said* they'd be delivering, what can I tell ya." Jesse looked at his gaudy gold watch. "Been an hour though. Maybe I should just go out and get it."

"Maybe you should," Dolores said. "I'll go with you."

"Forget it, you don't even have any decent clothes. In fact, I'll see what I can pick up for you. What size are you?"

Dolores wasn't sure she wanted Jesse picking out her wardrobe. "Now I *really* have to go with you."

"I'll just pick up a T-shirt and jeans so you can go out and get yourself some real clothes later, okay?" Jesse said. "You got any money?"

"Just credit," she said. "If anyone is still accepting it. I don't want to wear a T-shirt and jeans, not my style."

"Damn it, lil' sister, can you see what's happening out there? What the hell difference does it make how you're dressed for the end of the world?"

"That's exactly why it matters more than ever," Dolores said.

Jesse shrugged in concession. "You got a point. I'll pick you up a dress and some panties, on me, so to speak—what size?"

Dolores gave him the requisite numbers and requested colors, as well as the keys to the Impala. She wondered if he'd actually come back. In a way, she didn't care. She just didn't care about anything anymore.

Jesse tried calling the pizza place one last time before he left. Their phone rang and rang without picking up. Now he was worried. Finally he hung up.

"Funny, the whole world is finally united for a common cause," Jesse said as he stared at the TV, idly jiggling the car keys. "Little late for that, though. Listen, if the pizza joint is closed, I'll pick something else up. Hopefully I can find a grocery store as well as a department store still open. Be back soon, lil' sister." He left, and Dolores's stomach flipped with anxiety as she heard him start off the Impala and drive off into the impenetrable darkness.

After Dolores made sure the windows were shut and the door locked, she tried to find the Esther Williams movie, but it was no longer on. No movies were being broadcast now. Coverage of the zombie apocalypse dominated the airwaves, pre-empting any semblance of normalcy. She sat and chain-smoked, staring with glassy, impassive eyes at scenes of global mayhem and destruction. Her stomach growled incessantly.

Moments later, there was a knock at the door. Nervously, she went to the door and said, "Jesse?" though she belatedly realized she hadn't heard the Impala return. Or any vehicle, for that matter. Maybe the screeching sounds of the television and her spaced-out state had drowned it out.

"Pizza," a voice said.

"*Shit*," Dolores said in whispered exasperation as she flung open the door.

It was Eugene, the desk clerk. He was grinning lasciviously, and he wasn't carrying any pizza.

Chapter Forty

Myrna the head nurse rode Nick like a bronco-buster on top of the hospital bed, her wavy red-dyed hair liberated from the nurse's cap, her bountiful bosoms liberated from her uniform, the bed creaking precariously beneath the weight of the copulating co-conspirators. She kept stuffing her fingers in her mouth to quell her orgasmic cries as Nick's big new scaly lizard dick thrust deep inside of her, his long reptilian tongue lashing out and licking Myrna's face, neck and breasts as he came repeatedly inside of her. She could feel her vagina tearing as he pumped her with his prickly, powerful piston, her blood mingling with his reptilian semen, but the pain was superseded by the pleasure.

After her umpteenth forbidden orgasm, Myrna finally dismounted, feeling like she was disengaging her sore, swollen, blood-and-semen soaked pussy from a cactus. She groaned from the sudden jolts of sheer, sharp agony, now unmitigated by any contrasting source of sexual release, ironically moaning louder than her muffled orgasms would've been. Nervously she glanced at the clock on the wall—it was a little after 2 A.M. She'd sent everyone else home, but she was conscious of the orderlies still on duty.

"*Now* you can go home to your cat," she said, buttoning up her uniform, sliding her shoes and panties back on, stuffing her hair back under her cap. Then she noticed the dried streams of blood and semen down her legs, and winced. "I have to go to the bathroom," she said, wondering if kinky sex with the lizard-mutant-man was really worth the pain and paranoia. As she limped out of the room, she recalled her many orgasms, more combined than she'd experienced in twenty years of marriage to a man she could no longer stand, and realized, yes, it *was* worth it.

"*Finally*," Nick said to himself after she'd gone, putting on his pants and getting ready to leave. He'd paid the price for his premature release from the hospital, which Myrna promised in exchange for a bout of bestiality. Nick's lizard libido was more than willing to accommodate that deal, but the whole time he was fucking Myrna, he was thinking of Dolores. And his cat. He couldn't wait to see poor Buddy.

Looking both ways down the shadowy hospital corridor, dimly lit by fluorescent lights, Nick left his room and tiptoed toward emancipation. As soon as he was out the door, Myrna called the cops to inform them the lizard man had just escaped. "He threatened me and told me he's headed for Mexico," she said before she hung up with a laugh, still mopping up caked bodily juices from her meaty thighs as she sat behind her desk. Their deal was done. But she already had a new one in mind.

Chapter Forty-One

"You got a phone call in the office," Eugene said to Dolores. "I was just kiddin' 'bout the pizza. I like to do that just to fuck with people sometimes. Sorry. Just bored, I guess."

"W-what?" Dolores stammered, simultaneously terrified, relieved and confused. "A call for me? In the office?"

"Yea, I'da put it through to your room, but the line was busy," Eugene said. Dolores assumed Eugene must've tried putting the call through when Jesse was vainly attempting to confirm their pizza order a few minutes before. "It sounds urgent," he added.

"Who is it?" Dolores asked.

"He wouldn't say."

Dolores's heart did a little mambo as she followed Eugene to the front office—was it Nick? It had to be. Who else would know she was here, or even suspect it?

Miles would. "Hi, doll. Remember me?" His voice sounded gravelly, but unmistakable.

Dolores felt the blood drain from her face, and the words choke up in her throat. "*Miles*…you're…."

"*Alive*, right. You can't shoot for shit, bitch. And I got news for you: Heaven's Devils ain't too happy with you, neither."

"They're *all* alive?" she gasped into the phone as Eugene pretended not to eavesdrop, filling out some pretend paperwork.

"Well, not *all* of 'em," Miles said. "In fact, *none* of 'em are still what I'd call *alive.* A few are still walking, though. And they seem hungry."

"*Hungry*?"

Just then there was an ominous pounding on the door.

"Hear that?" Miles said. "I do, all the way from here. Sounds spooky."

"Is that you, Miles?" Dolores said shakily as Eugene went to the door and peered through the peephole.

"No, that ain't me," Miles said with a cackle. "You should be so lucky. I'm calling from a payphone nearby. Those are your friends, what's left of 'em. I just dropped 'em off out front of the motel. For some reason, they still listen to me! They're like live people—they follow anybody who just takes charge and talks louder than anybody else. I should run for office! Maybe when this all blows over, if I still have some influence over all the dumb sheep out there, I'll go into politics. Anyway, these undead bastards couldn't quite manage to get on their hogs in their condition, see, only the ones you shot in the brain never got up again. These two you only got in the neck or chest, not good enough. I can't explain it, but it's happenin' all over, apparently. Dead people gettin' up and eatin' the livin', just like in one of Nick's stupid movies back at the Omega. Me, you shot my ear off but didn't quite finish the job, just enough to royally piss me off, so I'm still technically among the living or so I can only *guess*."

Eugene screamed and Dolores dropped the phone. "What is it?" she asked in abject terror. She could hear Miles laughing on the dangling phone, like a broadcast from Hell over a transistor radio.

"I don't know, but it don't look good. I'm gettin' my shotgun," Eugene said. "Wait here." He ran into the back room and came back seconds later with the shotgun. "I keep this handy just in case zombies show up. You never know, the way the world is these days."

As Dolores let out a scream, Eugene flung open the

door and started blazing away. But there was no one there. He was firing at nothing.

Then cold, undead, muscular hands, already blue and stiff from defiant rigor mortis, reached for Eugene from both sides of the door, tearing at his flesh. Eugene screamed as he fired off two more shots, missing his attackers, but as they wrestled him down to the ground in the doorway of the office, Eugene went into convulsions, frothing at the mouth and making ungodly noises. Dolores, pressed up against the wall holding a lamp for possible protection, assumed he was having an epileptic fit. She eyed the shotgun but it was too close to the action for access.

Eugene was not having an epileptic fit, however.

Right before Dolores's incredulous eyes, Eugene began transforming. His nose extended into a snout, his hair became a mane, his teeth became fangs, his fingernails became claws, and his screams became growls. Within seconds he was tearing back at the zombie bikers, ripping off their limbs with savage fury, but they kept coming at him, moaning and groaning, so he kept tearing at them, as they tore at him. Finally, he ripped their heads off and flung them into the night. Their bloody torsos collapsed into harmless heaps of fetid flesh.

Eugene the werewolf licked the gore from his paws as Dolores stood in the corner frozen with fear, desperately holding on to the lamp, her only defensive weapon, staring at him with awe and dread, wondering if she was next. Instead, Eugene, sitting erect on the floor, panting, gradually transformed back into his human self. Then he stood up, stretched, cracked some stiff bones in his back and arms, and looked back at her.

"You hit me on my way to work, bitch," Eugene said to Dolores as he walked past her into the backroom to dress his wounds.

Dolores thought: *Zombie bites werewolf. That can't turn out well for anybody.*

Chapter Forty-Two

I was a teenage amateur filmmaker. Now I'm a middle-aged exploitation filmmaker. I don't consider that progress.

I first met Dolores Summers—as she called herself by then—at a party in Palm Springs. She's an actress. I'm a filmmaker. I had a project that was perfect for her. It was only natural we should get together.

I asked her if she'd consider doing nudity if the part required it. She laughed. She had been educated and professionally trained as a Shakespearean thespian back in Manhattan, at NYU, though she'd been raised in New Jersey, just outside of Atlantic City. Diction classes had completely eradicated any trace of an accent, however. Her educational background was in live theater, not movies, which she had once considered beneath her talents. Now she had bills piling up and was considering anything that paid well enough to keep the demons of destitution from her doorstep. Lately she'd been making a decent living doing commercials and voiceover work. She told me she'd consider nude scenes if they were done, as they say in the trade, "tastefully." *And* if she was in the proper physical shape, leading me to believe her hesitance was more an issue of vanity than morality. "Better than being a waitress or shilling for soap," she said. She'd done both—and worse, she told me. At the time I wasn't sure what she meant. I'd find out soon enough—though ironically, also too late.

The party in Palm Springs took place at a motel called The Capri, a few blocks off of Indian Canyon Drive. It was a mid-century modern oasis, in the middle of a mid-century modern oasis. It consisted of nine theme rooms forming an "L"-shaped border around a figure-8 pool. There was a canopied bar beside the pool that served "Capri-tinis" every evening at 5PM, which you could sip while relaxing in the soothing water. The themes of the rooms ranged from "Lounge Lizard's Lair" to "Tiki Hula Hut" to "Luchador Lounge" to "Space Age Launch Pad." There was even a "Zombie Fortress" with fake boarded up windows, stocked with zombie films. All the rooms came with vintage-looking TV sets hooked up with DVD players and their own selections of films suiting the room's particular theme. The furniture in all the rooms riffed off the original designs of Arne Jacobsen, Eero Saarinen, and Charles and Ray Eames.

I first proactively encountered Dolores in the "Zombie Fortress," where she was looking at a mannequin in the corner made up to resemble a zombie. It spooked the hell out of her. I went up and asked her if she liked it. "Hell no," she said. "Let's go to another room."

Since the film studio that was actively courting me at the time had rented out the whole motel, all the rooms were open for partying. We next visited the "Tiki Hula Hut" where an aloha-shirted bartender was mixing Mai Tais at a bamboo bar in the corner of the room. An old scratchy Exotica music LP played on a real turntable—"Moon Mist," by the Out-Islanders. The walls were lined with grass cloth, behind fake Polynesian masks and a velvet painting of a voluptuous half-naked island girl. The bases of the twin lamps were carved to resemble tiki gods. Dolores and I spent some time there marveling at the décor but even as we chitchatted and gossiped and bitched about the many woes, pitfalls and drawbacks of "the industry," I mentally removed her glittery gown and had my way with that luscious body beneath. I am pretty sure she knew it, too.

Next we checked out the "Private Eye's Office," a study in *film noir* with blinds you could never fully open, a vintage girlie calendar on the wall, a drugstore rack full of classic pulp fiction, and naturally a small bar in the corner. I asked the bartender for a Manhattan and asked Dolores if she wanted one, too, with a cherry in it, and whether it should be served neat or on the rocks. "No cherry for some time now, and I like it messy." But as I began to make the drink, she said, "Oh, you meant *that*? Yes, straight up with a cherry, thanks." I was already half in love with her. The other half was on standby. She seemed too good to be true. The more we talked, the more we realized how much we had in common, in terms of both interests and backgrounds. We shared a penchant for the previous century's pop culture, and felt somewhat out of place in our own time. "The only thing you'll ever need to know about me is that I'm the biggest Elvis fan in the world," she said to me.

Finally the conversation got around to my current project.

"It's about a pulp fiction writer whose life becomes even more outrageous than the story he's writing," I explained to her as we sat together poolside, sipping Capri-tinis to chase our Manhattans. I sat casually poised on a bar stool like a jazz musician while Dolores sat on the very edge of the pool, dangling her pretty feet and shapely calves in the shimmering moonlit water, her snake skin high heels sitting beside her. "I plan to film both stories, the one he's living and the one he's writing, like they're existing simultaneously in parallel dimensions. Eventually, you won't be able to tell which is reality, and which is fantasy." The warm night sky was crystal clear and full of stars, the tall mountains stark and majestic, rising like monsters from the desert, casting foreboding imagery amid the radiant ambience of the evening. It felt like mystical mating magic was in the air.

"Sounds ambitious, what's your budget?" Dolores asked me, pretending to know what she was talking about.

"Not much, I'll have to be creative," I said. "But hey, if anyone can stretch a buck, it's me."

"So you think there's a part in there for me?" Dolores asked me with perfectly feigned ingenuousness.

"Yes, the female lead, of course."

"The lead?" Dolores laughed so hard she almost spilled her drink. I loved the fact she was flirting with me, even if she did have an obvious ulterior motive, which I was gladly giving her, anything to hold her attention. All the men and many of the women at the party were coveting her company. I felt both lucky and despised. I was used to that feeling.

"Sure," I said emphatically. "Why not? You're an actress, right? And a very beautiful, sexy, intelligent woman. I can only assume you're talented as well, given your credentials. Why wouldn't I want to cast you as the lead in my movie?"

"Well, wouldn't you prefer a name actress?" She all but batted her fake eyelashes at me.

"Not on my budget," I said, and we both laughed.

"Now I get it," she said. "So when can I read the script?"

"Soon as I finish it," I said. Truth was, I hadn't even started on it at that point. "But I do have a title."

"Which is?"

"'*One-Way Ticket to Thrillville*.'"

Dolores smiled and nodded in approval. She gently splashed her feet in the pool water, like a mermaid playfully flipping her tail fins. "Nice. Well, you can send it to my agent, I guess, and we'll take it from there." She looked down as she said that. I think she may have been blushing. For a bombshell like her to blush was quite extraordinary, I thought to myself. Her lack of confidence was showing along with her bra strap. At any second, she could fall completely apart. Suddenly she seemed vulnerable, so I went in for the proverbial kill.

"How about I just drop it off at your place?" I asked confidently.

"Maybe," she said. "Here's my card, it has my cell number, just call me and we'll set up a, um…."

"A date?"

"An appointment," she smiled slyly, locking eyes with me and sending a shiver of sexual tension down my spine and right through my loins.

Later that night when we reluctantly parted, taking cabs to our separate hotel rooms, feeling light-headed from boozin' 'n' schmoozin', I had a wet dream about a mermaid trapped on a rock in a stormy sea, surrounded by ravenous zombie sailors, whom she was fending off with her tail fins. I tried swimming through the dark, choppy waters to rescue her, but before I could reach her, a zombie pulled her down into the depths of the sea. I dove under the surface to find her, but all I could see were the hordes of zombie sailors. Frantically I began swimming away from them, back toward the surface. A bright light seemed to shine through the water like a beacon from above. I felt the decaying hands of the zombie sailors grabbing at my legs, trying to pull me down into the depths, but I managed to break free and rise above the surface of the sea. I climbed up out of the water and found myself poolside at what seemed to be The Capri. No one else was around, and there was no moon so it was very, very dark and scary. I walked around calling Dolores's name for some reason. I thought I heard her screaming in one of the rooms, the Luchador Lounge, or rather its remotely recognizable dream-world equivalent. I burst inside to see her being gang-banged by a bunch of muscle-bound guys wearing Mexican wrestling masks. I had another chance to rescue her and I took it. I ran toward the bed but something—*someone*—was holding me back. I turned around and saw it was a guy wearing a *lucha* mask, and when he took it off, I could barely see his face, though I vaguely recognized it. Then I woke up.

The identity of that intervening phantom in my dream remains a mystery, but I remember waking up in a cold sweat, my boxers soaked with nocturnal emissions, going directly to my laptop, and beginning the outline for my screenplay, for the film I'm shooting now. It was all so clear to me at the time.

Action.

Chapter Forty-Three

When Nick got back to his studio apartment, he found Buddy and picked him up and hugged him for dear life. It was the middle of the night and nobody was around, not even the strippers down below at Zombieville. It was very still and quiet. He felt safe for the first time in what seemed like an eternity.

Nick replenished Buddy's bowl and gave him two doses of Prednisone to make up for those he missed. Buddy was very needy, purring and rubbing against Nick's shins as he paced the apartment, wondering what to do next. Now he was a fugitive, like the guy in his story, also named Nick. Maybe he should've changed his name.

That was it. Nick needed to write. When in doubt, write. Write your characters into a corner, and then just let the characters write themselves out of it. That had always been his M.O.

Nick went to his computer and began to type, his thick leathery fingers causing him many frustrating typos and angry rewrites. He kept typing into the wee hours of the morning, Buddy cuddled up around his feet. Every now and then Nick would glance over at the sofa bed and picture Dolores there, reading what he had written so far. This vision kept him inspired. Every now and then he got up to go the bathroom, but never looked at his own reptilian waste, unlike he once did, when still human. He was too afraid of his own excrement, what it might look like now. And wiping his new bleeding, rough-skinned anus was literally a pain in the ass.

A little after dawn, there was a knock at the door. Nick froze. Cops already? It was natural they'd look here first.

He ignored the knock and kept typing. And whoever it was kept knocking, and knocking…

"Nick, open up!" said a female voice. "It's me. Myrna. I got your address from the hospital records. The police are on their way here. Come with me and I'll hide you."

Reluctantly, Nick got up and opened the door. "Come in," he said with exhausted resignation.

"There's no time," Myrna said frantically. She was still wearing her uniform. Then Nick heard the approaching sirens, blending with the Theremin in his head until he couldn't distinguish them any longer. This was just like his story. Only worse.

"What about Buddy?" Nick asked.

"Um, can you bring him?"

"I don't know, that may freak him out. I'll go with you a little while, then come back here, okay?"

"Whatever, let's hurry!" Myrna literally grabbed Nick by the arm, but he gently pulled away and went over to pick up Buddy and give him a kiss. "I'll be back soon, little guy," he said to him sadly. Then Nick left with Myrna.

They went downstairs to her car, still idling by the curb. It was a 1960 Impala. Myrna had some class, at least.

"Believe it or not, this was my parents' car, Eugene and Yvonne Mansfield, no longer with us," Myrna said off-handedly as they got in and sped off. In the rear view mirror, Nick could see the red flashing lights descending like angry mutant fireflies on his apartment building.

Chapter Forty-Four

"Safely" back in her room, Dolores again locked the doors in a complete panic, tottering on the verge of a nervous breakdown after witnessing that shocking scene of supernatural slaughter.

The phone rang in her room. It rang and rang. Finally, she answered it, knowing full well who it was. "Your zombie assholes are now *really* dead, Miles," she said, sucking neurotically on a cigarette. "You can count on that."

"More where they came from," Miles said without missing a beat. "But you know who also *ain't* dead? I mean sorta but not *really*? Buddy. Your sax player. The one Nick shot. You know, 'by accident.' He'd like to talk to Nick, and he *still* has the hots for you! He's literally *dyin'* to give you a hot beef injection, or I guess now it's just a cold cut, like salami. Anyhoo, have any idea where we can find him?"

"*You're fuckin' insane*!' Dolores screamed, slamming down the phone several times until it broke apart; then she ripped the cord out of the wall, turned off the turbulence on the TV, and sat in silence for what seemed hours, or eons.

Finally, she fell asleep.

When she woke up, she was still alone, but the sun was shining brilliantly through the blinds. She sleepily went to the door and opened it. Fleecy, cumulus clouds hovered gracefully in the azure sky. She could hear birds chirping. There was no sign of anyone else around. The pool in the center of the complex was very still and peacefully inviting. She didn't recall there being a pool at this motel before. Maybe it had been too dark too notice, or she had been too tired. The entire layout of the Motel Capri seemed totally transformed from how it appeared in her memory. Still, she instinctively knew she'd been here before.

She went back into the room and tentatively turned on to the television. Talk shows, news, soap operas. The usual. No evidence of a zombie apocalypse, Elvis-spawned or otherwise. She looked in the mirror and touched her forehead. No bloody crescent shaped wound.

Then she finally looked around and noticed that the décor of the room was also completely different than she'd imagined—all decked out in bamboo, with tiki statues and velvet paintings of hula girls.

Had it *all* been a goddamn *dream*? What kind of cheapjack *Dallas* narrative gimmick bullshit was *that*? Still, this explanation beat the alternative.

She returned outside and walked around, leaving the door and her mind wide open. Beneath the Motel Capri sign was another sign that said NO VACANCY. The parking lot was full of cars. Her Impala was parked right outside her room.

Feeling a flush of bold relief, Dolores walked up to the main desk. An attractive older woman with granny glasses and silver hair was sitting there. She was wearing a pink blouse with a name-tag that said "Myrna Mansfield, General Manager." She smiled benevolently as Dolores walked in. Dolores vaguely recognized her, but couldn't quite place her.

"May I help you, dear?" the woman named Myrna asked.

"Is Eugene here?" Dolores asked.

"Who?" the elder woman said with furrowed brow.

"Eugene. The night clerk, I guess."

The elder woman looked nonplussed. "Nobody here but me, dear. Even at night. My name is Myrna." She pointed to her name-tag with pride of ownership. "Is there something I can help you with?"

Dolores felt suddenly delirious and almost giddy. This was too good to be true. "Um, the gentlemen I checked in with, is he still here?"

Myrna looked down her nose through her glasses at the guest registry. "Hmmm, what was his name again?"

"Jesse Mancini."

Myrna frowned as she scanned the list of names. "Well, according to this, dear, you checked in alone, just last night."

Dolores's heart sank again. This was seemingly pleasant, but still too confusing to fully appreciate. "I'm sorry, I guess I'm a little shaky. I haven't had my morning coffee."

"Oh! Well, we're still serving complimentary breakfast."

"No, no, that's okay, M-Mother, I mean, um, Myrna, um, maybe in a minute, I need to, um..." Suddenly Dolores caught a look at herself in a mirror behind the office desk. She was wearing a red halter-top and tight, low-hanging, hip-hugging, cut-off blue jean shorts. She looked down at her legs and noticed shiny white knee-high boots, Nancy Sinatra-style. She looked like the All-American bombshell. Wonder Woman in Wonderland. "Ummmm....."

"Are you sure you wouldn't want some coffee, sweetheart?" Myrna asked her again. "You seem a little out of it."

Dolores massaged her temples. "I do feel a little woozy."

"Well, have a seat, I'll bring you a little something." Myrna got up to help Dolores sit down in a very comfortable Egg chair in the corner of the stylishly appointed office. The walls, like the rooms, were painted in pastel shades of blue and green. Myrna looked like she may have been a pin-up queen back in the day. Despite her age she carried herself with a certain understated but unmistakable *va-va-voom* mystique, sashaying to the adjacent breakfast nook and preparing Dolores a tray of pick-me-up, with various fruits, a bagel with cream cheese and lox, and fresh coffee.

Dolores was hungrier than she initially thought. She hastily ate up the food before sitting back in the Egg Chair and sipping her coffee, listening to the music playing over the sound system, a combination of classic jazz and lounge, more Mancini than Musak. Henry Mancini, that is.

Apparently there was no such person as Jesse Mancini. Not any more.

Just then somebody burst through the office door that she recognized, and suddenly, it all came back to her.

It was Buddy West, whom she somehow recognized as her theatrical agent. "Hey, doll—the film crew is waiting. Ready to shoot the next scene?"

Fuck, Dolores thought to herself.

Chapter Forty-Five

"My husband is out for the night," Myrna explained as Nick nervously looked around her neatly arranged and tastefully appointed retro ranch-style suburban home. "So just make yourself at home. They won't look for you here. Eventually they'll really think you're on your way to Mexico." Nick noticed she not only had some dried blood left on her shins, but some cuts and bruises as well. What a freak, he thought to himself. After a brief tour of the model suburban home, they sat on her plush sofa and relaxed.

"Hey, aren't you worried my condition is contagious?" Nick asked her belatedly.

"No," she said simply. "The tests were inconclusive, but whatever you have doesn't appear to be a transmittable virus. It's a self-contained affliction of some sort. Fascinating, really, from a strictly medical point of view. You're going to be famous one day. You should be on TV."

"Wait—how do you know all this?" Nick asked incredulously. "So my blood work *did* come back? Why didn't you tell me?"

"Well, *some* of it," she explained as she drew all the drapes then went to the wet bar and poured him some whiskey, which she handed to him. "You tested negative for anything scary or fatal or communicable. I didn't tell you because, like I just said, basically the tests were inconclusive, other than ruling out certain possibilities and theories. Frankly, we don't know what the hell is wrong with you. And I for one don't care. I haven't felt like this since I was a teenager!" She put her foot in his crotch and tried tickling his marble-like balls.

"I'm just a freak," Nick said with a sigh as he took the drink and sat down on her plush sofa. "Like you," he then added under his breath. He felt like he was on the set of the ultimate '60s sitcom: *The Dick Van Donna Duke* Show. Everything was perfectly in place. The air even smelled sweet and musky, either from organic domestic euphoria or from store-bought artificial enhancement. The messy memory of their torrid tryst collided incongruously with the pristine image of his sedate, serene surroundings. They required his corresponding corruption.

"Wanna fuck some more?" he said suddenly.

"Okay!" she said cheerfully.

Myrna led him by the scaly hand to the bedroom. On the way they passed framed photos of her two handsome twin sons, Johnny and Jesse, both teenagers. Rather than turning him off, the idea of further defiling the mother of these pleasant photos turned him on, appealing to his sense of anarchy. The Theremin blared in his brain, swelling in tandem with his boner. He really was turning into an animal.

In the dark, plush bedroom, Nick tore off Myrna's uniform and fucked the hell out of her for hours and hours. The bed sheets were stained with blood and semen but neither seemed to care as they wallowed in their own bodily fluids. Nick used his long lizard tongue to innovative effect while performing cunnilingus on a perpetually orgasmic Myrna.

"Are you part frog too, hon?" she moaned.

"*Hmmph*?" Nick mumbled, mouth full of cougar pussy.

"That tongue of yours."

Nick retracted his tongue and lifted his head up, startled by the notion. "I don't know," he said simply after some contemplation, then immediately sending the tongue back deeper inside of her, flicking it all around the interior of her unseen nether region, like a randy reconnaissance probe. Myrna bucked and cried out in ecstasy, squeezing Nick's scaly face between her ample thighs, the sharp edges cutting into her cellulite, the sting of which augmented the already overwhelming cascade of physical sensations. Her pink-painted toes twitched over Nick's shoulders in shell-shocked spasms of bestial bliss.

Sometime during this sensuous session, it dawned on Nick—who was taking out his refuge from the outside world in trade—he was now a professional male hustler. A male *monster* hustler. He'd finally found his true calling in life.

Afterwards, as Nick sat at the dining room table while Myrna prepared some midnight macaroni and cheese, Nick ran his fingers through his hair and to his horror, some strands came out in his hands. His felt his blood freeze, though in his reptilian state, it was probably already cold. He got up and turned on the television and flipped channels, stopping when the image turned black-and-white. *The She Creature*, starring Marla English, American-International Pictures, 1956. Perfect. One of his favorites, and one he hosted at his midnight show only a few months ago. He suddenly thought of the Omega Theater in ashes, and felt sadness for the first time. Wait, no. The Oasis Theater is the one that burned down—the *Omega* Theater was the one in his story-in-progress, still standing, at least in his dreams. The borders in his brain were increasingly blurring.

Nick sat watching *The She Creature*, trying not to worry his scalp was succumbing to scaly submission. His hair was all his fragile ego had left, his final connection to his rapidly diminishing humanity. He hoped Myrna had merely loosened some during their hours of hardcore fucking.

The theremin on the film's soundtrack seemed to echo the Theremin in his head, and Nick grew increasingly dizzy. Myrna showed up wearing her leopard nightgown and slippers with two plates of mac 'n' cheese. She cuddled up beside him and merrily chowed down, giddily watching the TV. Without makeup—which had smeared off due to her tears of unbearable passion—she seemed older, though still attractive. Nick felt like he'd been banging his own mother, though since he never knew his own mother, as he had been abandoned to an adoption agency shortly after birth, the reference was obtuse at best. Anyway, Myrna was far too young to be his long, lost mother, *wasn't* she?

"How old are you, if you don't mind my asking?" Nick asked her suddenly, quickly adding, "I mean, you seem so *young* to have a house and family and all."

She looked shocked, but not offended. "Fifty-six. Why? How old are *you*?"

"Forty-two." Mentally Nick did the math. He figured she deducted at least two years from the truth, so she was probably more like fifty-eight, which meant they were separated by sixteen years, too close for comfort…

"So, are those your *only* children?" Nick asked Myrna, pointing to more photos sitting on the coffee table, depicting her well-scrubbed twin sons at younger ages.

"Yes, technically, but let's not talk about them right now," Myrna said with chilly resolve in her voice. She reached for the remote and turned down the sound of the television to a barely audible level. "Right now we need to talk about how and when you're going to kill my husband."

Nick projectile-vomited green, pea soup-like bile all

over the coffee table, framed photos, and shag rug, reaching as far as the television screen while Myrna casually lit up a cigarette and obliviously blew smoke rings into the sickly-sweet, musky air.

Chapter Forty-Six

Myrna Mansfield, manager and owner of the Motel Capri, called the hospital to send an ambulance after Dolores passed out cold on the floor of the office.

"Is she okay, has she been acting strangely?" Buddy West, Dolores's agent, who always traveled with her on location since he was secretly obsessed with her, asked Myrna, who cradled Dolores in her lap, applying cold compresses to her forehead.

"I'm sure she'll be fine," Myrna said. "Just a touch of the nerves. "

"Good, we gotta start shooting our movie," Buddy said emphatically.

"What movie?" Myrna asked, completely clueless.

"The movie we're filming *here*," Buddy said with exasperation. "The producers sent their scouts out here a while ago and set everything up with you, right?"

"No," Myrna said simply. "I don't know what you're talking about."

Buddy—a big man, former failed boxer-turned-failed saxophone player-turned failed-actor turned about-to-fail agent—paced and ran his fingers through his tousled black hair. "This doesn't make any sense. The whole crew is here, hasn't anyone checked in with you yet?"

"*No*," Myrna repeated. "I'm sorry. This is the first I've heard of it."

Dolores stirred and began to come to. She opened her eyes warily, and then sat up groggily.

"Where am I?" she said.

"That's what I'd like to know," Buddy said. "What's

going on, Dolores?"

"Who are you?" Dolores asked Buddy.

"Who am *I*?" he yelled. "Only your god damn *agent*!"

"My *agent*? Oh, yes…I'm an actress…and I sing, too…" Dolores tried to get up but then fell back onto the sofa next to Myrna. They were in the back room behind the office, where Myrna kept a bed, some furniture, a kitchenette and a television. "Where's Nick?" Dolores suddenly asked no one in particular.

"*Fuck Nick*!" Buddy blurted.

"Hush now," Myrna said to Buddy sternly. "Enough of that talk. Can't you see she's disoriented?" Myrna then said to Dolores, "Don't you worry now, hon. The ambulance is on its way."

"Ambulance?" Dolores said. "What for, Mother?"

"You," Myrna said. "You're obviously not feeling well. And I'm not your mother, dear. Not *here*. Just try to relax."

The siren of the ambulance became audible in the distance, closing in fast. Dolores stood up and wobbled out of the back room into the front office, Myrna and Buddy right on her shapely, fucked up ass.

"You'd best sit down and relax now, dear, or you'll pass out again, and then who knows where you'll wake up?" Myrna said mysteriously to Dolores.

Dolores turned around and faced Myrna. "What the hell does *that* mean?"

"Fuck this, we got a movie to shoot, I'm tired of *both* you bitches!" Buddy shouted. Myrna looked at him disapprovingly but didn't say anything, focusing her attention on Dolores.

"I want to know what in the name of living fuck is going on here!" Dolores screamed, freezing Buddy and Myrna rigid. She continued speaking in a trace-like daze,

"Last thing I remember…Eugene, the desk clerk, turned into a werewolf and killed the bikers, the biker zombies trying to get in and eat me because I shot them after they gang-banged me…Miles was still alive because he called and told me the bullet missed his brain…Jesse went for pizza and some clothes…but before that…Nick…Nick was bleeding to death…"

"Sweetheart, you're not making any sense," Myrna said to Dolores. "You'd best lie down."

"That's the scene we're supposed to be shooting *right fucking now*!" Buddy yelled. "The fucking *zombies* are already in fucking *makeup*!" Myrna turned around and smacked Buddy across the mouth.

"Now, that's *enough*!" Myrna said to a startled Buddy. "You'd best leave here, mister. I'll take care of Dolores."

"But she's got a scene to shoot—right *here*, you old bat!" Buddy yelled.

"Get *out*!" Myrna said to him without raising her voice, but in a forceful tone as she shoved him out the front door, just as the ambulance pulled up.

Dolores felt woozier, then passed out again, falling hard on the office floor.

When she woke up, Jesse was hovering over her.

"Hey, lil' sister, you musta passed out while I was gone," he said. "Did I miss anything?"

Dolores sat up, whiffing fresh pizza and looking at the raging zombie apocalypse still unfolding on the television screen. Ratings must've been through the roof for just about every station out there, she thought, though some were no longer broadcasting anything at all. Then she noticed a red halter-top and a pair of blue jean cut-off shorts draped across the Womb chair in the corner. At the base of the chair was an open box with the tops of white go-go boots hanging over the sides.

"Sorry, I couldn't find a nice dress in your size, hope those duds are okay for now, even though it's sort of a Seventies look," Jesse said with a lop-sided grin. "And I didn't even need any money! Downtown was totally deserted, I just walked in and took 'em, nobody around. The pizza place was still open, though. They were just afraid to leave the shop, with everything goin' on, in fact they were just gettin' ready to close up when I pulled up, they just gave me the damn pizza for free, so it's a good thing I went when I did, things are just getting' worse out there, and I'm afraid it's all my brother's fault. He's shakin' up the whole world all over again."

As Jesse droned on in his pleasantly oblivious drawl, Dolores stood and walked in a somnambulistic manner to the window and peeked through the blinds. Outside it was dark. Very dark.

Chapter Forty-Seven

My pursuit of Dolores Summers, classically trained dramatic actress turned "Hollywood hooker for hire," as I awkwardly joked that night we met in Palm Springs, began slowly, like a lion circling its quarry before the fatal pounce. I immediately fell in love with her, but I sensed a delicate sadness emanating from her soul, despite her outward show of sophisticated confidence, and decided to proceed with caution, to protect both of our wounded hearts.

Thanks for letting me open up like this, by the way. It helps, plus it's cheaper than a shrink and more fun than a guru. I'm very comfortable with your company now. I hope the feeling is mutual.

I'd been briefly married once before, to a recovering alcoholic named Gloria. She was a sassy Southern belle with a brutal wit and a lovely singing voice she never used in front of people. She'd been raised in Memphis, Tennessee, and, like Dolores, was a loyal Elvis fan. That was one thing we always had in common, and that bond often saw us through tough times. Though never clinically diagnosed as manic-depressive, her mood could go from sunny to suicidal in the blink of an eye, without warning. At first I found this mercurial quality attractive, as if I was her personal Messiah sent from above to save her from herself. My self-glorifying gallantry was often rewarded with resentment and hostility, however, and I soon learned to distance myself from her when she became overwhelmed by her own demons. An avid follower of the AA steps program, she finally fell off the wagon one night after a tryst with a stranger she met at the club where she stripped. Yes, Gloria was a stripper, in a titty bar that served booze. The situation was a ticking time bomb, and I kept the fuse lit, warily waiting for the inevitable explosion and its painful fallout. The truth was, I was addicted to her body. We had great sex, plain and simple. No amount of neurotic, chemically imbalanced behavior could throw a damp chill on our heated sessions, often sensually sublimated anger and frustration. Whenever we had a fight, we'd fuck ourselves free. This always seemed to work, until that night she was seduced by Miles, my former best friend.

Miles Conroy and I grew up together in South Philly. His mother, Irene, a plump Irish woman, was best friends with my mother, Myrna, a high school beauty queen. They were both nurses at the same hospital where Miles and I had been born. Both of our fathers were losers: his was a two-timing mechanic who took car repairs out in trade; mine, named Stewart, a jack-of-no-trades who mainly lived off my mother, until he got bored with her. They both left when we were still too young to really notice, and we were both raised as only children, so in a way, we grew up as brothers. Literally. Miles assumed his mother's surname after his father, whose last name was Orowitz, split. My mother Myrna left me when I was still in single digits age-wise, too, abandoning me to live with Miles and his mother Irene, who unofficially adopted me. I never even got to know her. Myrna still sent Irene checks from someplace far away, I never found out exactly where, though due to some secretly discovered postmarks, suspected it was somewhere in the Northwest. At an insane asylum.

As far as the authorities were concerned, she was still my legal guardian; AWOL thought she might have been. She was still devastated by my father's cruel absence.

That was her excuse for leaving me behind. I only reminded her of the life she'd never have now. Irene seemed to understand.

Miles and I just grew closer after I moved in, playing baseball and basketball, swimming in the Delaware River, hanging out on South Street, going to school together. He loved Geno's, I loved Pat's, both located catty cornered from the other, not far from our brownstone flat, but despite this cheese-steak rivalry, we always got along, bonded by our mutual love of Marvel Comics (I also liked some D.C.), doo-wop, busty women, and most especially, movies. He was a fat, homely kid who grew into a fat, homely man, and sometimes, I got the distinctly disturbing feeling he resented me, for some odd reason he never came clean about.

We moved to Manhattan together as young men to somehow break into the film business. Miles wound up managing a "speakeasy"-style art-house in Greenwich Village called The Omni, located upstairs from the strip joint where I met Gloria. The Omni was tiny, and could only project 16mm, the image thrown onto a pull-down screen, but it was outfitted with cozy sofas and beanbags, and Miles would illegally supply the patrons pizza from a nearby Italian restaurant, as well as run drinks from the strip joint below, which was called the Lunar Lounge. It had once been a popular burlesque house before the original owners sold it to the Mob, at least that's what we suspected at the time, based on much of the clientele and some of the people who had "business meetings" in the back booth. In any case, when the joint changed management, which was long before we took on The Omni, pasties were swapped for g-strings, real boobs for silicone watermelons, jazz sax for rock guitar. It was a shame, really, but it was definitely a savvy business move.

You have to roll with the times, or just get rolled over by them.

The Omni was basically like a 42nd St. grindhouse with delusions of grandeur. The NYFD, as well as the NYPD, would've shut us down had it not been for the kickbacks Miles arranged via a cousin on the Force, or something like that; he never really revealed the details of his arrangement to "protect me," he said. I should've never been involved with such a shady operation, but I needed a job, nobody was even reading much less buying my film treatments and half-assed screenplays, so the way I saw it, I had no choice, unless I wanted to bus tables for a living, which is no way to live at all.

Miles hired me to program The Omni, and I obtained most of the 16mm prints from private collectors, or from professional film collector catalogues which were packed with profitable product in those days, before video killed the market. Miles worked the door and ran the projector, and we both took orders for pizza and drinks once the show started. Since we never bothered to pay any money to the rightful distributors of any of these titles, we kept all the door cash for ourselves, splitting it right down the middle. Our only overheard was rental of the space to some Italian guy who never asked any questions. It was a sweet set-up. At least until that night when it all fell apart.

At The Omni, not only did we re-sell fresh pizza and booze, adding our own delivery surcharges, along with frequent and generous tips, but bringing one's own pot was often encouraged as well. The place was insanely popular considering it was a strictly underground operation without an official operating license, much less permission to serve alcohol. It only comfortably seated about sixty people but on many nights, when we'd show real crowd-pleasers, we'd pack over a hundred sweaty, happy, drunken film nerds in there. Our most popular films, which I amassed for our personal archives, included, just off the top of my head: *Plan 9 From Outer Space*, *Forbidden Planet*, *Barbarella*, *Faster Pussycat Kill! Kill!*, *Night of the Living Dead, Dawn of the Dead, The Texas Chainsaw Massacre, Bring Me the Head of Alfredo Garcia, Flesh Gordon, Tommy, Phantom of the Paradise, The Rocky Horror Picture Show, A Clockwork Orange, The Man Who Fell to Earth, Eraserhead,* and *Pink Flamingoes*. Along with the features we screened dozens of vintage cartoons, newsreels and *Three Stooges* shorts, always delighting the stoned audience. Again, this is to name but a few highlights from our bootleg vaults. I have no idea what became of all those prints. Miles probably unloaded them all on eBay by now.

To further earn my keep, once a week I would host a subjectively selected cult film, mostly favorite B flicks I discovered in my own youth, like *Invasion of the Saucer Men, It Conquered the World, This Island Earth, I Was a Teenage Werewolf, I Was a Teenage Frankenstein, Blood of Dracula, How to Make a Monster, The Amazing Colossal Man, Tarantula, The Hideous Sun Demon, The Alligator People, The She Creature*, *Astro Zombies,* and *The Incredibly Strange Creatures Who Stopped Living and Became Mixed-Up Zombie*s, to, again, name but a few. Sometimes I'd even recruit a few strippers from The Lunar Lounge to dance as part of a half-assed pre-show, wherein I asked the audience a little trivia and for prizes, gave away comic books donated from a store nearby, in exchange for free booze and admission for the owner. I called it "Thrillville," since I dressed up like a '50s beatnik, wearing a beret and dark shades and playing bongos whenever I hosted it. I called myself "Nick the Beatnik" and eventually, I had my own little fan following. It got pretty wild sometimes. Sometimes I wore a red-and-yellow *lucha libre* mask with little devil horns on it, and showed Mexican monster movies starring El Santo, Blue Demon and Mil Mascaras, calling myself "El Diablo." I know for a fact many of the patrons who attended these weekly midnight shows wound up copulating on the sofas and even the floor. I'd often let them crash there, like it was a hotel room for an itinerant rock group. I even had my own groupies. In fact, Gloria was one of them.

Sometimes celebrities would show up, like Debbie Harry or Iggy Pop or Andy Kaufman. At least I *think* they were famous people—not always easy to see their faces in the dark. Eventually, due to my ascending rep as a local underground celebrity of sorts in my own right, I scored a freelance gig as a movie reviewer for *the Village Voice*. Miles seemed to grow increasingly jealous of my independent success, though he never said anything negative outright, aside from snide comments here and there about my lowbrow film selections. Suddenly he became a snob. Already the fabric of our fragile partnership was beginning to unravel. By the time Miles fucked Gloria in the toilet stall at the Men's Room at the Lunar Lounge that night, after getting her stoned on coke and whiskey, our life-long friendship was running on fumes. Combustible fumes.

The business began to tank as videos became more affordable and both rare and popular titles became accessible for convenient home viewing, so The Omni began to branch out into other media, like experimental live theater, poetry slams, a daytime rehearsal space for rock bands, and even a fuckpad where the more ambitious strippers downstairs brought their johns. This was Miles' idea. He'd run porno flicks while the strippers/hookers did their business. Miles charmingly called it "Fuck-O-Rama," and it became more popular and profitable than my "Thrillville" gig ever was. By that time I'd quit doing my Nick the Beatnik routine anyway, desiring bigger and better things for my life. The johns loved it and paid Miles extra cash for the service and space, like he was the strippers' pimp, which, in effect, he was. I should've left once that practice began, but the cash still flowing under the table made it hard to simply split, and for some reason, Gloria didn't want to quit her job, even though she had been offered a job as a singing waitress uptown. She just didn't have the confidence to grow up, and I didn't have the strength to make her. I was still growing up myself.

It took Miles getting Gloria drunk then fucking her to knock some sense into my head, or least to begin the process. Still, despite my broken heart, I didn't leave right away. I actually gave them both a second chance, for the sake of sheer sentimentality. I still loved both of them. Miles, obviously ashamed, wouldn't even talk to me and avoided me entirely, not even showing up to work for the next few days, but Gloria, who told me about Miles fucking her in the toilet stall, responded to my patience by bringing home four bikers from the strip club one night and letting them gang-bang the shit out of her in our own bed. I came home to this. One threatened me with a broken beer bottle when I interrupted the session and protested, so I left and went back to The Omni and sat watching movies by myself all night, crying. That was finally it, though. I took my stash of cash, bought a plane ticket to Los Angeles, filed remotely for divorce, which Gloria gladly granted now that she was back on the bottle, and I never looked back. I never fell in love again, either, even after I managed to finally graduate from a gofer to a set designer to a film editor to an assistant director to a director of my own scripts, most of the resulting low-budget product going straight to video, ironically enough. No matter. I'd finally established myself as an exploitation filmmaker of reliable renown, at least in certain circles, and I got plenty of pussy until suddenly my heart just wasn't in it, and when I tried to introduce my heart to the party, everybody left. Sincerity was not part of the game.

I went through a long dry spell until that night in Palm Springs when I met Dolores, and everything changed. First for the better, then for the worse, but I had no way to know that when I rang her buzzer one bright Santa Monica morning and she answered wearing nothing but a see-through bathrobe and slippers, her nipples boldly peeking out from the behind the silk, her long dark hair dripping wet from the shower. For some reason she still reminded me of a mermaid.

Wearing a smug smile, I handed her my script for what I considered to be my ultimate masterpiece, "*One-Way Ticket to Thrillville*."

"Done already?" she said, genuinely surprised to see me, as well as the completed screenplay. "It's only been four days! I thought you were going to drop it off at Buddy's office, like I said."

"I lived it, I dreamed it, then I just wrote it down," I said, ignoring the bit about her agent. Buddy had been the name of my dear departed cat, so I didn't appreciate the painful association. I'd planned home delivery all along anyway, it was part of my impetus to finish it so fast, and then I'd have an excuse to see her again as soon as possible. "It was easy. The hard part will be getting it made."

"How do you plan to do that?" she asked, slyly showing some leg.

"For one thing, I have an investor. Old friend from

New York, named Miles."
Action.

Chapter Forty-Eight

"I may be a monster, but I'm not a murderer," Nick said to Myrna as they sat on the sofa trying to ignore the stench of puke and sin. "I'm not going to kill your fuckin' hubby, sorry. The sex was good, but not *that* good. My life is complicated enough. I gotta go." Nick stood up, gingerly stepping over his own vomit, and headed toward the door. Myrna just laughed.

"You can't go anywhere that's safe, other than here, and if you try to leave, I'll call the cops on you," Myrna said with bemusement. "You may not think you're a murderer, but that's not what the cops think. I should know. My husband is chief of police."

Nick stopped in his tracks and said over his shoulder, "In that case, he may not take kindly to getting knocked off. It's against the law, y'know."

Myrna sighed. "So is beating and cheating on your wife. Or it should be. It's against Myrna's law, anyway." Myrna stood up and went over to Nick. He turned around and she struck a match on his tough, leathery cheek and lit a new cigarette. Then she casually blew the smoke in his face. "I'm taking the law—*my* law—into my own hands now. Or rather, *your* hands, lizard man."

"You're out of your fuckin' mind," Nick said, heading for the door again. "I'll take my chances out there, better than being locked up in here with you."

"When they come looking for you, you'll have only one place to hide," Myrna said. "You'll be back."

"Why would I hide in the police chief's home anyway?" Nick said as he opened the door and looked back at her. "That would be pretty stupid. We've met. He doesn't like me."

"That's why you have to kill him first—otherwise, I can't protect you," Myrna said.

"No dice," said Nick, and he left. He could still hear Myrna's wicked laughter as he headed down the primrose pathway.

Chapter Forty-Nine

"Elvis is undead and taking over the world with an army of zombies," Jesse intoned dramatically, yet matter-of-factly, as he sat eating pizza in front of the increasingly monotonous scenes of slaughter beaming from the television screen. Dolores just stood staring through the blinds at the eternal night, her eyes glazed over, he face expressionless, her limbs rigid—like a zombie.

"I don't care," Dolores said as if in a trance. "I don't care about anything anymore. I just miss Nick." A tear escaped her eye. She ached with paralyzing loneliness.

"Aw c'mon now, lil' sister, don't fret," Jesse said, rising from the bed and bringing her a slice of pizza. "You gotta eat, ain't you hungry?"

"Not any more," Dolores said.

"Hey, are you cryin'?" Jesse compassionately placed a fleshy, fake-bejeweled hand on her shoulder. "I'll protect you from those fuckers, man! And my brother ain't gonna mess with no friends of mine, I can tell you that!"

Dolores shrugged off his beefy hand and walked over to the clothes draped over the Womb chair and picked them up, along with the boots on the floor. "Thanks for these. I'm going to put them on, and then we have to leave."

"And go where?" Jesse asked.

"Anywhere but here," Dolores said. "Does it even matter anymore?"

"Well, all due respect, we should just stay here for the time being, since ain't no zombies around here, not yet, anyway, none that I seen that is," Jesse said. "Just the rumor of 'em, is all. They'll be comin' eventually."

"Exactly. And they *were* here. You just missed 'em." Dolores went into the bathroom with the clothes and shut and locked the door behind her.

Jesse walked up to the bathroom door and said, "Huh? What are you talkin' about?"

"While you were out," Dolores said passively as she put on the red halter-top and tied it behind her shoulder blades. "They attacked me and the desk clerk, but then he turned into a werewolf and killed them. Or whatever. He's the one we hit on the way here, by the way."

"You gone loony tunes on me, girl?" Jesse said. "That don't make no damn sense! That's just plain crazy talk, don't fall apart on me, now! We gotta keep our heads on straight if we're gonna make it."

"Welcome to my fuckin' world," Dolores said, abruptly opening the bathroom door. "And you're just livin' in it," she added, looking directly into his eyes as she brushed by him. She looked like a refugee from a '70s car chase flick. The cut-off jeans tightly conformed to her curvaceous hips, and the halter-top revealed enough cleavage and navel to give Jesse a spontaneous, involuntary boner. She looked cheaper than ice, and twice as cold.

Dolores opened her purse and pulled out the gun and held it aloft, without pointing it anywhere in particular, and said, "I'm outta here, old man. You going with me or staying here? Your choice, but decide now." Then she turned and pointed the gun at the television set, beaming unimaginably horrible images of the Elvis-spawned zombie apocalypse, and fired a single bullet into the LCD screen, which exploded in a cloud of shards and smoke. "Enough of that shit already," she said.

Jesse grinned a lop-sided sneer. "That's what I'm

talkin' 'bout now, lil' sister. Definitely, let's leave the building."

He collected his things and they peeled out of the parking lot and down the deep, dark road into the beckoning blackness. She was hell-bent determined to find Nick, dead or alive or undead, in this dream world, or the next.

Chapter Fifty

Dolores's little Santa Monica apartment, blocks from the beach, was neat and clean, like my suit, and bright and warm, like her personality. A couple of Mondrian prints adorned the walls, adding bright, bold colors to the otherwise dimly lit room.

"No wonder you like Palm Springs," I said to her as we sat sipping coffee on the sun-drenched terrace. "Suits your style. It's weird we met there and not back in New York."

"I'm much younger than you, remember?" she said, her legs crossed strategically so that her silk robe exposed most of them, one heeled slipper dangling from her red-painted toes. "We probably didn't run in the same circles. So your old partner from back there wants to help you finance this film?"

"Yea, he made a fortune in the porn racket back there, after our business broke up, and wants to help me out, for old times' sake," I said, carefully avoiding any subtext. "He also wants to move out here and beef up his resume, so it's not all altruistic. We haven't spoken in years, so it was kinda weird to hear from him, out of the blue."

"Did you have a falling out?" Women's intuition.

"Sorta, I don't want to go into it, though," I said. "It doesn't matter anymore, anyway. Let's talk about you. I don't even know anything about you."

"I told you, I love Elvis," she smiled. "That's all you need to know."

"There's gotta be more than that," I said. "You ever been married? Engaged?"

"Well, that's cutting to the chase," she said with a laugh. "I've been knocked up a couple of times, but nothing that was ever formalized."

My gut did a little jig at that impromptu revelation. "Go on," I said with as much blasé attitude as I could muster.

"Go on where?" she asked, cutely raising her eyebrows.

"To wherever the hell it is you're going with this story," I said.

"That's where I've been, not where I'm headed," she said, getting up from the table as if suddenly uncomfortable. "More coffee?" she asked, heading back inside. A chill wind blew, signaling a fog front moving in on the Pacific coast. I loved when that happened in L.A. It was so rare, and made the normally smoggy, sunny city seem so surreal, like a civic doppelganger from an alternate dimension. Everything would look the same, but feel totally different.

I followed her into the kitchenette. I'd follow her anywhere.

I sat on a stool at the counter facing her. She poured me a fresh cup of java, which I sipped in silence for a few moments, contemplating what she said and what I should say next.

"You seem like you're in shock," she said simply, sipping her own coffee.

"No," I lied, "not really. It's just you've got a past you'll only hint at, whereas I'm here spilling my guts."

"I didn't ask you to," she correctly observed.

"True," I admitted. More tense silence.

Then she said, "Listen, I really don't have anything to hide, I just don't like talking about myself in the past tense. I'd like to think all my best stories are in front of me."

"They are," I said, nodding back at the script sitting on the coffee table in the living room behind us.

"Sometimes…." She seemed to drift off.

"Yea?" I prodded.

"Well, sometimes I have these dreams, and I'm not sure whether they're from my past, or my future, but I always recognize the places and people in them, even though when I wake up, they seem unfamiliar to me. Does that make no sense or what?" She seemed vaguely disturbed by the recollection.

"When you're talking about dreams, nothing makes sense," I said. "That's part of their appeal."

"Or their horror," she said, which stunned me.

After some bullshit chitchat about which cooking shows she liked to watch, we went into the living room and sat on her sofa together. I couldn't take my eyes off her nipples, and she noticed.

"Excuse me while I slip into something less comfortable," she said, rising again.

"For you, or for me?"

She didn't respond, just left me alone while she went into the bedroom to change. Outside it began to rain. It hardly ever rained in Los Angeles. Rain was even scarcer than fog in that dusty town. Felt like fucking *Blade Runner*. She seemed to be taking her sweet time in there.

Listless, I finally stood up and idly scanned her selection of books and movies, always telling of one's true personality. Books included novels by Barbara Kingsolver, Gabriel Garcia Marquez, and Alice Walker; theatrical manuals by the likes of Lee Strasberg and Anna Deavere Smith, and some glossy tomes on Mid-century Modernism and design. Now on to the good stuff: DVDs. *All About Eve, One Flew Over the Cuckoo's Nest*, *Grease*,

Sophie's Choice, *The Breakfast Club*, *The Dick Van Dyke Show, That Girl*, and naturally a few choice Elvis titles: *Jailhouse Rock, King Creole, Blue Hawaii, Viva Las Vegas, That's the Way It Is*. It was innocuous and predictable enough fare, so far. As I dug a little deeper, however, one disturbing title in particular caught my eye, since it was hidden behind her copies of *The Women* and *Stage Door*: it was called *Orgies at The Omni, Volume 11*.

It *couldn't* be.

I grabbed the case off the shelf and looked at the credits on the back. "Directed by Miles Conroy." It was a sample of the lucrative amateur porn that Miles had thrived on after I'd left New York, selling hundreds if not thousands of home-made DVDs over the internet, all shot at The Omni and edited out of his home office, or so I'd heard via the grapevine.

Overcome with anxiety, I popped the disc into her player and turned on the television. When Dolores finally returned to the living room, wearing a smart, yellow, Doris Day outfit, apparently ready for the tennis court or a stroll along the Third Street Promenade, I was sitting on the sofa, weeping but aroused, watching a very young Dolores being eaten out by my ex-wife Gloria on the floor of The Omni Theater while some naked, hairy, burly men stood around them in a circle-jerk, ejaculating all over both of them. One of the masturbating men was Miles.

Dolores had played dumb with me this entire time. What an actress!

"Got any popcorn?" I asked her.

Action.

Chapter Fifty-One

The Theremin was shrieking so loudly in Nick's brain he thought his head would explode like an asteroid hitting the Earth, sending thousands of reptilian scales flying all over the firmament. That seemed like a fitting resolution to his torment, one he almost hoped for, except for one driving impetus: the search for Dolores.

Nick managed to make it to the lake, avoiding contact with anyone, since it was late at night. Allegedly, this was where authorities had initially found her, as a cold corpse washed up on the shore. But then she disappeared *again*, apparently walking, or rolling, right out of the morgue, reborn as a zombie mermaid. Yea, right. Like something like *that* could ever happen. Stupid fucking cops.

He sat on the lakeshore sadly contemplating his horrific reflection on the moonlit surface of the water. As he despondently ran his hands through his scaly scalp, more and more strands of hair began to come out between his thick fingers, and he felt nauseous, fearing he would vomit again. This hopelessly distressing situation reminded him of a recurring lifelong dream wherein all of his teeth would gradually fall out, and he'd wake up in a cold sweat, desperately feeling his mouth for his missing molars. They were always there, to his relief. But he couldn't wake up from this current nightmare, it seemed, no matter how many times he closed his eyes and reopened them. He tried drowning out the Theremin with his own inner soundtrack, playing the song "All By Myself" by Eric Carmen in his mind, mixed with Paul Dunlap's moody score for *I Was a Teenage Werewolf.*

They both reminded him of his childhood, which seemed so long ago, it may as well have been a dream.

A fish swam by in the water and without even thinking about it, Nick lashed out his long frog-like freak tongue and snatched it up. It landed in his hand and he bit into the squirming creature, taking off its head and gnawing it between his increasingly sharp teeth, which were still very much intact. In self-disgust, he spit out the bones and blood and tossed the headless fish back into the water. Maybe it was not such a good idea that he found Dolores. He may repulse her. He was already repulsing himself.

Nick thought of his story, how he'd left his doppelganger bleeding to death on a motel bed. He wished he could trade places with *that* Nick. Rocking back and forth with neurotic intensity as he sat on the shore, sobbing, Nick prayed for a miracle to Whoever may have been listening.

Just then, a familiar voice called out to him, from somewhere *in* the lake.

"*Nick, come with me,*" the ethereal voice said. He looked up. It was Dolores. Her smiling face was radiant. Her pert breasts were fully exposed. She was swimming in the nude! He couldn't believe his yellow eyes.

"*Nick, come swim away with me*," she said repeatedly, beckoning him hither with her finger and a girlish giggle, then diving beneath the gently swaying surface of the lake, kicking up and revealing her legs, which were not legs at all, but a fully formed flipper with emerald tail fins that glistened in the moonlight. The Theremin suddenly stopped, but his life wasn't any less weird.

Then just like that, she disappeared beneath the scintillating surface of the lake, and was gone. *Again.* With renewed resolve to live, he dove in after her.

Chapter Fifty-Two

Dolores felt like she had a rash on her legs, which she kept itching as they drove through the night toward the Elvis-spawned zombie apocalypse engulfing them like a plague of piranhas in a whirlpool. "I need to stop and pick up some lotion, this is driving me nuts," she said to Jesse, who just laughed.

"I think it's a little late for that," he said. "Just nerves, is all. You probably got a bad case of the heebie-jeebies, or as I like to call 'em, the jivey-hiveys. I don't blame you none, neither." Then Jesse pointed out the windshield with familiar finger configuration. "There's a gas station, let's pull over and fill this sucker up while we got a chance."

"This is all a dream," Dolores said. "And it's not even *my* dream. I'm stuck inside somebody else's messed up head. That's the fucked up part of it. I can't wake up until the asshole dreaming this shit does."

"I used to think I was living a bad dream," Jesse said, "and my brother was living the *good* dream. Now things have kinda flipped, like the B-side of the record becomes the hit after the A-side has been forgotten. I've been tourin' around makin' my livin' as an Elvis impersonator since the Seventies. Before that I often worked as his stunt double in his movies. He got me that gig but changed my name to Toby. Toby Kwimper. That was his original name in '*Loving You*' before it got changed to Deke Rivers. Nobody ever picked up on it. He felt responsible for me and always took good care of me." Jesse seemed suddenly wistful, overcome by sentiment as he recalled his past.

"So, why didn't he just tell the world who you were?" Dolores asked. "Why didn't *you*?"

"I didn't wanna hurt him," Jesse said. "He wanted to just let the world know the truth, but I said, El, there's only room for one King in this world, and that's you. You got the crown, man. Plus I didn't want the hassle. I've always been a loner type. I couldn't handle fame the way he could—at least until he couldn't no more. I'd grown up with some nice folks who sheltered me from my origins until my brother got really big, and then one day my Papa Mancini took me aside and told me not only was I adopted, but this hellcat dancin' up a storm on the TV was my kinfolk."

"Wait, so why do you talk like you're a hick from Mississippi if you were raised in New Jersey?" Dolores asked. "Though you do dress like a goombah. None of you fits together, dude. It's one reason I have trouble believing anything you say, though I do find it interesting. And distracting from all this other crazy shit that makes no sense."

Jesse laughed and said, "Oh, I picked up this accent, I guess you could call it, when I was in Georgia, as a little kid, before we moved on to Jersey, and then later, when I decided to earn a livin' impersonatin' my brother, it just got into a groove, plus I was spendin' a lot of time with Elvis, mostly when nobody else was around, so he wouldn't have to explain my presence, and, well, this way of talkin' just sorta stuck." Jesse seemed awed by his own tale. He continued, "Y'see, once my Papa Mancini told me the truth, I high-tailed it for Memphis and looked my brother up. See, my adopted folks was real poor and my old man was into the Mob for some serious gambling debts, I thought maybe my bro' could help us out."

"Did he?" Dolores asked.

"Not at first. Naturally he didn't believe me, and I wasn't sure myself till I got the blood tests confirmin' it, then our Mama and Papa Presley sat us all down and laid the entire scoop on us. It was pretty painful. But once it was all out, and I promised to sort of lay low, my brother always looked after me. I promised not to embarrass the family, and I never did. But, sorry to say, I think the guilt may have driven our Mama to that early grave. Elvis didn't think so, but I don't know, she just got so sick so sudden like, not long after I showed up. I always felt guilty about that, no matter what my brother or my daddy said. Hope they all ain't out there walkin' around together now, lookin' for me..." Jesse stopped cold. That thought had never even occurred to him before.

A neon gas station sign shone eerily in the blackness. They pulled into the lot. Nobody was around but the pump still seemed operable for self-service. Jesse got out with Dolores's credit card and filled up the tank. Somebody forgot to turn off the system on the way out the door. Just as Dolores restarted the engine, they heard a loud wailing sound from within the apparently abandoned gas station convenience store.

"You think somebody needs our help?" Dolores asked.

"I'll check it out," Jesse said. "Gimme your gun and stay put."

Cautiously, Jesse approached the convenience store, which was still lit up for business, though no one was inside. Just when Jesse was about to open the door, a horrific crash made him spin around to see the Impala flying across the lot into a dumpster after being rammed by a speeding '59 Cadillac convertible. The violent impact mangled metal and sent shattered glass flying in all directions. Jesse ran toward the scene of the crash and dragged Dolores out of the totaled Impala. It seemed like a miracle she was still breathing, since the rest of the car had been completely destroyed by the big Caddy, which just slowly backed up from the wreck, disengaging its front fender from the Impala's rear, then coming to a contemplative stop a short distance away.

Cradling a bloody, barely conscious Dolores in his lap, Jesse pulled the gun and aimed it at the driver of the Caddy, who got out and casually strolled toward them.

"Easy there," said the driver. "I know this lady. My name's Miles. And these are some of our mutual friends."

From inside the convenience store lurched two more biker zombies, the one with the leather vest and the one with the black *lucha* mask. Despite their intimidating physiques, they were decomposing rapidly, and Jesse felt like he was about to lose his composure as well.

As Miles stood over them, with Jesse keeping his gun trained on him, despite the approaching biker zombies, Dolores began to deliriously murmur something, over and over. It sounded like, *"Nick, come swim away with me..."*

Chapter Fifty-Three

"I was young and stupid and needed the money and I didn't tell you because I didn't want to hurt you," Dolores rambled in a quivering voice, after she ejected the disc and flung it across the room. "I totally forgot that stupid fucking piece of shit video was still in there, it must've fallen. What you don't know won't hurt you, Nick. Just walk away and forget all this. Please. We'll both be better off."

"So, you didn't just happen to be at that party in Palm Springs," I correctly deduced, still sitting on the sofa, with no plans of walking any time soon.

"It was Miles' party," she said. "He sent me there. He wanted me to talk to you, to get to know you, what makes you tick. You're a mystery to him. He still cares about you."

"Bullshit," I said. "That party was arranged by the Mickey Mouse studio that wants to distribute some of my films."

"Miles *owns* that studio now," Dolores said. "Monogram International. Or rather he co-owns it as a silent partner. One of their secret subsidiaries distributes his porn. It's the only reason they're still solvent. He didn't want to tell you earlier. He's been keeping track of you for years. That's why he wants to finance this film of yours. He feels guilty about what went down back in New York. He knew I was your type and you'd approach me, which would make my 'surveillance' job easy. Mind if I smoke?"

"I don't care if you burn," I said reflexively, repeating an ancient *Honeymooners* gag. When in pain, I often resort to nostalgic references for consolation. "What did he promise you to seduce me?"

"Nothing," she said. "Just that he'd keep quiet about some of these movies. They wouldn't look good on my resume."

"And I thought you were the high class, educated type," I said.

"Fuck you and your judgmental bullshit," she spat, beginning to cry. "It was easy money, I admitted that already. Anyway, what makes you so much better than me, or anyone? I've seen your films, Nick. The only difference between the shit you and Miles make is that *his* movies make a lot more money."

"Less overhead," I said. "Or maybe more head all over. I'm not judging you, Dolores, but you have to admit, I feel a bit betrayed."

"It's not like I promised to marry you," she snapped, sucking on her cigarette.

"Well, would you?" I asked.

"Would I what?"

"Marry me?" I was serious.

She laughed through her tears. "You don't even know me."

"I feel like I know you a lot better than I did a few minutes ago," I said. "After all, we've both been with my ex-wife. We're married by proxy."

Dolores took a long drag on her cigarette and said, "She still loves you, you know. Gloria."

I shrugged that off and asked, "Do you?"

"Do I what?" she snapped.

"Still love Gloria," I said snidely.

"That wasn't *love*, Nick, it was *sex*," she said coldly. "It was just plain sex. For *money.* I never loved anyone until…."

“Until what?”

“Until I met you the other night,” she whispered, looking away at the rain.

I went over to hold her. At first she resisted, but finally she succumbed to my genuine compassion, and we embraced, then we kissed, gingerly, tentatively, then passionately, and then we went to bed. I still had my boner from watching her eat out my ex-wife, and as I ate Dolores out, I couldn’t help but think of Gloria, as if our mouths had merged. But when I looked up, I was so happy to see Dolores’s smiling face, and not Gloria—happier than I’d ever been in my entire life, despite Miles, despite Gloria, despite everything. To hell with them all. Amid all this filth, I’d finally found my heaven on Earth, no matter whether Dolores was an angel of the morning or a devil in disguise.

Action.

Chapter Fifty-Four

When Dolores opened her eyes, she was underwater, but breathing naturally. She kept swimming through the murky depths punctuated with moonbeams penetrating the surface above. Finally, disoriented but delighted, she headed up towards the light, and when she broke the surface of the water, she saw someone on the distant shore, apparently searching for her. She instinctively knew it was Nick, even though his countenance appeared strange and monstrous, at least from her distant vantage point. She waved frantically and called out his name, but he could no longer see nor hear her. She had drifted too far away. She dove back under the surface and swam towards the shore, rapidly propelled by her tail fins, which she looked back and noticed with both awe and immediate acceptance, but when she surfaced again, near the shore, Nick was gone. She dove back underwater to look for him there, but after a vain search, she headed back to the surface and instead of the moon, found herself staring into the blinding fluorescent light of a hospital room.

"What the fuck kinda fucked up dream was *that*?" she exclaimed as she sat up, feeling wobbly.

By her bedside was Buddy West, her agent, and Myrna, owner of the Motel Capri.

"You all right?" Myrna asked her, brow furrowed.

"Mother?" Dolores said groggily, looking at Myrna.

Myrna just smiled. "I'm not your mother, dear. But you're in a safe place now."

"What?" Dolores said. "Where's Jesse?"

"Who?" Buddy said. "You mean Johnny?"

"*Jesse*!" she screamed. "*Jesse! Nick! Help me! Somebody, anybody, help me wake up*!" Dolores bolted from the bed in hysterics, but then, feeling suddenly woozy, collapsed once again.

When she opened her eyes, she was looking into Jesse's worried face.

"Lil' sister, do you know this asshole?" Jesse said, motioning with his chin toward an arrogantly posturing Miles and the moaning, slobbering biker zombies by his side, still training the gun vaguely in their direction. "'Cause he just nearly killed you."

Through blurred vision Dolores looked impassively at Miles and the biker zombies, then back at Jesse. Her vision wasn't impaired from head trauma, but from an onslaught of tears. "Where's my Nick?" she whispered, before passing out once more.

Then she just continued swimming through the moonbeams, keeping her eyes wide open beneath the surface of the water, trying with all her mental might not to wake up from *this* dream…

She could hear Nina Simone singing, "Wild is the Wind" from somewhere up above, the celestial sound somewhat warped and muted by the intervening waves, but unmistakable and strong. It gave her impetus to keep swimming through the murky depths of her own dream.

Chapter Fifty-Five

Nick swam back to shore after plunging into the cold waters of the lake to find his mermaid Dolores. He reluctantly returned to the shore and lay down in the mud—cold, wet, sad and tired. The stormy deluge had finally stopped. He closed his eyes and drifted off to the old Mr. Acker Bilk tune "Stranger on the Shore" as performed by his inner Theremin.

When he opened his eyes, he was staring at the ceiling of a motel room. It seemed vaguely familiar, though hard to pinpoint. He lifted his head and shook off his grogginess, then looked around. This was exactly how he'd imagined the room at the Motel Capri, where the other Nick, the one he'd just made up for his story, had been tied up and left to bleed to death.

Instinctively, Nick tried to move his arms, but could not because, as he suspected, they were tied to the bedpost. He kept struggling until he managed to loosen the rope around his left wrist, and once freed, he untied the other arm, and then both of his legs. He rolled off the bed, searing pangs of sharp agony throbbing in his bloody shoulder where Miles had plunged the knife blade, and looked at himself in the mirror. No scales or any evidence of monstrous metamorphosis. His face appeared totally normal, though wan and pale from loss of blood. He was obviously dreaming, but had somehow slipped into the subjective viewpoint of his own fictional character. Or so he surmised. At least his fictional counterpart was finally free to go out and find his fictional Dolores. If he couldn't find and reunite with Dolores in his real world, he'd find and reunite with her in his dream world. And then never wake up.

Nick washed his face and dressed his wound using motel soap and towels, took a shower, and headed out the door.

Outside it was dark. Very dark. He overheard the screeching sound of a car radio emanating from the parking lot. Something about the dead returning to life and devouring the living. People screaming in terror. But he didn't have time for that right now. He had to find Dolores, and then everything would be made right again, he was sure of it. She was his personal Missing Link.

Nick went to the front office. A middle-aged, dour-faced guy with dark hair and dark clothes was sitting behind the counter. He was wearing dark sunglasses and a dark cowboy hat, and there were several band-aids on his pasty face, neck and hands—all areas of exposed flesh. Apparently he'd been in some sort of accident, or was suffering from some awful, degenerative disease. His name-tag said "Eugene Orowitz, Manager." Nick then noticed a mop and a bucket in the middle of the slippery floor. Obviously the clerk had just cleaned up some sort of mess, too. Nick ignored all of these potentially troubling details. He wouldn't allow himself to be distracted from his quest.

"Can I help you?" Eugene asked in a gravelly voice.

"I'm looking for my friend, her name is Dolores, I checked in with her a while ago. I'm wondering if she came back here, looking for me."

Eugene seemed puzzled. "Hey, you look messed up, friend," he said without a trace of irony. "What room are you in?"

"Eleven, I think," Nick said, avoiding commentary on the clerk's own obviously unhealthy condition.

Eugene looked through his guest registry. "Can't be, that room has been vacant since the cops showed up and took away the body."

"*Whose* body?"

Eugene shrugged as he sucked on what appeared to be a toothpick, though it was actually the bone of a human finger. "Beats me, I just got on duty a little while ago. I can tell you, a woman named Dolores split on her tab just a few hours ago."

"What?" Nick felt light-headed and confused about his own identity, his place in the world, whatever world he happened to be in. "Where'd she go?"

"Beats me, took off with some Elvis-lookin' dude, an old man," Eugene said. "Ask me, they're into some kinky shit. I tried running her credit card but our system ain't workin'. Must be 'cause of everything goin' on."

"What's going on?"

Eugene gestured to the television mounted in the corner of the office. Apocalyptic scenes of zombie horror flickered through the snowy screen. Reception was becoming increasingly poor as communications broke down. The very fabric of society was being torn to shreds like so much mortal flesh and blood in a meat grinder.

"Oh," Nick said, unfazed. "Anyway, thanks for your help."

"Anytime," Eugene said. "Good luck out there, Nick."

"Cheers," Nick said, and he walked back out into the night. The fact that the clerk had called him by his name, without a formal introduction, didn't register right away. Instinctively, he knew the clerk as well. But right now he had a job to do. He boldly approached the car with its radio blasting news of the end of the world. It was a pale blue two-seater Thunderbird, the new model. Two young people were fucking in it. The keys were in the ignition.

Nick opened the door and forced them both out, threatening them with physical violence.

"Hey man, it's the end of everything, we're just getting one last rock off before it's all over!" yelled the blonde teenage boy, obviously stoned, sitting on the ground with his pants around his ankles.

"Yea!" said the blonde teenage girl, perky breasts hanging out of her frilly top, panties down around her tanned, taut loins. "What the fuck do *you* care?"

"I don't give a shit what you do, get a room, take mine," Nick said, flipping them the motel key still in his pocket, "Number eleven. We'll swap." Then Nick climbed in the driver's seat and started up the engine.

"*Hey, that's my dad's car*!" yelled the kid, but Nick just ignored him as he backed up, nearly running over both of the drugged teenagers, who barely rolled out of the way of the Thunderbird as it peeled out of the lot and sped down the dark road. The first place Nick would look was the Omega Theater. He just hoped he was in time to stop the porn massacre, unsure where he was in the timeline of his own made-up story, which no longer felt very fictional.

Nick drove and drove, but no signposts or landmarks indicated he was going in the direction of his destination, The Midnight Lounge.

He had been driving for some time when some sort of large animal leaped into the road in front of him. Nick swerved to avoid it, and the Thunderbird skidded off the side of the road and came to a halt when it hit a scarecrow pole, which fell on top of Nick, knocking him senseless. He couldn't hear the growling and howling of the beast closing in on him.

Chapter Fifty-Six

Dolores put on a CD and I heard Nina Simone singing "I Put a Spell On You" as I took a shower. Then I came out into the living room wearing nothing but a towel around my waist, and we sat on the sofa together, quietly listening to music. She had the CD player on random. The next song was "My Buddy" my Mel Torme. I began to weep uncontrollably.

"Why are you crying?" she asked me, hugging me.

"My cat," I said. "My dead cat. This was our song. One time…one time I had a dream, we were swimming in a pool together. As we reached the end, I lifted him up and onto the side of the pool, and then he was gone. His journey with me had ended. His name was Buddy. Like your agent." My voice was choked with sobs. It came on suddenly, and just a moment before, I'd felt so content. Music can have that affect.

"I'm so sorry," she said, gently caressing my face, kissing away my anguished tears.

I regained my composure and, just to change the subject, said, "Miles said he thinks he could get Mickey Rourke for my movie, at least in a small role, to help sell it."

"I thought it was low budget," Dolores said. "I'm one thing, but Mickey Rourke is an actual movie star."

"It is, and he is, but Miles knows Mickey from the New York days," I explained. "Mick used to frequent The Omni now and then when he was in town." I felt a pang just referring to that hellhole. "He knew *everybody*, it seems," I added with pointed irony.

Dolores gently stroked my forehead and hair. "I'm so

sorry we met this way," she whispered. "But at least we met." Nine Simone was singing "Since I Fell For You."

"Yes," I said, still teary-eyed from thinking about my dead cat. "As long as you're not faking that you like me."

"That would make me a whore," she said flatly. "I don't sleep with just anyone. Not anymore, anyway. And I'm not *that* good of an actress."

I thought of the DVD I'd just watched. I had to take her word for it.

"Did you ever strip?" I asked her boldly. "You know, downstairs from The Omni, in the Lunar Lounge."

Since we'd just been intimate, I'd bought myself enough slack and good credit to avoid getting slapped. Just barely. "*No*," she said emphatically, keeping her indignation in check, though I didn't see why stripping was any less dignified than having lesbian sex in front of a camera while guys stood around you, jerking off. "Though I did try burlesque dancing, old school stuff, at some other little clubs in Manhattan. I gave it up, though."

"Why?" I said. "You got the figure for it. And the creativity, I'm sure."

"It took dedication I didn't have," she said. "You're not just taking your clothes off, you're performing. It's an art form I didn't have the natural talent for. And what I really wanted to do was sing. And act. In live musical theater, off-Broadway and eventually *on* Broadway. But that never happened, either. I was in some small plays, here and there, though. I also did do quite a few burlesque shows before I got around to retiring from it. Then I was a singing waitress for a little while, till I quit that too. And a model sometimes, though I wasn't nearly skinny enough to work regularly. And then…."

"Then what?" I asked knowingly.

"Excuse me," Dolores said abruptly, getting up and

going into the bathroom, ostensibly to avoid the trajectory of the conversation. She certainly liked to spend a lot of time in there, I noted. I took the opportunity to swipe the *Orgies at The Omni* DVD and stick it in my suit jacket, hanging on a rack in the corner of the living room. I couldn't wait to get home and whack off to it, even though I could also have Dolores in the flesh. Sometimes fantasy was better than reality, and I could escape in that world, without any rules, without any regard for the restrictive perimeters of acceptable reality. This is how I felt when I made movies. I could create any alternate reality I chose. Within a budget, of course. And with the consent of my actors and distributor. But when left to the devices of my own imagination, the sky—or the sewer—was the limit.

Feeling both ashamed and confused, I got dressed and walked out of the apartment without even saying goodbye. For some reason I couldn't fathom myself at the time, I just had to get out of there. In retrospect, it was an instinct I should've kept following.

Action.

Chapter Fifty-Seven

"Dreams and memories eventually merge in the imagination, and since both are equally intangible, both are equally real, or unreal, relative to the touch of the present moment, which is fleeting, blending with our dreams of the future and memories of the past before we can capture and hold onto any of them—it all just slips through our grasp like so much sea mist..."

Dolores wasn't sure where those spoken words came from, but she was quite sure of their phantom articulation, resonating in her ear like a book on tape, as she instinctively swam toward their mysterious source. She mentally flashed back on a very clear memory of waking up in a morgue, with a sheet over her head, then just getting up and walking out, stark naked, into the dark night, through the pouring rain, intuitively returning to the lake, where she'd drowned after diving in, thinking she was a mermaid because of the stiffness of her scaly legs, only this time, when she dipped beneath the surface of the lake, she found her newly formed emerald tail fins were fully functional, and she was able to continue swimming, and breathing underwater. It was glorious. She felt like herself for the first time in her life.

But she missed Nick, her newfound soul mate. Her heart yearned for him. She had left his apartment via the fire escape to get away from Miles, racing instinctively for the lake, where she just jumped in. Then she found herself too far from the shore to swim back safely, everything going black; then she woke up in the morgue, and once again, snuck away back to the lake. But she knew Nick was probably looking for her too—unless he thought she was dead. Despite the glorious rush of aquatic emancipation, she had to return to the shore and find him, even though she wasn't sure how she could navigate land in her completely transformed condition. She headed for the light anyway, guided by the seemingly omnipresent voice of Nina Simone.

Suddenly, just as she broke the surface of the water, she was looking in a mirror, a towel wrapped around her head. The Nina Simone music seemed to be coming from the next room. She walked out into the strangely familiar yet lonesome and empty living room and said, "Nick?"

But Nick was gone. She felt dizzy and laid on the sofa for what seemed an eternity.

When she opened her eyes, she was staring into a starless sky. She felt motion, pain, and nausea. She slowly deduced she was in the backseat of a moving car. She smelled something foul, like decaying flesh, and then looked into the dead eyes of the zombie whose muscular but cold and stiff shoulder she was leaning on. He had long, stringy hippie-hair held in a bandana, and a leather vest with no shirt, revealing powerful if putrefied pecs. A huge wet bullet hole gaped in his throat. She screamed.

"Hey, darlin'" Miles said from the driver's seat. Another zombie, the one wearing the black *lucha libre* mask, concealing his facial but not bodily decay, since he was shirtless, sat passively in the passenger seat. The top to the Caddy was down and the warm night air felt thick and musky, humid and cloying, with very little breeze for relief from the dark heat. "'Bout time you came to. I gotta get you cleaned up so we can finish the movie."

"M-movie?" she murmured. "Where's Nick?"

"Nick?" Miles said. "Oh, he's dead. At least he *was*. In any case, not my problem, or yours. Like I said, I need to finish our movie so I can show it at the Omega once all this zombie non-sense blows over. See, I think it's a plague, a virus, but somebody will beat it, and when they do, when scientists figure it out, or the government stops experimenting, 'cause they're probably behind it all, using us like guinea pigs, the sick fuckers, things will get back to the way they were before, folks will want their normal lives back, and I'll have just the thing they'll want—*zombie porn*! This is even better than I coulda hoped, and I don't even have to spend money on makeup effects! Not even on you—I'll just pretend you're a goddamn zombie bitch, too, gettin' gang-banged by these undead horny fuckers! That's right, baby, you're gonna be a star—a necrophiliac star, but a star nonetheless." Miles laughed as he took another swig of his beer, finally finishing it, crunching then chucking the can, and opening another one, handed to him by his biker zombie slave.

"J-Jesse?" Dolores said, looking around for her friend.

"Oh, him? The Elvis impersonator?" Miles said. "Oh, *that* old fuck is gone too. My boys here ripped him to shreds and ate his heart and brain. He won't be a bother to us, either. It's just you and us, baby." Miles drank more beer and kept driving. Dolores noticed his head was covered in bloody bandages from where she'd shot him, unsuccessfully, back at The Midnight Lounge. She vowed to herself that next time her aim would be truer.

Dolores stared out into the night, closed her eyes tightly, and concentrated. But when she opened them again, she was still in the backseat of the Caddy, speeding towards a future she wanted desperately to escape. For now, she just settled back, feeling the blood caking around her head wound, suddenly recalling the horrific car crash that led her to this painful predicament, and she just waited to either wake up, or go back to sleep. She closed her eyes and imagined she was a mermaid, as she had done so many times before.

Chapter Fifty-Eight

"This is how it's been my whole sorry loser life," Nick thought to himself: "I just can't ever seem to make all the pieces connect into one satisfying picture."

He was saying this to himself as he opened his eyes. He was no longer driving the Thunderbird. He was back on the bank of the lake. He touched his face. Scaly. Hideous.

Nick mentally readjusted, resigned to his suddenly shifting realms of reality, chalking up most of it to hallucinations caused by his mysterious malady, and sat up to take in his surroundings. He lingered lake side for a while before he decided to give up on the idea of Dolores re-emerging from the deep, her mermaid metamorphosis apparently complete, and returned to his studio apartment to feed and care for his beloved Buddy. When he arrived at his apartment building, his monstrous appearance and murderous reputation attracted a small mob of curious onlookers. "*Leave me alone*!" he yelled at them, and they dispersed like frightened pigeons. He didn't care whether the cops were upstairs waiting for him. They weren't, though one of the strippers from Zombieville admonished Nick some serious-looking plainclothesmen had been around looking for him earlier. Nick nodded and trudged up the stairs as if she'd told him the landlord had been looking for the rent money, which was also true.

Buddy was very happy to see Nick. The two animal-beings embraced. Buddy was not deterred by his master's new face. Nick still smelled and sounded the same. The cat was not fooled or swayed by outside appearances. He knew Nick's loyal heart still beat reliably beneath all that scaly skin. They looked into each other's eyes and saw into each other's spirits, and neither felt lonely, though the knowledge of imminent parting saddened their souls.

"You'll always live inside of me, no matter what happens, my little friend," Nick whispered to Buddy as he held him, after giving the cat his daily dose of medicine. Now that Dolores may have been gone forever, Nick cherished his friend Buddy more than ever. And now that he was an animal too, Nick felt especially bonded with Buddy in a way he hadn't been before. He could relate to his animal nature.

Then Nick noticed cat vomit on the floor. Not a good sign. Nick held back tears as he cleaned it up. Wherever he went now, he'd have to take Buddy with him. He couldn't just wait for the cops to come take him away, because then they'd separate Buddy from him forever, send him to the animal shelter, or worse, have him destroyed. They both needed new sanctuary from the outside world.

Reluctantly yet resolutely, Nick put Buddy into his carrier, threw some cat food and an open sack of litter into a grocery bag, pocketed the bottle of Prednisone pills, snuck downstairs then outside with him in tow, and headed quickly for Myrna's house.

Chapter Fifty-Nine

When I got back to my Buddy-less apartment in Westwood, my cell phone was ringing. I'd left it behind on purpose, so I wouldn't be disturbed while visiting Dolores. I picked it up and answered. Caller I.D. indicated it was my old pal Miles. Just whom I wanted to talk to right then.

"Our deal is off," I said. "Two-timing bastard. No, *three*-timing bastard!"

"Nick, it's me, Gloria," said the voice of my ex-wife, echoing from the past.

"What the hell?" I said, genuinely shocked.

"I took Miles' phone when he wasn't looking, I knew you wouldn't pick up if you thought it was me," she said. She sounded drunk. That's how I could be sure it was really her. I thought I could hear a baby crying in the background.

"I barely wanted to pick up thinking it was him."

"Sounds like it," she said. "How are you?"

"Peachy," I said. "Remember a girl named Dolores?"

"Dolores?" she said. "Dolores who?" I could tell she was lying. Always could.

"The one you had sex with at The Omni," I said. "Anyway, we finally have something in common besides our tastes in music. Where is Miles, anyway?"

"I don't know," she said. "Nick, I didn't call to talk about Miles or anybody else, whoever you're talking about. I called to talk about *us*."

"Nothing to say."

"Nothing to say? It's been *years*."

"Exactly," I said. "And nothing's changed. Except for

me. You're the same, Gloria. I've seen the evidence caught on tape. Goodbye, Gloria. And tell Miles I'm on to him, and the deal is *off*."

"Nick, please let me say..."

I hung up on her, though after I did, I was rather curious what she had to tell me. We hadn't spoken since the divorce had been finalized over a decade before. At the time it didn't occur to me what an odd coincidence it was to hear from her, right after seeing that video of her with Dolores. That's because I didn't believe in coincidence.

I took out the *Orgies at The Omni* DVD and began watching it from the beginning.

It started off innocuously enough, with Dolores and Gloria portraying two movie patrons—obviously college girls, probably sorority sisters—giggling and gossiping as they watching a movie at The Omni, with only a few burly, hairy guys sitting in the back row of sofas. On the screen was an old Doris Wishman flick, *Bad Girls Go To Hell*—my own 16mm print that I'd left behind. The two giggling gals gradually grew aroused watching the vintage black-and-white sleaziness flickering in front of them, and began to make out. I didn't feel turned on this time, even as they began to slowly then voraciously undress each other, and even when the big burly hairy men—and Miles—suddenly showed up and sprayed semen all over the writhing women. It was like watching something clinical, both riveting and reviling, like open-heart surgery. Just a bunch of intertwined body parts and mingling human juices. Despite the fact I recognized three of the faces, it felt more like I was merely a voyeur distantly watching an anonymous gathering of fellow perverts. I went over and touched the screen, and my fingers hit glass. I could not penetrate into this alternate dimension. I couldn't touch them, only myself, and they couldn't touch me, either. It may as well have never happened, except it was happening, right in front of my eyes, even if the activity was intangible. If I closed my eyes, I could picture much more disturbing—and arousing—images than the ones "preserved for posterity" on this disc. But I didn't. I was too transfixed by the seductive horror of it all.

I thought: we were all just globs of flesh and fluids wandering lost, lonely and afraid on a ball of dirt floating in a big, empty void. What did any of it matter. Unless we had spirits that lived on, but they were just as intangible as the images on the screen, or in my head. I noted how the grunting ghosts on my television screen had been initially filmed against the screened background of different cinematic images filmed many years prior to this particular occurrence, creating this looped, self-reflexive, visual odyssey: disparate eras resonating and ultimately merging with the other, forming one single moving visage impacting me mysteriously here in the present, where I was alone, with nobody to touch but myself. And even that wouldn't last.

Finally, in morbid, self-pitying, philosophically indulgent disgust, I popped out the DVD and tossed it aimlessly, and then went to my room and lay face down the bed. I missed Buddy. I was lonely. How could I have a future with Dolores? For what purpose did Miles set her up with me anyway? There had to be more to this sordid story, which I probably didn't want to discover. Maybe it was none of my business. I hardly knew any of these people: my best friend, my ex-wife, and the new love of my life. All total strangers to me.

After a while I got up and went into the corner of the kitchen and looked sadly down at Buddy's bowl, which still had some dry food in it. Next to it was the little toy mouse stuffed with catnip he had once loved to play with. I picked it up and began to cry, uncontrollably, for what seemed like hours, out of sheer loneliness.

Someone rang the doorbell. I opened it. It was Dolores, still wearing her deceptively cute little Doris Day outfit.

"Did you steal my DVD?" she asked playfully.

Without saying anything I went and retrieved the disc off of the floor where I'd aimlessly flung it, turned back around, and handed it to her. "Yea, it must've fallen in my pocket when I left," I said.

"And you did leave suddenly," she said, without taking the disc from me.

"How'd you find me, anyway?"

She held up my script for "One-Way Ticket to Thrillville" and pointed to the address printed on the bottom.

"Ah, so you're a detective," I said. "Come in?"

"If I were a detective I'd have figured out why you left without saying goodbye," she said, standing pat. "Still mad at me, I take it?"

I wasn't sure how to respond, because I wasn't sure what the truth was. I didn't know why I had left. Fear, I supposed. Not of the past. Of the future. With her. Or worse, without her.

"Did you bother to read it, or are you just swapping it for the DVD?" I said, still holding it in my hand.

"I don't want to give you back your script, I like it too much," she said softly, and sincerely.

"Well, I like your movie too much," I lied.

"So I guess we're at an impasse," she said.

"Yea, I guess so," I said. "But you can come over and watch your movie whenever you want to."

"You can come over to my place and watch yours, too,

especially if I'm in it," she said.

"I don't think that's going to happen now," I said.

"Why not?"

"Because, I'm going to tell Miles to go to hell, so that means no financing for this piece of shit," I said fatalistically, but hoping she'd jump in and stop me, "and nobody else will bankroll something so ambitious and weird and fucked-up, so there ya go."

She did jump in, but she didn't stop me. "We can do it without Miles," she said. "But first, you have to finish the script."

"What do you mean?" I said. "It *is* finished."

"But it just sorta *ends*. Like you just ran out of ideas, or ink. No resolution. And it doesn't make any sense in the real world."

"That's the point," I said, though my artistic ego was taking a hit, and she knew it.

"Well, that's just my opinion, of course," she said.

"Well, wanna come in and discuss it?"

"Okay," she said, tentatively entering my domain.

She gave my place the visual once-over as I mixed us a couple of Vespers. She asked if I could make a French 75 but I didn't have the champagne for it, so she settled for whatever I was making. She made note of the framed Bettie Page pinup, the framed print of Edward Hopper's "Nighthawks at the Diner," the shelves of movie books and pulp fiction novels, the massive DVD, CD and LP collection. None of it seemed to surprise her. She just took it all in like a schoolgirl playing hooky and spending her day at the Natural History Museum.

Then she noticed the bowl of dry cat food in the corner of the kitchen. "I thought you said your cat was dead," she said.

"He is," handing her the drink. "Here's to Buddy.

Cheers."

She accepted my toast, I put on some Sinatra, and then we sat together on my sofa. *"I'm a Fool to Want You,"* Frank crooned. She was still clutching the script like it was a top-secret manual for making bombs. Actually, maybe it was going to be a bomb, eventually.

"So I don't understand why you don't like the ending," I said to her.

"Because it's not an ending," she said.

"It's a beginning," I said.

"In a way," she said, "but you haven't resolved the situations of the main characters."

"Which ones, in which story?" I asked.

"Both," she said. "And shouldn't you change the names?"

"Why?"

"*'Nick and Dolores'*?" she laughed. "Isn't that a bit too obviously autobiographical?"

"But the story—stories—are so outrageous," I pointed out, "that it doesn't matter. I'm just using those names for now, anyway. It helps me get into the zone I need to be in when I'm writing. I may change them later. But overall, you liked it?" My insecurity was showing.

"Yes," she said, though after further contemplation, she added, "but it needs some work."

"Oh, and I guess you're the one to help me with that," I said.

"Yup!" She sat erect, getting excited by our still unofficial, one-sided "partnership." She was so damned cute, though, I couldn't resist her enthusiastic pitch. "First of all, why don't you have the stories merge into one story?"

"That's *ridiculous*!" I said. "How could that even happen? It's not science fiction. I mean, not *really*. The story the pulp writer is *writing*, or imagining in his head, is like a horror *noir* story, and then the one the pulp writer eventually *lives* is a sheer B movie fantasy, but none of it is actually explained, so it's not science fiction. It's just a romantic flight of fancy. There's not supposed to be a point to it, per se. Just two tales of crazy shit happening to the same poor sap. Get it?"

"Yea, yea, I got all that," she said, waving her hand dismissively, impatient with the overly obvious analysis of my own imagination, "but neither story is really resolved. You still need to let the audience know how it all comes out, even if it keeps going—that's where the *sequel* comes in! But meantime, I was thinking, if the two Nicks somehow merge into *one*, *that* would be the resolution. It was all one story all along!"

"I don't get it," I insisted, just playing with her. Frank was crooning "Angel Eyes."

"You will," she said, taking me by the hand. "Let me give you more inspiration." She then led me into my own bedroom and fucked my brains out. Her plan was to literally pick my brain —off of the floor, that is, after she'd banged it out of my head, then rearrange the pieces, and put them back exactly the way she thought they should work. My brain was already swimming in gin, vodka and Lillet Blanc, so her work was easy.

Afterwards, naked in bed, she flipped on my television and stopped when she came across an old Esther Williams movie, *Million Dollar Mermaid*, on TCM. "One of my favorites," she said. "We can work on our script later. Let's watch this. Fix me another drink?"

"*Our* script?" I said, backing it up a bit.

"Yes," she said, "*Ours*."

She owned me completely. I heard Frank singing "Witchcraft."

Then she disappeared into my bathroom for a long time. I called several times to see if she was all right, and she responded that she was fine. Why did she spend so much time in the bathroom? It was becoming a troubling trend.

"You spend more time in the bathroom than Elvis Presley," I said to her when she finally emerged, "and look what happened to him."

"Well, you're going to find this very coincidental," she said, "but I have this strange rash on my legs."

My blood ran cold. "I don't believe in coincidence," I said.

Action.

Chapter Sixty

When they arrived back at The Midnight Lounge, Miles ordered the biker zombies to drag Dolores inside. Miles was taking no chances; he wanted to get as much usable stuff on film as possible while he still could, before his main actors completely decomposed. He was investing in a future that may never happen. Dolores couldn't believe she was back here again, in the same exact situation—only *worse*. This time, she'd be gang-banged by *corpses*. It was all a recurring nightmare that kept looping back onto itself, or a movie with no ending. She'd have to write the proper resolution to this self-recycling situation herself.

And Miles had one more surprise up his sleeve: Buddy, the undead sax player, came staggering from the back of the bar as they came in. His neck wound was still bleeding, Dolores noticed. She also noticed he had no pants, and was erect, his pecker stiff with more than rigor mortis. She screamed. Miles laughed.

How could she have known when she plugged these assholes the first time—or when Nick shot Buddy—that an undead Elvis Presley was going to raise an army of the dead and take over the entire planet? You can't really plan your day around things like that, they just happen, and then you have to adjust and rearrange your own little agenda accordingly. Dolores was flexible. She'd go with the flow. *None of this was even real, anyway*, or so she forced herself to believe as the three slimy, slobbering ghouls began to grope at her bruised, battered, bloody, and now bare body on a pool table in the back of the lounge. At least they were wearing condoms this time, administered by the director, who didn't want his star infected with the zombie virus via unprotected intercourse with the undead.

"Be careful with the biting, fellas, don't wanna hurt our star" Miles reminded them with a wary grin from behind the camera. Miles was now playing Marilyn Manson's version of "I Put a Spell On You." Dolores felt their rotting tongues on her flesh, and puke swelled in her throat.

Miles was quite disappointed when one of the ghouls, the one with the long hair and leather vest, attempted penetration, but his decrepit cock bent when it hit Dolores's thigh, and then it broke off like a breadstick. He backed off and whined like a wounded bitch, holding his gory crotch. Dolores took the opportunity to bite off the Mexican wrestler biker zombie's cock that had been forced into her mouth. She spit out the grisly, rancid stump, and then ripped the black *lucha* mask off of the zombie like it was a used condom. He wailed with anguish, covering his disfigured, decomposing face with one hand, the geyser of blood gushing from his loins with the other. Laughing maniacally, Dolores then karate kicked Buddy the zombie in the head as he lustily lunged at her, and he went down. She picked up his saxophone and literally beat his brains out with it. Dolores then ran toward Miles, still petrified with shock, and with all of her might, slammed his big, fat ass to the ground. Then she picked up the video camera and fiercely beat him with it until his face caved in, busted machine parts flying along with bits of shattered skull. Miles wouldn't come back this time, dead or alive. She'd make damn sure of it. After pounding him ruthlessly with the now-broken video camera, she pounced on his lifeless torso and began beating his pulpy face, or what was left of it, closing her eyes and screaming with savage fury, splattering herself with the remnants of his unrecognizable countenance.

When she got up off the bloody heap of broken bones that had been the man known as Miles only moments before, she instead saw the inert body of Jesse Mancini, or at least, someone who looked just like him. Instead of a jogging suit, he was wearing a bejeweled Elvis-style jumpsuit. He sat erect and sneered at her, then stood up. "You through now?" he said congenially as he dusted himself off. She looked down at herself, and saw that her red halter-top was clean, except for some dust, but no grisly stains of collateral carnage.

Dolores heard laughter and looked around. There were more cameras, and more people, but it was bright daylight, and she was no longer in The Midnight Lounge. She was somewhere in the middle of a desert, with no buildings around other than a few trucks and trailers. Near the side of the road was a vintage '50s Cadillac that looked like it had been in an accident. Blinded by the sudden glare, she squinted as if someone had just shone a flashlight in her eyes. A film crew was standing around watching. Some were laughing. The guy who looked like Jesse said, "Next time, don't hit me so dang hard, ma'am, I'm getting' too old to take a punch." He massaged his jaw for effect. "I'll be in my trailer. Let me know when you're ready for the next take."

Dolores felt a hand on her shoulder. It was Buddy, her agent. "That was great, honey, but the director wants another take—and this time, don't beat up on the poor guy so brutally. Remember, you're also in love with him, because of the Elvis connection. Let's go grab a bite and discuss your motivation, okay? Great job, considering."

"Considering what?" Dolores was completely dazed.

"Well, considering you just came out of a coma!" he said with a nervous laugh.

As they walked to her trailer, Dolores noticed several actors in zombie makeup and biker outfits. One guy was tricked out as a werewolf, being coached by the director for the next scene. The director's chair read *Miles Conroy*. The guy she thought she had murdered. *Twice.*

She then noticed a scene marker board under the arm of one of the crew-members. It read: "One-Way Ticket to Thrillville."

Chapter Sixty-One

Myrna opened the door and laughed in Nick's scaly face. "I *told* you you'd be back," she said. "And you brought your kitty, which means you plan to stay a while, I take it? Well, hurry up, we don't have much time."

"What do you mean?" Nick asked as he stepped inside with Buddy in the carrier.

"My husband will be home soon, we have to hurry with our preparations," she said.

"Preparations for *what*?" Nick asked.

"Killing him, what else?"

Nick groaned like he'd just been assigned homework. "Whatever," he said. "Where can I put Buddy where he'll be safe? I don't want him to get outside."

"You can use the guest room, upstairs, all the way down the hall to the left," Myrna said. She was wearing a black silk robe and no undergarments, so her ample cleavage was generously exposed. Her torrid perfume permeated the thick, musky air. The whole house felt sensuously stuffy. She'd obviously been expecting him.

Myrna stopped him at the stairs and kissed him. He thrust his long tongue down her throat and she squirmed with illicit pleasures. Then when her mouth was free, she said, "There's something else I should tell you."

"God damn it, now what?" Nick said.

"That fire at The Oasis Theater?" she said.

"Yea? What about it?" Nick said. "They trying to pin that on me too? I was nowhere *near* the joint. I got an alibi, too."

"You mean your girlfriend, Dolores?"

“Yea, matter of fact,” Nick said. “One more reason I have to find her. *Again.* But I probably never will.”

“Probably not,” Myrna agreed cryptically.

“What do you mean?” Nick asked nervously.

“My husband wants her to stay missing, because he knows she’s your alibi.”

“Oh come off it,” Nick said, picking up the cat carrier and his bag and pushing her aside, heading up the stairs.

"Even if that’s not true, this much is: my husband set that fire, and now he’s framing you for it,” Myrna called after him.

Nick stopped halfway up the stairs and turned around to face her. “Why would a police chief burn down a movie theater?” Nick asked wearily.

“The insurance,” Myrna said.

“It wasn’t his theater,” Nick said.

“Yes,” Myrna said, “it was. Your friend Miles is just the front man. My husband’s name is on the deed to the property. You’re a stranger in this town, what do you know? I’ll tell you what you don’t know: They’re running drugs and hookers out of The Moonlight Lounge, too. My husband is a very bad man. And so is your friend Miles. I’m doing you a big favor. I’m doing the whole *town* a big favor.”

Nick sighed and said, “Nice,” then continued up the stairs.

“Come down soon so we can make plans!” Myrna shouted after him. “I’ll make coffee.”

The guest room was small and dark but sufficient, with its own adjacent bathroom. Nick transformed a shoebox into a litter box and poured some cat food in the soap dish. Buddy went and hid in the back of the closet. After trying to coax him out into the open, Nick gave up and sat on the bed and put his increasingly hairless head in his hands, and sobbed.

Then he noticed another framed photo next to the bed. He turned on the light to get a better look. It was a beautiful young woman wearing a cap and gown. A formal high school graduation photo. At first he thought it was a younger photo of Myrna. But it wasn't.

It was Dolores. She was Myrna's daughter. The guest room was once *her* room. Suddenly it dawned on him: everybody was a liar, and everything was a lie.

Before the ramifications of the revelation could even register, he heard a car pull up in the driveway outside. He went to the window and peered down though the tree branches partly blocking his view of the front lawn. He couldn't quite make out whom it was, but he fearfully assumed it was Myrna's police chief husband, Dolores's father, marked for a violent, untimely death in his own home. They'd *all* run out of time.

Chapter Sixty-Two

"I've had this rash since before I met you, don't freak out," Dolores said as she sleepily, sexily reposed on my bed and resumed watching *Million Dollar Mermaid.* "I think it's from nerves."

"I make you nervous?" I said. "Must be my manly charm. C'mere." I turned on the light and checked out her shapely gams. There did appear to be some sort of goose pimples on her shins, and she'd scratched them so hard, some were bleeding. But she wasn't growing fins. Not yet, anyway. I sighed in relief, got up, and found some Aloe Vera lotion in the restroom cabinet. I returned and proceeded to slather her legs with it. She laid back and sighed as the soothing effects of the lotion seeped into her skin. I then gave her a full body massage, and she moaned blissfully.

She looked so serene. I leaned over and kissed her. This was too good to be true.

It was.

The bedside phone rang. It was my old pal Miles. I didn't know how he got my landline. We hadn't actually spoken on the phone for months, communicating mainly via email, and we had spoken on the phone, it had been very brief and terse, business only. It was still that way.

"Gloria says you're lookin' for me, and you're missed," he said simply, sans any sentimental salutations. "You got my email offer, I take it. And now you wanna chuck it back in face? What the hell's wrong with you?"

"How'd you get this number?"

"I got friends," he said. "So do you."

"Who is it?" Dolores whispered, and when I mouthed

"Miles" to her, she just got up and left the room, stark naked. I let her. Her immediate presence would only further complicate an already complex conversation.

"Guess who's here?" I said acidly to Miles.

"Dolores, yea, I know," he said. "She told me she was headed over to your place."

I cringed from the psychic gut-shot. "So you're keeping tabs on me with her. Nice."

"Why not? She's just your type," Miles said. "Ain't like you're not gettin' anything out of this deal. I still know you well, my friend."

"You're not my friend, and you're not my partner," I said, rising to pace the floor as my decibel tone increased along with my anxiety level. "I don't know why we ever got back in touch, you haven't changed, still fucking me over like we were total strangers. We grew *up* together, man! How can you repeatedly stab me in the back like this?"

"Calm the fuck down," Miles said. "Listen to me, because we're both in big trouble, and I have to admit, it's all my fault. But we don't have time to dick around bickering about old times right now. Our lives are in danger. Seriously."

"What the hell are you talking about?"

"Well, remember the Lunar Lounge, the strip club under The Omni?"

"Yea, yea, of course, so, what about it? I thought it folded."

"It did. It became an Italian restaurant, called Gourmet Guido. But it still has the same owners. You know who I mean."

"Yea, so?" The Mob.

"Well, the long and short of it is, I'm into them for some bucks. And so are you."

"What the fuck do you mean, Miles?" I felt sweat dripping down my neck, and my legs felt suddenly weak. I sat down on the edge of the bed.

"They bankrolled my porno racket, just enough to get it up and running, but then they made themselves my senior partners, without my consent, if you know what I mean."

"I *don't* know what you mean, Miles. Spell it out for me."

"Anyways, they—I mean we—took the substantial profits from The Omni porn DVD line and bought a share in this company, I don't want to name it, but a subsidiary of that company is Monogram International." He paused for effect.

I didn't like where this was headed. "Go on," I said.

"Well, the company isn't doing all that well, with the economy being what it is and all," Miles continued. "Now, I didn't tell you I was a silent partner in M.I. because I wanted to protect you from my *other* partners."

"How big of you," I said dryly. "I still don't see how any of this is my problem."

"Well, because I named *you* as a partner, too. See, I absconded with some funds and now my partners want it back. I told them I used it to finance your film, without their consent. They're still pissed, but if I make good on that so-called secret investment, we're both off the hook. Now you *have* to make that film, Nick, only, ironically, without my help, since I ain't got no more of the loot, I spent it all."

"On what?"

"Not what. Who. Gloria. We're married now, Nick. She called to tell you that. We even have a kid, six months. I told her to call you and make it seem like it was all her idea. And there's something *else* you don't know."

I was so beyond giving a shit at that point. "Thrill me," I said.

"Dolores's father is the senior partner. He owns that restaurant. He owned the Lunar Lounge. And now he owns us. Dolores's last name isn't really Summers. It's Mancini. Her old man is..."

"Tony 'the Man' Mancini," I said. He was the reputed head of the Manhattan crime family. Now it was all making some kind of warped sense.

"You got it," Miles said. "Dolores changed her name to Summers when she got out of college. It's her stage name. Thing is, the truth of it is, she isn't really keeping tabs on you for *me*, Miles. She's afraid of him as much as anyone. I mean, hell, it was his sick idea to put her in the porn we were distributing! I never figured that out, but it wasn't my call. Bottom line is: she's working for her old man, and like it or not, so are we."

"You're all a bunch of fuckin' liars," I said bitterly.

"Yea, I guess so," Miles said. "Sorry, my friend."

"My friend, *my ass*!" I exploded. "We fuckin' grew *up* together, man!"

"I guess we grew apart," Miles said coldly, after a chilly pause. "I was always jealous of you, Nick. You had the looks and talent. I just had the ambition. But it got me where I needed to be, eventually. I guess I always wanted what you had, or what I thought you had: the world by the balls. Now I got it. And now, you got what I have. A disease called Tony Mancini."

"Miles, I'll talk to you about this later," I said, suddenly weary. "Right now I have to talk this through with Dolores." He tried to say something else but I hung up him. First he fucks my wife, then he marries and knocks her up. With me she never even wanted kids. They all sucked. I mean the whole damn human race. Just a bunch of cowards out to save their own hides at any cost, pursuing their own pleasures even if it meant sacrificing their own integrity and loyalties. I guess I wasn't much better. I missed my cat more than ever. Fuck it. So what. So fucking what. I didn't care as much as I wanted to.

It didn't really bother me that Dolores had lied to me about her name. Hell, Nick Winters isn't even *my* real name. It didn't even bother me her old man was a Mafioso. That sort of turned me on, actually. It also didn't bother me she had lied to me. Again. Or that Miles had been lying to me for years. Everybody lies, everybody cries, everybody dies. Those are the inescapable Laws of Human Nature.

What *really* bothered me was, how the hell I was going to get "One-Way Ticket to Thrillville" financed without Miles' help, especially with the added pressure of a potential Mob hit on my ass. This would require some creative thinking. Right *now*.

I heard music. I put on my robe then went into the living room fully expecting to find Dolores gone. But she wasn't. She had gone into my CD collection—I guess she owed me that—and was belly dancing stark naked to Natacha Atlas singing "I Put a Spell On You," tears streaming from her closed eyes as she lost her herself in the music. It was a bizarrely seductive sight. Mesmerized, seduced, I let it go on without interruption. As she danced, strange images danced in my brain—horrible, sexual, nightmarish. Beautiful.

She stopped suddenly when she noticed me, and turned down the music. "I'm so sorry," she said. "I'll leave if you want me to."

"Don't leave," I said. "You're the star of my movie. And now I know you can dance, too. I need you now more than ever. But right now, you and me need to figure out where we're getting the money to make this movie."

"I have an idea," she said. "But you won't like it."

"Thrill me," I said.

Action.

Chapter Sixty-Three

"So where the fuck is Nick anyway?" Dolores asked Buddy as they sat in her trailer, eating craft service sandwiches. "You keep evading my question."

"Honey, that fall you took at the motel really banged you up good," Buddy said, stuffing his mouth and spitting out chunks as he talked. This was a real pet peeve of Dolores's. In *any* dimension. "I've answered that same fuckin' question five hundred times, you just don't like the answer. But it's not gonna change, so give it up already."

"Motel?" Dolores asked. "Which motel?"

"The Capri," Buddy said impatiently. "Remember? The old lady and I picked you up and hauled your carcass into the ambulance after you hit the floor. You were out for almost two whole goddamn days. Don't you remember? You seemed okay when I picked you up last night. Docs say they couldn't find nothin' wrong with you. Hope you're not havin' a relapse, we don't have time for any more setbacks, we're on a schedule here."

"Um, no, no, I'm fine," Dolores said, nibbling on her sandwich, but hardly hungry under the circumstances. "So what about Nick? Is he all right?"

Buddy just stared at her. "You got amnesia. Right after we wrap, I'm takin' you back to the hospital. In L.A., that is. You're seriously fucked up, baby." He stuffed the rest of his sandwich in his mouth and stood up, wiping his hands together, then cleaning them off on his suit jacket. He was wearing an open collared shirt, revealing a robust chest and a silver chain around his thick neck. Rings adorned most of his fingers. He was one pretentious motherfucker, Dolores thought to herself, hoping she'd never fucked him, and then:

"*God damn it, where the fuck is Nick*?" she screamed.

"Whoa, whoa, take it easy," Buddy said. "He's in the same place he's been the past two months or so, doll. Six feet fucking under. The *ground.* Where he fuckin' belongs."

"He's *dead*?" Dolores said, stunned. "How? *Why*?"

Buddy gestured with frustration. "*You* know…"

"No, I don't fucking know, asshole, so fucking tell me before I fucking scream *again*!"

Still flustered, Buddy said in a barely restrained, but loud, whisper, "The robbery, Dolores, the fuckin' *robbery.* He got fuckin' shot to death during the robbery, already a couple months ago now. Okay? *Remember*? Man, your head is fucked *up*! Now let's get back out there and finish this fucker, the heat's gettin' to me and I think it must be gettin' to you, too."

"That doesn't make any sense," Dolores said slowly, still in a daze. "None of it does." She stood up and said, "I want to go home now," she then said, child-like.

Buddy grimaced. "*Home*? You nuts?"

"Or back to the motel. Where's Jesse?"

"You mean Johnny, the guy *playing* Jesse?" Buddy said.

"*Johnny*? Who the hell is *Johnny*?" Dolores asked.

"Johnny fuckin' Burroughs, you silly cunt, the guy playing Jesse, Elvis's brother!" Buddy said, increasingly frustrated.

"*Playing*?" Dolores said, equally incensed by the lack of real communication. "He's not *acting*, you idiot, he *is* Jesse! And don't call me a silly cunt, you fuckin' *prick*!"

"Then don't *act* like one!" Buddy said, miming quotation marks. "You're fucked up," he said, tapping his own temple.

"Never mind, fuck it, let's go," Dolores said, putting on her sunglasses, momentarily stumbling in the dim light of the trailer, before bursting through the door and out into the middle of the lake, where her limbs felt instantly liberated, floating freely in the deep, dark waters.

She was swimming again, free and alone, powerfully propelled by her tail fins. She swam for dear life, rapidly, desperately away from the blackness swirling behind her like the ink spray of a giant squid, and toward the light beckoning before her like a torch-bearing angel.

Chapter Sixty-Four

Nick crept to the guest room door, cracked it open, and listened to the banal, terse yet tense conversation below:

"I thought you'd be home later," he heard Myrna say.

"I just stopped in for a bite, you mind?" said a male voice, which Nick assumed was that of her husband, the police chief. "Last I checked, this was my house, too."

"You should've called," Myrna said. "I don't have anything ready."

"I'll make myself a sandwich," the male voice said. "Why'd you make coffee?"

"Because I wanted some," Myrna said tersely.

Then all Nick could hear was some rummaging around the kitchen, followed by angry footsteps, and then the sudden sound of sports from the television.

He was startled when Myrna suddenly appeared at his door.

"What the hell?" he whispered, letting her in then gingerly locking it behind them. Then he grabbed her viciously by the arm and led her to the photo of Dolores in the cap and gown.

"What the fuck is *that*?" he said, pointing at it.

"My daughter," Myrna said simply, then she began to sob, and sat on the bed. Nick sat beside her. "I forgot it was there, I'm so sorry."

"Why didn't you tell me?" Nick asked.

"We never see her," Myrna said. "It's like she's no longer our daughter. She hates us. All we have left are the twins."

"Why?" Nick asked, though he could understand why.

"My husband used to molest her as a child," Myrna said. "For years, until she was a teenager and she rebelled. Then she seemed to block it all out, and things were normal for a while. Then when she was in high school, she suddenly became depressed and suicidal, so we took her to this shrink, Dr. Brandon, who hypnotized her and brought up all these suppressed memories of all this shit that happened, which I knew about, but ignored. I was afraid of my husband, just like she was. When Dolores came out of the hypnosis, she forgot everything again, and created a whole new identity for herself. She changed her last name, and pretended she didn't even recognize or remember us. Now she lives in the same town like a stranger. I never see her. My husband even visits her at the tiki bar, and she pretends she doesn't know who he is. The doctor says its just more suppression, a form of psychosis, but I know it's just her hating us. I don't blame her. My husband told Dr. Brandon he thinks Dolores is just making this mind block up, out of spite, then he stopped taking her to the shrink. I think he threatened him into silence, too. That's his whole M.O. He rules this town like a gangster."

Nick didn't know what to say. "I had no idea. I thought she was a stranger in this town, like me."

"It's all her father's fault," Myrna said.

"And yours," Nick said. "For not stopping it."

"We have to kill him *now*," Myrna said lowly, but forcefully, ignoring Nick's accusation. "I can't take it anymore. He's *such* an asshole! You have *no* idea! Even if he didn't molest his own daughter! You love Dolores, don't you, Nick?"

Nick flashed on fucking Dolores's mother, and felt hopeless. "What do you expect me to do, just go down and strangle him?" Nick said.

"Yes," Myrna answered emphatically. "With your fucking *tongue*!"

Nick recoiled in disgust. "Well, hell no, I'm no killer, I told you."

"But *he's* a lowlife criminal two-timing perverted piece of *shit*," Myrna said, punching her finger into his chest. "He *deserves* to die. *Badly*."

"Who the hell are *you* to judge?" Nick said. "You're cheating on him, too. With *me*. And *look* at me. I'm a *freak*!"

"I think you're beautiful," Myrna said, tears welling abruptly in her eyes. "*He's* the monster."

Then she continued sobbing softly in his arms. The Theremin blared in Nick's brain, like a warning siren. But he ignored it.

"Okay," Nick said finally. "For Dolores's sake, then. Let's go get this over with."

Nick went over to the closet to offer Buddy some comforting baby-talk remarks before embarking on his murderous mission with Myrna.

They tiptoed downstairs and crept up behind the unsuspecting man of the house. His name was Stewart Mansfield (which meant Dolores was originally Dolores Mansfield, before she changed her name to Summers). Their family had been in this town for generations. His father had owned the property where the movie house was built for decades. Stewart's father and grandfather had both been cops, though. They had no interest in the movie business, though they often frequented the place, and allowed the entire force to watch movies there for free. Of course, the entire force only consisted of four other cops, with two deputized citizens on stand-by, in case of an emergency. It was a very small town. But suddenly too big for all three of them.

Chief Mansfield had been the cop who had initially locked up Nick, so when he rose from the sofa to get a glass of milk, he instantly recognized the horribly deformed interloper standing beside his fake-quaking wife. But he was still frozen with shock. Nick finally recognized him as one of the cops who picked him up.

They just stared at one another for one long, awkward beat. "You killed my daughter, you sick, ugly bastard," Stewart said, but before he could elaborate on his baseless claim, Nick suddenly lashed out with his long, elastic tongue, encircling Stewart's neck, tightening its grip like a python as he grew closer. Myrna screamed with both joy and horror, much like she had during sex with the lizard man. Stewart's face turned blue as he gasped his final breaths. He saw his reflection in the mirror on the wall as he lay dying, the monster's tongue around his throat, choking the life out of him, and felt both fear and revulsion. He knew he wasn't going to a better place. And then suddenly, the reflection in the mirror could no longer see itself, because its eyes were dead.

"You better be right about him molesting Dolores *and* burning down the theater," Nick said after it was over. But he suspected his overwhelming impulse to kill Stewart had little to do with Dolores or the theater. It had nothing to do with anything except sudden, uncontrollable outburst of sheer rage against humanity. But the remainder of his sanity required the justification.

"I lied about that," Myrna said simply. "*I* burned it down. Or rather, I had it burned down. Gave some vagrant scum fifty bucks and a pack of cigarettes. But I wasn't lying about Dolores, or all the drugs and the hookers, so don't feel *too* bad."

"Huh? Why did *you* burn down the theater?"

"For the *insurance*, dummy. Now I'm the sole

beneficiary, and I'm totally free to spend it, alone, without that creep in my life. Get it? Now let's get rid of the body, or do you care to just…*eat* it?' Myrna threw back her head, feeling madly triumphant, and she laughed and she laughed. Finally, after recovering from her malevolent mirth, she said, breathlessly, "And now you better high tail it out of here before I call the cops."

"Call the cops?" Nick said incredulously, but weakly. He felt his voice cracking, changing, like the rest of him. "You just *killed* a cop!"

"No, fool, *you* did. And that's exactly what I'm going to tell the 911 operator—that the monster man broke in, strangled my husband, and *raped* me." She lifted up her robe to show off her thighs, scabbed and bruised from passion. "And I've got the *proof*. I've got enough of your semen slopping around inside of me to sink a ship. I don't want you raping my daughter next. You think I want you even touching her, you slimy piece of shit?"

He began walking towards her, and she backed away with mild trepidation. "You should've saved your daughter from *this* monster," Nick said with a newly intimidating growl to his voice.

Myrna was nervous, but not quite afraid just yet. She still felt like she had Nick under her power. "I tried, but..."

Impulsively, instinctively, Nick's tongue lashed out one final, fatal time, and after a few blissfully brief moments, in which Myrna experienced her very last orgasm, moaning ambiguously and writhing with both ecstasy and agony as the life slowly drained out of her, she lay dead beside her husband.

Quickly, Nick ran upstairs, grabbed Buddy from the back of the closet, put him in his carrier, picked up the bag of food and litter, ran downstairs, and into the dark night. Now he really was a fugitive from justice. And a true monster.

Chapter Sixty-Five

"My parents split up when I was a baby," Dolores said to me as we drove down to Venice Beach in search of a peaceful place to rest and reassess our situation. "My mom was a cocktail waitress in an Atlantic City casino, and my dad was a button man in the Manhattan family. They got together when he was on vacation. Both being Catholic, they married after he knocked her up, but by then he was already banging a bunch of other broads, to put it in his parlance, and my mom asked for an annulment soon after the ceremony. I never really knew my dad, but I was raised with his name, and his money. My mom never worked again. He set her up, and always took care of her, even when he remarried and had four more kids, whom I've never even met."

"Did he come down and visit, at least?" I asked, genuinely curious.

"Not often, he was too ashamed of me. And of himself," she added cryptically. "See, my mom—Esmeralda was her name—was Cuban."

"So?" Italian-Cuban, I thought to myself: That bloodline explained her mercurial temperament.

"She wasn't a wop," Dolores said bluntly, "and I wasn't a boy, so I wasn't considered that worthy of him. He wanted a purely Italian son to carry on his name. A Sicilian. You know, it's the Mafia's way. Now he has three sons, and one other daughter, by some wop chick from the Bronx named Maria."

"And you've never even met your half-siblings?"

"Hell, no," Dolores said. "Not like I'd get invited to any of the family get-togethers at Thanksgiving or

Christmas. He treated me pretty much like a bastard child, a mistake from his misspent youth." Tears formed in her eyes, but she kept talking. "I know he loved me, though, in his own creepy way, even though he made me *do* things for him sometimes." I let that go. "And my mom really inspired me to make something of myself. She had wanted to be a performer when she was younger, too. We both loved music, and musicals. She imparted her special love of Elvis to me. Sometimes we pretended *he* was my real father! My grandparents were nightclub singers in Havana. I never met them, either, since they were both murdered when she was young, a teenager, and she fled Cuba for Miami, and then eventually Atlantic City. I'm still not sure why my grandparents were killed, but I think the nightclub where they worked was run by gangsters, and they must've fucked up and pissed them off. My mom never wanted to talk about it. It didn't matter, she was all the family I needed. She gave me a lot of encouragement and insisted I get an education. I owe her a lot. And my dad paid for it, so there you go."

I patted her on the knee, which seemed patronizing, though I didn't mean it to be. "That's good," I said. "I never really knew my father or my mother, so you got one up on me."

We parked along the beach. It was a beautiful, blistery day. We sat in a sidewalk café and ordered breakfast. We'd already been up talking most of the night. But the conversation was far from over.

"I have a confession to make, too," I said to her over our lattes.

She bristled with apprehension. "Yes?"

"I killed my cat."

"Oh, I don't believe that." She seemed relieved it wasn't something worse. But for me, there was nothing worse.

"No, really. Not on purpose. I went to Hawaii to shoot a movie, and left him behind with some dry food. He was on meds for intestinal cancer. The person I trusted to take care of him flaked. When I got home, I found Buddy dead. He had died from a combination of starvation and the cancer, which advanced quickly without the daily doses he was meant to get."

"Oh my god," Dolores said. "That's horrible. But it's not *your* fault. It's the fault of the fucker who let you down."

"Well, this person didn't exactly flake. She was an actress I was fucking at the time. I was sort of in love with her, but not really. I just liked her sexual company a helluva lot, made me forget how lonely I really was, without actually resolving it. You know what I mean?"

"I know exactly what you mean. Go on."

"Anyway, she was injured in a bad car accident while I was gone, which put her in a coma. But the reason she got into an accident is she was blowing some other dude in his car at the time. So it was hard for me to feel sorry for her. Buddy died because she was cheating on me, or at least, not being straight with me. I think she was pissed I didn't cast her in my movie."

"Good thing you're not making that mistake again," Dolores said with a wink. "Anyway, I'm sorry, but you have to stop blaming yourself for Buddy. It was an accident."

"Then why am I always looking over my shoulder?" I said. "It's like someone is coming after me for a crime I didn't mean to commit. I can hear Buddy crying in my head constantly, like a, like a….*Theremin*."

"A *what*?"

"Well, it doesn't sound exactly like that, it's definitely

the wailing of a cat in pain, but…you know, the Theremin. That instrument they used in all those old B sci-fi movies."

"I didn't watch those, I liked musicals," Dolores said. "With Carmen Miranda. My mom and I would watch 'Weekend in Havana' and cry together."

I nodded impatiently. "Okay, you know the Beach Boys' song 'Good Vibrations'?"

"Uh, yea. That wasn't a Carmen Miranda cover, though."

"Yea, I know, smart-ass, but they used a Theremin in that song," I said. "The '*woo-woo'* sound."

"Oh, *now* I get you," Dolores said. "I know what you're talking about. They used it in 'Lost Weekend', too."

"You only watch movies with the word 'weekend' in the title?" I asked.

"Yes," she said, "and only on weekends."

We were madly in love, anyone could tell that.

Feeling the heat of the moment, I kept talking. "Anyway, the guy who invented the Theremin, a Russian dude actually named Theremin, Leon Theremin, no kidding, anyway, he came over to the States during the Twenties, and lived a real swingin' life in New York, and he invented this instrument you could play simply by manipulating airwaves." I gave her a mock demonstration with hand gestures. "So anyway, at some point the KGB showed up and dragged him back to Russia, where they kept him for years. Finally, decades later, in like, the Eighties, he returned to New York and reunited with his old flame. Most of his friends were gone, and he had no idea his invention has become this popular instrument."

"Wow, that's a crazy story," she said. "You should make a movie of it."

"Somebody did already, a documentary," I said, "but I often listen to Theremin music for inspiration. In fact, like I said, I seem to hear it all the time, but it sounds like Buddy crying."

"You should get that checked out," Dolores said playfully.

"Strangely enough, I'd miss it if it suddenly disappeared," I said. "It's all I have left of Buddy. His voice in my brain, converted into a Theremin."

"That's some weird shit, man," she said.

"Hope I don't scare you off," I said.

"Fat chance," she said. "I'm a lot more fucked up than you are."

"That's true." Then I kissed her, my kindred spirit, two lost souls briefly united, a romantic respite from our solitary sojourns. "You taste a lot like my ex-wife," I said after our lips had disengaged.

"Fuck you," she said.

"I can't believe she married Miles," I said. "Gloria, I mean."

"She did it out of guilt," Dolores said. "She felt bad about cheating on you with him, so she married him."

"And had his baby," I said snidely. "That's a lot of guilt."

"Yes, it is. But that's what I think. The kid's name is—get this: Nick."

"Cute. So anyway," I said, getting back to things that still mattered to me, "what's your big plan to score some cash for this movie so your dad doesn't bump me off?"

She suddenly grew serious, disturbingly so. "You know, despite everything, in spite of *me,* he *will* kill you if he thinks you ripped him off."

"That's comforting," I said, "but the fact is, I *didn't.* Miles did."

"That's not what my dad thinks," she said. "And what he thinks is what counts. He's expecting this film to get made so Miles can justify giving you all that money he embezzled."

"Which he didn't," I said. "Give to *me*, that is."

"I know that, you know that, *Miles* knows that, but my dad *doesn't*," she said. "I'm afraid you're screwed."

"Not the first time, not even by Miles," I said. "But the irony is, the fact remains, I really want to make this movie anyway, regardless of the circumstances. It's been developing in my head for years. It's just that now my motivation has changed. But I'm back to square one—financing."

"That's where my plan comes in," she said quietly.

"Why are you whispering?" I asked.

"Because my plan is dangerous," she said. "And illegal. Maybe even immoral."

"I've done all those before," I said. "So, what is it?"

"A robbery," she said, staring intently into my face so I'd know she wasn't kidding.

Still, I said, "You gotta be kidding."

"I'm not." She took out a cigarette, which I lit for her.

We sat in silence for a few moments, and then I naturally asked, "Rob what?"

"Not what," she said. "Whom."

"Okay, whom should we rob? A bank."

"No," she said. "My father."

I sat back and laughed, though not amused by her suggestion. "You're crazy. I can't even imagine how we'd begin to pull that off, but forget it." The irony of the concept did appeal to me, though I didn't let her know that right away.

"Well, we wouldn't be robbing him directly," she said. "We'd just hit a place he has an interest in."

"Being?"

"His restaurant in New York. I happen to know he stashes *all* of his cash in that safe. It's his little secret, but he made the big mistake of telling me about it once."

"Gourmet Guido, formerly the Lunar Lounge?"

"The same." She blew smoke into the clean ocean air.

"Shit, you *are* nuts," I said. But again, my sick sense of irony was being seriously seduced. Plus it made perfect sense not to shit in our own backyard. Fly back East, knock over the joint, fly back, *voila*! We've got our financing, from the same source it was originally intended to be, with nothing to trace us back to the robbery—as long as I trusted Dolores to cover our tracks.

"You're nuts too," Dolores said. "That's why it can work."

After a pause, I said, "Okay, fuck it, let's do it. When?"

She smiled. "Our flight leaves tonight."

Action.

Chapter Sixty-Six

Against her will, Dolores broke the surface of the water and walked smack into the blinding sunlight of the isolated desert shoot. "God *damn* it!" she shouted at the cosmos.

"What the fuck's the problem now?" Buddy asked, closing the trailer door behind them. "Jesus, you're one moody broad lately. I think the doctors are dead wrong—there is *definitely* something wrong with you!"

"Oh, go to hell," Dolores said, storming off, toward the director—Miles. But before she could reach him, the guy in the Elvis jumpsuit she had assumed was Jesse Mancini, not some copycat dude named Johnny Burroughs, stopped her.

"Ma'am, may I speak with you a moment in private?" the man dressed in the Elvis jumpsuit said.

Dolores stopped and just stared at him. "What's your name?"

"Huh?"

"I said: what's your fuckin' *name*, dumbfuck! Just tell me, I'm in no mood to mess around."

"Uh, Johnny. At least that's what I tell people. That's kinda what I wanted to speak to you about, ma'am."

"Stop callin' me 'ma'am,' you're old enough to be my goddamn grandfather," Dolores said. "Okay, Jesse, yea, sure—let's talk."

"Jesse?" the man said, curling his lip. "My name isn't really Jesse either."

"Yea, well I'm Glenda the Good God Damn Witch, pleased to meet you—whoever you are. We've talked *enough*." Then she continued on her path towards the occupied director's chair. Miles was still talking to "the werewolf."

The man in the Elvis jumpsuit grabbed her by the arm and said, "What if I told you I'm playing I'm playing my own dead brother in this stupid movie?"

Dolores freed her arm from his grasp and said, "*Now* you're talking. Let's go someplace private."

They walked away from the crew and the trailers and the cameras. Dolores heard Buddy calling her name, but she just flipped him off in response, without even turning to face him.

Once they were at a safe distance, Dolores said to the man who would be King, "So, exactly what the fuck are you saying to me, Jesse?"

"I'm *Elvis* Presley," he said. "The *real* one. That's what I need to tell you, tell *some*body. I'm just *playing* Jesse, my dead twin brother, who's really alive, at least in this stupid movie." He sighed. "Man, it feels good to get *that* off my chest!"

"That's fuckin' impossible," she said. "The real Elvis is dead. Been dead for decades. You *are* his twin brother, Jesse. Remember? I can't even believe I'm saying that! I mean, even *that's* impossible, since he's been dead longer than you, I mean, his brother, but frankly, I give up trying to make sense out of anything anymore. It's all a blur. Just don't fuck with my head, okay? I can't take any more."

"Sorry, but my twin brother was stillborn, ma'am, I mean, Dolores."

"That's what *you* say," she said, "but I know differently. Or at least I know a guy who claims to be your dead twin brother Jesse, not just a guy *playing* him. I just don't know anymore."

"Dolores—I've always liked that name, by the way—Dolores, the truth is I *am* dead. As dead as my twin brother, Jesse." He wiped off some light brown makeup from his seemingly tanned cheek, revealing a ghoulish pallor beneath. "I just woke up, and here I am. I know it's confusing. Imagine how *I* feel. But trust me, I'm *not* Jesse. I'm his equally dead brother, Elvis. The one and only. The one and only one *here*, anyway."

"Yea, whatever" Dolores said with a fatalistic sigh, unfazed by the revelation. "I sure know *that* feeling. We're both lost in a dream, Jesse. I mean Johnny."

"*You* can call me Elvis," he said. "But not in front of nobody else, and don't tell anybody else about me, either. They just wouldn't understand. I knew I could trust you, though, because I could tell you were someplace else when we were shootin' that last scene. You kept calling me Nick, and asking me to go swimmin' with you, or somethin'm then you just went wild, makin' these weird sexual kinda noises, but sorta sounded like you were in pain, and angry too, and I just knew you were someplace else, is all. The crew thought we were just playin' around between real takes. But I knew different: You're slippin' around like an eel through time and space at random, across alternate dimensions of reality. Like me. My friend Larry Geller used to give me books about this kinda stuff, but I never really believed in any of it. Till I died, and came back."

"Wow," Dolores said. "I don't know if you're who you say you are, or say you *aren't*, or even if *I'm* who I think I am, but this is some seriously fucked up shit."

"And I thought my life *before* I died was somethin' else," Elvis said. "I mean, look at me. I died then woke up in a movie playing my dead twin brother. You just never know where you'll wind up next."

Chapter Sixty-Seven

Nick stared into the moonlit lake surface, his tears dripping into his own softly rolling reflection, merging with the endless black water. From somewhere beyond his immediate perception, he heard Nina Simone singing "Sinnerman." Buddy the cat was mewing inside his carrier. Every now and then Nick would feed him a treat and offer him some calming words of affection.

"We have to wait for Dolores to come back," Nick said to Buddy. "Or we have to go to her. She's the only one that can save us now."

Nick ran his fingers across his scaly scalp, and what was left of his precious hair came out in his hands. He let the few remaining strands drift in the air before they settled down and floating on the water. His brain throbbed with reptilian thoughts. He was losing himself.

Suddenly he heard the wailing of sirens. But he was too sad and tired to move. He just sat and waited, for either the mermaid or the cops, whichever showed up first.

Maybe Dolores had turned into a mermaid and then drowned, Nick thought. But that was impossible. Mermaids can't drown. Unless she stopped being a mermaid too far out into the lake to swim back safely to shore. The thought chilled him. The sirens grew closer, and closer. The water seemed to grow blacker, and blacker.

Hearing the screeching sounds of patrol car wheels and cocked guns behind him, then seeing the flashing red lights of the sirens bathing the lake in an eerily pulsating crimson glow, Nick suddenly grabbed the cat carrier and plunged into the lake. The cops—all six of them, riding in both of the “force’s” patrol cars—ran towards the shore and opened fire, sending several potentially lethal rounds into the lake where Nick had jumped.

Minutes passed. Nick didn’t resurface. The cops fired a few more shots into the water out of sheer frustration, and then retreated to their vehicles, calling their report into dispatch, vowing to drag the lake for the body in the morning. Nobody could’ve survived being underwater for that long, especially while dodging a barrage of bullets. Nobody human, anyway.

Chapter Sixty-Eight

"My dreams have been getting stranger," Dolores said to me on the red-eye flight to New York, the lights dimmed, most of the passengers asleep around us, the seat beside us thankfully vacant. "I can't tell if they're based on things that have already happened, or will happen, or might happen."

"Like what? Explain," I said, staring at the monitors showing the classic movie *Gilda,* starring Rita Hayworth—a truly unusual choice for an in-flight film, since most airlines showed crappy recent movies you missed the first time on purpose, badly edited, no less. It added to the surreal mood I was in, on a *kamikaze* mission with a woman I barely knew, but was madly in love with. Being on a plane is like being in a dream, I silently observed—floating in space, above the clouds, strangers clustered and cramped together in this claustrophobic metallic shell, vulnerable to the elements as well as manmade mechanics, subject to the undiscerning whims of nature, fate, and basic human fallibility. Conversations on a plane took on an equally unreal quality in this hyper-conscious context, this alternate dimension in the air.

"Well, just now. I dozed off, and I was in a desert, talking to *Elvis*," Dolores said, breaking my contemplative spell.

I laughed rather too loudly. "I'd say that was definitely the past, not the future. You're thinking of the Jesse character in the script."

"No, it was Elvis," Dolores said emphatically. "Definitely Elvis."

"Well, what did Elvis say to you?" I said, trying not to

sound like I was condescendingly humoring her.

"I can't remember," she said softly, like a little girl.

I reached over and kissed her lightly. "It was only a dream. Go back to sleep."

"I'm afraid to," she said. But then she drifted off again, and I heard her murmuring something. I leaned over and she was repeating, over and over, "*Come swim away with me...*" She was subconsciously repeating a line from the script. How sweet.

In *One-Way Ticket to Thrillville*, the character named Dolores becomes a mermaid in one of the parallel stories being told, serenely and safely swimming away into the sunset at the very end (though her doppelganger doesn't fare so well in the alternate world of the film), while the character named Nick...well, I don't want to give it *completely* away. In any case, I was already thinking of how to morph the two tales into one, as Dolores—the *real* one—had suggested. As it was, both ended somewhat inconclusively, setting up a possible sequel. You had to think franchise to have any lasting financial security in this business. My movie was meant to be pure exploitation, with not only living mermaids but things like zombies, werewolves, biker gangs, undead rock stars, monster men, gunfights and a *lot* of gratuitous sex. I wasn't going for any awards here. I was just trying to make a living. And yet, I did sense that beyond my economic goals, something deeper was motivating me. I wanted to do this for Dolores. I wanted to make enough money for us to retire from this whole insane scene, from the whole mad world. Forget the sequel. I wanted this to be The Last B Movie. The End. But first I had to make it, and for that, we needed money. After meeting her that night in Palm Springs, I'd knew I'd do whatever I needed to do to get it. I just never imagined I'd go this far.

The plot Dolores had concocted was simple enough. As the Don's daughter, she had free access to the restaurant, even off-hours, so getting in late at night and opening the safe would be relatively easy, especially since she knew the combination, or thought she did (she wouldn't tell me but again, I trusted her).

When she woke up again, she touched my arm and said, "There's something I need to tell you."

"What now?" I said with apparent apprehension.

"Okay, you know how I was in that movie? The porn movie."

"Was there another one?" I said with escaped sarcasm. She shot me a disapproving look. "Okay, sorry. So why is that relevant now?"

"It was my father's idea. To appear in a porn movie."

"Oh," I said, as if Miles hadn't already told me that.

"I've always wanted to kill him," she said simply.

"I can understand that impulse," I said, not wanting to delve too deeply into what was obviously a touchy subject, one I had taken pains to avoid. I kind of wanted to kill the bastard myself, but Dolores had enough unresolved issues as it was. "But..."

She continued, now on a confessional roll, "I think he always had a little thing for me, though he never touched me. He knew my mother would kill him. So he waited till she was dead—I told you she died young, from a heart attack in her fifties, right?—though she was drinking and doing a lot of coke by then—*any*way, he waited till she croaked to make me do porn. Just that once, I swear. But he said if I didn't do it, he'd make sure I'd never make it as a real actress. Ten or so years later, look at me now. I basically did it for *nothing*. He made a lot of promises he obviously never made good on, or else I'd have a real career by now."

"Okay, I can see you had no choice, he's probably a very scary guy," I said gingerly, tap dancing around the discomfort and mounting tension, "but..."

"This will be our chance," she said flatly, over-riding my bullshit sentiment and cutting to the proverbial chase.

"*Our* chance? To do what?" As if I couldn't finish that thought on my own. It hit me that she waited till we were already on the plane to lay these extra details of the plan on me, along with a somewhat more fleshed-out back-story.

"Kill the asshole, what else!" she exclaimed.

"*Kill* him? Wait a minute, one crime at a time, baby."

"*Listen,*" she said, squeezing my arm. "I know exactly when he's at the restaurant, late at night after it's closed, in the upstairs office, where The Omni used to be, counting his money. He only trusts himself with the restaurant's haul and he skims some off the top for himself. He's a total psycho when it comes to money. So we're just going to go in, take the money, and kill him. That way it'll look like a real robbery. No one will suspect me of patricide. I'm a Theater major, for Christ's sake!"

Some old man with mutton chop sideburns pretending to sleep in front of us was cocking his ear in our direction, trying to eavesdrop on our conversation, and I motioned for Dolores to lower her goddamn voice, especially if she was going to detail a conspiracy to murder, with me as an accomplice.

"Keep your voice down," I said sternly.

"Miles will be with him, too," she continued, in a lower voice, but unabated. "Two birds with one stone."

"How do you know Miles will be there?" I whispered. "Miles now lives somewhere in California, he told me." Most likely with Gloria, I realized—talk about too close for comfort. "You should know, since you've been in touch with him recently, I'm assuming."

I was cautiously sidestepping the issue of parlaying a relatively simple, walk-in/walk-out robbery into a double homicide, especially when the victims were close to us, in both a familial and friendship fashion, as fucked-up as they were. "Family" never meant shit to me, though. My relatives, especially my parents, the only ones I really knew, however briefly, never gave me anything but grief. Flesh and blood relations were ephemeral, anyway; only spirits mattered, because only spirits lasted, and only spirits could merge in eternity. That's where one's consciousness—and conscience—truly mattered, because that's where one's essence survived the physical realm, or realms. Or so I chose to believe. The fact remains, nobody really knows anything about Life or Death; we *all* just make it up as we go. I know more than you, though.

"Doesn't matter where you think he is," Dolores said. "I know Miles will be there with my father because I just dreamed the whole thing. The money, the killing, the clean getaway, our lives together, *all* of it, in just a few minutes, it flashed before my mind." She squeezed my hand reassuringly and said, "It's going to work out perfectly. I just know it is."

Then she closed her eyes again and smiled with malevolent contentment. I felt shivers riding my spine like an electric eel slithering up and down a stripper pole. I stared out the window at the clouds, wondering which world, which optional reality, awaited us beneath them.

Action.

Chapter Sixty-Nine

Dolores couldn't believe she was hanging out with the real Elvis Presley, even if he was only a zombie.

"Your secret is safe with me, whoever you are," she said to him as they walked back toward the outdoor set to re-shoot the scene. "I have my own secrets, God knows. I even have secrets from *myself,* apparently."

"Thank you, thank you very much," Elvis said. "Do you remember the scene we were doin' before you tuned out?"

"I think so," Dolores said. "It's weird, I seem to know everyone around me, I recognize Buddy, even though I don't know how, or why, like, I'm two people in one, or something, but with one single mind, one shared *soul*. Or something. You know what I mean? Like, it just takes me a few seconds to reacclimatize to my different surroundings, wherever they are, even though I still feel somewhat disoriented, suddenly finding myself in a whole different…*what*? Dimension? Time warp?"

"Beats me," Elvis said. "All I know is, one minute I'm dead, sittin' on my own toilet, and next thing I know, I'm *here*, makin' a movie, playin' myself! It's like all those people, all the fans, God bless 'em, who wanted me still alive, sorta brought me back, like some kinda crazy voodoo curse."

"You've lost a lot of weight," Dolores noticed.

"Thank you very much," Elvis said. "Death'll do that to ya, I guess."

"So did you know your brother is still alive someplace?" Dolores asked.

"That's nice to know," Elvis said. "I talk to him sometimes. Maybe he hears me."

"How long have you been *here*, in *this* dimension?" Dolores asked.

"I'm not sure," Elvis said. "Time's kinda lost all meaning. In fact, this ain't the whole only place I been. There's another world where…"

"Yes?"

"I can't talk about it," he said. "It's too horrible."

"Okay," she said, "I understand," thinking of The Midnight Lounge, and the world where it still existed.

They approached Miles, sitting in the director's chair, talking to "the werewolf," and Dolores wasn't sure what to say to him, since she wasn't sure which "Miles" he was. But then she assumed, since she maintained her basic identity, whether she was swimming underwater or walking above ground, in either world, that Miles maintained his identity, too. Her consciousness remained constant across time and space, but did his? Maybe he wasn't even aware of his actions in the other dimension. Dolores seriously considered clueing him in. But first, she'd feel around for indicators of his true identity, or identities.

"Hello, Miles," she said to him. "Remember me?"

Miles looked at her and grinned, crudely massaging his crotch. "Let me guess," he said. "Raquel Welch?"

"Close enough," she said. She gestured over toward the actors in biker zombie makeup, just standing around, smoking and laughing. She couldn't be sure because of the facial prosthetics, but one of them appeared to be the famous movie star, Mickey Rourke. "Those your guys?"

"My guys?" Miles said, grimacing.

"You know, your henchmen."

"They play zombie henchmen, if that's what you mean," Miles said. "You should know."

"You're not gonna make me have sex with 'em, are

you?" Dolores asked bluntly. Elvis—or "Johnny"—shuddered at the suggestion.

Miles laughed out loud, "Hey, your ex wrote the script, not me! I'm just going by what he wrote, in honor of his memory, which is just what you wanted, isn't it?"

Dolores's heart fluttered. "His memory?"

Miles looked at her intently, squinting in the sun even though he was wearing shades, then said, "Buddy told me you've been actin' kinda loopy lately. I think he's right, these local quacks don't know shit. You should get your noggin checked out when we get back to L.A. You okay to keep filmin' for now?"

"Just peachy," Dolores said confidently, yet secretly wondering which "Nick" Miles was speaking of in the past tense. She tried to keep her voice from shaking. She didn't want to reveal any vulnerability to Miles, just in case his ultimate, ulterior motives were less than noble, per his inter-dimensional track record. "Let's roll it," she said.

"Okay, everybody," Miles yelled through his bullhorn, standing up from his chair. "Let's get back to work. Everybody in place for Scene 24, Take 2."

Dolores followed Elvis to the spot where they were before, when she was straddling and beating him up, Tura Satana-style. As the crew set up lights, camera and sound, she tried recalling this fatal "robbery" Buddy had referred to, but it was all a blank. She could only recall bits and pieces of her past—her childhood, growing up just outside Atlantic City; her Cuban cocktail waitress mother turned junkie alcoholic; her father, a Mafia Don—wait, was that last part really true? The thought resonated with a certain kind of intuitive veracity, but she couldn't be sure. Too many pieces were missing, especially the piece concerning Nick. She closed her eyes and tried to remember everything, and when she opened them, she was back in The Midnight Lounge, sitting on top of a very dead Miles Conroy, his face pounded into pulp.

Chapter Seventy

When Nick opened his eyes, he was sitting in the crashed Thunderbird he'd stolen from the copulating teenagers, engine still running, on the side of the desolate road. He tossed off the scarecrow lying across him, along with the smashed pieces of the windshield. He vaguely recalled swerving off the road to avoid hitting some sort of animal that had thrust itself in his driving path. There was no sign of it now.

Realizing where he was, Nick checked out his reflection in the cracked rear view mirror. No sign of scales, but a full head of hair. Nick sighed with relief. He was back within the relative sanctuary of his own story. But casually, then frantically, he looked around the ditched car for the cat carrier, but it was nowhere to be found. Buddy had not made the trip with him. Now he was truly all alone. Unless, of course, he could find Dolores. At least one of them. He only needed one.

It was strange yet somehow contextually acceptable how real and tangible everything seemed in his own story—equally real and tangible compared to his "other" existence, the one where he turned into a murderous monster man. The line between his life and his fiction had finally disappeared. Now both Nicks were one.

Instinctively, Nick knew how to get to The Midnight Lounge, even though he kept getting lost in the murky maze of his own mind. Navigating the bi-ways and catacombs of one's own imagination shouldn't be so difficult. After all, he made the map. All he needed was reliable transportation. The T-bird seemed in good enough shape, despite a few dents. He revved it up and started back toward the road.

Suddenly he was attacked from behind by something with claws and fangs. Nick could smell and feel the hot, foul breath of his attacker as its thick, slimy saliva dripped on his neck and down his back. He turned and swung a wild punch that sent the attacker backward, but not very far. Then Nick confronted his attacker face to face: a zombie werewolf. Nick instantly knew what it was, since he was in fact its creator. Now that Nick was safely trapped within the dimension of his own imagination, he optimistically assumed he was still in complete control of the situation. And yet, despite that assertion, the fact remained he was still fighting for his very life, the only one he had, wherever he was. Fantastical origin notwithstanding, this world that Nick had created was now as real, and as potentially dangerous, as the one he'd just escaped from. The rules of the game were the same; only the arena had changed.

The beast's face was mostly covered with dark, mangy fur, but some had fallen out due to the decomposition of the flesh beneath it. One eyeball was dangling from its socket. Blood dripped from its crooked snout. Several fangs were loose, or missing. Its animalistic movements were jerky, obviously challenged by advancing rigor mortis. The beast lashed out furiously at Nick, scraping his face and chest with its crumbling claws, a couple of which broke off and became embedded in Nick's flesh.

Nick pulled out the claws and swung savagely at the zombie werewolf, which was somewhat compromised by its undead condition. It just wasn't as powerful as it had once been, and it whined and whimpered with painful frustration as it struggled to maintain its strength. Nick almost felt sorry for the horrid thing. Its weakness reminded him a bit of Buddy, his sick, missing cat.

Though suffering further deep bites and scratches, Nick finally gained the upper hand in the intense physical combat, and the poor beast finally relented, and simply lay panting heavily on the ground next to the Thunderbird. It still gnashed and ground its loose fangs, which reminded Nick of his recurring dreams of losing his own teeth. The thing pawed vainly at thin air. Nick could've finished it off, and considered putting it out of its own misery, bashing its head in with a rock or something, but then the beast's visage began to change, reverting to its human form, its alternate alias. Nick could relate to both its internal and external agony, its identity crisis, the feeling of losing power over one's situation.

Finally, the sad, wan, zombified face of Eugene Orowitz the desk clerk was revealed. "Kill me," he gasped. "If I had killed you first, I'd live forever. Now it's all over. Or now, I just *want* it to be. Just end it. Stop my pain. You made me, man. Now *un*make me. Please. *Please*."

Struck by the fact that Eugene recognized him, meaning he had known who he really was all along, ever since they "met" at the Motel Capri, Nick removed the keys from the ignition, went back to the trunk of the T-bird, and looked inside for a weapon. He found a tire iron, walked back over to Eugene, exchanged tearful eye contact, and then with several quick, vicious thrusts, crushed the accursed skull of the miserably warped, deformed creature.

Afterward, Nick flung the tire iron aside in self-contempt, kneeled beside Eugene's mangled body, and wept, mourning the murder of his own creation, feeling hopelessly lost and utterly alone within the claustrophobic confines of his own twisted, tormented subconscious.

At least, in *this* world, he could no longer hear the

Theremin, supposedly because he was now one with it in his own mind. In a way, he missed it. Maybe he'd finally be able to find its source now.

Chapter Seventy-One

After touching down at JFK, we took a cab into the city, checking into the Parkway Hotel in Greenwich Village, a former beatnik hangout and now drunkard's dive with a funky, folksy espresso bar downstairs still called The Moonlight Lounge, just a few blocks from the site of the former Omni —now "offices" for Gourmet Guido downstairs, a place we planned to visit late that very evening. Dolores already had an afternoon rendezvous planned with her anonymous gun source. Meantime, it was still a pleasantly innocuous morning, the hazy sunlight beaming off the buildings with that filtered intensity seemingly endemic to the perpetually gray island of Manhattan, the air pungent with traffic, trash, hot dogs and hedonism, tourists and natives mixing and mingling in the street below, rushing toward the subways and the stores, as if a terrorist attack could happen any second and obliterate the urban tranquility of this cosmopolitan paradise, or cruel hellhole, depending on one's disposition and current cash flow.

The room was serviceably seedy, with poor lighting, well-worn furniture and a musty stench, redolent with the residue of generations of lovelorn alcoholics, desperate junkies, heartbroken hookers, itinerant jazz musicians and struggling poets still haunting the hotel like celestial transients with no place else to go, because nobody else would have them, in death as well as in life. We belonged there, I thought. I chose it primarily for its proximity to our target. Dolores loved it because she fantasized about being a Beat poetess herself sometimes, she told me.

I flipped on the television, which is what I always do as soon as I check into any motel or hotel, to make myself feel more at home, and *Neptune's Daughter* starring Esther Williams and Ricardo Montalban was on. Satisfied, I relaxed in the dingy but comfy corner lounge chair and casually watched the movie with the sound turned down low, while Dolores blissfully bathed. She had left the bathroom door open. She was humming a tune I didn't recognize.

"What's that you're singing?" I asked.

"Song I made up," she said.

"What's it called?" I asked.

"'One-Way Ticket to Thrillville'," she answered, then resumed humming.

"That name's taken," I called back playfully.

"Not for a song," she said.

"I'll sue anyway," I said.

She suddenly stopped humming and started singing the Nina Simone standard, "Feeling Good."

"That's more like it," I said. "You have a killer voice." Poor choice of words, I realize in retrospect.

She still took it as a compliment. "I used to get great tips as a singing waitress," she said, somewhat sadly.

"I guess you missed your true calling," I yelled, but this time, she didn't respond. I could almost hear her thinking, "Fuck you."

I got up and walked to the bathroom and found her ensconced in bubbles. "Wouldn't a singing waitress be better than a prisoner on Death Row?" I asked her.

"No," she said quickly, briefly interrupting her own singing.

"We don't have to do this," I said. "There are other ways."

She stopped singing, looked at me seriously, and said, "Like what?"

"I don't know," I said. "Get a job?"

She laughed. “Yea, right. Doing what? Singing in my dad’s restaurant?”

“Not a bad idea, really,” I said.

“That would take way too long, and anyway, I wouldn’t give him the satisfaction,” she said bitterly. “Last time I performed for one of his enterprises, I regretted it.”

“So you regret being in that porn flick?” I asked her.

She looked at me and softly said, “I do now.”

I bent down beside her in the tub, and we embraced, and I got sopping wet, so I removed my wet shirt, then my pants, and climbed into the bathtub with her while she giggled with delight. I scrubbed her back, and the she scrubbed mine. We would’ve seemed obnoxiously cute to an outside observer, the proverbial fly on the wall. They’d have never have guessed we planned to kill someone in just a few hours.

Action.

Chapter Seventy-Two

Standing up from the truly dead body of Miles Conroy, ex-pornographer and former tiki lounge/movie-house proprietor, Dolores turned and lunged for the gun still in her purse next to the pool table, and with two quick, well-aimed shots, blew out the brains of the two pathetic, dickless zombies still standing around, moaning. It was finally over. It had to be. Those were her last two bullets.

Stepping over Buddy's saxophone, drenched in his own blood and brains, Dolores put the halter-top, skirt and boots back on, and when she got to the front door of The Midnight Lounge, Nick was standing there, waiting for her, his torn shirt hanging in shreds from his clawed, bloody torso.

"We gotta get you some classier clothes," Nick said.

She ran up to him, unfazed by his wounds, or by hers, and they embraced and kissed passionately. Before Dolores knew it, she was naked again, and making love on the cold, bamboo floor of The Midnight Lounge with her long lost lover, Nick, obliviously surrounded by the rank remnants of pornographic carnage and grisly evidence of a zombified zeitgeist. Tiki gods watched over them with voyeuristic omniscience in this poor man's pagan Polynesian paradise. They no longer noticed nor cared about their surroundings, in any place, or in any time. They had found each other at least, against all odds, across inter-dimensional space. "Taboo" by Arthur Lyman played on the jukebox as they happily fucked. Nothing would separate them now.

"What's all this?" Dolores asked Nick as they

entwined on the floor, intoxicated with post-coital ecstasy.

"What? You look pretty beat up yourself, sugar."

"I was in a car accident then raped by zombies," she said simply, now accustomed to such things, "but what about *you*? What's all this from?" she asked, touching several of the tender, open wounds on his neck, shoulders, and chest. "You look like you've been attacked!"

"No big deal," he said dismissively. "You were raped by zombies, and I was attacked by a zombie werewolf," Nick said casually. "But hey, at least he didn't *rape* me, so it could've been worse. He's dead now, just like your boys, so don't worry about it anymore, okay?"

"But have you been infected?" Dolores asked nervously.

"By what?"

"The *bites*, Nick. You could become a zombie, or a werewolf. Or a zombie werewolf." She laughed derisively at the concept, despite the grisly realness of the wounds, or the possibility of this prospect actually being realized in *this* world. She wasn't quite ready to ask him why he'd put her through so much grief, if this really *were* his dark little world, and she was merely another of his captive pawns. They'd discuss that later, after she convinced herself all of this was actually happening.

Nick sighed and shook his head. "I'm not changing again," he said. "For some reason I'll never know, probably, *this* world, the world in my head, which I only tapped into when I was writing about it, began bleeding—*literally*—into my other world, my *real* world, and things that were supposed to be impossible in my real world suddenly became possible, so the distinction between the two began to blur, then finally merge. But I'm still *me*, which must mean I'm still in control of *this* world, in a way I could never be in what used to be my real world.

You understand? I've left that world behind. Now I'm safe inside my own head. It's a crazy miracle, Dolores. We've *both* somehow escaped the real world, and now we're alive inside my own head. We're safe here. We're *free*."

"Are you sure?" she asked, caressing his torso and arms lovingly, yet tentatively, growing uneasy about their relative and ultimate security in this strange, dangerous, unpredictable dimension.

He looked deeply into her eyes and said, "This is *my* dream, and I can make anything happen. Or *not* happen. I'm in charge now."

"How do you know it's not *my* dream?" Dolores asked. "I mean, I feel like I'm real and in control, too. At least of my own actions."

Nick rolled back over and stared up at the nautical fish floats and glowing puffer fish hanging from the ceiling. "I guess I don't know anything for sure," he said in a monotone, after a pensive beat. "None of us do. We can just pretend that we do, that's all. I got my theory of existence, you got yours. Impossible to prove or disprove either one. I guess we're not meant to figure anything out. All I know for sure is, wherever we are, I'm still *me*."

"I don't even know which Nick you are," she whispered with a tinge of fear in her voice.

He looked back into her glistening eyes, and said, "The *only* one."

"How can you be so sure?" she asked, desperately yearning for a single, simple, satisfying answer to everything, all at once—the basis of all manmade religions. But Dolores wasn't religious, and neither was Nick. Spiritual, maybe; but not religious. "Maybe there are a *lot* of Nicks, somewhere in time and space…and a lot of Dolores's…"

"I know I can be sure I'm the *only* Nick now," he said,

"because the *other* Nick, the only other one I know of, is dead. It's like we traded places. He drowned himself, and his cat, *my* cat, sad to say."

"Why?"

"Looking for a mermaid," he whispered.

Dolores leaned over and began sucking the blood from his garish wounds.

"What the hell?" Nick asked, stopping her.

"Whatever you got, I want too," Dolores said. "I'm not taking any chances of being separated from you again."

Nick lied back and Dolores not only sucked the blood from his wounds, she sucked semen from his cock, swallowing all of it, desiring to fill herself with his essence, however toxic, so much so that no matter what happened next, in whichever world they found themselves, their spirits would merge, and they'd be eternally bonded, no matter how turbulent the sea that continually attempted to separate them.

"Mermaids can't drown," Dolores said huskily to Nick, licking his bodily fluids from her moist, glistening lips. "I'm only wet on the inside now."

He smiled because he wanted to believe her.

Chapter Seventy-Three

We met with Dolores's gun connection, a thuggish, twenty-something half-black, half Puerto Rican punk called Domino, uptown in Central Park. He was wearing a paisley handkerchief around his shaved head, a gold chain around his thick neck, and a sports jersey with sweat pants and sneakers when we saw him leaning against a tree across from the Museum of Natural History, casually smoking a joint. He already knew Dolores, so they just nodded at each other with comfortable familiarity. I got a sick feeling they knew each other pretty intimately at some point.

"You ever go in there?" Domino asked us both, rather rhetorically, as a greeting, nodding toward the museum. "Fuckin' amazing place, man. All those stuffed animals 'n' dinosaurs 'n' shit. I been goin' there ever since I was a kid. Fuckin' place still blows me away, just like I was a little kid again. It's like a whole 'nother world in there, frozen in time. Nice to know some things never change." He gazed longingly into space. "Sometimes I'd sit in the museum café for hours, reading comic books, *Spider-Man, The Avengers*. Man, those were the days."

"I was a Batman guy," I said, trying to find common ground with this intimidating stranger.

"Spider-man could've kicked Batman's pansy DC ass," Domino said. "Marvel ruled."

"I liked Marvel too," I said, "but my favorite was Batman." I'd had this same silly argument with Miles since we were eight years old.

"Shit, Spidey was *real*, man," Domino said. "Peter Parker was just a regular guy, but Bruce Wayne was this rich fuck Republican, could buy anything he wanted. Spidey had to get down with the *people*, know what I'm sayin'? He was for *real*."

"How do you get that Bruce Wayne was a Republican?" I said, bristling defensively, even though I was basically apolitical. Life was so much bigger than politics, which was just one more pointless distraction from things that truly mattered, like movies and sex. "He was a philanthropist whose parents got killed, so he spent his fortune helping the masses. He spread his own wealth for the common good."

"Spidey could've still kicked his ass," Domino said after a beat, suddenly confused and alienated by the political implications of the discussion.

"I doubt it," I said firmly.

"Spidey had like super spider-powers, really strong, he could swing around, with his, y'know, webs. Batman ain't got shit but a cool car."

"Batman had a superior intellect," I said. "That was his super power."

"*Girls,*" Dolores interrupted. "We got business to attend to. You can geek-talk later. We're not little kids anymore, none of us."

That put things into depressing perspective, so I changed the subject. "Kind of conspicuous place to hand off a piece," I said to Domino.

"Let's take a walk," he said. "Follow me."

We followed him further into the Park. In a suitably secluded area, Domino casually reached behind his waistband and handed me a .44 caliber handgun. It felt heavy and sickening in my grasp. I couldn't imagine firing a bullet into another human being, especially one I'd never even met, much less someone I grew up with, no matter what our differences were over the years. Suddenly, stricken by a belated attack of conscience, it all seemed so *wrong*. I was just letting my life slip down the drain. I was chilled by the notion Dolores seemed to be taking this whole self-perpetuating situation in stride.

"Have you done this before?" I asked her, and they both laughed.

"No, really," I said.

"Really, I gotta go," Domino said. "That shit's as untraceable as Jimmy fuckin' Hoffa. Been real." Dolores shook his hand and he took the cash in her palm, then he leaned over and kissed her flush on the mouth, tonguing her in the process, revealing several gold-capped teeth. Then he nodded at me solemnly and took off down the wooded path, vanishing like he was never there.

Now it was just us. Dolores put the piece in her purse, then put her arms around my neck, and kissed me.

"You ever fuck that guy?" I asked her after she let go.

"Not lately," she said.

"Have you ever killed anyone?" I then asked her.

"Not lately," she said.

"You're beginning to bug me," I said to her. "I can't believe I'm here."

"Maybe you aren't," she said.

We headed back to the Parkway Hotel, ate sandwiches and coffee at The Moonlight Lounge downstairs, like we were out on a date, just killing time, before it *was* killing time. I kept looking at my watch with an increasing sense of dread and doom. Dolores was eerily serene and calm.

Back upstairs, I flipped on the television and found *Hand of Death*, starring John Agar. It had been considered a lost film for years, only recently unearthed in the Fox studio vaults, and unceremoniously tossed on the air with little fanfare. It was about a scientist who turns into a hideous mutated man-monster due to exposure to radiation. He walks around in a fedora and trench coat, resembling Ben Grimm, AKA "The Thing" from *The Fantastic Four.* Theremin and bongos blared on the soundtrack. It was my kind of movie. I thought of Domino as a little kid, reading comic books and going to the museum. How do people get so fucked up, just by growing up?

I was just beginning to relax and forget our impending date with Fate when Dolores emerged from the bathroom, wearing a leopard coat, red dress and white go-go boots. She was one badass pistol-packin' mama. "Let's go," she said. "Turn off the TV. Time for *our* reality show."

Reluctantly I rose from the chair. "But I'm watching '*Hand of Death*'," I said. "It's never been released on DVD, and this may be my only chance to..."

She reached for the remote and flicked off the set, suddenly all business, and said, "'*Hand of Death*'? What's that, a documentary about masturbation? Let's go, Nick. It's getting late and I don't want to miss Daddy." She said it like we were going over to his house for Thanksgiving. As we left the Parkway Hotel, I knew my life would never be the same again. No more comic books for baby.

Action.

Chapter Seventy-Four

Lying on the floor of The Midnight Lounge, wearing nothing but an official bar tender aloha shirt, standard issue, drinking extra strong Zombies he'd mixed from the bar, Dolores dozing under his arm, the jukebox silent, Nick suddenly heard what he thought was the Theremin, and he cringed with dread. But then he realized it was only the wail of a police siren. They were closing in on them, once again, only this time, they were out of bullets, or so Dolores said.

"I can fix that," Nick said.

"Of course you can," she said.

Nick went back into Mile's office and moved aside a velvet painting of a nude Tahitian girl. Behind it was a safe.

"But do you know the combination?" Dolores asked.

Nick grinned and said, "Baby, I know *everything* in *this* world."

He flipped the knob deftly and the safe door popped open. Inside were wads of cash in large and small bills, a .44 caliber handgun, and pump action rifle, with several rounds of ammo. Miles was one paranoid fuck, in any incarnation.

"Did you just imagine that was there?" Dolores asked him.

"I must have," Nick said, scooping out the cash and the weapons and placing them all on Miles' desk. "Or else it wouldn't be here, right?"

"Maybe you should imagine us some new clothes while you're at it," Dolores said.

"Just wear what you have on for now," Nick said. "I got this shirt, and my pants are okay. Hell, who would care if we just ran around naked?"

"Not me," Dolores smiled.

Nick said, "Well, the world I created already exists. I'm not sure I can make up any more of it. It is what it already is. We'll find nicer duds for you once we get out of here, assuming there's a 'there' out there."

"Is that why the sun never shines here?" Dolores said.

"I guess so," Nick said. "I don't know, really. Maybe it represents the darkness in my own mind."

"You guess a lot for someone so sure of himself," Dolores said.

"All I'm really sure of is that I love you," Nick said, "whoever and wherever you are."

Dolores flinched, feeling tears well, then she smiled, but avoided a direct rejoinder. Instead she said, "Maybe this world existed before you thought of it," Dolores said. "You just discovered it by accident. When you mentally visit it, it tells *you* what's happening, and you just report it. Or you used to, when you were on the outside looking in."

"Maybe," Nick said wearily, suddenly feeling dizzy. He massaged his forehead and scalp, and then smacked his own cheek. "But it's still my show. At least for now. Let's go." Dolores was concerned about his strange behavior.

Then they went outside and silently sat at the bar, listening to exotica tunes on the jukebox, simply waiting for the cops to show up, weapons loaded and ready, idling ominously beside the cocktails. The sirens seemed to multiply as they grew closer, like spontaneously mating fireflies.

"Can they hurt us, even here?" Dolores asked Nick, who had tuned her out, lost in his own internal, eternal sea. She continued, trance-like: "Everything seems, and feels, so real, whichever world I'm in, at any moment. I can't get a *grip* on anything. It just slips through my fingers like vapor. Only the pain survives the transition from place to place."

Nick didn't answer. He was staring into his tiki mug, as if transfixed.

"Nick?"

He looked back at her. "Huh?"

"Are you all right?"

"I think so," he said lowly and slowly. "I'm just having trouble focusing…" Was that a siren or a Theremin he heard? Suddenly, he was unsure. His vision was growing blurry. He attributed it to the alcohol. "What are we doing here?" he asked, genuinely confused, feeling lost.

"Where?" she asked, crinkling her brow.

"*Here*."

"In The Midnight Lounge?"

"The what? I thought this was The Moonlight Lounge." Nick got up and stumbled around, disoriented and dazed, bumping into the chairs and tables, knocking some over.

Dolores tried not to panic, "Nick, what's wrong?"

"I'm losing control, " Nick said. "I can't breathe…like…I'm underwater…drowning…" He fell to the floor, clutching at his throat, gasping for air.

"Nick!" Dolores screamed, over and over. "Nick, don't leave me, not *again*, not *ever...Nick*!"

It was no use. The two Nicks had not only merged consciously, but subconsciously; by now, one could no longer distinguish itself from the other, so Nick's frame of reference was distorted, his memories blending into one common whirlpool of images, thoughts and impulses. He still recognized and adored Dolores, though, and instinctively wanted to protect her, so when the cops fired warning shots outside, Nick ran for the pump action rifle, and opened fire, initiating a mutual barrage of bullets, back and forth.

Dolores screamed, then grabbed the handgun and ran to the nearest window, joining the fierce battle. Nick was too busy at the other window to notice at first, and when he did, it was too late too halt her feverish frenzy. She was already in this fight, to the finish. Fresh wounds began joining Nick's old ones. Before long, Nick was a bloody mess all over again. Dolores wasn't faring much better, taking harsh hits in the shoulder and side. But she kept pumping bullets out the window at her faceless foes.

There were a total of six patrol cars outside The Midnight Lounge, since the town had brought in reinforcements from outside their jurisdiction. Fourteen armed policemen were in various positions of aggression, loading and reloading sundry forms of firearms, including two machine guns. The scene was very hectic, very violent, and very, very real. Or so it seemed. That's all that mattered to anyone trapped there at the moment.

Then the zombie hordes arrived, led by Undead Elvis, and all hell seriously broke loose.

Chapter Seventy-Five

It felt very, very strange and surreal, approaching the site where The Omni once illicitly thrived. It was late at night, though being Manhattan, a good number of people were still out and about, which only served to increase my anxiety, even though it seemed as if I were floating through their ranks like a ghost. We walked by a bar and heard Nina Simone singing "Wild is the Wind" from within. I assumed it wasn't live, and we just kept walking. The song stuck in my head, making me feel even more desperate, sad, and alone, yearning for Dolores, even as she clutched my hand and smiled into my fearful eyes. I felt like the tides were taking her away from me. Or maybe I was the one being sucked into the depths of the sea. I held onto her hand like it was a life raft.

When we got to the Gourmet Guido, I just stopped and said, "I can't do this."

"I need you," Dolores said, eyes glistening. "The man is a monster. He deserves to die."

"But do we?" I said.

"No," she said, "so we won't."

The non-descript door to the defunct Omni—which never even had a sign—was padlocked. Dolores took out her personal keys to the restaurant, which had closed about an hour earlier, at midnight, so the staff were all gone by now, and let us inside. She went straight to the alarm and punched in the code.

"How do you know all this?" I asked.

"I pay attention," she said simply. "I've been planning this a long time."

I didn't like the sound of that. We were drifting apart, we just couldn't see that yet. I stupidly went where the current took me, without resistance.

The restaurant was purposely old school, framed pictures of The Rat Pack and *The Sopranos* on the wood paneled walls, along with Tony Bennett, Joe DiMaggio, Placido Domingo, Al Pacino, Robert DeNiro, and other great Italian celebrities, past and present. Some of the photos were signed, mostly "To Tony." One was from Marlon Brando. The guy got around, I gave him that. All of the tables were covered with red-checkered tablecloths. The stripper runway was still in the center of the room, but the pole was gone. Dolores told me they now used it for fashion shows. How respectable. I wished we were just going there to eat. I bet the food was good. I'd never know.

Dolores took me to a back stairway that led upstairs to the offices, where The Omni used to be. This was the same route Miles and I used to take when delivering outside food and drink orders to our patrons. When we reached the top of the stairs, Dolores knocked on the door.

"Who the fuck is it?" a voice from within asked gruffly.

"It's me, Daddy," Dolores said. "Surprise!"

Miles opened up. We just stared at each other, both stunned.

"Hi," Dolores said rather brightly. "Daddy here?"

Miles was visibly stunned. "Yea, why didn't you *call* first? Had no idea you were even in town. Who's that with you?" Miles peered into the dark and made me. "*Nick*? What the fuck are *you* doing here?"

Dolores suddenly reached into her purse and took out the .44 and shoved it in Miles' face, backing him up into the office that had once been The Omni. I barely registered the fact that Dolores was already brandishing a weapon in her father's presence, and I was right behind her. Why was I even there? What the hell did she need me for? I guess I should've asked that sooner. But I was already under her spell before I realized it. She was like a sea siren, luring me, the gullible sailor, to my watery grave. It was all just a wet dream to me. And I was about to wake up, but too late to save myself from drowning.

"Hi, Daddy!" she said to Tony, who instantly reminded me of the old actor Henry Silva. He was impeccably dressed in a gray sharkskin suit, but his black tie was loosened, and he appeared sweaty and agitated. His desk sat in front of the wall where the screen once was. There were other desks and file cabinets in the room, very neatly organized. Posters of *The Godfather*, *Angels With Dirty Faces, Scarface* and *Goodfellas* were framed on the walls, invoking the room's previous incarnation as a makeshift screening room. The formerly beat-up beige walls had been covered with wood paneling, giving the room a cozy amber effect in the dim light.

"Dolores," Tony said with a grin, apparently bemused rather than surprised by the suddenly tense situation. "What the hell? Put that thing down. Who's *this* joker?"

"It's Nick, my partner," Miles said, wide-eyed, starring down the barrel of the gun with trepidation. "I didn't invite 'em here, Tony, I swear. I don't get this."

Tony carefully gave me the once over. "Oh yea," Tony said, "I kinda remember seein' you around the strip joint when you was younger. So you got my money? And you're gonna make more money with it? Dolores, sweetie, put that fuckin' thing away, playtime is..."

"Just beginning," Dolores said, suddenly pivoting from Miles and firing a round into Tony's shoulder. She didn't want to waste time with any preamble, giving her father time to figure out the score. She was here for one reason, and she got right to it. She fired again but he ducked the bullet. Miles ran towards the exit, shoving me out of the way, but Dolores screamed at him, "Miles, you're not fuckin' goin' anywhere!' She fired another shot into the air, and he froze in his tracks.

Tony reemerged from behind the desk with his own gun, also a .44. Must've run in the family. He was clutching his shoulder, tears of pain and shock in his dark eyes. "Dolores, what the fuck is *wrong* with you, I'm your *father*!"

"I know," she said, "and you pimped me out like a whore. You abused then abandoned me when I was only a child. You left my mother to die alone. So, for all that, and more…fuck *you*." Then she fired another shot, taking him off guard, hitting him squarely in chest. A red splotch suddenly appeared on his white shirt, like he'd merely spilled red wine on it. It felt like a movie—only this time, I was on the wrong side of the camera.

Tony felt himself slipping away, and aimlessly fired his gun once more. But whoever his intended target was, he didn't hit Dolores. He hit *me*. Right in the forehead. I barely felt it. Nice shot, even if it was an accident. I went down like a zombie, lying in a pool of my own memories and dreams.

As everything faded to black, I felt Dolores crouched over me, sobbing, and I heard Miles saying, "He'll never know this was the plan all along," as he put Dolores's gun in my dead hand after wiping off their own prints. I looked at the wall where the screen once was, and hallucinated I was watching *The Day the Earth Stood Still*, with Bernard Herrmann's Theremin score resonating in what remained of my brain. The last words I heard in this realm were "*Klaatu Barada Nikto*." Then I was adrift in time and space, where I remain, lost in eternal limbo, no longer a member of any physical dimension, my identity absorbed by the cosmos.

Action.

Chapter Seventy-Six

No matter where they went, something was out to destroy them, and Nick was helpless to stop it from happening. There was no escaping his fate.

The zombie hordes were being led by none other than Elvis Presley, the Undead King of Rock 'n' Roll Re-Animation. Elvis was wearing a badly torn and stained white jumpsuit, glistening with gore and rhinestones, his face ashen and misshapen almost beyond recognition, his famous curled lip smile distorted into a permanently crooked grimace, revealing decaying gums and missing teeth, his gray hair thin and disheveled. He pointed toward the cops and Midnight Lounge with that trademark finger configuration, and yelled in a booming but broken baritone, "*Kill…them…all*!"

Hundreds of zombies poured onto the terrified cadre of cops, who turned their gun sites on the marauding masses of decomposing corpses, killing many with shots to the head, but mainly just wasting bullets in an attempt to stave off the inevitable outcome of this confrontation: the cops were torn apart and devoured, while still alive, screaming in agony as they helplessly watched their own innards ripped out from beneath their bellies and chests, then eaten by the foul-smelling, horribly mangled ghouls. The cops—already feeling anonymous and peripheral to the main arc of this story they lived in, as if they were merely decorative objects in someone else's house—pictured all of the Christmases and summer vacations they'd never take, as their vital organs and entrails were removed and devoured. It was an awful way to die, but they prayed they'd wake up in a better place, not just relegated to background noise, which at the moment happened to be the sounds of their own tortured screaming.

Once the zombies had finished with the cops, they headed *en masse* into The Midnight Lounge, even as Nick and Dolores tried fending them off, first with the remainder of their ammunition, and then, as the zombies burst through the door and the windows, with anything handy: chairs, tiki mugs, bottles of booze. It was no use. They were surrounded in minutes by ravenous demons, hungry for their flesh and guts and souls. Nick and Dolores held each other behind the bar, and waited for the end. Dolores noticed Nick felt very clammy, covered in a cold sweat. She looked into his pale face, and saw the dark circles beneath his eyes. She assumed it was from the stress of imminent, violent death, torn apart by his very own creations. But it wasn't.

"I'm dead anyway," he said to her, and she felt her spirit slipping away.

"*Hold it!*" commanded Undead Elvis Presley, who staggered to the front of the monstrous mob, holding up a bejeweled, skeletal hand as a halting gesture. "*Theessse are mine...*"

"*You* hold it," said a similar voice from behind Nick and Dolores. Jesse emerged from the back room, holding a .45 he'd taken from the office safe, which Nick had left open. "Been a long time, brother," Jesse said, training the gun on Elvis, tears steaming down his face.

"*Jesssseeee,*" Elvis hissed in a frightening yet pathetic rasp. His body twisted and jerked spasmodically as he spoke, like a puppet with a few strings cut. "*You...finally...found me. Thank...God...now...free me....Pleassse, brother....free me from thisss place...I want to go home to Mama...pleassse....only you can free me, becaussse only you know my sssoul...pleassse, my brother...let my sssoul go free...I can't sssstop myssself from thisss horror...I want to go home now...I miss Mama....pleassse, brother...pleassse...Don't Be Cruel...Return to Sender...It's Now Or Never..."*

Jesse nodded in sympathetic yet stoic accord, choked back a sob, and fired a single bullet into his brother's forehead. Gray hair, bits of skull and the brain that had transformed popular culture blew out onto the bamboo floor. The zombie hordes moaned in confusion and disappointment. Then slowly, they turned and trudged off, lost and leaderless, gradually fading away, like ascending spirits, or rock fans leaving a stadium after the concert has ended, vanishing through the walls of The Midnight Lounge. Now all of the world's lost souls had been emancipated, thanks to Jesse Garon Presley Mancini.

"It's *over*!' Dolores exclaimed, turning to embrace Nick, but it was too late. He had already transformed into a zombie werewolf, drooling hungrily as he gazed with bloodshot yellow eyes upon Dolores's succulent flesh, his face twisted into a hideous amalgam of rotting flesh and matted fur. He was just about to tear Dolores's throat out when Jesse fired one more round into Nick's head, and he slumped on the bar, dead, his tongue hanging out of his hairy, malformed jaw, his brain splattered into a tiki mug.

When his human features returned, Dolores went over to him and kissed his peaceful face, or what was left of it. "Goodbye, my love" she said. "I'll see you in the next dream." Then she drank his bloody brains from the tiki mug, digesting his dreams, absorbing his consciousness, merging his memories with her own, preserving them for eternity. Now they were one.

Chapter Seventy-Seven

It was all coming back to her now. The original "plan" *wasn't* for her to shoot her father, and then frame Nick. The plan was to shoot her father, then frame *Miles*. She should've told Nick that part beforehand. But it wouldn't have mattered. Tony Mancini's "misfire" changed everything, irrevocably. Nick was dead. And it was all her fault.

She looked down at the newspaper in front of her. The headline screamed sensationally: "B MOVIE MAKER AND MOB BOSS KILLED IN NY SHOOTOUT." She didn't bother reading it. Beside the newspaper was a worn script, whose cover read, "*One-Way Ticket to Thrillville,' by Nick Winters*." She wondered why she still carried around the screenplay of a film that would never get made. She looked down at her legs. No tail fin, just fishnet stockings. Wiping the wet mascara from her cheeks, she just got up and left the dressing room and stoically went outside to the film set.

Miles, the director, was waiting for her. No biker zombies, no werewolf. Just guys in aloha shirts and, oddly, multi-colored Mexican *lucha libre* wrestling masks, but no pants, simply standing around jacking off. Then she saw one stud without a mask, but sporting a slick pompadour, Elvis-style. He even had on Elvis-style shades. And nothing else. She knew exactly where she was, and it wasn't anybody's notion of heaven.

"C'mon, baby, we gotta shoot this baby," Miles said impatiently. "You ready?"

"Poor choice of words," Dolores said. She looked around at the elaborate set, a mock tiki lounge. A clapper read "Midnight Lounge, Scene 7." The crew was small, and sleazy-looking. "I don't think I can do this right now," Dolores said, as if disembodied.

Miles sighed, then said to the crew just milling about, "Okay, let's call it a night, pack it up, c'mon." Then he said to Dolores, "Honey, let's have a drink and talk about this thing."

The bar was fully stocked with real alcohol. There was even a bar tender, wearing an aloha shirt, but no mask, who mixed cocktails for them, two Zombies, extra strong. They were very well made, using fresh juices along with premium rums. He must've been a professional. Then she recognized his face. At first she thought it was her father, but it wasn't, only someone who resembled and reminded her of him. In fact, it was Buddy West, her agent. Her pimp.

"You're still hung up on that loser Nick?" he said to her. "It's been fuckin' *week*s, Dolores. Get over it already."

"Let us have some private time," Miles said to Buddy, who reluctantly left the set, staring at Dolores with a mixture of lust and disgust. "Insensitive prick," Miles said after he'd left, and he was all alone with Dolores on the tiki lounge set.

"I shouldn't be drinking," Dolores said, slurring her words after only a few sips. "Maybe I should go to a meeting."

"Fuck that, bottoms up," Miles said. She was no good to him sober. He could only control her when she was drunk on Zombies.

"Nobody will ever love me like he did," Dolores whispered into her drink.

"I love ya, Buddy loves ya," Miles said.

"You know what I mean," Dolores said.

"Dolores, this was the *plan*," Miles said with gentle frustration. "It was all *your* idea! I don't get this now. I was in hock to those killers, you've been wantin' to take out your old man for how he treated you and your mother for years. This was the only way. Nick knew the risk of what he was getting into."

"No he didn't," Dolores said. "Miles, I should tell you something."

"Yea?"

She was about to tell him her *real* plan—to shoot *him* with her father's gun right after she killed the old man, and put it in Miles' dead hand, not Nick's, and that she'd still had that impulse, even after Nick was accidentally shot instead of Miles, but by then, her spirit was broken, and the urge to kill had left her. She wanted to tell Miles all of this now, so he'd feel like shit, and realize just how much she hated him, and her life, even without her father in it. But she didn't. She didn't tell Miles anything. No point to it now. No point to anything. She was all alone in this world now. Nick was gone, framed for a murder he didn't commit, his reputation forever notorious, his name infamous and ingloriously, unjustly sullied, though he had a cult reputation on the internet, the cops and public thought of him as a hero, and his films were selling better than ever. He would've loved the irony of it all. But she missed him too much to appreciate any of it. Maybe he still lived somewhere else, in some other alternate dimension of reality, and they were still together, eternally, laughing at all of it, as if it were only a movie.

"Leave me alone, Miles," she said. "Just leave me the hell alone."

He patted her shoulder gingerly, downed his drink, and then got up from the stool, saying, "I'm goin' home to Gloria. You two have your big scene tomorrow, so you take care and get some sleep. See you in the morning. And don't be *mourning*." On his way out, he turned on the jukebox, so she'd have some company, at least.

Chapter Seventy-Eight

Dolores stood looking at Nick's lifeless body for a few moments, then Jesse gently took her by the hand, and said, "It's time to leave the building now, little sister."

She looked into Jesse's wrinkled, friendly face. He'd been crying, of course, having just shot his brother Elvis dead in the head, but it was the only way to stop all this madness, once and for all.

"Miles told me you were killed by the biker zombies," she said.

"They tried," he said. "They attacked me and while I was preoccupied wrasslin' 'em off, Miles dragged you away in the car. So I ran, hopin' to live to fight another day. That day is today, though it feels like it's still yesterday, or maybe tomorrow. I'm all confused. Anyway, I just kept walkin' and followed the road till it ended here. Looks like I made it, just in time." He hugged her and kissed her forehead. "I'm sorry about your man. I had to do it."

"I know," she said. "Thank you. But I'll see him again someday. And you may see your brother again too, in a better place."

"I hope so, lil' sister. And I hope I don't have to shoot him in the head again. I know it wasn't really him no more, but still, he was my flesh and blood. And his soul was trapped in there someplace. Now he's finally free to go on to the next world, wherever that is." Jesse took her by the hand and led her outside into the warm, brilliant sunshine and clean desert air.

"Jesse, this is beautiful," she whispered in awe.

"Thank you very much, but I keep telling you: Jesse is dead. I'm just *playin'* Jesse."

Dolores turned and stared into the undead face of Elvis Presley, the real one, or at least, the *other* "real" one.

They were still standing together in the sunshine, but when Dolores turned around, there was no Midnight Lounge, riddled with bullet holes and saturated with blood. There was only her cold, sterile trailer. She was back on the desert set of *One-Way Ticket to Thrillville.*

"Oh," Dolores said softly. "I understand. It's all coming back to me now." She leaned over and kissed Elvis on the cheek, tasting makeup and dead flesh. "Goodbye," she said, looking into his sad, dead eyes, touching his cold face with her warm hand, then she went back inside of her trailer, put her head down, and wept herself into the depths of dreamland, where she finally swam to the surface, and everything became crystal clear to her at last, Sarah Brightman's "Captain Nemo" echoing in her brainwaves.

Chapter Seventy-Nine

An hour or so after Miles left, Buddy burst onto the set of *Midnight Lounge*, Miles' *porno noir* opus, an ambitious attempt to bring hardcore eroticism back into the mainstream. It was, in fact, midnight. Dolores had been drinking heavily, all alone at the makeshift bar. "Lujon" by Henry Mancini was playing on the fake jukebox. The *faux* tiki bar was convincing in context but somewhat surreal and strangely, boldly colorful, resembling a set from a 1960s Seijun Suzuki *yakuza* flick. Like many illusions, it looked better than the real thing, but proved ultimately unsatisfying due to its ephemeral nature.

"Nick's dead and he's not coming back," Buddy said, "in this world, or in any other. I'm here, and I want you. You're a whore, anyway. Always were. You're lucky *any*body wants a piece of that ragged hole now. At least nobody's paying *me* to fuck you on camera, you goddamn slut. I'll do it right now. Give you the fuck of your miserable life. For *free*. Take it or leave it."

"Just take me," Dolores said to Buddy, finishing her fourth drink of the night—straight rum. "I don't care anymore." She shakily got up off the stool, pulled the Polynesian dress off over her head, unhooked then flung off her bra, slipped her panties and fishnet stockings down and off her feet, then kicked off her leopard skin high-heeled fuck-me pumps, all of which Miles had picked out just for her, using her Daddy's credit card, of course, and then she climbed up and lay prone on the bamboo bar, staring stoically up at the glowing puffer fish dangling from the ceiling, her legs spread open. Buddy hurriedly removed his shirt and let his pants drop down around his ankles, then climbed on top of her. He was too anxious and desirous to completely disrobe. He wanted to have her willingly, or he'd need to take her by force. In any case, it was going to happen. This way, he wouldn't feel so bad about it.

Dolores could feel Buddy penetrating her pussy with his pulsating penis. She mechanically caressed his sweaty muscles, trembling with unbridled pleasure. He grunted like a pig, and she involuntarily moaned in response. His enormous cock was tearing the lips of her morally conflicted vagina. He voraciously licked her tears of lonely agony, which he mistook for tears of sensual ecstasy, off of her face, then licked his own drool off of her throat, as he thrust deeper and harder inside of her, owning her body even as her spirit drifted away, Eric Carmen's "All By Myself" echoing from beyond, like a celestial jukebox. Buddy quickly shot his Blob-like wad inside of her, where it dripped and spread like an alien invader, merging with all of the other alien substances feeding on her insides, but he kept thrusting, still erect, still hungry, like a sex zombie. She felt like she was suffocating —drowning. *This story needs a better ending*, Dolores thought. So she made one up, a typical male fantasy of which Nick would approve.

Chapter Eighty

I burst into The Midnight Lounge wearing a silver Santo *lucha* mask and shot Buddy West dead, twice in the back of the head —and this time, it wasn't an accident. "Only room for one 'Buddy' in this world, anyway," I said, thinking of my dead cat. Dolores rolled Buddy's heavy, lifeless body off of her, and it hit the floor with a pleasing *thump* of finality. I removed my Santo mask, which I'd picked up while hiding out in Acapulco, and which I'd worn to infiltrate this nefarious pornography ring and rescue Dolores.

"Nick, *you're alive*!" Dolores screamed in exaltation as my true identity was revealed to her. "*How*?"

"Don't believe everything you read, baby," I said, then she jumped into my arms, and we passionately kissed, then danced, as Henry Mancini's "Lujon" played on the jukebox. She put on her Polynesian dress and grabbed her shoes. I was wearing a green sharkskin suit and a skinny black tie. I looked and felt great, better than ever, thanks to the miraculous experimental combination brain and plastic surgery that had saved my life, performed by the mad but benign scientist who rescued me from the morgue. I still had a nasty scar on my forehead, and a metal plate in the back of my skull that was concealed by a very naturalistic wig, but otherwise, I was tiptop. As we left, I put my Santo mask back on to conceal my identity from the outside world, where I may be recognized due to my newfound notoriety as a gangster killer; then we got into her Impala and fled the scene of the crime, never looking back, sirens wailing in the distance, headed for the Motel Capri, our sanctuary, the place we'd first met, before any of this nightmare had even begun. "Feeling

Good" by Nina Simone was playing on her car stereo. Once we were far enough away, having eluded our pursuers, I removed my mask. We were free to be ourselves at last.

Supposedly still on the road to Palm Springs, Dolores and I finally pulled over and stopped at a signpost on the side of the desolate highway. It said, "Welcome to Thrillville—Population: Unknown." Overheard in the starry firmament, a flying saucer began final descent into its designated destination, disappearing just beyond the not-too-distant horizon, glowing pink in the purple twilight.

We got out of the Impala and walked to a scintillating swimming pool surrounded by majestic palm trees, located alone and isolated in the middle of nowhere, like an oasis. Next to the pool was a fully stocked bar covered by a bright green awning. The bartender wore a bow tie and white jacket and looked a lot like a young Ricardo Montalban. He was already shaking up some cocktails, apparently in anticipation of our arrival. On the other side of the pool, a strange, beautiful woman in a sparkling scarlet evening gown was playing Martin Denny's "Quiet Village" on the Theremin. She resembled Rita Hayworth in her heyday. Despite the setting sun, the weather was warm. We stripped down to nakedness and jumped into the cool, soothing water. As we did laps, I looked over and saw Buddy the cat was serenely swimming alongside of us. Dolores flipped her tail fins playfully. I turned into a lizard man, and we made love underwater, my scaly member perpetually penetrating the moist aperture in her scaly groin, lost in our own private sea of aquatic erotica.

I was home at last, with no return ticket.

That's a wrap.

CODA

Dolores lifted her heavy head, opened her swollen, puffy eyes, and stared at the blinking cursor on her computer, where a solitary phrase was still waiting for a pointless period, just like her barren womb: "*A man without a future met a woman with a past...*" A torn picture of her parents, Miles and Myrna, lay at her feet. She finished her drink, and then the sentence: *and together, they made a present for themselves.* With a weary sigh, she shut off the computer, finally ending the MP3 of her favorite song, "Mermaid," by Elysian Fields, which had been playing in a continuous, obsessive loop; picked up her cat, Elvis, and went to bed, crying herself back to what she privately referred to as "The Midnight Lounge," her personal dreamland, where the stranger she called Nick was waiting to rescue her from the dark depths of the suffocating sea.

THE END
Fade to Black…Roll credits….

FREAKS THAT CARRY YOUR LUGGAGE UP TO THE ROOM

A Nightmare in a Novella
by Will "Bizarro" Viharo

Will Viharo

To my beloved Bubba,
And all my friends over the rainbow

WELCOME TO VIOLENCE

People who checked into L'Hotel du Frisson always checked each other out, too. It was a sexual nexus of neurotic eroticism. The guests were consumed by lust and loneliness, because these intoxicating interludes distracted them, like all of humanity, from their real obsession: a collective fear of death. Morality was no match for mortality. These primal passions erupted one night when a beautiful, seemingly ageless Latina movie queen named Estrella Margarita Moreno, renowned for her promiscuity on and off screen, decided to take a vacation from her native town of Tlaquepaque, Mexico, a suburb of Guadalajara, traveling across America, where she could literally get lost, maybe even disappear. She settled on L'Hotel du Frisson because it sounded foreign and exotic, even though it was located in a typical American town. She had once lived in Paris, years ago, until a scandal, involving an important politician, drove her out, exiling her from the country of France forever. She never got over it. In fact, she wanted to die. But first, she wanted to fall in love, one last time.

The desk clerk on duty recognized her right away, because her picture was in the magazine he kept under the counter, next to the gun, which he always brought with him for safety, since he worked the night shift, and sometimes shady, dangerous types would lurk in the adjoining Cafe du Frisson, though they were the least of his worries, especially tonight.

The cafe was somewhat more contemporary in appearance than the three-story hotel, since most of the furniture had been replaced in the 1960s, at odds with the 1930s decor of the hotel, which had never been updated. The mid-century modernist style of the cafe, in pastel blues and greens, also both complemented and contrasted with the Art Deco fashion of the building in which it was housed. Together, it was an architectural, aesthetic haven for bygone styles that didn't clash so much as copulate. This unique atmosphere made L'Hotel du Frisson a global destination for world-weary travelers. The desk clerk did not share this love for his place of employment. He was only here temporarily, anyway. He'd be moving on once he suspected that the people pursuing him were in uncomfortable proximity. The desk clerk's name was Danny. A regular in the cafe known as "The Mantis Man," from New York City, where he had once worked as a headhunter and hung out in coffee shops with his good friend, the late filmmaker John Cassavetes, had warned Danny that, via the underground grapevine, his enemies were getting closer, and it may be time for him to leave, very soon, strongly advising him to just walk off the job *tonight*. But after meeting Estrella Moreno, the famous Mexican porn star (though her sensuous, surrealistic movies with titles like *Iguana Sexo* and *Mi Gata Quieres Amor* were shown in mainstream art houses), he didn't want to abandon his post just yet. She was worth the risk, he figured.

"They're having a little party for you," The Mantis Man had told Danny earlier that evening, rather sardonically. The Mantis Man was called such because of his thin, insect-like appearance. "Because you made a mistake. What kind of a mistake? A *bad* mistake. Now they have to resolve this mistake that you made. You're invited to this little party, Danny. You should RSVP for this party that they're throwing for you. You're the guest of honor." The Mantis Man's beady eyes lit up with an odd sort of enjoyment as he described Danny's plight.

"I'll just leave town again," Danny said.

"You can run, but you can't hide," said The Mantis Man. "I should know. I was a headhunter. It was my job to find people."

"Not me," Danny said.

"*I* found you, didn't I?" The Mantis Man cackled.

"But you weren't even looking for me," said Danny.

"Well, there you go," said The Mantis Man. "Imagine if I *were*. That's how easy it is. You should have changed your name."

"I did."

"Well, I guess that wasn't enough. My contacts tell me that your trail has heated up and your friends could be arriving shortly. It will be a very fun party, I'm sure." The Mantis Man lit up a cigarette.

"Please smoke outside," Danny said irritably.

The Mantis Man nodded and walked away.

"I have nothing better to do than die," Danny whispered to himself.

Then Estrella Moreno showed up, and changed everything.

When Danny had first arrived for his shift that evening, the clerk he was replacing, a rotund, clean-cut, red-faced fellow named Franklin DeWitt, was in one of the rooms, masturbating on the bed, then carefully cleaning up after himself. This was his usual routine. Franklin desperately wanted to sleep with L'Hotel du Frisson's owner, a buxom blonde nymphomaniac widower named Clara Cleaver, but then so did most of the desk clerks, as well as the guests. Clara sometimes obliged them, taking the hotel tab out in trade, but she never slept with her employees, as a strict policy. Franklin had to settle for photographs he surreptitiously snapped of Clara taking a shower in that very room, which Franklin had taken through a small, secret hole in the wall, drilled for this perverse, voyeuristic surveillance. Clara was very sexy, an ex-stripper (stage name: Clara Belle due to her enormous, and very real, breasts, which men loved to "milk" by ejaculating between them), who had married a wealthy businessman that in turn died of a heart attack on their honeymoon, following a strenuous sexual session. She was never even sure what exactly he did for a living, since he'd just picked her up at the club where she worked and proposed the next morning. He left Clara his entire fortune, which she wisely invested by purchasing this hotel. That was ten years ago. Some say the businessman's spirit haunted this hotel, but then so did many spirits, many in liquid form. The hotel's legendary reputation as a graveyard for ghosts was part of its appeal. Clara always played that up on brochures. It was an effective marketing scheme, whether it was true or not. Clara was as shrewd as she was lewd.

"Now that you've soiled that room, I can't rent it," Danny complained to Franklin, sweating and reeking of his own semen. "It's our only vacancy. The maids are long gone."

"Yes, you can, I always clean up after myself," Franklin said.

"Zip up your god damn pants and dry that spot on your crotch, you fat, filthy bastard," Danny said. Franklin just snorted and laughed.

So when Estrella checked in, Danny had no alternative but to give her Room 101, the closest one to the front desk. It was known as The Purple Room, because it was decorated in purple. All of the rooms had a unique color scheme. A white stain on a plush purple bedspread would definitely stand out. If only Franklin had used The Yellow Room, but that was occupied by a man from out of town, a salesman, who rarely ventured out during his regular visits.

FREAKS THAT CARRY YOUR LUGGAGE UP TO THE ROOM

The bellhop on duty, a deformed dwarf from Russia named Boris Yakov, once a successful surgeon, until he botched an operation due to his incessant trembling, carried Estrella's baggage to her room, even though it was heavier than he was, and the room was nearby. Danny did not let Estrella know that he recognized her, but she could tell that he did.

"Are you here all night?" she asked him. "In case I need anything?"

"Yes," he said.

It was 3 A.M. and Danny, pretending to read a detective novel, was having trouble staying awake, despite his date with either impending doom or the fuck of his thirty-year-old life. The sounds of classic jazz emanated from the café's sound system, as it did around the clock since, like the hotel, Cafe du Frisson never closed. That's when Danny noticed the two familiar men in the mirror, which reflected the cafe. They were wearing sunglasses in the middle of the night. That's when he knew he had to run.

"Cover for me," Danny told Boris, who was sound asleep. Boris had been the one who had drilled the hole in The Purple Room, and told Franklin about it. Danny brought his gun with him.

He knocked on Room 101, and Estrella let him in, closing the door behind them, and locking it.

"I need a place to hide," he said.

"I was going to call you anyway," she said.

"Why?" asked Danny. Up close in person, he marveled at how much she resembled Raquel Welch, his wet dream girl, in her glorious prime.

"There is a strange stain on my sheets, and my bed smells like *sex*. Also, there is a hole in the wall of the bathroom."

"I'm sorry," Danny said. "Would you like me to

plug your hole?"

She was wearing a silk robe that was untied, revealing her pointy, perky brown breasts with their large nipples, which he recognized from the magazine. She said, "*Sssshhhh*," then took him into her meaty arms and enveloped him in her warm, soft flesh. He removed his black suit, white shirt, shiny black shoes, and thin black tie. They made violent love for hours. Estrella cried because she had found her final fling.

When Danny woke up, the sun was streaming through the blinds, and it burned his skin. He got up and closed the curtains. Estrella was still on the bed, her eyes wide open, her skin cold to the touch. She was dead.

Danny went to the bathroom and noticed two puncture wounds on his neck. They hurt when he touched them. There was a knock on the door, then two men suddenly kicked it open, and fired their guns at Danny. But he just stood there and took it. He then walked up to the two men, ignoring his own gun on the bedside table, and snapped their necks, one in each hand. Then he dropped them on the ground and returned to Estrella's side, and wept. Estrella opened her eyes, and smiled, licking the bloody saliva from her lips. She carefully covered Danny in the blankets, told him to stay put, walked to the window, opened the curtains and blinds, and burst into flames.

NOTHING BETTER TO DO THAN DIE

There's nothing worse than dying alone. This is what Estrella Margarita Moreno believed, and since the only for her way to die was to commit suicide by sunshine, she felt she could control the destiny of her ultimate demise. Loneliness was normally lethal when left untreated. In her case, it was merciless torture, not a fatal illness. The only way to kill her loneliness was to kill herself.

She'd first been infected with blood-lustful immortality while making a monster movie in Mexico City, way back in 1962. The actor hired to play the vampire wore phony fangs and a cape. This only served to disguise the fact that he was a *real* vampire, as Estrella discovered one dark, sensuous night after the movie had wrapped. The movie, entitled *La Lucha Contras El Vampiro*, about a masked wrestler battling the undead, was a cult favorite. Estrella was only twenty-four at the time. She had made the film under her real name, Maria Munoz, but changed it in 1974 when she appeared in her first "art" film, *Estrella Estrogena*. Critics and audiences marveled at how she hadn't aged very much since that film was made, and she denied she was the star of *La Lucha Contra El Vampiro*, claiming that was her deceased cousin. Her friends in the Mexican drug cartel—big fans of her work—helped fabricate credence to this cover story. Many of her criminal friends were vampires as well. The ruse worked. Estrella actually wore makeup in public to make her appear somewhat older, but not so old as to eschew erotic love scenes, her stock-in-trade. She was indeed a living miracle. Actually, an undead miracle. But she was lonely, and she wanted it to end.

Though she had many, many lovers over the years, she had fallen in love only once, with a member of the French Parliament, in the late 1970s, whom she'd met at Cannes where one of her films was premiering, but he was married, and when intimate photos of them surfaced, she was denounced by her lover as an evil temptress and effectively ostracized from that country, though her fans still loved and worshipped her. Her lover later committed "suicide," found hanging from a balcony, drained of blood.

Estrella fled France and traveled next to Spain, where she lived and loved and worked for many years, appearing in several films for the director Jess Franco. But despite her many affairs, she was very lonesome. The fact that she often fed on her lovers disturbed her soul, and she was convinced she still possessed one. Her spirit was just trapped. Only love could free it from this prison of undead flesh.

She returned to her childhood town of Tlaquepaque and decided to retire, sleeping by day, painting by night, feeding only on small animals, mostly mice and possums, but never cats, because she loved them too much. She often stole human blood from hospitals as well. Her sudden disappearance from the screen concerned her many fans worldwide, but her films gained new audiences and popularity via video and then DVD. She could live on these royalties alone. She became a restless recluse. That's when she decided to travel.

Danny Falco was on the run from people in Philadelphia to whom he owed a lot of money. Danny was a gambler and a drifter from Pitman and then Atlantic City, New Jersey, though his last address had been in Chicago. He took odd jobs to survive as he wandered the country. He'd finally quit his gambling habit via GA—Gambler's Anonymous—only to replace one addiction for another: sex. This was an easy addiction to fulfill, since he resembled a young Elvis Presley. He always thought he'd die young, too. He just didn't think he'd live to tell about it.

When Estrella dissolved into dust before his very eyes, Danny instinctively swung into action. He hid the bodies of the two dead hit men in the bathroom, because of the sirens in the distance. Then he returned to his post, though the morning clerk, a suave poseur named Dick Reid, who was obsessed with Japanese women, was already on duty, talking to the police, who were responding to reports of a disturbance in one of the rooms. Dick had already given the cops all the guest logs, including Estrella Moreno. Danny decided to play it cool. Mendacity had become a lifestyle for him

"What's up?" Danny said. "I fell asleep in one of the rooms, sorry, man."

"These policemen said someone called to report some loud noises, possibly gunfire, in The Purple Room," Dick said as he checked his hair in the mirror. He was swarthy and handsome and quite vain. His suit was neatly pressed and he smelled strongly of expensive cologne.

"That was me, sorry," Danny said. "I was watching 'The Untouchables' on TV, too loud, I guess."

"Can we see the room?" asked one of the policemen.

"Ahm, I'd rather you didn't," Danny said.

"Why?" asked the cop suspiciously.

"I wasn't alone," Danny said.

Dick smiled. "So that was the *real* Estrella Moreno you checked in?"

"Yes," Danny said.

"The Mexican porn star?" asked one of the cops, wild-eyed.

"Art films," Danny said. "She doesn't make porn."

"Whatever you want to call it, works for me," Dick said.

"I'm sorry someone complained," Danny said.

"You work here?" asked the cop.

"Yea, I'm the night clerk."

Dick winked at Danny, who ignored him.

"Okay, well, we only had one call, and it seems quiet now," the cop said.

"It is," said Danny.

The cops left. "You look pale," Dick said to Danny. "She must've drained you dry."

"Where's Boris?" Danny asked, unaware that Boris had tipped off the men looking for him. Boris knew Danny must've been in Estrella's room. He planned to go watch her taking a shower later on, through his customized peephole, but then Boris didn't know Estrella was dead. Boris had keys to all the rooms. He lived in the basement of the hotel, where, when he wasn't reading or watching pornography, he conducted his secret experiments on stolen corpses from the local morgue.

"He was already gone when I got here," Dick said. "Nobody was here. *Nobody*."

"I was only gone a few minutes before my shift ended," Danny lied. "Sorry."

Dick shrugged. "Just cover for me next time I'm late. I met this fine Japanese lady last night, I need to tell you all about her…"

"Not now," Danny said. "I'm too tired."

An Afro-haired part-Jewish, part-German, half Cuban would-be musician from Miami named Mortimer Schmidt, though his friends just called him Morty, or they *would* if he *had* any friends, accosted

Danny. Morty frequented the café on a daily basis, careful to avoid The Mantis Man, with whom he did not get along. "What happened?" he asked Danny in his usual pushy manner.

"Nothing, mind your own business," said Danny. "I need to go get cleaned up."

"You look like shit," Morty said. "Why were the cops here? Something happen?"

"I said mind your own business, man," Danny said.

"Okay, okay, okay, okay, okay," Morty said. "Just askin'."

"Poke that big nose up somebody else's ass," Danny muttered as he returned to Room 101 to find a way to clean up his mess.

But when he got there, he only saw Boris the dwarf, with his pants around his ankles, sitting on the bed.

"I am sorry," Boris said. "I come here to pleasure myself, to smell the people that have stayed here as I imagine having sex with them, because no one will have sex with me for real. I thought you had left. I come on the rug. There was dust on rug. The dust came to life. My semen, it brought the dust to life. Like semen *should* do, create life. She was a beautiful naked woman, full grown. She went into the bathroom, and ate the bodies in there. She ate them *all.* Even the bones, very quick. Then she kissed me." Boris wiped his mouth.

Danny gulped. "Where is she now?"

"Beneath this bed," he said. "I am very sorry. I need to go now."

Boris hopped off the bed, pulled up his pants, and left the room. When he was gone, Danny peered beneath the bed and saw Estella resting peacefully in the cool darkness. Danny smiled. He was in love. Feeling weak and nauseous, he climbed underneath and lied down beside her, and soon fell asleep.

"I have something better to do than die now," he said to her as he drifted off, though she could not hear him. She was dreaming of her own death, which had once again eluded her.

At dusk, when she awoke, she leaned over and kissed him. He opened his eyes and smiled.

"Estrella," he whispered, kissing her hand.

"Call me Maria," she whispered. "That is my true name."

"Are we dead?" he asked.

"Not quite," she said. "I was dead, at least, but now I no longer wish to die, now that I've found you."

"Am I like you?" he asked.

"Not yet, but soon."

"Forever."

"Yes," she said. "Forever." A tear escaped and ran down her cheek. He kissed it off.

"I'm not afraid," he said.

"You should be," she said.

"But now, we're safe," he said. "My enemies cannot harm me."

She kissed him. "Let's go above the bed, and make love."

He looked at his watch. "I have to go to work soon. Would you like to have dinner with me?"

She suddenly looked forlorn, and stroked his thick, black hair, then kissed his forehead. "That's the hard part," she said. "Feeding the *thirst*."

"Did you really come back to life because the dwarf jerked off on your remains?" he said.

"Yes," she said. "Blood and semen. I live on these fluids. They are liquid life. I do not *have* to consume human flesh and bones, except when I must dispose of evidence from a kill. I try to choose my victims carefully."

"But why did you try to die?" Danny asked. "Especially after last night?"

"Because I wanted it to end perfectly," she said.

He kissed her. "Now it will never end," he said.

"But it won't be perfect," she said.

"I don't care," he said, and then they climbed up onto the bed and made love. He was very hungry when 11PM rolled around, and, after taking a shower, he had to report for work, and the pizza that Juan and Carlos, the Mexican cafe workers, offered to share with him just didn't appeal to him.

"Estrella Moreno is staying here?" asked Carlos, whose raucous laugh often filled the cafe.

"May I meet her?" asked Juan, who sent his entire paycheck home to his family in Mexico, living on his tips and some male hustling on the side. They would be quite impressed—and appalled—to know this famous Latina star was residing in his place of employment.

"Maybe," said Danny. "She may be staying here for a long time." He tried not to notice the veins in their necks. "Here," he said. "Take the pizza with you."

"You not hungry?"

"No," Danny lied. "Just thirsty. Bring me some sangria. Please."

The Mantis Man was watching Danny from the cafe. He went to the phone booth and made a call to a private eye named Vic Valentine.

THE HEADHUNTER

The Mantis Man was alone in his room at L'Hotel du Frisson, the only one that didn't have its own color scheme, other than Gloom, dreaming of better days, which would be *any* day prior to whichever one he was currently living. His isolation and dementia were progressive, and linked, but he didn't see it this way. He loved living at the hotel, even though it was somewhat expensive, despite the bargain rate deal he had worked out. The hotel only had a few indefinite residents. The Mantis Man had amassed considerable personal wealth before retiring from his career as a headhunter and moving to this town, and he lived fairly simply, rarely venturing outside the confines of the hotel and adjoining café. He had nowhere to go, and no one to love. He subsisted on a steady diet of denial. And burritos.

He was eating one now, brought up from the cafe, while he watched an old Mexican horror move with the sound down low. The female star seemed vaguely familiar; he assumed because he'd seen her in another movie before, or maybe even this one. The Mantis Man was losing touch with reality. He didn't miss it much.

After finishing his burrito, he went to his closet and pulled out his customary trench coat and derby hat, hanging just beside the row of shrunken heads he'd collected from his side gig as a voodoo priest. He knew how to raise the dead. He just didn't see the point in prolonging anyone's agony. He wasn't quite that sadistic. It was raining heavily outside, but that was not an issue. He hardly ever went outside. There was nothing out there for him anymore.

The phone rang, and, cursing, he put down his

burrito, got up and answered it. It was Dick, up at the front desk.

"There's a phone call for you; shall I put it through?"

"Yes." The Mantis Man lit a cigarette and took a drag on it.

"Hey, it's Vic," said a voice on the phone. "I tried calling your cell, but there was no answer."

The Mantis Man took a puff and said, "Yes, the battery is low."

"I can relate," said Vic. "I'm tired so I'll make this quick. Your boy Danny Falco? The guys who want him are well connected, back in Jersey. I know people who know them. Not nice."

"I *know* all that," The Mantis Man said. "I'm familiar with their ilk. That's not what I wanted to know. What I want to *know* is..."

"Why they want him, I know, yea yea yea," said Vic. "Gambling debts, and some other things."

"Like *what*? Details, details. That's why I hired you, Valentine. The rest of it I could *guess*, for Chrissake."

"Well, apparently, he fucked some wiseguy's fiancée," Vic said. "I know the type. I'd love to kill him myself. Maybe I should be a hit man for hire instead of a private dick?"

"I'll take care of it from here. Goodbye," The Mantis Man said, and abruptly hung up. "I should've just hired the ghost of Johnny fucking Staccato," he muttered to himself.

The Mantis Man then went to his closet and pulled out a trench coat and derby hat, relics from his youth, hanging just beside the row of shrunken heads he'd collected from his side gig as a voodoo priest. He knew how to raise the Dead. He learned a lot of tricks from his Haitian masters when he lived in New Orleans back in the 1950s. He just didn't see the point in prolonging anyone's agony. He wasn't quite that sadistic. He'd rather see everyone just die and leave him alone, anyway. It was raining heavily outside, but that was not an issue. He hardly ever went outside. There was nothing out there for him anymore. He often wore his coat and hat, anyway. It made him feel like he had someplace to go, even if he didn't want to leave. *Ever*.

The Mantis Man reached down, picked up and opened a shoebox at the bottom of his closet and took out a little blonde male doll with overalls, that he called "Chumpy Walnut." He removed it and set down the box.

"We're going to have a party for our friend Danny," The Mantis Man said to the doll.

He sat back down and finished watching the Mexican monster movie, completely unaware that the actress on the screen was now in the room right below him, a half century after the film had been made but just as youthful and beautiful, feasting on the life-giving fluid she sucked from Danny Falco's cock, biting his groin to add the crucial nutritional supplement of blood to her meal. Unfortunately, she could not live on sex alone—violence was also part of her diet. Blood and semen: the secret of Life, and the alchemy of the Damned.

The Mantis Man cackled to himself, holding the doll and repeating to himself as he watched the film, "We're having a party for you, Danny. Because you made a mistake. What kind of mistake? A *bad* mistake. Now we have to resolve this mistake that you made." He despised Danny Falco for something Danny had unwittingly done to him, for breaking his heart, and he vowed to send the kid's soul straight to Hell, but Danny's soul had already been spoken for.

FREAKS THAT CARRY YOUR LUGGAGE UP TO THE ROOM

THE SINFUL DWARF

Boris the bellhop rubbed his grimy little hands all over the nude, voluptuous body of his boss, Clara Cleaver, as she lay strapped, nude and unconscious to a dirty table in the basement of L'Hotel du Frisson, with bloody pieces of rotting corpses strewn here and there around the dank, dark "dungeon," amid tables full of glass jars containing human organs floating in strange fluids. Once a prominent surgeon, Boris Yakov lost his practice, his career, and his Russian citizenship when he botched the heart surgery of a prominent Russian ballet dancer who had suffered a near-fatal seizure after overdosing on diet pills, and whom Boris happened to be secretly in love with. He blamed the tragedy on his nervousness, since he couldn't stop shaking as he operated on her. He had been shaking ever since her death, which everyone blamed on Boris, including Boris. His self-loathing ran deep in his tortured soul.

Clara had been hidden down here for nearly two days, and Boris knew he'd have to release her soon, before suspicion was aroused. She often vanished for days at a time anyway, away on trips to undisclosed locations, drinking and fornicating, or so the stories went. Clara was very lonely as well. Not only had her husband died on their honeymoon, leaving her a small fortune with which she purchased this very hotel, but she had lost several babies, some via abortion, some via miscarriage, and two that were stillborn. She felt cursed by the universe, and often wanted to die. Instead, she had random, unprotected sex with eager strangers, hoping one would impregnate her with a child that could be brought to term. It was a procreative crapshoot.

The dwarf, Boris, was in love with Clara and knew of her birth-challenged plight, and he wanted to help her by helping himself. He had drugged her by spiking her customary morning latte from the cafe, then lured her down to the basement, where she never ventured, knowing Boris had lived there for years, before she purchased the building, and she was afraid of what she'd find. He always creeped her out, but she couldn't find it in her heart to fire him. Perhaps she would if she regained consciousness while he licked her bosoms and torso and legs and feet, running upstairs to masturbate in one of the empty rooms when he became aroused beyond endurance, because he didn't want to defile her, not while she was unconscious, anyway. He wanted her to love him, and he knew if he could cure her barrenness, however surreptitiously, she would love him forever, just like Katarina, the beautiful ballerina who died on his operating table back in Moscow, twenty years ago.

There was a thunderstorm raging up above, which Boris could hear through the basement's single window, the lightning illuminating horrible things. Boris paid off the local mortician for access to corpses on which Boris could conduct mindless, pointless experiments. The problem was, Boris had no idea what he was doing. He had a vague notion of bringing the Dead back to Life, but was unsure exactly how to go about it. He paid the mortician with money he stole from the seemingly endless stash of cash hidden in the back of the closet of one of the residents, whom everyone called The Mantis Man. Boris had seen The Mantis Man's hideous collection of shrunken heads, but didn't think much of it. Since he had keys to all the rooms, Boris could come and go as he pleased, and he wound up searching all the guest's rooms during their stay, when they weren't in the rooms, of course, stealing whatever he could, but mostly just sitting on their beds and masturbating, often with whatever feminine undergarments or lingerie happened to be handy. He hoped The Mantis Man never discovered that he was constantly stealing his cash, which The Mantis Man apparently never counted. The worst thing that could happen? The Mantis Man might kill him. That wouldn't be so bad, really. Boris just didn't want to die a fifty-eight year old virgin.

In her coma-like state, Clara was dreaming of her past, as a hot young stripper in various nightclubs on the Eastern seaboard, including Atlantic City, where she once had a one-night stand with a young Elvis impersonator, now named Danny Falco. She had been engaged to a Jersey mobster at the time, but he broke it off when he discovered her many affairs. He didn't kill her, though, because he loved her too much. He just sublimated his heartbroken rage by killing everyone she had ever slept with. Except for Danny, who disappeared without a trace. Clara was in love with Danny and offered him sanctuary at the hotel, under an assumed name. His real name was not Danny Falco. He had changed his name so many times he didn't remember what it used to be anymore. It didn't matter. He never knew himself very well, anyway, and was always open to change on his journey of self-discovery. He told Clara he loved her, even though she knew he was lying, just so he could rest for a while under auspices. She just wanted him close to her, to perpetuate the illusion of romance and domestic stability that had always eluded her. Clara was thirty-eight, eight years older than Danny, who truthfully claimed he had never been in love with anyone. They still had sex sometimes, even though their trysts often left her lonelier than ever. So much sex. So little love.

Clara suddenly moaned as Boris was eating her pussy, and he stopped suddenly. He had another erection and wanted to go back upstairs and relieve himself, but now all the rooms were booked, except for the room where Clara slept, which was as sacred as her womb and could not be violated, so he had no choice but to go to his own little bathroom and jerk off in the sink, which he hated to do, mainly because he had to stand on a stool to do it. He didn't want to ejaculate anywhere near, on or inside Clara, not until she was in love with him, and ready to bear his child. Boris knew Clara was in love with Danny, which is why he had told those gunmen where to find Danny. He wanted Danny out of the way, preferably permanently.

Sensing she was snapping out of it, though she would not be able to recall anything following her first sip of the spiked latte, Boris whistled and a very large mute brute, chained to the corner of the basement, stirred. The mute brute, like Boris, was horribly deformed, not due to the fickle cruelty of Nature, but as a result of Boris's bizarre experiments. The brute had once been just another guest at the hotel, a disgraced football player, kicked out of the league for steroid abuse. His name was simply LeRoy, born African American, but now his skin color had been lightened via Boris's various injections, so now he resembled an albino. He had no mind of his own. He was simply Boris's slave.

"Take her upstairs and leave her in The Scarlet Room," Boris told him as he unlocked the shackles. "Be careful, it is late but someone may be about. Use the secret staircase. Hurry, before she comes to."

The seven feet tall LeRoy nodded sadly and walked toward the table in the center of the room as Boris undid the straps. LeRoy lifted Clara's nude body and entered the service elevator, which he rode up to the third floor. The Scarlet Room was left unlocked so LeRoy could deposit Clara inside quickly, then return to the basement undetected. As a reward, Boris often fed LeRoy scraps of human flesh, for which LeRoy had developed quite a taste.

After LeRoy gently laid Clara down on the scarlet bed, he stood and admired her beauty, then put his tongue on her bosoms, then on her face and mouth and neck, and was working his lips down her body when she suddenly opened her eyes, and screamed.

THE UNHOLY HOLE

Clara was in love, and feeling pregnant, even if she hadn't actually conceived—*yet*. But her many hours of rapturous lovemaking over a period of what felt like months with this huge albino stranger gave her hope, more hope than she'd felt in a long, long while. His member was so tirelessly aroused that he was able to maintain an erection even after ejaculating within her multiple times, and she came so violently and frequently that by the tenth or twelfth orgasm per session, she simply passed out from pure pleasure. Whenever she awoke the next morning in The Scarlet Room—which she kept reserved for her own private use—the albino stud was gone, evaporating into thin air like mist in the sunlight. Then she would go about her day, wondering if it was all a wonderful dream, Boris would bring her a cafe latte, and next thing she knew, she was back in The Scarlet Room, completely nude with no clue what had happened to her clothes, the leering giant towering over her, already drooling on her gloriously exposed flesh, but never speaking, so she had no idea where he came from. She only cared that he came *inside* of her, forcefully and repeatedly, and that eventually, she would bear his child. The phenomenally primal sex with this monstrous male creature was so powerful that procreation seemed inevitable. It felt like the eternal forces of Nature were at work. And even if she never got knocked up, it was still worth the effort. Clara had never felt so physically sated in her entire life. LeRoy could boast the same, if he possessed the vocal or literary tools to do so.

Clara, conversely, was quite communicative while LeRoy was furiously fucking her, moaning deliriously, caressing his muscular if misshapen form as she cried out in ecstasy, then clutching his white Afro hair, clawing his hard, expansive back, and biting his ear till it bled as he pounded her pussy mercilessly, until it bled as well, and he sobbed with joy as she huskily whispered in his ear, "Love me…love me…*love me…*"

Of course, Boris was oblivious to this torrid trysting, going about his bellhop duties at all hours of the day and night, when not toiling away on his experiments, masturbating in one of the rooms, or sleeping for a few hours at a time (he was "on call," summoned by a bell that rang in his basement lair, wired up to the front desk). Boris truly had no idea what was happening once LeRoy took Clara back up to The Scarlet Room, after Boris had systematically drugged, kidnapped and molested her nude body as it was strapped to the dirty operating table, on a semi-monthly basis, for over a year now, often keeping her two or three nights, feeding her intravenously.

Clara attributed her frequent blackouts to drinking, but she sought no help from a medical doctor, a shrink, a priest, or a substance abuse program. She had lost track of time, dazed, disoriented and barely functioning outside of her hotel duties, and in fact, Danny did most of the bookkeeping and bill paying. She had been so miserable that this bizarre, hallucinatory new lifestyle didn't bother her at all. Now at least, she had something to live for, even if it *wasn't* real.

The reality was, LeRoy only spent an average of ten minutes fucking the hell out of Clara whenever he got the chance—it just *seemed* like many blissful hours to her, in her semi-drugged state, still groggy from the effects of her spiked café latte. But LeRoy stayed erect for the entire ten minutes, coming almost continuously, in one long gush that leaked and spilled out of her vagina onto her thighs, staining the scarlet sheets, leaving behind a rich puddle of evidence for her to ponder the next morning when she awoke, wondering if it had all been a wonderful dream, lapping the leftover semen from the sheets and gargling it in her mouth before swallowing it, savoring the salivation of her own salvation.

Sometime Clara was still completely unconscious when LeRoy dropped her onto the plush scarlet bed in The Scarlet Room, but he'd soon arouse her with passionate penetration, and she'd often wake up coming. LeRoy always returned to the basement after no more than ten minutes, careful not to arouse the dwarf's jealous suspicion. Though Boris couldn't even imagine that Clara would ever willingly submit to the hideous brute's lust, much less that LeRoy would be bold enough to rape her, the dwarf eventually began to wonder why LeRoy was taking so long each time he took Clara upstairs. Since LeRoy was mute and could neither read nor write as a result of the dwarf's mindless experimentation on his magnificent body, he could not communicate anything to anyone, except in the universal language of sex. LeRoy pantomimed for Boris, explaining that he had been taking a dump in The Scarlet Room toilet all that time, even though the basement was equipped with its own filthy bathroom, which LeRoy was permitted to use only once daily. For lack of a more sensible, alternative alibi, Boris bought LeRoy's story. But LeRoy knew that he would not be able to hide his secret passion for Clara indefinitely.

Chained in the corner of the basement except when his nocturnal transport services were required, LeRoy was continually forced to watch Boris violate his beloved Clara, feasting on her flesh with his tongue and mouth and grubby little hands. But it was only when Boris decided to actually penetrate her sacred hole with his proportionally large, wart-covered penis that LeRoy became visibly enraged, yanking angrily at his chains as Boris succumbed to his own deepest, darkest desires, and ejaculated inside of Clara for the first time, while she was unconscious. Once he started, he could not possibly stop. He was addicted to her body.

"*I give you child, my love,*" Boris whispered huskily as he stretched enough to slobber on her breasts as he repeatedly thrust his grotesque penis inside of her unconscious vagina. "*I give you child that make you love me, love me, love me…*"

LeRoy's growing animosity towards his master was becoming palpable, but he refrained from outright rebellion, for fear of jeopardizing his own opportunities to make love to Clara. If only he could tell her what was *really* going on, but then perhaps she was better off not knowing.

Six months later, after being injected with the infected semen of both Boris and LeRoy many dozens of times, Clara indeed became pregnant. But by whom, she could only guess, and in her mind, the only possible candidate was LeRoy. She prayed she could carry his child to term. And Danny Falco no longer appealed to her. She didn't care what happened to him now. Or so she told herself. He was looking very pale and unattractively unhealthy recently, anyway.

Meanwhile, Danny had spent the past six months harboring Estrella Margarita Moreno—or as he called her, Maria—in The Purple Room, bringing her blood from a blood bank after bribing the nurses with charm and cash. They would both sit in The Purple Room on the bed, naked after another intense bout of lovemaking, sipping their packets of blood and watching vintage television shows and classic films, like an old married couple. They felt like they had created their own little salacious slice of perverse

Paradise on Earth. "Love me, love me, *love me*" Estrella cried as Danny made love to her with *Abbott and Costello Meet Frankenstein* or *The Honeymooners* playing in the background. Danny filled her with the semen that, together with the blood he bought, sustained them both. He no longer had enough of his own blood left to offer her—only his semen replenished itself, for a constant supply. Often she would French kiss Danny after giving him head, swallowing most of his seed, but sharing a little with him, too, so that he might also benefit from its magical properties. Danny felt odd, licking the taste of his essence off of his own lips, but it did add some spice to the blood. He feared what would happen if his source ever cut them off.

Naturally, Danny spent his nights working the front desk, and his days entombed in The Purple Room, all on Estrella's tab. He even gave up his apartment to move into the room with her, carefully hiding this fact from Clara. But Estrella was running out of funds, and Clara was growing increasingly suspicious about why she never saw the occupant of Room 001. However, she was distracted by her own sexual escapades and obsessions, and didn't pay much attention to the matter, ultimately oblivious to the coming and goings of both staff and guests, lost in her own private whirlpool of passion and now, impending motherhood. Life at L'Hotel du Frisson otherwise went on in normal fashion. Everyone seemed happy at last.

Everyone except Franklin DeWitt, that is, reduced to masturbating in the café bathroom now that all the rooms were booked, with Clara's clandestinely obtained shower shots from The Purple Room (where she resided before moving to The Scarlet Room) taped to the wall as he spit in his hand and massaged his member, fantasizing about propping Clara up on the sink beside him, hiking up her dress, and humping her till she wept with disgust and pleasure. "Love me…love me…*love me*," he whispered feverishly to himself, until he shot his wad and had to clean up the toilet and then his pants, waiting for the spots to dry before he could return to his post and waiting customers that in turn were impatient and infuriated by the fact no one was on duty to assist them. Franklin didn't care, and Clara seemed too distracted lately to notice or respond to the occasional complaints left in the guest book, which Franklin often edited, anyway.

Franklin bonded with Boris the bellhop because they were both social misfits obsessed with their boss. They would exchange disgusting scenarios involving the sexual degradation of Clara, except Boris was relating actual events, unbeknownst to Franklin, who was merely sharing his most lurid fantasies.

One day Boris decided he must kill Franklin, because he needed fresh meat for his experiments. His morgue connection had been arrested, so his supply of corpse parts had been cut off. Also, Boris, who had shared his Purple Room peephole with Franklin, was growing weary of Franklin describing his delusional yet despicable desecration of his beloved in such vivid detail. Plus, Franklin was so fat, his carcass would yield more flesh and organs than the usual emaciated cadaver to which Boris was accustomed.

"Would you like to come downstairs and look at my Playboy magazines?" Boris asked Franklin one day. "Very old, classics, from the nineteen sixties."

"When women had *real* boobs—like Clara!" Franklin said, wiping the sweat from his brow and loosening his tie.

"How you know they real?" asked Boris with furrowed brow.

"They are when I imagine them, and they *look* real enough," Franklin said. "Though she did used to be a stripper, I've heard, so maybe they're fake after all?"

"Not fake," Boris said emphatically.

"How do *you* know?"

"I see her in shower, yes?"

"Yea, me too. I guess you're right. They *do* look real."

"So you want to come down to my little room? It just, as you say, a 'hole in the wall,' but it is nice. Cozy. I bring us coffee from café, and pastries."

"Sure! I'm off soon. Danny's taking over at eleven."

"I'll come get you and lead you down there. It'll be fun! See you then!"

Later, in the basement, while Franklin was poring over Boris's collection of 1960s *Playboy* magazines, LeRoy snuck up from behind and strangled Franklin until he spit up his own guts, then placed his fat sweaty corpse on the table, where Boris stripped off his clothes and chopped him into many pieces with a hatchet, depositing the gory parts in the jars which Boris had emptied, feeding the old scraps to LeRoy. He even sliced some meat off of Franklin's corpulent torso for LeRoy to chew on. LeRoy appreciated the freshness of the blood as well as the flesh. The warmth and the taste reminded him of Clara, who had yet to inform Boris, or any of her employees, of her maternal condition. She was waiting until she could be positive this one would be carried to term, after the many heart-breaking failures. Meantime, the dwarf continued to drug and rape her, and LeRoy continued to make love to her upstairs in The Scarlet Room, until one night, she told LeRoy he was going to be a father, and he lay in her arms, weeping, and she held him like a baby.

"That does not mean we must stop making love," she said. "Feed me, feed our child, pour yourself inside of me, my love."

LeRoy fucked and wept, fucked and wept, as Clara cried and came, cried and came. He was happier than he could ever remember, though his life before the dwarf had mutated him with drugs was now only a distant echo in the murky catacombs of his damaged brain.

It was then, after this revelation, that LeRoy decided it was time to kill Boris, and then devour the remains, erasing all evidence of the dwarf's pathetic existence, shit him out, and flush him, like he had never been born. But he would discover that the essence of any life could not be destroyed.

THE HEP CATS

Two clairvoyant cats lived at L'Hotel du Frisson, for free. They were fed by staff and residents alike, and were quite personable and beloved by all. Their names were Pheromone and Endorphin. Pheromone was a beautiful female "torby"—a tortoiseshell/Tabby mix—and Endorphin was a handsome black Tabby male. Of the two, Pheromone was the more aggressive and emotional, whereas Endorphin was docile and reserved in temperament. Clara adopted them when their owners tragically died in one of the rooms after smuggling the two kittens inside, though pets were not normally permitted. It was an unsolved case involving two of the temporary tenants, a married couple, discovered dead after only a single night's stay, despite the fact they had paid ahead for a month. Some suspected it was an act of unbridled passion, and others claimed the couples' ghosts still haunted the hotel. Both claims were true.

Pheromone and Endorphin had free reign of the hotel and café. Unbeknownst to the humans who shared their space, the cats had the ability to read people's minds. They understood every word. They just pretended they didn't, because their stupid animal act got them room and board. They could also telepathically communicate with each other. Overall, they were appalled by the antics of their benefactors, but they put up with these severely flawed, inferior beings as long as their physical needs were met.

The cats also frightened off the aliens, who had been living secretly amongst mankind for centuries, infiltrating their oblivious ranks at all levels of society, plotting their eventual hostile takeover. They strategically mated with Earth's women, propagating their own kind, or at least hybrids that could blend in even easier with the pitifully ignorant population. The aliens assumed very handsome male bodies and since they already possessed superior intellects, took high-paying jobs that would attract the most desirable women for their nefarious purposes. The cats were hep to all of this, and the aliens knew they were hep, so when one of the aliens checked into L'Hotel du Frisson one afternoon, the cats hissed at him, and he hissed right back. For years his Earth name had been Ramon Navarro, and he played the role of a wealthy Spanish playboy. He was looking for Estrella Margarita Moreno, with whom he had an affair, many years before. Neither had aged since then, so he knew he'd recognize her if he saw her. His alien sources had informed him that she was here at L'Hotel du Frisson. His mission was to destroy her, since supernatural beings were harder to control than normal humans. Or that's what he told his superiors. The cats were hep to his agenda, and went to tip her off.

Wishing to remain anonymous and disguise his presence in the hotel, the alien checked in under the name "Paul Birch." He wore a dark suit and a dark fedora and a dark tie and dark sunglasses, but was otherwise inconspicuous. Except to the cats, who scratched on Estrella's door until she let them inside.

She could tell from the felines' expressions that danger was lurking, once again. Danny was in bed, not feeling well. He needed to feed.

Estrella thanked the cats, then followed them to "Paul Birch's" room. She knocked on the door, and when he answered, pretending to be happily surprised at the "coincidence," she attacked him. The cats followed her inside the room, and transformed into panthers, one black and one spotted, joining the assault.

The alien didn't have a chance. He didn't even have the opportunity to scream.

While the alien was lying near death, bleeding green blood onto the carpet—which was fine, actually, since he was in The Green Room—Estrella massaged his penis, made it erect, then climbed on top of him and rode him until he came inside of her. Despite his pain, Paul Birch was helplessly stimulated by the sight of her perfectly formed naked breasts in such proximity to his human face. While inhabiting this body, he was susceptible to its basest desires. However, his alien fluids still ran through the veins of his assumed identity, so he gushed a gallon of green fluid into Estrella's vampiric vagina. She then licked some of his green blood and held it in her mouth until she returned to Danny, where she French kissed him, sharing the alien substance with his mouth, infusing it into his emaciated form. Then she laid spread eagle on the bed while he licked and swallowed the alien's green semen from her undead pussy. He was feeling much better afterward, refreshed and invigorated. The alien fluids were even more beneficial than those from a human.

"Whose blood is this?" Danny asked as he face was buried in her muff.

"It's not blood, it's semen," Estrella replied, "from an alien I used to make love with, a long time ago."

"That's pretty old semen," Danny said. "Is it still, y'know, *good*?"

"I just fucked him a few minutes ago, so it's fresh," Estrella said. "*Before* I killed him, that is. Or maybe it was after. It's all a blur already."

Danny lifted his head. "So why was he even *here*?"

"He's not anymore, that's all that matters," she said. "He came to reclaim me, I suppose. He's been following me, *stalking* me, for many years. I don't know how he found me, but it doesn't matter now."

"Would he have hurt you?"

"No; he loved me, at least in his human form. But enslaving me would have been a kind of death. He wanted to take me back to his planet, forever."

"Fuck that," Danny said, continuing to lap the substance oozing from her lips. Danny was so turned on while performing this nutritional fellatio that he had an orgasm simultaneously with Estrella.

"This will give you everlasting life," Estrella said.

"I thought I was *already* immortal, thanks to you?" Danny said.

"Yes, but you could be killed much easier. Now your powers are almost boundless."

"Is that how you came back from the dust?" he asked.

"The dwarf's semen was enough to revive me from the ashes, but I too am empowered with this alien's blood, from when we were lovers before. That was his power over me. He was a dealer, and I was a junkie. That's how love often works, anyway."

"If he could offer you so much, why did you leave?"

"I did not love him in return. Unrequited love is a tragic waste of energy. He got what he deserved." Estrella then kissed Danny, licking the sticky residue of her own vaginal juices mixed with the alien semen from his lips, told him she'd be right back, and returned to The Green Room to join the cats in devouring the remains of the alien. She ate the bones after they'd been licked clean by the panthers, which then reverted to domestic cats, and returned to their posts in the café, as the silent, secretly savage sentries of L'Hotel du Frisson.

THE MAN IN THE WHEELCHAIR

The man in the wheelchair was very wealthy but unable to have sex due to his disability, so he paid other men to have sex with his young, beautiful wife while he watched. He wasn't even able to achieve orgasm because of the spinal injury that had left him paralyzed from the waist down. But he had been suffering this indignant misfortune since age twenty-four, after recklessly driving drunk. Fortunately, he was heir to a massive fortune and did not have to work for a living, so his handicap did not affect his economic status. Since he had no physical prowess, his original dreams of becoming a football player were out. But he did purchase a professional team. In fact, the star quarterback was named LeRoy Johnston, whose career suddenly ended after a steroid scandal. The man in the wheelchair was named David Stern, now sixty-two years old. His wife was named Daphne D'amato. She was twenty-five, with long legs and round hips and small perky breasts and the sculpted perfect face of a demonic angel. She was an aspiring actress and model. But for now, she was getting by as a hooker for hire, pimped out by her own husband. It was all part of her plan. Unfortunately, David knew exactly what that plan was. But he didn't let it bother him.

The couple checked into L'Hotel du Frisson intending to set up a temporary fuckpad, bringing men back to the room to defile Daphne while David wept in the corner. They also brought with them Daphne's two new kittens, named Bella and Benjamin, who would later be renamed Pheromone and Endorphin. The cats didn't care what humans called them. They saw Life as merely a liquid illusion through which they swam.

Their spirits were eternal, and they recognized their bodies as mere temporary confinements. However, their feline nature extended to their souls, and their temporal bodies were manifestations of their true forms, the size and shape of which they could adjust at will. The kittens watched the erotic escapades of their caretakers with detached bemusement, especially since both had been fixed at three months of age. For them, physical pleasure was the main benefit of the corporeal form, to be relished, which is why they luxuriated in their own primal playfulness. They figured the humans were doing the same, except for the man in the wheelchair. Both kittens often sat in his lap and consoled him with purring love and sympathetic nudging. Except, of course, when he watching his wife being fucked by two or more men, and sometimes women. Then his physical and emotional intensity made his lap a most inhospitable place, like sitting on a volcano that could not erupt, despite its pent up fury, because its point of release had been permanently blocked. During these sessions, the kittens hid under the rocking bed until it was all over.

David Stern hired men to fuck his wife for a twofold purpose, both of which he considered altruistic, with Daphne's best interests in mind. One reason, he rationalized, was that he hoped these perverse scenes would result in his libido being psychologically and vicariously stimulated to the point where his penis would regain full function. The other rationale was that his wife could experience the sensual pleasures he was unable to offer her. Daphne had no problems with this unscientific experimental voyeurism. She was on the pill and refused to let the men wear condoms. She loved the sensation and scent of semen flooding her every orifice, and she also loved the soft, warm touch of feminine flesh, so she figured she was getting the better end of the bargain. She also loved David, as a father figure, and initially worried about his potential jealousy interfering with her own enjoyment of these experiments, but ultimately she was able to ignore his tears in favor of her own orgasmic releases, which were legion, induced by multitudes of strangers, different ones, night after night. Her husband even wrote about some of the more eventful evenings for Penthouse Forum. She felt like a star.

On their initial night in L'Hotel du Frisson, David had his ex-star quarterback LeRoy Johnston check into an adjoining room, inviting some of his former teammates over. David had a proposition for him.

"I want you to fuck my wife while I watch," David said to LeRoy in The Black Velvet Room.

"I can't do that, sir," LeRoy said, as Daphne lay sprawled on the bed in her black silk nightgown. She kicked off her high heels and peeled off her stockings as LeRoy and his two teammates watched.

"I can," said one of his teammates, named Edwin.

"Me, too," said the other teammate, Dwayne. Both were big, black and beautiful and Daphne was more than ready to rock and roll.

"I will pay you," David said. "More than your present salary. Five thousand dollars. Cash. Each. For each time my wife comes. And if I come, even once, I'll give you each an additional ten thousand dollar bonus. In any case, if any of you ever tell anyone of this, I will have you all killed."

"My lips are sealed," said a drooling Edwin.

"Meow," said the cats in unison.

"I have too much respect for you, sir," LeRoy said.

"If you respect me, fuck my wife," David said. "Because obviously, I cannot."

"I won't do it."

"Fine, then maybe your teammates will," said David with exasperation.

They all watched as Daphne stripped off her nightgown and writhed seductively on the bed, moaning and masturbating. David hit the "play" button on the CD player, and "This Corrosion" by Sisters of Mercy began to blare. It was their favorite music.

Next door, The Mantis Man beat on the wall, screaming for them to turn the music down. Whenever *any* guests played loud music in the hotel, it was *always* the same tune. It had become the theme song for L'Hotel du Frisson.

Finally, Dwayne and Edwin took off their clothes and climbed into bed with Daphne. Within minutes, all three had come several thousand dollars worth. LeRoy just watched, refusing to participate, despite his arousal.

David got an erection, stroked his improbable hard-on, and came in a gush, a back-load large enough to fill a bucket. It was the miracle he had prayed for over these many years. He sobbed as he came, leaking profusely from both heads. Then, after the last drop dripped from his cock, he died instantly of a heart attack. His body was simply unable to handle the sudden shock.

Meanwhile, oblivious to the effect the wild sex was having on her husband, Daphne literally choked to death on Dwayne's enormous cock, her throat already clogged with both the men's semen, and she died almost simultaneously with David.

All three gridiron giants screamed at once.

Sirens wailed in the distance, a common ambient sound in this dirty town. The Mantis Man, in the room next door, had already called the police. Because of the music, not the screaming.

LeRoy could not move, paralyzed by the horror of what had happened.

Edwin and Darwin ran out of the room. The desk clerk at the time was Franklin DeWitt, who was not at his post since he was masturbating in the bathroom, so no one saw Edwin and Dwayne exit, just as the cops pulled up front. The two running backs evaded detection and capture, escaping into the darkness.

Boris the bellhop emerged from his basement when he heard the sirens. The cats led him to the scene of the crime, which was wet with blood and semen, making a striking contrast against all the black velvet. Since the cops were already swarming the lobby, The Mantis Man ready to lead them upstairs, Boris offered LeRoy asylum in his basement sanctuary. Already fatally traumatized by this series of terrible events, LeRoy panicked and accepted the offer, following the dwarf down the secret elevator, never to be seen nor heard from again by the outside world.

The popular theory, perpetuated by the lazy media and law enforcement officials quick to blame any violent crime on a minority, particularly a high profile offense like this, was that LeRoy Johnston, whose name was indeed on the hotel registry, had disappeared after killing David Stern and brutally raping and killing his wife Daphne D'amato. But the cats knew differently. They just weren't talking. Not in a language the cops could understand, anyway. Nor could anyone hear the tormented wailing of the damned ghosts of David, finally freed from his wheelchair, and Daphne, who haunted the hotel for the remainder of its existence. Ironically, the cats, which did not differentiate between the corporeal and spiritual realms, were their only terrestrial connections.

FREAKS THAT CARRY YOUR LUGGAGE UP TO THE ROOM

THE MIDNITE SUN NEVER SETS

The atomic swing of Count Basie, circa his "New Testament" era, righteously resounded in Café du Frisson throughout the wee hours. "Lil' Darlin'" played as the employees, Juan and Carlos, wiped down the counter, pretending to look busy. Dick Reid the desk clerk was watching Japanese porn on his smartphone, though he never masturbated, always saving his boner for whatever Japanese girl he was dating at the moment. Meantime, a homeless teenage girl was sitting on the sidewalk outside in the rain, longingly peering into the sleekly stylish, brightly lit Space Age sanctuary of the café, her stomach grumbling with acidic emptiness. Her name was Lila, no last name at present, and she was a werewolf, a *hungry* one. She was shivering in the cold like a lost puppy, her tears indistinguishable from the raindrops dripping down her filthy, but pretty, face.

Lila was only eighteen years old, but she had been on her own for two years already, after running away from a foster home, where she'd been beaten and abused. They were all dead now, though. Figuring she'd be better off on her own, she hit the streets, and got by with petty crimes and some sexual hustling, both male and female, whoever would pay her for sex. She wanted to change careers, and was hoping she could get a job in the café. But she was a mess, convinced that no one would hire her in her current state. She needed a bath and a change of clothes. Someone needed to take pity on her, and that someone was The Mantis Man, the café's lone customer, who was watching her from his seat inside. When he went outside to smoke a cigarette, he asked her to come to his room, where he bathed and fed her, both by hand.

"What would you like in return for your kindness?" she asked him coyly as she leaned back on his bed, wearing only a hotel towel, luxuriating in the sudden comfort, her reddish blonde hair billowing across the pillows.

"I want you to kill someone," The Mantis Man said.

"Who?" she asked him, without batting an eye.

"He lives here in the hotel. He's a desk clerk. He calls himself Danny, though that is not his real name."

"Why do you want to kill him?" she asked, opening her legs so he could see her vagina.

"Because he broke my daughter's heart, and she killed herself as a result. She was only your age, too. You remind me of her."

"Does that mean you don't want to fuck me?"

"No. You can blow me, though. I won't mind."

Lila removed her towel and The Mantis Man sat on the bed and unzipped his trousers. She took his long, pale, veiny cock into her mouth and sucked it hard. He came in her mouth a minute later.

"Thanks," he said, standing straight up and zipping his pants back up.

Lila swallowed The Mantis Man's load of semen in one gulp, making her eyes tear as she gagged. "You didn't seem to like it very much," she said sadly.

"No, it was fine. I just wanted to test you, anyway. The best way to get to this person is to seduce him. I want you to bite off his cock, and bring it to me."

"My teeth aren't sharp enough," she smiled wryly.

"Yes they are," he said, rubbing his crotch.

Her yellow eyes danced with devilish delight. "Can I stay here if I kill him?"

"No."

She pouted. "But I have no place to go."

"I don't take in strays. Against house rules."

"But I'll suck you anytime you want."

"No dice."

"Then I won't kill the desk clerk."

"Then get the fuck out. I have no further use for you."

"You are a sad, bad man."

"So what?"

Lila lay back and stretched seductively, nude and nubile. The Mantis Man was not aroused, because he'd already climaxed. He knew he wanted to get that out of the way, so he was no longer distracted from his homicidal scheming. The little slut was the ideal assassin, he figured. As long as she agreed to the plan.

"Okay, I'll kill him if I can spend the night at least," she said.

"Fine. You can sleep on the floor."

"Wow, you are *such* an asshole. How did you get so mean?"

"Practice."

"When do you want me to kill him?" she asked.

"Sooner the better. He's on duty at midnight. Maybe you can just get it over with now."

"It would better if I wait a couple of days," she said. "When the moon is full."

"What the fuck are you, a werewolf?"

"Yes," she said with a giggle.

The Mantis Man's eyes lit up at last. "Well…that's even better. You'll have to get him alone just before you change, though."

"I can arrange that." She hadn't expected him to believe her, but then she didn't realize he was a voodoo priest, and quite familiar with the supernatural underground.

"Maybe I'll ask him to come up here, to fix something, only I'll tell him I'm going out, so he needs to do it while I'm gone."

"Okay," she said. "Then I'll seduce and kill him."

"Bite his cock off first," he said. "If his cock is lying on the bed when I return to the room, I'll let you stay a week."

"Can I sleep on the bed?"

"Yes."

"Okay, deal. But tonight I get the floor?"

"Yes."

"All right. Good night."

"Good night."

"What is your name, anyway?"

"None of your goddamn business."

"Mine's Lila."

"I don't give a shit."

She curled up at the bottom of the bed. He took off his clothes and climbed beneath the covers. He pretended to snore, but that was only to drown out the sounds of her soft sobbing.

Two nights later, The Mantis Man walked by the front desk and asked Danny to fix the leaky faucet in his room. It was dusk, and Danny was working a double shift, covering for the missing Franklin DeWitt, so The Mantis Man got lucky.

Danny went to the room, opened the door, and turned on the light. Lila was laying spread eagle naked on the bed. Danny got a boner, took off his clothes and fucked her. Lila had lied about the full moon. She only turned into a werewolf when sexually aroused. She'd learned this when her foster father continually raped her. Normally she was too filled with disgust to respond pleasurably, but the one time he ate her pussy till she finally came, for the very first time, she made the change, and violently wiped out the whole family, much to her satisfaction. She'd inherited the lycanthropy from her unknown father. The hereditary condition was only, and always, triggered by hormonal stimulation. Whenever she had an orgasm, she turned into a werewolf. As a street whore, she killed most of her johns (and janes) and took their money. That's what she'd been planning to do to The Mantis Man, except he'd refused to fuck her, a circumstance she was not used to. She only made the change when she had her *own* orgasm, which she found she was unable to achieve via masturbation. She always needed another body to make it happen.

Handsome, virile Danny made her come right away, after only a few thrusts of his experienced cock. She was a very sexy werewolf, retaining her voluptuous human contours, but covered from head to toe in smooth reddish brown fur, same hue as her human hair. Her drooling fangs were quite sharp, however. But she didn't bite off his penis. It was much more useful to her attached to his body.

Accustomed now to mating with monsters, an unfazed Danny just flipped her over and finished fucking her doggy style, in her pussy and then up her heart-shaped hirsute ass, and they both came in howling unison. Then he casually took a shower and returned to his post. He never even checked the faucet, which wasn't leaking anyway.

When The Mantis Man got back to his room, Lila the werewolf attacked him, but The Mantis Man, ever paranoid, was ready. He stabbed her with a silver pocketknife, and she collapsed on the floor in a pool of blood, whimpering as the life drained out of her, reverting to her human form.

"Goddamn Danny Falco," he muttered. Then The Mantis Man called Boris the bellhop to come collect the garbage, wrapped in a blanket, sitting just outside his door. This was a common practice, and no questions were ever asked. The Mantis Man always left a generous tip with his garbage, even though Boris helped himself to The Mantis Man's secret stash of cash anyway.

He'd lied to Lila, too. It wasn't his daughter who killed herself. It was his "wife," or at least the woman he imagined to be his wife, even though he'd only seen her once while she was alive, on a train to New Orleans, from afar, and their eyes locked for one brief, intense moment; but he never even got the chance to speak with her, since immediately afterward she hung herself in her private compartment for reasons never explained, at least publicly. The Mantis Man's obsession with this beautiful stranger lead him to rob her grave near the French Quarter and cut off her head, so he'd have some memento of the single glance they exchanged in the dining car that day. His entire life with her had been a fantasy in his fevered brain.

The Mantis Man lovingly contemplated the shrunken head of his long dead love, hanging in the closet with all the other shrunken heads, which he kept as souvenirs of other encounters throughout his long, lonesome life, of both an amorous and a hostile nature.

Then The Mantis Man sat down in his easy chair and placed the shrunken head of his dead love, whom he referred to as his "wife," at least to himself, in the crotch of his pants, and wept with longing and loneliness and the lingering sense of lost opportunity, verbally vowing to one day destroy Danny Falco, who had never even met his late wife, was probably not even born when she died. The Mantis Man bobbed the shrunken head on his penis until he came in its mouth. He let it dry. It was already sticky from many layers of his semen. He was glad he had killed Lila. That was his way of atoning for his unfaithfulness. Now he had to find another way to kill Danny, his wife's alleged lover and killer, at least in his stubbornly delusional mind.

Boris sent LeRoy up to the room to carry Lila's naked human form, wrapped in the bloody bedspread, back down to the basement. The dwarf figured he could use her parts for experiments, after he violated them, of course. Unfortunately for Boris, Lila wasn't entirely dead, only wounded by the cheap knife, since it wasn't made of *real* silver, like the street merchant had told The Mantis Man. He'd been gypped. While strapped to the table, naked and unconscious as the dwarf furiously fucked her with his abnormally large, wart-covered penis till she came, Lila suddenly regained consciousness mid-orgasm and turned back into a werewolf, breaking the straps, growling menacingly at the dwarf and the albino giant.

"I thought you are dead!" Boris exclaimed defensively. "I only make love to corpses, I am so sorry! Well, except for Clara…but she is my *love*." It was like trying to negotiate with a rabid dog.

Boris tried to cover Lila's drooling fanged mouth with a drugged cloth, but it was too late. Lila was now completely a werewolf, incapable of human speech, so a conversation was not forthcoming. The dwarf screamed and LeRoy obediently responded.

She fought LeRoy viciously, wrecking the basement lab, test tubes full of useless but combustible chemicals crashing to the floor, creating small fires which the dwarf put out with an extinguisher as the battle continued around him, snarling and roaring and tearing and biting, equipment being smashed, but eventually the brute overpowered the she-wolf, strangling her into unconsciousness. LeRoy then tossed her limp form over his shoulder and threw her in a cage in the corner.

"We have a new pet now, LeRoy," Boris said, locking the cage as Lila growled and banged against the rusty bars.

LeRoy grunted impassively, looking forward to his date with Clara later that week, wondering if this unwelcome guest would interrupt the usual abduction-and-seduction schedule. Boris surveyed the mess, then instructed LeRoy to clean it up.

Upstairs, feeling like a caged animal herself, Estrella was pacing the floor of The Purple Room. She called Danny at the front desk, her fingers shaking as she dialed, her voice trembling with undead Latina fury

"Where were you when I called earlier?" she demanded.

"Fixing a faucet," he lied dryly.

"You better be telling me the truth," she hissed.

"I am."

"Fuck me on your break?"

"You bet."

Then he went to the bathroom and threw up buckets of green blood. He'd been suffering stomach cramps ever since Estrella had fed him alien juices from her pussy. He also felt the claw marks on his back, wondering how he'd explain them to Estrella. Then he noticed the bloody hickey.

Count Basie's celestial orchestra continued to play blissfully and obliviously as Danny continued to vomit, filled with fear of his own fading future.

BLOOD-SPLATTERED BREASTS

Lila picked the lock and escaped from her cage in the basement lab one day when Boris was on duty and LeRoy was up in The Scarlet Velvet room, nursing the pregnant Clara, who lived on room service, though LeRoy kept his presence hidden. Juan and Carlos left platters of food from the café on her doorstep. Clara rarely left the room now, leaving Danny in charge, but he wasn't really feeling up to the task. His skin was ashen and his eyes were sunken and his stomach was growling, and the illicit blood bank withdrawals weren't satisfying his craving. He ate Estrella's pussy until it was raw, and bit her flesh viciously, which turned her on, but still, he remained oddly ungratified. A crucial ingredient was missing from his diet, and he felt himself slowly slipping away.

When Lila escaped the basement, she snuck into The Purple Room, again picking the lock, a skill she had picked up living on the streets, after no one answered when she knocked on the door. Estrella greeted her warmly. The two were immediately attracted to one another and began making love. Lila turned into a werewolf as Estrella ate her pussy, and then they bit and clawed each other with wild, animalistic passion, their beautiful breasts covered in each other's blood, which they licked and sucked sensitive body parts, screaming with mutual pleasure, turning up "Gimme Shelter" very loud to drown out the sounds of their frenetic fornication. After her fifteen orgasm, Estrella offered Lila permanent asylum in the The Purple Room, and they became lovers, allowing the decomposing Danny in their bed, after he returned from his shift that morning, and joined the monstrous *ménage au trios*.

"Now we're even," Estrella said later, as Lila slept peacefully between them, bits of Danny's decomposing cock stuck to the lips of her swollen vagina, which was also sticky with the blood oozing from puncture wounds left by Estrella. "She's *both* of our bitch now."

"Okay," said Danny, wheezing slightly after the physical exertion.

"Things will be better now. We are a family."

During the day, they all cuddled beneath the bed. When Danny awoke, he felt like he had a hangover, and he looked awful.

"What is happening to me?" Danny asked Estrella as he dressed for his shift the following evening. "*You* did this to me!"

"Your body was still trying to process the alien *and* the vampire blood," Estrella said professorially. "When you suddenly added werewolf blood to the mix, your immune system broke down, and now it's *all* fucked up. The alchemy has been irreversibly corrupted."

"Why didn't you fucking *tell* me that!" Danny cried.

"*Because I didn't think you'd be fucking a werewolf, at least not so soon after your exposure*!" Estrella screamed as Lila sat back and smiled. "You did this to *yourself*, Danny, you vain, unfaithful fool. Now you're becoming something *else*. Not a werewolf. Not a vampire. Not an alien. Certainly not *human*."

"So if I'm not a werewolf, or a vampire, *or* an alien, what the hell *am* I?"

"A zombie," Estrella said, embracing Lila in the crook of her arm. They both laughed, then French kissed and made love as Danny stared at his deteriorating visage in the mirror, his stomach growling as his hunger grew. Not for blood. For flesh.

"We must go out and hunt human food now," Estrella said to him as he returned to the bathroom, straightening his tie and picking bits of rotten flesh from his face, dropping them in the sink, then flushing them down the drain.

"Fuck that," Danny said. "I couldn't even drink blood, at least unless it was from the blood bank. I can't *kill* people. It's not in my nature."

"Not yet," Estrella said. "Your nature is not what it used to be."

"*Please*, Maria."

"Don't call me Maria. Call me Estrella. Maria is *dead*. Estrella is eternal, and now, so are *you*, my love…"

Even though he was turning into a zombie, Danny had never been more sexually satisfied. He felt emotionally torn, but that was better than feeling completely empty, which was how he had spent most of his useless, transitory life, now fading from his zombified memory. Estrella gave him a reason to live, to die, and then to live again.

But Estrella had been growing increasingly distant lately, and Danny noticed. He assumed it was due to his rapidly deteriorating appearance. His vanity had suffered a crucial blow. He'd taken to wearing makeup to cover the decay, but it was becoming so severe that customers were noticing, and recoiling with revulsion. It was a good thing Clara was bed-ridden with a mysterious malady, the nature of which she refused to share with the staff. It was basically Danny's hotel now, even though he was literally falling apart. Danny in turn tapped Dick Reid as General Manager, and Dick agreed as long as he likewise got his own room. Not surprisingly, he chose The Yellow Room, which meant the traveling salesman who normally preferred that room was shit out of luck. Dick used the room as his own private fuckpad, tying up and sexually torturing his Japanese dates, that tied up and tortured him right back. Despite her lack of experience, and at Estrella's request, Lila was also hired as a full time desk clerk. Danny exclusively worked graveyard shifts now, befitting his zombie status. During the day, the vampire, werewolf and zombie fucked, and fucked some more. But they were all growing very hungry.

"If we do not feed soon, we will die," Estrella announced. This preoccupation was the reason she hadn't been as affectionate as usual. "We must go out into the night, and hunt. Or you can *bring* us customers, Danny."

"I'll check people into this room during my shift," Danny said. "But they'll check out the hard way."

"That sounds fine," Estrella said. "I will kill them, then drink the blood and semen, while you and Lila can devour the flesh and bones, which I've never enjoyed. That way there will be no evidence, and you will not have to kill anyone yourself."

"Okay," said Danny. "But word might get out eventually, to the wrong people."

"You must destroy all records of any of our victims checking in here. Be selective. We can make one body last a week, if we have to."

"Depending on what we use it for," Danny pointed out. "Y'know, this isn't how I saw my life turning out. *Or* my death."

"Welcome to my world," Estrella said.

THE THING FROM THE WOMB

Nine months after having sex with both the albino mutant giant and the hideous dwarf—the latter unwittingly—Clara gave birth to a malformed monstrosity, equally composed of LeRoy and Boris's damaged genes. It was pale and sickly and covered in warts and completely hairless, whining and shrieking with the agony of new life in a horribly disfigured form. But Clara *loved* her baby. The doctors at the hospital were mortified, figuring this ghastly, pathetic little thing was the product of severe drug addiction or some other hereditary horrors that had gone undiagnosed. After a few days in the hospital, Clara took her infant mutation home to L'Hotel du Frisson. She named him Tobias, but just called him Toby. It had been her father's name.

A few days later, a weary, weakened Clara died in The Scarlet Room. Her body had been fatally ravaged by the incubation of this creature. But passed away peacefully in her sleep as the baby also slept silently on the bed beside her and LeRoy, whom she presumed was the one and only father.

Before Boris could discover the tragedy, LeRoy took the infant down to The Purple Room. He knocked politely on the door. Lila answered, wearing a lavender see-through negligee. She recognized LeRoy and growled, but he merely handed her the infant, and walked away. He went back to The Scarlet Room, made love to Clara's corpse one last time, tore her from limb to limb, and devoured her raw, bone and flesh, so no trace of her bodily presence remained. Clara became just another spirit haunting L'Hotel du Frisson. Now free to wander the rooms and corridors with ghostly grace, Clara was shocked but not surprised to find out what was *really* going on behind all those closed doors.

Estrella and Lila raised Toby as their own, while Danny, a hybrid of viral horrors, continued to rot, and Clara wistfully watched from beyond the grave, secure in the knowledge her baby had found a good home.

A grief-stricken LeRoy went down to the basement, picked a startled Boris up by the neck, strangled him, then ate his remains, except for his head, which he put in a sack.

Then he returned upstairs, knocked on the door of The Purple Room, and showed the head to Danny. It was his way of asking for a job. Estrella insisted that LeRoy be hired, as a reward for bringing them Toby.

"Fine, you're hired, I never liked that little creep anyway," said Danny, looking better now after a few weeks of feasting on unfortunate patrons, shared with his female roommates. "But in addition to being a bellhop, you'll need to go out into the night and bring us back people to eat. I want you to pick out the scum of society—criminals, especially those that live in nice neighborhoods. Also vagrants, thieves, murderers. Bring them back here, to this room, unconscious but alive. I will cover for you during my shifts. Can you do that, LeRoy?"

LeRoy nodded and grunted.

"Here," Danny said, handing him back the sack with Boris's head.

LeRoy knew just what to do with it, too. He went up to The Mantis Man's room, knocked on the door, and presented it to him.

The Mantis Man did not recognize LeRoy, but took the bag anyway, and peeked inside. "Thanks," he said. He then performed a quick ceremony in his room, shrunk the dwarf's already small head, and hung in it his closet.

"That's for stealing my money, asshole," The Mantis Man said as he closed the closet door, leaving Boris's shrunken head in darkness, alongside the rest.

When LeRoy attempted to leave the grounds to scout for involuntary human sacrifices as directed, his body was suddenly wracked with unbearable agony, and he was forced to return to the sanctuary of the hotel. The same phenomenon began to affect the other monsters as well. This strange, inexplicable fact limited their food supply to guests alone. Their food would have to come to *them*. Another plan would have to be developed eventually, or they might all ultimately starve, Estrella feared.

Months passed, and Toby was growing abnormally fast into an exceptionally ugly little boy: quite corpulent, his folds of pinkish flesh covered in boils and warts and acne; one eye bulging out of his misshapen head, while the other was welded shut by pustules; his yellow teeth crooked or missing; his dark hair sparse and stringy; but he was surrounded by love, so he was happy, watching Betty Boop cartoons in The Purple Room night and day. His caretakers—Estrella, Lila, and Danny—could not die, unlike his true, unknown mother on the other side of the Void. They envied one another, as the endless cycle of sex and death continued.

Will Viharo

ORGY OF THE UNDEAD

The older man, named Elias, nearly seventy but quite virile with a full head of curly graying hair, removed the beautiful young woman's high heel shoes and licked her red-painted toes and inhaled the scent of her perfumed feet, pressing them against his face, his penis growing erect. He then grabbed her and licked her face and neck, salivating on her smooth, olive-hued flesh. The young woman reluctantly responded, repulsed as she was, kissing his mouth and chest and arms as he unzipped his pants. Next he shoved her head into his crotch as he sat on the edge of the bed, and she took his throbbing penis in her mouth and sucked it till it was very hard, jism and saliva dripping from her lips and down her chin, kissing and licking and sucking his balls as he closed his eyes and moaned with ecstasy. He slowly removed his shirt as she sucked him, stroking her pointy firm banana-shaped breasts, squeezing her hard nipples; then he gently lifted her head by her tousled, dark brown, wavy hair, kissed her mouth with his jism on her lips, then laid her back and took off her panties and ate her delicious pussy as she moaned loudly and got very wet, her juices dripping down his chin. He loved how she tasted as he stuck his tongue deep in her pussy and licked her clitoris, and she writhed with pleasure, chewing on her own fingers. Then she sat up a little and wriggled off her dress and he sucked her tits as he fingered her and she bucked some more as she came. Then she hungrily sucked his cock again as he fondled her breasts and kissed her neck and back. He couldn't hold it any longer and he came with a gush down her throat and even though she didn't normally swallow, she did, delirious with unbridled lust, and then she sucked him hard again and mounted him and rode him until she came screaming as he sucked her tits and they French kissed, drunk on disgust and desire. He laid her on her back and fucked her till she bucked and came again, shooting a bucket of jism deep inside her pussy. He had never come so much and so hard.

Then the younger man, a swarthy body builder nicknamed Cody, pulled him off and ate the cum from her wet pussy and she came again as the younger man massaged her tits then climbed on top of her, kissing her throat and face, and she sucked on his muscular arms, and he fucked her hard till he shot a huge load inside of her, and she came yet again, with her legs wrapped around his muscular torso, the older man kissing and licking and smelling her feet. Her pussy was sore and wet and dripping semen as they both kissed her whole body, absorbed in her scent and sweat, then they made a sandwich as she lay on top of the younger man and inserted his huge cock into her pussy as the older man mounted from behind and slid his medium cock into her heart-shaped ass, and she came multiple times as they both came inside of her pussy and ass, and the semen dripped down her thighs and soaked the sheets. Then she sucked the younger man's cock as she felt his muscular arms and chest and he came again in her mouth. She was full of semen, dripping from both ends, and she craved more. They took a short break, smoked and drank and then fucked some more. Afterwards she lay spread eagle nude on the bed, smoking a cigarette, soaked in semen, inside and out, as they kissed her beautiful feet.

Then the young woman, named Adele, told the men she had to clean the room now, after she cleaned herself, so it was time for them to go. She was the head maid for L'Hotel du Frisson.

However, she didn't mean it was time for them to leave the Ivory Silk Room, which was indeed an ungodly mess by now. It was time for them to leave the Earth. She'd had her fun, and now she had to get back to work. But first, she had to finish soiling the room.

There was a knock on the door, and to the men's embarrassed surprise, Adele got up to answer, still completely nude, stopping only to crank up the volume of "Gimme Shelter," playing loudly in a loop on the CD player atop the dresser. It was Estrella. The two kissed each other on the lips, and the men grinned with carnal approval. Estrella closed the door with a sly smile, stripped off her own dress and high heels, and then each of the women began sucking each of the men's sore cocks until they were hard again. Suddenly the women sunk their fangs deep into the men's cocks just as they were ejaculating, hungrily swallowing the nutritious mixture of blood and semen. The men passed out after their cocks and balls were literally torn out of their groins and spit out onto the white carpet, which would require industrial strength bleach.

Estrella had left LeRoy behind in The Purple Room to baby-sit little Toby, the mutant offspring of the late Clara Cleaver, who nonetheless watched over her child in celestial form from beyond the grave. That left Danny and Lila free to join the party. After the two men had been castrated via fellatio, Danny and Lila quietly entered the room and ate the penises and testicles off the carpet like they were appetizers as they patiently waited for Adele and Estrella to finish draining the bodies of blood. While they waited, lying nude on the floor, Danny ate Lila's pussy, her thighs tightly squeezed around his badly decomposed face, till she came and turned into a werewolf. Danny picked one of his teeth out of her hairy vagina and tossed it into the wastebasket. "There goes another one," he said wistfully, before Lila the werewolf kissed him on the mouth, biting his thin cold lips and licking his gums, now soaked in his own blood as well as her vaginal juices, both of which dripped down his rotting chin.

Once Adele and Estrella had their fill of fluids, Danny and Lila devoured the flesh and bones, so there was nothing left of the two hotel guests—father and son, owners of a nearby strip club that served as a front for a drug-and-prostitution racket. They thought that Adele had lured them to L'Hotel du Frisson so she could "audition," not to fuck then suck them dry so the resident zombie and werewolf could feast on their remains.

Oh well.

Adele, back in her standard issue maid's uniform, then went to the front desk and told Dick Reid, in her phony Spanish accent (she was actually half Portuguese and half Arabian), "Room 205? Is *cleeeeeean*!"

"Good," said Dick without even looking up. Adele was hot, but not Japanese, so not his type.

"You're lucky to be alive, asshole," she whispered as she disappeared into the night. She loved her job, especially since her promotion.

WILL VIHARO

THE DEMONIC DUO

Dick Reid, wearing nothing but black socks, was in The Yellow Room, tied to the bed as a gorgeous young Japanese dominatrix with long, silky black air, perky breasts, a thin waist, round hips and ample thighs, wearing nothing but leather boots, lashed him with a whip, "This Corrosion" blaring on the CD player, obscuring his screams of painful pleasure. The woman's named was Kiko. Dick had picked her up in a local tiki bar. She was visiting from Japan, and Dick, who was fluent in her language, charmed her with his knowledge of her culture. Dick had been an Army brat, raised in Japan, beaten by his father on a regular basis. Dick's father had died in the gas chamber for killing his mother after he caught her in bed with another woman, when Dick was twelve. Dick was then raised by his father's Japanese housekeeper, Aimi, who took Dick's virginity when he was only fourteen. Ashamed of deflowering a minor, even though she justified it as an act of pity for a lonely orphan, Aimi killed herself, leaving him all alone. Since then, Dick, who schooled himself before returning stateside, had dated Japanese women exclusively, trying to replace Aimi in his broken heart, but to no avail.

"*I love you*!" he shouted at Kiko through gritted teeth, as the lashes across his chest, stomach and legs continued to leave bloody stripes.

"*I hate you*!" she retorted in a thick accent, and he laughed.

Kiko had fled Japan after the Great Tsunami, and was hoping to marry an American so she could remain in the United States. Dick was the sucker she'd been praying for. But as it turned out, she wouldn't need him. She wasn't going anywhere, rendering things like national citizenship irrelevant.

LeRoy burst the door open, smacked Kiko unconscious, and then Danny entered and bit Dick on the fleshy part of his right thigh as he screamed with shock, confusion and agony. LeRoy carried the unconscious Kiko down to The Purple Room, where Estrella and Lina made love to her. Then they both bit her, and Kiko became a were-vampire. Dick, in turn, became a zombie. Together they killed and ate all of the permanent hotel residents except The Mantis Man, because he had signed a fifty-year lease with the previous owner, Clara, and Danny wanted to honor that. Plus nobody wanted to eat much less fuck someone so despicable.

Café du Frisson was also considered off-limits as far as victims went, since it generated too much revenue, and was useful as a front for the depraved debauchery going on inside the adjacent hotel. One of the café patrons was named Barney Doolittle. He was allegedly an art dealer, who boasted that, aside from the occasional business trip, he never left the block on which he lived, which happened to include L'Hotel du Frisson. He was destined to *never* leave it.

Dick applied the same flesh-toned makeup that Danny wore, giving him a grotesque, clown-like appearance that many found startling, but they were afraid to comment for fear of offending the friendly Dick. Except for Barney, that is, who brought it up as he sat in an egg chair across from the front desk, sipping his latte.

"You look like shit, Dick," Barney said.

"Thanks, you too," Dick said good-naturedly.

"Except for your hair, of course." Actually, Dick's beloved hair, his greatest asset, had been gradually falling out since he'd been turned into a zombie. He was considering wearing a wig. Meantime, he kept it creatively combed.

"Your hair looks terrible, as usual," Dick said to Barney, whose hair indeed resembled a rat's nest, complementing his overall slovenly, unkempt appearance.

"I don't care," said Barney. "I'm not trying to pick up any women, am I? It would undermine my male dominance. That is why I prefer to masturbate. I could have sex any time I wanted. But I deny women the satisfaction of exerting their feminine sensuality over me. Speaking of which, whatever happened to Clara?"

"She left the country," Dick said, concentrating on his work.

"Really? How come?"

"Nobody knows."

"So who's in charge now?"

"We all are. It's a collective."

"How nice."

Barney continued slurping his latte, rhapsodizing about his carefully guarded male dominance. "I've jerked off buckets worth of come fantasizing about Clara," he said. "*Buckets*. But she has no power over me."

The spirit of Franklin DeWitt winced as he reached for his untouchable pecker.

"That's very sweet," Dick said. "I need to work now."

Barney kept babbling, though, and Dick was growing increasingly annoyed. Something would need to be done, and soon, to shut this poor man up for good.

Kiko, who had been hired as an assistant maid, came up to the desk, wearing her cute little pink uniform. She told Dick that all the rooms had been cleaned. It was Adele's day off.

"Are you the new maid?" Barney asked, his boner

bulging.

"Why, yes," said Kiko. "Adele needs some help, since we're so *busy* lately."

"Would you like to see Kiko's work?" Dick asked Barney.

"Her *work*?" said Barney, imagining her naked.

"One of the rooms she just cleaned."

"I've never even *seen* a room here. It would be an honor."

"Well, now's your chance. Kiko, care to show Barney here The Yellow Room?"

Minutes later, Barney was tied to the yellow bed, as Kiko savagely rode his loins. He came inside of her many times. It was the first sex he'd had in years, and the best ever. Which was good, since it was also his last.

After they'd both come in unison multiple times, as Barney tore at his wrist and ankle restraints and Kiko gnawed on her own wrist during each intense orgasm, she turned into a werewolf-vampire hybrid, hungry for both flesh and blood, her own flesh only partially covered by smooth black fur, and she tore Barney's throat out, then drained his body of blood. She rang the front desk and Dick took a break, leaving a sign for guests that said "Be Right Back!," walked down the hall whistling, entered the room, and ate Barney's remains. Clara's ghost looked down at the scene, and laughed. Then when Barney joined her in the spiritual realm, he felt very embarrassed, but frustrated, since he still couldn't touch the object of his lustful fantasies, bound as they were in this ethereal limbo.

Dick and Kiko made love in the shower, then casually resumed their posts.

The cops came looking for Barney a few days later, but there was no trace of him anywhere. He'd simply vanished.

After the cops had left, Danny called a staff meeting, and told them, "We need a new business model. We're running out of guests."

"I have an idea," said Lila. "Let's not *give* away our services. Let's *sell* them."

"To whom?" asked Dick.

"People who want to fuck and die, and get it all *ove*r with," said Lila. "We offer the hottest products on the market, for cheap: Sex, and death. Because that's all there is, and it's all that ultimately matters. Everything boils down to one or the other—politics, religion, entertainment, and even love."

Outside the wind howled, like it knew something they didn't.

Soon word spread through the underground that anyone who was weary of life *above* ground and wished to die could go out with a bang by volunteering to be sensuously sacrificed at L'Hotel du Frisson. For the meager price of a one-night stay, the morose guest would be treated to the greatest sex of his or her life, and then promptly turned into vampire/werewolf/zombie food. It was suicide by sex.

Danny could barely keep up with the deluge of requests.

With Lila's creative input, Danny arranged some clever marketing for their new venture. Tag lines like "Bring Your Baggage, Leave Your Load" and "A Different Kind of Room Service" were printed on the new, simple, black brochures, which contained only these words in white lettering along with the hotel's website URL, www.thrillville.net, which was also designed by Lila. The site simply sported a photo of the hotel's innocuously inviting yet sinisterly seductive façade, and a space to join the hotel's "mailing list" for further information regarding reservations and accommodations. At that point, the prospective client was screened, and if he or she passed the test, they would be sent further instructions. The brochures were distributed surreptitiously amongst a cult-like network of fans, most of which adopted the Goth lifestyle, a subculture embraced by Adele as well as Kiko, who both frequented the clubs, and whose circle of friends volunteered to promote their business. Word of mouth traveled quickly, though customer satisfaction was only a matter of hyperbolic hearsay, since no patrons ever lived to post a review on Yelp. Nonetheless, the hotel was booked nightly for months in advance. The café even offered "The Last Meal," a special selection prepared by Juan and Carlos, catering to individual palates. They were directed to keep the coffee and jazz coming, 24/7, and they'd be handsomely compensated with sex, but no death. Business was so good, everyone got a raise.

Each member of the hotel staff had been turned into some sort of monster. The café workers had been spared in order to help keep up appearances to the outside world, since the café had its own separate set of paying patrons, who simply wanted coffee and pastries, not sex and death. At first, The Mantis Man had no clue what was going on, because he tuned it all out. He was too wrapped up in his own little web of isolation and anger to notice or care what was happening around him. Since the hotel was continually booked, only suicidal sex fiends could gain entry, so The Mantis Man was constantly surrounded by screaming and both "This Corrosion" and "Gimme Shelter" blasted at full volume, though he'd given up and taken to wearing earplugs. It was a murderous/suicidal sex spree that went on for many years. Soon the hotel was overrun with the spirits of the dead, but only the cats could see and communicate with them. It was getting very crowded, at least on a celestial plane. Physically, the turnstile never stopped, and nobody stayed for long.

The specters haunting the hotel were sexually frustrated, watching all this fornication without any way to appease their own lusts. Clara's spirit tried masturbating, but could feel nothing. It seemed like eternal damnation. At least she could watch over her son, Toby, from an omniscient vantage point.

Still, despite their reliably sated appetites for food and sex, the basic needs of physical existence, a melancholic malaise was manifesting amongst the monsters.

"What is the secret?" Danny asked Estrella one night after a typical feast of fucking and flesh-eating. Lila and Toby slept blissfully between them.

"Of what?" Estrella asked dreamily.

"Life. And death. And sex. *All* of it."

Estrella carefully considered her answer. She had spent many years poring over religious doctrines and spiritual texts from every culture on the globe, trying to piece together at least one solid clue to the puzzle of existence, uncover one tiny key to unlock at least one riddle of the universe. Finally, she whispered, "I don't know."

The specters hovering over them all laughed, then collectively wept, because they still didn't know the secret, either. Whether dead or undead, no one found ultimate peace, it seemed. The only respite was Love, even if it was merely just another illusion. The souls of the departed, who had paid for their seemingly endless state of voyeuristic limbo, as well as Boris, Franklin and Clara, all felt gypped, but they had nobody to complain to, nobody who could hear them, anyway, except for the cats, who didn't give a damn.

"What about the loved ones of the ones we kill?" Lila asked Estrella. "We are not being fair to them."

"No, we're not," Estrella said. "But this world has always been a cycle of life and death. We are pawns as much as perpetrators. Look at nature. One beast kills another in order to survive. We are predators, at the top of the food chain. Accept your fate and your role in this cycle, and consider yourself lucky."

"I still think we are committing sins," Lila said.

"Perhaps; I don't know all the answers," Estrella said. "In fact, I don't know *any*."

"Will we be punished for our sins?" Danny asked

Estrella anyway.

"Look at us," she said. "We already are."

"Is there a Hell?" Lila asked.

"Yes, wherever I can't be with both of you, my loves."

"This will *never* end?" Danny asked, feeling a touch of ennui.

"Not unless we *make* it end," Estrella said. "But I don't *want* it to ever end, to be alone, and without you; to simply cease to exist, or to exist for eternity in loneliness. Do *you*?"

"No," Danny said tentatively. "Though eternity trapped in this horrible body seems like a pretty goddamn long time, too. I wish I could just take a simple shit again." It was true; none of the monsters urinated or defecated, because none of the flesh, blood, semen and bones they digested went to "waste," being totally absorbed into their voracious supernatural systems.

"But at least you'll always be safe with me, and I love you," Estrella said. "Your enemies from your past can never harm or even find you. Your present and your future have forever merged."

Danny nodded, popping his left eyeball back into its socket. "That's nice."

"There's nothing worse than being alone," Lila said, holding them both. "I am afraid to die, because then I might be all alone again, and forever."

The spectator-specters laughed some more, but bitterly. They craved the relative solitude of their corporeal counterparts, craving relief from the crushing company of their fellow incarcerated souls in this shameless but saddening sanctuary from righteous retribution.

CHANGE OF HABIT

LeRoy had become L'Hotel du Frisson's number one stud and most requested prostitute. He could fuck faster, longer and more intensely than anyone else on the staff, and he had no preference, bringing both men and women to such exquisite heights of pleasure than when the time came to snap their necks so the feast could begin, they all died with a smile on their faces. The rest of the staff relished LeRoy's life-giving leftovers, particularly the females, who lapped up gallons of LeRoy's semen from the cunts of the corpses with which he had copulated. Danny and Dick contented themselves with the flesh and the bones. It was a good deal for all.

But LeRoy himself was unhappy. He still missed Clara, who woefully witnessed his raunchy rituals of hedonistic homicide. The spirit of Boris watched and wept as well, out of eternal envy. Boris's jealousy was sheer, unabated agony, but at least he shared the spiritual sphere with Clara, whose soul still shunned him, especially now that she knew exactly what he'd been doing to her body. However, the dwarf did share parental bragging rights, if not responsibilities, with Toby's "Uncle" LeRoy, so Clara sometimes tolerated Boris's celestial company. After all, neither one had anyplace else to go, since they were both ghostly prisoners of the hotel forever, or so it seemed.

Estrella had taught LeRoy some basic literary skills, so he could communicate with notes, not just grunts and gestures. He hardly ever slept, working by day as a bellhop and by night as a lethal fuck machine. Since all the guests who checked in now knew the hotel was a place to love and let die, LeRoy's freakish appearance alarmed but did not dissuade them. In fact, the muscles rippling beneath his uniform often succeeded in selling his meaty, murderous merchandise.

Toby was still young, but LeRoy did not want Toby to know that he was his natural father, especially since some of Boris's genes were in Clara's son as well. One day, there might be a revelation, but for now, Toby was content being raised by an entire family, who all shared custody.

Then one night, LeRoy fell in love all over again.

Clara had finally figured out a possible reunion strategy. She would inhabit the body of one of LeRoy's lovers just as it exited the body, then she could be rejoined with both her true Earthly love and their baby son.

The body she chose belonged to a depressed, lonely nun who had renounced her faith because the horrors of the world, which she'd witnessed while aiding the poor and the sick, defied the existence of a conscientious Creator. Beneath her habit and gown was an exceptionally voluptuous but untouched body, which LeRoy greatly enjoyed fucking, viciously violating her every orifice as she screamed with delight, the giant coming inside of her again and again, as the nun, a forty year old virgin, continually cried out in blissful tandem. LeRoy strangled her to death during her tenth orgasm, as prearranged (one for each Commandment she had broken), but just as her spirit ascended, Clara ducked inside, and the nun's watery eyes reopened, and LeRoy recognized his Clara in them. The beautiful nun's name had been Nina, but now she was Clara, the ex-stripper, reborn into the body of Nina the ex-nun. They continued to make passionate love till dawn as Nina the nun looked down and sobbed, because she was still so lonely, even amongst so many other equally lonely spirits.

LeRoy did not want to service any more strangers, handing in his resignation to Estrella via a scribbled note, then taking "Nina" down to the basement, where he still lived, fucking her over and over. He did, however, retain his daytime bellhop duties, carrying luggage up to the rooms, a task which he enjoyed. He always enjoyed meeting new people, but not always fucking then killing them.

Estrella was not pleased with LeRoy's decision, and threatened to destroy him if he didn't capitulate and copulate. Anticipating this backlash, LeRoy kept "Nina" hidden in the basement, for fear they'd attack and destroy her, and he'd lose his Clara all over again.

Nina/Clara desperately wanted to hold their son LeRoy, but for now, while she was in hiding, that was not possible.

"You must return to work," Nina/Clara told him as they were wrapped in other's sweaty, naked bodies on the cold lab table, where Boris had once violated Clara's body on a regular basis. Boris looked down and frowned. He had lost Clara again to that ungrateful bastard LeRoy. After all, Boris figured he had saved the brute's worthless life, by harboring him as a fugitive from the law, even though LeRoy was innocent of the charges, anyway.

Silently vowing monogamy, LeRoy shook his head, but Nina/Clara kissed him, and said, "I will not be jealous, my love. I promise."

Under intense pressure from his fellow employees, LeRoy finally resumed his whoring assignments, greatly pleasing Madam Estrella. His first client of his first night back on the job was a black ex-football player named Tank Lewis. It was one of LeRoy's former teammates, but Tank did not recognize LeRoy at first. Tank had always been conflicted by his sexuality, kicked out of the league after a locker room incident, and then ostracized by his own people, who shunned him due to his homosexuality. LeRoy's memories of his prior life were muddled, but he recognized Tank from somewhere. He just couldn't place him.

Tank was as big as LeRoy, and in the midst of their lovemaking, Tank suddenly recognized LeRoy's cock. He'd tasted it before, in the football stadium locker room—before they got caught by the coach, and LeRoy cried "rape," ruining Tank's career. Once this dawned on Tank, he began to savagely beat and strangle LeRoy, eventually killing him. Just as LeRoy's spirit left his battered body, Boris the dwarf's spirit entered it, and with renewed vigor and a sense of vengeance, Boris, as LeRoy, mangled and dismembered Tank, then called on the others to finish him off, while LeRoy/Boris went to the basement, and reclaimed Clara as his own, now that she was accessible in the lovely body of the unfortunate nun.

Clara/Nina shrieked in terror, sensing the spiritual swap, but it was too late. After raping her repeatedly, Boris/LeRoy threw her in the cage once occupied by Lila. Nina/Clara was now his sex slave. Boris would continue his experiments with the bottled cadaver pieces in his lab, attempting to bridge the gap between life and death, especially now that he'd experienced it from both sides, hoping he could freely navigate between the two realms, and possibly inhabit a more attractive body in the future, even if he had to make it himself.

Meantime, from above, LeRoy's spirit wept and wept, as Nina's true spirit tried to console him.

HOUSE OF PAIN

The hotel staff eventually caught incurable cabin fever. Though the steady supply of humans was satisfying, they grew restless, and yearned to return to the outside world, if only for fresh meat and new experiences, even a change of scenery. However, it was still the case that whenever they tried to venture outside the confines of L'Hotel du Frisson, under cloak of night, they were stricken with severe pain, and had to return to the restrictive boundaries of their home, which had become their prison. There was no escape from the hotel for the undead, as well as for the dead. Something had slowly then suddenly changed, something that trapped them within this self-made hell; a force of evil, or perhaps of good, but most likely neither. Whatever its origin or purpose, the supernatural barrier was accessible from without, but impenetrable from within. Even Boris, inside LeRoy's body, was unable to leave the accursed premises.

The weather seen through the windows was persistently autumnal, overcast and gray, with frequent thunderstorms, the wild winds whipping the brown and yellow leaves from the trees, whose branches never grew bare. Inside the hotel, the only movies available on the "cable system" were decadent horror and sex films, from the 1960s and '70s, the "grindhouse" era. They were trapped in a warped existence of their own deranged design that knew neither time nor space. Juan and Carlos worked the café constantly, day and night, never tiring, like machines. The Mantis Man sat in the café drinking espresso, pissing it out, then refilling his bladder. The classic jazz music never stopped. At least, this is how it all appeared from their internal perspective, seen through the windows and doors through which they could never exit, an alternate reality created by their own perverse deeds, from which they was no apparent escape.

The Café du Frisson still received the daily newspaper, though Juan and Carlos, who couldn't read much English anyway, seemed oblivious to the ever-evolving news of the outside world, as they worked and worked and worked, with only food, bathroom and cigarette breaks. They forgot their former lives in Mexico, or anywhere. They lived as if in an endless trance. They were under Estrella's hypnotic spell—not quite dead, but stuck in time, ageless and ceaselessly subservient.

From an outsider's viewpoint, the hotel still existed in a world where the seasons changed, people lived and died, and time went on. The guests who checked into L'Hotel du Frisson left this world behind forever, plunging into the perpetual purgatory of this dismal domain. This was not advertised on the web site.

In The Silver Room, an old, mournful man that had lost his wife to cancer after thirty-two years of blissful marriage, was being fucked senseless by Lila, who continued to fuck the man as he wept and she came and turned into a werewolf, finally slaughtering him. But his spirit was not reunited with that of his dead wife, because his spirit was trapped within the hotel, wandering its crowded corridors, while her spirit had ascended to its ultimate destination. He had no way of knowing this beforehand, though. It was yet another raw deal.

In The Mahogany Room, a young girl had lost her beloved cat, and wanted to die with love. Danny and Dick fucked her till she cried, then devoured her while she was still alive, until finally she found release from this plane of existence, but not from her torment, since her spirit did not find her dead cat, because the only cat spirits on this property of the condemned were Pheromone and Endorphin, and they were still in their bodies. The two cats could see and communicate with the dead girl's spirit, though, and offered her comfort when possible, relaying communiqués from her own cat that was somewhere beyond the rainbow.

In The Azure Room, a middle-aged man who had lost his job after his company folded, forcing him to burn through his savings, and whose family was living with relatives, gave all he had left to offer—his sperm and his soul—to Estrella, who swallowed the sperm, but spit out the soul.

And up in The Black Velvet Room, Boris, in LeRoy's body, gleefully raped, tortured and killed all of his lovers, leaving the bodily remains for the others to feast upon, only nibbling on scraps to keep his zombified body going, or stealing parts for his ongoing experiments in the basement. Boris only wanted the sex and the power, not the food. No one could figure out what, or who, had gotten into LeRoy lately, whose personality had undergone a noticeable change, but as long as he completed his assigned tasks, they left him alone.

Meantime, unseen and unfelt, the ghosts of the guests continued to haunt and cohabitate with the living and the undead. LeRoy's lonely, mournful spirit was bonding with Nina's sad and disillusioned spirit. *Where is God*?, she wondered. The spirits did not relate to each other in verbal language, since humans and in fact all species spoke in tongues created for their earthbound bodies, whereas the language of the infinite required no words. However, Nina was able to wordlessly hum the gospel standard "Just a Closer Walk With Thee" as a lullaby to LeRoy, giving his tortured spirit some peace, and hers as well.

The radios inside the hotel only played certain classic rock songs, like "Hotel California," "Stairway to Heaven," "Another Brick in the Wall," "We Will Rock You," "In-a-Gadda-Da-Vida," "Freebird," "Light My Fire," "Werewolves of London," "Black Magic Woman," "Witch Queen of New Orleans," "House of the Rising Sun," and course "Gimme Shelter." There were no DJs. The music was played loudly over the constant acts of carnal carnage, with the final, fatal orgasms always occurring in tandem with the musical crescendo of any given number. The only respite was the cool classic jazz playing 24/7 in the café, where Juan and Carlos had lost all sense of time, digging the ageless sounds of Duke Ellington, Miles Davis, Chet Baker, Dizzy Gillespie, Charles Mingus, Dave Brubeck, Art Pepper, Vince Guaraldi, and Stan Getz, to name a few. But the food was always fresh, and the coffee was always hot. Nobody on either side of the counter seemed to notice the hours ticking by, or the fact that the jazz did not come from a radio or a CD player. It was simply in the air. Customers of the café came and went, as long as they didn't check into the hotel. This went on for a long time, or so it seemed. Life, and death, was very monotonous, though not monogamous.

VOODOO DREAMS

The Mantis Man spent most of his days in the café, sipping espresso, munching on croissant sandwiches, reading the paper, muttering to himself, smoking, and scheming to kill Danny, who looked like he was slowly dying anyway. The Mantis Man simply wanted to expedite the inevitable process.

Mostly, The Mantis Man was insufferably lonely, suffocating in his self-imposed isolation, but didn't want to admit this fact, because that would imply a sense of vulnerability The Mantis Man could not abide. If he remained willfully ignorant of the symptoms, he could deny the diagnosis, as well as any possible cure.

He called Vic Valentine on his cell phone, just because he needed someone to talk to, even a disembodied and frankly apathetic voice.

"Vic, something strange is going on around here," The Mantis Man said. "I mean, stranger than *usual.*"

"What now?" asked Vic with an impatient sigh.

"I can't put my figure on it. For one thing, the music is always too loud. Rock music. I hate it." The café's jazz music was like a sonic tonic.

"Call the cops and complain."

"I tried, no answer."

"They must be busy."

"And my cable channels only play horror movies and pornography—*old* porno, from the sixties and seventies, ancient Times Square/42nd Street kind of shit. I can't watch any of my regular shows anymore. No more 'Johnny Staccato.'"

"Too bad, I *love* that show," Vic said. "I get it just fine where I am. Call the cable company and complain."

"No answer."

"Hm. Well, guess what'll happen next time you call *me* to complain?"

"Fuck you." The Mantis Man hung up on Vic, robbing him of the satisfaction to do it first.

The Mantis Man went up the counter to order more espresso, and said to Carlos, "Why is it you and Juan are *always* here? Don't you ever go *home*?"

"This *is* our home," Carlos said as if hypnotized. "What may I get you?"

Just then Mortimer Schmidt walked in. The Mantis Man detested him, even more than he detested most people.

"What do you *do*, anyway?" The Mantis Man asked Morty as he walked by with his cappuccino. "You're a Jew who comes out here and just sits around complaining and whining? *Why*? What good does *that* do anybody?"

"I'm just here to enjoy my coffee, and the music," said Morty, sitting on the opposite side of the café with his newspaper, which he customarily shredded upon finishing the comic strip section.

The Mantis Man got up and followed him, sitting at his table. "Let me ask you something, my fellow outcast. Do you notice anything *funny* going on around here?"

"Besides *you*?"

"You think I'm *funny*, do you?" The Mantis Man squinted his already beady eyes.

"Not really," said Morty. "Leave me alone, why don't ya? I'm reading."

"You're a self-loathing Jew asshole," The Mantis Man said, rising to his feet.

"Fuck you, Mantis Man," said Morty.

"*Asshole*."

The Mantis Man went upstairs and pulled out his

"Chumpy Walnut" doll out of the shoebox in the closet. He refashioned the face to resemble Morty's, then he stuck his cigarette in its belly.

Down in the café, Morty was doubled over with agonizing stomach pain. "What the hell did you put in my coffee?" he screamed at Juan, who helped him up. Morty was vomiting as he exited the café. The Mantis Man looked down at Morty, through the rain on his window, even though it was a clear night with a full moon when Morty went home and died painfully while playing his guitar, tears steaming down his face, dreaming of Cuba and his lost dreams of youth.

Then The Mantis Man once again tried changing the countenance of the doll to resemble Danny Falco, poking pins in the doll's head, back, stomach and legs. As usual, it didn't work, because Danny was at the front desk when The Mantis Man checked up on him, and he seemed fine. The guy wasn't responding to The Mantis Man's typical tried-and-true spells.

"How do you feel?" The Mantis Man asked Danny, eyeing him closely. "Headaches?"

"Fine," said Danny. "Why do *you* give a shit?"

"You don't look so good."

"I've had the flu."

"The flu? Like headaches, maybe?" pressed The Mantis Man.

"*Every*thing hurts," Danny said.

"Sorry to hear that. Feel better."

"Thanks."

But The Mantis Man knew Danny wasn't suffering as a result of the voodoo rituals secretly conducted at his expense. Ironically, The Mantis Man hadn't tried his voodoo on Danny until the night Estrella Margarita Moreno had checked in, and changed everything. Now Danny was impervious to the voodoo spells, since he was already *un*dead. If The Mantis Man had tried it only one day earlier, Danny would be *really* dead, lingering among the spirits haunting the hotel. But The Mantis Man hadn't hated Danny then. Not much, anyway. Not any more than the rest of humanity, anyway. The Mantis Man only began to truly *hate* Danny when his wife's shrunken head told him that she had killed herself after her affair with Danny, which had never actually happened. But The Mantis Man believed whatever the dead head said. She was his only companion. Most of the shrunken heads hanging in the closet next to her had once belonged to her alleged "lovers." At least they could keep her company while he was out, he figured.

The Mantis Man returned to his gloomy little room and put the customized voodoo doll, which he called "Chumpy Walnut" after a book he read once, back in the shoebox, and then he removed his wife's shrunken head from the hanging rod.

"I cannot seem to kill this one, my love," he said to the head, polishing off a bottle of wine from the café.

"Because he is *already* dead," the head said.

"Really? I never thought of that. He must be a zombie then. That would explain his obvious illness, and refusal to just fucking *die*. Then what must I do?"

"Wait. An opportunity will present itself. And don't hang me next to the dwarf head again. He creeps me out."

"Why, that little fucking pervert! I'll *squash* it!"

"No! First you must rid this hotel of his spirit, or he will haunt you forever."

"But he is *dead*. That's for *sure*."

"His spirit still lives here, hiding inside a body that is not his own. I can feel it. He means you and everyone in this hotel great harm, if he completes his experiments in the basement. Remember what I told you: *everybody* is your enemy, because chances are, at some point, I fucked them once."

"Nothing is ever what it seems," said the drunken Mantis Man.

"No shit," said his wife's shrunken head.

THE END OF LONELY STREET

Danny and Dick, who still dressed to the nines while on duty at the front desk, sporting shiny vintage suits with skinny ties, had stopped wearing makeup to cover up their deteriorating facial features due to their advancing zombification. Nobody seemed to notice or care anyway, so there was no point to perpetuating the laborious charade. It was business as usual. They went about their regular routines, reading comic books—particularly reprints of *Tales from the Crypt, Eerie, Creepy, Vampirella* and *American Splendor*—and casually chatting with the café customers, including frequent patron Deacon Rivers, founder of the local chapter of the Church of Elvis, who was convinced that Danny was the real thing.

"Just admit it, you're The King, in hiding," Deacon Rivers said to Danny, who was sipping a café latte from the café, even though he no longer got a caffeine rush from it. It was merely an old habit. Some of the coffee even dribbled out of this sagging mouth and down his crusty chin. He was careful not to spill any on his suit, skinny tie, or pocket square, though. Today Danny was reading an anthology of the old black-and-white Marvel Comics magazine *Tales of the Zombie*.

"No, I'm not," said Danny. "Though I used to be an Elvis impersonator, back in Atlantic City." His memory of that part of his life was very hazy, and that was most of what he could recall.

Just then two men wearing dark sunglasses, dark suits, and dark Fedoras walked in. "Does a Danny Falco work here?" one of the men asked Danny.

"No," said Danny.

The two men looked at Danny's zombie face, nodded, said "thank you," and left.

"That proves it," said Deacon Rivers, sitting in the chair opposite the desk, sipping his own café latte. Rivers had long red braided hair and wore a T-shirt that simply said MIKE STONE MUST DIE.

"Proves what?" said Danny.

"You just denied you were Danny Falco to those two guys, meaning you're not *really* Danny Falco, right?"

"I was lying. They didn't recognize me because I'm a zombie now and my face is falling apart."

"Why were they looking for you then?"

"To kill me."

"Oh yea, how come?"

"I fucked a lot of their girlfriends and wives back in the day. I also owe a lot of gambling debts. At least, I *think* I did. Anyway, they come in every so often."

"Same guys?" asked Deacon Rivers.

"Different guys, sent by the same guy," Danny said, adding with a shrug, "I guess."

"So wearing zombie makeup is the perfect cover."

"I'm not wearing makeup," Danny said. "Not any more."

"So this isn't just some sort of promotional Halloween shtick?"

"It's not Halloween," said Danny.

"It always *feels* like it in here, though," Deacon Rivers observed.

"True," Danny agreed.

"Funny how Halloween is so popular," said Deacon Rivers. "It's all about monsters and scary stuff. Makes you wonder."

"People want to fuck what they fear," Danny said. "It's like Life beating Death at its own dirty game. Just human nature, man."

"How do you know?"

"I used to *be* human."

"So you're telling me you're a real zombie, but *not* the real Elvis Presley?" asked Deacon Rivers.

"Of course," said Danny. "How could I be *Elvis*? That's *ridiculous*. He's *dead*, not *un*dead."

"Well, how could you be a zombie?" asked Deacon Rivers. "Like that's any more credible."

"Because I fucked this gorgeous vampire woman from Mexico that later fucked an alien dude from Outer Space and then she fed me its blood and semen because I was only a vampire then and needed the extraterrestrial boost to my system, but then I fucked a really hot young werewolf teenage runaway, and the combination of those strange fluids all at once broke down my body and turned me into the living dead. Then I bit Dick and turned him into a zombie, too, so I'd have company."

"Whose dick?"

"Dick Reid, the desk clerk."

"No, not who *is* dick, but *whose* dick did you bite?"

"I told you."

"You bit *Dick's* dick?"

"No, just his leg. The fleshy part."

"Oh, I see," said Deacon Rivers dryly. "Makes perfect sense now. Thanks for clearing that up for me."

"No problem."

"Explains a lot, actually."

"I'm glad."

Deacon Rivers silently sipped his café latte for a while, smirking as he watched Danny read his comic book.

"Why do you think I'm Elvis anyway?" asked Danny finally. Deacon Rivers was beginning to get on his nerves.

"Because you look just like him, or you did, before you became a zombie."

"So you believe I'm a zombie."

"I believe what I see."

"And what do you see?"

"An Elvis zombie."

Just then Kiko came up to the front desk and said to Danny, "Room 205 is clean!" she said in a sing-songy voice.

"Kiko, would you like to show Deacon Rivers here our new Elvis Suite?"

"Of *course*!" Kiko said with a beaming smile, careful not to show her fangs.

"You have an Elvis suite?" asked Deacon Rivers. "I didn't know that."

"There's a *lot* you don't know," said Danny. "We're trying theme rooms as part of our new makeover."

"Nice!" said Deacon Rivers.

Kiko, whose luscious cleavage was clearly visible because she always kept the top buttons of her pink maid's uniform undone, took Deacon Rivers by the arm and led him to The Blue Room, since that reservation—a young, troubled girl named Judy Spreckles, whom Danny was planning to fuck and kill personally later that evening—wasn't due to arrive for a couple of hours yet, so they had time to soil it before she cleaned it once again.

"Ladies and gentlemen, Deacon Rivers has left the building!" Danny announced to nobody a half hour later, though in fact, he had not, and possibly never would.

Danny began playing John Carpenter's theme to his 1978 film *Halloween* on his iPod in a continuous loop, hooking it up to the lobby speakers, setting the proper mood and preparing the naïve guests for the unspeakable horrors within.

LAST ROOM ON THE LEFT

Judy Spreckles was young and beautiful, with long thin dirty blonde hair and very soft white creamy skin and big blue innocent eyes and perky breasts and, unlike most of the morbid guests, a cheery disposition. Danny loved making love to her so much he had to ask her, "Why do you want to die?"

"I don't," she said. "Fuck me *again*!"

"But, I'll *have* to kill you, that's the *deal*," Danny said. "It's in our *contract*."

"My master won't permit it," she said.

"*What* master?"

Just then a lanky, middle-aged man with a long thin dirty brown hair, a thin brown beard and wearing a tie-dye gown and sandals, flanked by several hippies, male and female, all wearing the same garb, walked into The Blue Room, brandishing knives and clubs. One closed and locked the door behind them.

"Jesus is here!" Judy cried, jumping up stark naked and throwing her arms around the intruder's neck.

"Jesus?" said Danny.

"Righteous retribution is at hand," said the bearded man. They were all part of a local cult of Jesus freaks.

"Actually, his name is *Hey-soos*," Judy said, making the phonetic correction. "But now he's just Jesus to us! I led him here so he could save you."

"From what?" Danny asked.

"Yourself," Jesus said as all eight hippies slashed at Danny, ripping his decaying flesh, splattering his blood out onto the blue carpets and bed sheets. The room suddenly reeked of Patchouli, dirty feet, sex and gore.

"*Now my children*," intoned Jesus with wide-eyed, trance-like intensity, "*suck the soul right out of this evil body*!"

Then Danny's severely damaged body was ravaged by the female hippies, including Judy, throwing him on the bed and taking turns fucking him, wiping his blood all over their faces and breasts and thighs as he came inside each one of them, too weak to fight back, and they didn't stop till they had each had several orgasms apiece, all to the tune of "Gimme Shelter," playing in a loop on the radio. Danny could feel himself slipping away as the hippies around the bed all chanted random verses from the Bible as well as Buddhist texts in hypnotic harmony as the savagely sensuous ceremony continued for several hours.

Finally, while Judy was still astride Danny's barely conscious corpse, Jesus suddenly shouted "*Death to the Devil!*," and bashed Danny's head to a pulp with a club, finishing him off as Danny's brains spewed all over Judy's tits and torso and she had a simultaneous screaming orgasm. Danny joined the legions of ghosts haunting L'Hotel du Frisson. He was not pleased with the transition, though his spirit was not zombified, which enhanced his self-esteem.

LeRoy and Nina, who were really Boris and Clara, burst into the room moments after Danny's skull had been smashed, wondering why they hadn't heard from him. LeRoy snapped necks, broke bones, tore limbs from sockets and heads off of necks, spraying the room with hippie blood, while Nina, now a vampire, drank her fill of the sanguinary fountains of flesh. The hippie chicks were especially nutritious since, besides their own blood, they were filled with Danny's semen, so there were like delicious cream-filled nuggets.

"They taste even better than that Satanic cult who invaded us last week," Nina said, and Boris nodded in accord. "Too bad about Danny, though. I loved him, once, long ago, it seems."

LeRoy nodded in accord as he hungrily munched on Jesus's bones, though inside his body, Boris's spirit was smiling with extreme satisfaction at the gruesome irony of it all. Danny was gone at last, through no design of his own. Perhaps the final barrier to Clara's love had been removed. It was Fate, beautiful Fate.

After the hippie Jesus cult had been destroyed and devoured, LeRoy brought Danny's remains to The Purple Room, showing Estrella what had happened. She screamed and wept, and Lila joined her, and Toby the baby, confused by the commotion, cried too.

Amid the mournful wailing, Nina breastfed the horrid little child in the corner of The Purple Room, rocking gently back and forth, humming a lullaby as the hideous creature sucked and bit her nipples till they bled, since Mother Clara had no milk to offer her infant son while in this stranger's body. Soon Toby was calm again, and Nina wept with joy.

Clara loved feeling close to Toby, even by spiritual proxy, which is why she had let Estrella turn Nina's body into a vampire in the first place, at LeRoy's impassioned request. LeRoy himself, inhabited by the spirit of Boris the dwarf, had likewise allowed his final transformation into a zombie, in order to also become physically immortal, being bitten by Dick, who was happy to oblige. Nina, possessed by Boris's beloved Clara, was now physically immortal, too, therefore forever fuckable. Nina was also just as attractive as Clara, perhaps even more so. Now LeRoy/Boris the albino zombie giant could live eternally with Clara's spirit trapped inside the curvaceous vampire body of Nina the ex-nun. And now that she was an official member of the undead hotel staff, Clara, as Nina, could experience all the sensations of Life once more, though she was unable to escape the hotel's confines, just like the others. In either spiritual or physical form, Clara found she was forever a prisoner of L'Hotel du Frisson, which was fine with her, as long as she could raise her beloved son and watch him grow into a fine young monster, which he quickly did. Plus Boris now *looked* like her long lost love LeRoy, so she could pretend it was really him as they made violent love, even though LeRoy's spirit could only watch in idle jealousy as Boris used his body to defile his beloved would-be bride on a regular basis.

When Toby was only five years old, though his body was that of an eighteen year old, Nina deflowered him one night while the others slept. Clara never felt closer to her own son, in body as well as spirit. Toby was not as physically imposing as his father LeRoy, but he was much, *much* uglier, warts and boils covering every inch of his misshapen, hairless body. Due to his abnormally accelerated maturity, at least in appearance, Toby, unholy spawn of an undead union, was hired by Estrella, the new general manager, as LeRoy's bellhop relief, and soon, Clara's offspring was fucking, killing and feasting along with the rest of the family, and soon, Nina and Toby became an inseparable pair of lovers. She loved popping his boils and sucking the slime out of his pustules, especially those on his penis, so that she could swallow his essence via several types of fluid, all at once. Naturally these trysts, normally conducted in the basement lab while LeRoy was on duty, were kept secret from LeRoy/Boris, who would've killed them both if he had found out his Nina/Clara was cheating on him with their own son.

Time did not exist in the spiritual realm, so the ghosts of the victims witnessing this profane progression of evil events unfold before them were unaware of any chronological passage. They merely viewed the many, many, many acts of extreme sex and violence as one morbid montage of frenzied flesh, and whether the screams of the living and undead came from pain or pleasure, the spirits were envious of the corporeal experience, since they were trapped in a dreamlike limbo, unable to find any relief from their perpetual state of ghastly, ghostly grief. Deacon Rivers thought it was pretty amusing when Danny suddenly showed up on his side of the spiritual divide, though.

In The Purple Room, Estrella wept in between increasingly lonesome sessions of sexual sustenance, once again wishing to die forever and reunite with her true love, wherever he was.

And in The Mantis Man's room, the shrunken head of his dead wife told him the good news about Danny, and he laughed and laughed, even though now, without blind hatred to occupy his time, his life had lost all meaning, and he wanted to die, too.

LOVE AND LET DIE

As its reputation spread beyond the underground grapevine, a variety of social groups from disparate subcultures began converging and attempting to lay siege to L'Hotel du Frisson, from gang-bangers to Hollywood talent scouts to the Mafia to Satanists to religious fundamentalists to the authorities. None were ever heard from again, and soon, the word on the street was to avoid this place like the plague, unless you wanted to die via sexually assisted suicide, in which case it was both heaven and hell on Earth, in that order. It was indeed The Last Resort for the frisky and the forlorn.

At various intervals, the police as well as gangsters missing loved ones and bounty hunters hired to find them would show up with guns, surrounding the hotel, and infiltrating it with violent intent. They were subsequently either seduced then killed by the beautiful women on this property of the condemned, or simply killed by the bulletproof zombie men. While all this was going on, The Mantis Man and other patrons would calmly sit in Café du Frisson, sipping espresso and eating croissant sandwiches. Juan and Carlos would turn up the classic jazz, which emanated from the air itself, to drown out the bothersome sounds of gunfire and screaming. The Mantis Man grew more and more suspicious that something strange was going on.

The monster women were so seductive that even homosexual men sometimes succumbed to their charms, though mostly, they preferred the hulking LeRoy, even though Boris, trapped inside of LeRoy's muscular body, found other men repulsive. He went through the motions anyway, to maintain his cover. The fact that LeRoy's body was also zombified did not repel requests for his fatal company. In fact, they only increased. The kamikaze customers of L'Hotel du Frisson liked the idea of literally being fucked to death by something that *looked* like Death. The only problem was death was not The End they had been seeking, and once their spirits left their bodies, they were trapped in the spiritual realm, so the peace they sought remained elusive, and no refunds were offered.

Eventually, those who came to destroy L'Hotel du Frisson were ultimately seduced by it. Soon the patrons *included* policemen as well as gangsters, all fed up with how things were going in the outside world, ready to give it all up for one final killer orgasm before ultimate emancipation, which ironically never came.

Group rates were offered, and Estrella, Lila, Nina, Adele, and Kiko, the vampires and werewolves, would each take on up to six customers at once, including cops and criminals alike, while LeRoy, Toby and Dick limited their guests/victims to one at a time, since they were zombies, and had to eat the remains of all of the women's victims, so they needed to save room. All of the monsters fucked and killed male and female humans alike, of all races and backgrounds. There were no discriminatory practices. All were welcome at L'Hotel du Frisson. It was an equal opportunity whore/slaughterhouse.

Once a gang of six Baptist/Neo-Nazi cops who all shaved their heads and wore tattoos of Hitler, Jesus, swastikas *and* crosses requested the services of all four women to accommodate them. Their plan was to ambush the monsters once they'd gone through regular channels to solicit their services, but it backfired. After they'd been fully drained of semen, the weakened men pulled out their concealed guns from their baggage and opened fire. Naturally, the weapons had no mortal effect on the women, who laughed deliriously as they ignored their own bullet wounds and added the men's blood to the copious amounts of nutritious semen already lining their stomachs and dripping from their gratified vaginas.

Later a gang of four Muslim fundamentalist terrorists, appalled at rumors of the decadent depravity going on at L'Hotel du Frisson, yet also intrigued like the other prurient party crashers, showed up to not only commit suicide, but take the entire place with them. They took off their clothes for Lila and Kiko, but their bodies were strapped with explosives. "*Praise Allah! Death to the Infidels*!" they screamed in unison, incredibly aroused by the naked monster women, and anxious to get to Heaven and fuck as many virgins as possible, per their promised reward. "*You look like lumps of clay compared to our women*!" one of them lied to the monster women, who just laughed. But before they could touch a single detonator, Kiko and Lila had slashed their throats, disarming them, first figuratively, then literally. Within seconds, Dick and LeRoy were on the scene, disposing of the bombs as well as the bones. The imprisoned spirits of the suicide bombers were quite dismayed to discover they'd passed up their last and best opportunity to get laid—*ever*.

Estrella made sure that what happened to Danny would never happen to any one of them again. Surveillance cameras had been installed, and sometimes the staff, which now rotated shifts as desk clerks and bellhops, would masturbate beneath the front desk as they monitored the various sessions. The hotel's walls seemed to be painted with blood, and the floors carpeted with dried semen; the essence of Life, seeped in Death, merging into a single torrent of titillating terrors.

Eventually, some of the more enterprising spirits took Boris's and Clara's lead and attempted to inhabit the physical forms of the departed just as they reached the final climax, since once all life functions completely ceased, seconds after the original soul departed, that body was eternally closed for business. Those who managed to enter the bodies at the split-timed juncture only wound up being killed all over again, despite the fact they cried for mercy, babbling about coming back from the beyond, and rightfully claiming the whole operation was a total sham. None of them got many words out before they were silenced. The staff assumed that these allegedly reincarnated spirits were really customers who had a change of heart once the sex was over, which sometimes happened, regrettably. Rarely, the monsters would form attachments to the guests they were fucking, and would balk at killing them, despite their contracts, but if they couldn't commit the kill due to emotional blockage, a fellow impartial employee would step in and complete the process. Some clients actually tried to buy their way out of the contract once they'd been sexually satisfied. These clients usually consisted of wealthy, arrogant businessmen or even young, drunken fools who simply wanted a wild weekend, without their deviant demise as part of the bargain.

There were to be no reprieves or refunds, however. A deal was a deal. The monsters could not be bribed, since they only used their profits to keep the hotel clean and running smoothly and to pay their fair share of taxes, just to keep the Government off their backs. Otherwise, they had no use for monetary wealth whatsoever, one reason the rates were kept attractively low. Human beings simply had nothing to bargain with, other than their bodies, which by that point belonged to the monsters anyway.

Boris had managed to strategically enter the body of LeRoy, one of the trusted staff, so he was never suspected of soul swapping, or so he assumed; and LeRoy, before Boris stole his body, had instantly recognized Clara's soul as soon as she entered Nina's body, and they agreed to keep one another's secret, so neither would be exposed and forced to face the wrath of Estrella, thereby risking their return to a coveted physical existence. But even if the other spirits had succeeded in claiming the physical form of a dying guest, once they attempted to exit the hotel, their borrowed bodies would have burst into flames, and their spirits once again returned to the property's personal purgatory. There just wasn't any checking out of L'Hotel du Frisson, in any form, once the guests had signed away their souls for one day, or night, of deceptively cheap thrills.

FAMOUS MONSTERS OF FILTHLAND

Eventually, the outside world gave up on trying to close down the brutal, blood-soaked brothel known as L'Hotel du Frisson, instead turning it into a celebrity-mongering multi-media sensation. The revelation of real life monsters, once thought to be mythological creations of artistic and superstitious imaginations, combined with the true stories of hardcore kinky sex and voluntary violent death, made L'Hotel du Frisson an instant legend, bitterly reviled and protested by religious and political groups, while whole-heartedly embraced by sundry social misfits, sexual deviants and counterculture iconoclasts from all corners of the globe. Camera crews, angry opponents and devoted fans alike camped in droves outside the property, interviewing the sad but horny suicide cases parading into their allegedly final destination. This concentrated convergence of curiosity-seekers actually scared off some potential guests who didn't want that type of attention and exposure, but the free worldwide advertising easily filled all vacancies and last minute-cancellations for years to come. Many guests actually reveled in the spotlight. On-camera profiles were conducted with the monsters themselves, who met with reporters and bloggers in Café du Frisson, which was as far as anyone whose name was not on the guest registry was allowed to venture. If anyone tried to sneak inside the hotel without a reservation, they were killed and eaten, but without getting fucked first. It wasn't long before these boundaries were consistently and universally honored.

Footage of the staff discussing their previous lives in the outside world, pre-monster, as well as recounting some of their more interesting encounters with guests, broke all cable ratings and internet viral records. The monster women could fuck and fuck and fuck and never worry about getting pregnant since, as undead beings, they could no longer foster true life. Their wombs were worthless sacks. Also, as basically copulating corpses, they were not susceptible to venereal disease. Though they could not propagate their own species via intercourse, only via selectively administered viral infection, they all smothered Toby with parental adoration to satisfy what maternal instincts they still possessed. This all became the subject of sensationalistic articles and academic journals alike, appealing to both lowbrow and highbrow sensibilities, though all on a commonly prurient level.

Lila told of her orphaned childhood and history of abuse at the hands of her would-be benefactors. Adele related tales of abject poverty and bigotry while growing up in a small town outside of Tucson, Arizona, where she had once been a schoolteacher, before she was driven out of town by hypocritical religious citizens who could not handle her bold sensuality, and wrongly accused her of seducing students. Kiko stunned audiences with stories of survival following the Great Tsunami back in Japan, where she had once been a secretary for a large corporation that crashed in the subsequent recession. Dick just talked about his dick. Estrella did not talk at all. She was still in mourning.

Estrella thought of it all merely as a distraction from her grief. Danny's corpse was still rotting in the closet of The Purple Room. She couldn't bring herself to let the lifeless, headless husk go. It was her solitary cherished remnant of her former *raison d'être.* Meantime, the show went on, preoccupying her mind and body, if not her heart.

"*They're just like us*!" was the responsive refrain from fervent fans. Except, of course, for the fact they were all undead fiends. Even The Mantis Man, the lone resident who wasn't a monster or a "one-night stand," enjoyed his own rabid following, of which he took full advantage. He had a reason to live again, at least until he got bored again.

Soon an official, exclusive reality series was given the green light, and select camera crews were allowed inside the rooms to film both the sex and the violence, uncensored, as long as the guests consented. There was no payment for the rights, since the monsters had no need for more money than they were already making. They only shared their sessions of erotic horror with the rest of humanity because the interest was there. It was immaterial to them whether anyone knew of their horrible activities, and in fact it was a relief not to have to hide in the shadows any more. Everything was now out in the open, except for the monsters themselves, who still could not leave the hotel without being stricken with unbearable pain that would surely kill them if they continued to drift beyond the perimeters of the property. They decided to let the world come to them instead.

Per the agreement drafted and signed by Estrella, all the networks as well as all the cable stations, in every major media market on Earth, picked up the show, simply called "Forbidden Thrills." The series became so insanely popular it eventually pre-empted every other program on the air as well as the web. It was the only thing anyone wanted to watch. The gothic grotesquery and explicitly exotic eroticism of L'Hotel du Frisson were without precedent, rival or equal.

The aliens who had planned to conquer the Earth began abandoning it in droves, calling off the systematic infiltration of humanity and subsequent invasion, and returning to their home planet. They wanted no part of a world that was so seriously fucked up. Mankind had no idea what a debt they owed these monsters, even if the alien threat had been inadvertently averted.

Meanwhile, audience demand for a steady stream of steamy programming was so insatiable that Estrella had all the windows in the hotel lined with tin foil, to block out the sunlight, so that they could perform 24/7, just like the sleepless human automatons Juan and Carlos, whose café business was booming bigger than ever.

"Forbidden Thrills" often featured individual interviews with each of the staff, now all famed cast members, including The Mantis Man, who served more or less as the program's human host, relishing his new role as Impresario of the Damned. He would laconically introduce each episode from his chair in the café, wearing a smoking jacket, puffing a cigarette and drinking coffee, welcoming viewers with his now-infamous tagline, "*We're having a little party….would you like to join us*?" Then he'd lead the camera to the first room, where a guest was either being fucked or killed, depending on which phase of the session was in progress. The Mantis Man became the most beloved television anthology host since Rod Serling. His fans were legion, and when he brought a female and sometimes even a male groupie back to his room, violating the rules of the house, LeRoy would burst in and kill them, but only after The Mantis Man had preyed upon their young flesh.

"Why do you stay, when you're the only one who can leave?" asked the young pretty blonde reporter, who was wearing a smile as big and fake as her breasts.

"This is my home," said The Mantis Man. "I have

no place else to go."

"No family or friends?"

The Mantis Man took a deep drag and said, "Not alive."

"Ironic that they call you 'Mantis Man.'"

"Why is that?" asked The Mantis Man, squinting his eyes in suspicious paranoia.

"Because in nature, the praying mantis kills after it mates. Except it's the female that kills the male."

"I never even thought of that," said The Mantis Man. "How annoyingly astute."

"The praying mantis is known for its camouflage, too," said the reporter.

"Camouflage?" The Mantis Man casually blew smoke in the reporter's heavily made-up face.

"The ability to blend in with its environment, so that it may strike from the shadows without warning."

"Well, that's just fucking fascinating," said The Mantis Man. "Aren't you a clever one. Your parents must be very proud of you and you're a credit to your college. But this isn't a fucking nature show, so can it."

"One last question," said the pretty reporter, still smiling. "Aren't you scared the monsters will kill *you*?"

"They don't even *talk* to me. I'm a voodoo priest, and I used to be a headhunter. John Cassavetes was a good friend of mine."

"*Who*?"

Later, back in his room, The Mantis Man rearranged his "Chumpy Walnut" voodoo doll's face to resemble the reporter's, and stuck two pins in its chest, resulting in an abrupt and ugly explosion of blood and silicone, like popped balloons, splattering one of the news vans parked outside.

UNEARTHLY DESIRES

The undead often took pity on those that no longer wanted to live, especially the destitute and the homeless, who came begging for release from their torment, despite the fact they had no compensation to offer in exchange for the hotel's premium services. For no charge, these poor souls were fed, bathed, fucked and killed, as acts of mercy. Some pleaded to join the ranks of the monsters, to be turned into a vampire or werewolf or even a zombie, but there was a hiring freeze in effect, since accommodations had to be reserved for paying guests, not more residents. Only The Mantis Man was permitted to stay, as long as he kept to himself, partly because he paid handsomely for the privilege, as well as the privacy, but mostly because he just didn't give a fuck, and the feeling was mutual.

Toby continued to grow at an alarming rate, until he was almost as tall as his secret daddy, LeRoy. Boris's spirit inside of LeRoy was very cold to Toby, however, and Toby noticed it, though Toby was unable to speak. However, Boris could now verbally communicate via LeRoy's thick tongue, speaking the same broken English he had in his dwarf body; he only pretended to be mute in order to maintain his cover.

"I am your father," LeRoy/Boris said to Toby one night in The Purple Room while the others were busy working in the rooms. "But I despise you. You are…abomination. You are…*horror*. I wish you not ever *born*. Your mother…is dead…but *lives*…I *love* her…I give her *you*, to express my love…but now, she does not love me…I wish you *dead*. And one day…*I kill you*."

Toby began to cry. Lila and Adele heard him as

they walked down the hall, and came in to console him in the only way they knew how.

LeRoy/Boris watched with jealous disgust as Lila sat on Toby's horrible face and he ate her pussy till she came and turned back into a werewolf, while Adele sucked Toby's pimply cock till he came down her throat, again and again. Adele, a vampire, drew blood as well as pus and semen from Toby's penis, mixing them in her mouth before swallowing the life-sustaining solution, the mixture of fluids dripping down her chin and onto her breasts. Kiko then walked in and joined the festivities, turning into a werewolf-vampire after her first orgasm, then riding Toby until neither could come any more, at least not for the rest of the night.

Nina suddenly walked in and tore Kiko off of Toby, then stopped herself, since Clara, inside of Nina, was afraid to reveal herself, too. The intervention aroused suspicion. LeRoy, also afraid his inner Boris would be exposed if Nina/Clara decided to confess her dual identity, quietly left the room.

"Why do you care if we have sex with Toby?" Lila asked Nina.

"He needs the practice, and he was crying, too," Adele said. "We were merely trying to make him feel better."

"And it worked," said Kiko, the were-vamp, wiping Toby's semen from her hairy thighs and licking it off her furry fingers.

"I do not care," lied Nina/Clara. "I am sorry. Here, let *me*."

Then she took the confused Toby into her arms as she sat on the floor beside him, and he greedily suckled her dry breasts as she beamed with maternal pride.

Toby suddenly coughed, choked and stopped breathing after typically wheezing through mucus-filled lungs and misshapen naval cavities, his face reddened with labored gasps, and Nina panicked. When Toby finally opened his eyes again, she saw that LeRoy's spirit had managed to inhabit the fatally flawed body of their son, which had succumbed to any number of diseases, its already weak immune system exhausted by the excessive orgasms. The stressful shock of LeRoy's confession accompanied by the strenuous sexual activity had simply proven to be too much for his fragile form to handle.

LeRoy's invasive spirit only kept Toby's body alive long enough to look into Nina's eyes and see Clara within them for a single fleeting moment of bliss, but after he touched her face, he too was gone again, and Toby's body, no longer able to sustain life, was without *any* spirit, just a lifeless lump of freakish flesh. Consumed with grief, Nina/Clara ate his remains herself, weeping as she devoured every inch of her ill-fated offspring.

She blamed the others, accusing them of killing her son, and claimed she could no longer go on with this freak show.

"I understand," Estrella said to her. "I know what it's like to lose a loved one. I will help you. This will all come to an end."

Estrella embraced Nina tenderly, then kissed her face and lips and breasts, and they made love, though their spirits cried out for release from this ephemeral realm of flesh, blood, and tears.

JUST A KISS AWAY

Boris, in LeRoy's body, had been quietly taking time from his duties to return to his experiments with life and death. He began stealing body parts from the dead guests, smuggling them down to the basement lab instead of eating them, in his obsessive attempts to re-create physical Life. Boris still had no idea what he was doing, and LeRoy's massive hands made the handling of some instruments problematic, but at least his fingers no longer trembled. Boris was determined to prove he could bridge the gap between the physical and spiritual realms, create bodies for other souls to inhabit, especially since he'd crossed over himself—*twice*. Few if any souls ever stole a second chance, much less a round-trip ticket.

Leaving Nina nude and asleep in The Purple Room, Estrella suddenly walked in on LeRoy while he was working in the lab. She was completely nude, holding the desiccated, skeletal corpse of Danny's headless body in her arms.

"I want you to revive my Danny in a new body, made from these parts," she said simply to LeRoy. "He needs a new head. Just pick one, I don't care."

"I cannot do that," LeRoy said. "And even if I could, I would not. I never like him. I glad he is gone."

"So you *can* speak, you fucking *bastard*," Estrella said. "That confirms what my inside sources have told me. You are *not* LeRoy. You really *are* Boris. Aren't you?"

LeRoy/Boris sighed and nodded in reluctant accord. "Yes," he said. "I stole this body."

"I know. We *all* know. *We have always known*. I let you live so you could continue your experiments and hopefully find a cure for our condition."

"What condition?" asked LeRoy/Boris.

"Loneliness."

"How could you know I am Boris?" LeRoy asked.

Just then Pheromone and Endorphin walked in the open basement door and rubbed lovingly against Estrella's bare ankles and shapely shins. LeRoy/Boris looked at them and scowled. *God damn cats*, he thought. She laid Danny's corpse on the table, and said, "*Do it*."

"I….I do not know what I doing," LeRoy/Boris said. "I only do this because…I lose someone I love, many years ago, and it was my fault…my fault…*my fault*…."

"Can you bring *you*r love back, at least?" asked Estrella.

"No, her body is gone, but…I am compelled to continue my experiments. I do not know why. I just want…an answer, even though the question is losing all meaning to me."

"It's all a dream," Estrella said in a trance-like whisper. "All a fucking dream, and when you wake up, you're in *another* dream. I am tired of living in dreams. We are all trapped."

"*I* am the one who is truly trapped," said Nina, abruptly walking in and standing behind Estella. "But I thought I would be emancipated. I am really Clara, you see."

"I know that too," said Estrella, and the cats meowed in unison.

"I love you," LeRoy/Boris said to Nina/Clara. "You are the only thing I love since Katarina."

"I *hate* you," said Nina, spitting on the filthy ground.

"Love is all that ever matters," Estrella said.

"Though it remains fickle and elusive for most. Still, the hope and search for someone to love is the only reason to continue drifting through these dreadful dreams."

"Then you understand," LeRoy/Boris said.

"Yes, but your love is not reciprocated," said Estrella, "so it is a selfish desire, not true love, which must be shared, not imposed."

"Why didn't you *say* anything, try to help me, if you knew who I really was?" Nina asked Estrella.

"Why didn't *you* say anything to *us*?" Estrella countered.

"Because I just wanted to be near my Toby," she said. "I didn't want you to kill me, and separate us yet again."

"Then there was nothing else I *could* do but welcome you into our family," Estrella said. "We only needed your sexually strong bodies to keep the hotel operating, giving us a steady supply of flesh, blood and semen on which to subsist; the souls within your bodies were immaterial to us. It was a business decision."

Nina began to sob. "Free me," she said simply. "You have lost your Danny, whom I once loved too, but now I am without both my Toby and my LeRoy. I am weary of this grim fairy tale. I have no more reason to be here."

Estrella suddenly turned and ripped Nina's head off. She held the head close to LeRoy's stunned face, blood and gore dripping from its jagged neckline.

"*You killed her*!" he cried. "*You killed my love—again*!"

"I merely freed her spirit, so she could be with Toby," Estrella said. "I will do the same to you if you do not help me, and you have *no one* who loves you on the other side. *No one*. Not even your ballerina, whose spirit has gone to a place neither of us have even dreamed of."

"*I stronger than you*!" LeRoy/Boris cried, lunging for her. "*I fuck and kill you*!"

They battled furiously, biting and punching and clawing. LeRoy/Boris eventually overpowered and raped her on the filthy floor. The spirits cheered, particularly Estrella's many victims, while the ghosts of Danny, LeRoy, and Toby wept, unable to intervene.

As LeRoy/Boris violently thrust his monstrous penis inside of Estrella, coming again and again, laughing, she came as well, sobbing. Finally, when LeRoy/Boris had been weakened by his many orgasms, Estrella took advantage of his vulnerability, and bit deeply into his skull, sucking out his brain through the puncture wounds, until LeRoy's body lost consciousness, and Boris's spirit began to depart, however involuntarily.

"*Now, my love*!" Estrella cried, but Danny's spirit did not wish to inhabit the body of this giant albino zombie. "*Now, please*!" she cried, doubled over in emotional agony. "*Please, before it's too late…*"

But Danny's spirit was too vain to once again occupy such a loathsome physical form, so he did not respond.

Meantime, Boris's spirit once again left the physical realm, and the spirits all laughed. The cats turned into panthers and ate LeRoy's putrid remains, then vomited them back up.

Estrella sewed LeRoy's head onto Nina's nude body, which she strapped to the lab table, and once again begged Danny's spirit to enter it, so they could be reunited in the physical realm. She had no skills as a surgeon, and her incessant tears obscured her grisly actions, so it was a particularly messy patchwork job. Along with the needle and thread she found in a drawer, she also applied glue and tape for extra adhesive power.

"*Please, my love....please come back to me....I know your spirit is here...please...or else, I will die too, and join you in the hereafter...free from this fetid flesh...*"

Danny still respectfully declined her invitation to inhabit this makeshift monstrosity. In disgusted defeat, Estrella ripped LeRoy's head back off of Nina's body and threw it on the ground, wracked with sobs as the cats tried to console her.

Finally, picking up the two bloody, decapitated heads from the filthy floor, Estrella regained her composure and carried them up to The Mantis Man's room, knocked on the door, and when he opened up, handing them to him, saying, "Two more for your collection."

"How do you know about my shrunken heads?" asked The Mantis Man.

Pheromone and Endorphin were once again at Estrella's ankles, purring.

"Fucking cats," said The Mantis Man, taking the heads and slamming the door.

Estrella then returned to The Purple Room, and saw Lila and Adele asleep on the bed. Dick and Kiko were asleep in The Yellow Room. Lila and Adele looked so peaceful, but Estrella knew they suffered from the quiet torment of self-loathing, as she did. She suddenly attacked them both, tearing them literally to pieces within a few horrible seconds, then devouring their remains, so that their souls would be freed from this cruel illusion of happiness.

Sobbing silently, but content in her resolve, Estrella opened the curtains and ripped the tin foil from the window panes, allowing the morning sunlight to stream into the room and burn her bare, glorious flesh, which smoked and sizzled, and then with a sad smile, she suddenly burst into flames, with nothing nearby to revive her ashes.

Now she would truly be with Danny forever, even if he had other plans.

THE THRILL IS GONE

The Mantis Man had grown weary of his fabled position as Impresario of the Damned, and returned to his misanthropic mindset. He was just sick of people in general, and wanted it all to end.

One night he shaped the voodoo doll's head into a globe that was meant to be Earth, and began randomly sticking pins in it. Since he no longer had a specific target for his hate now that Danny was gone, he decided to take out his tireless rage on the true culprit behind the tragic loss of his dear departed wife: *the entire world.*

The truth was, The Mantis Man had never been married. He had led a solitary life, never finding true love, and it had driven him mad with bitterness and resentment against all of humanity.

Around the planet, catastrophes struck randomly and fatally: earthquakes, floods, tsunamis, plagues. No one could account for it. It felt like the Apocalypse, out of the blue, though some found confirmation in numerology and other contrived clues hidden and open for interpretation in various doctrines.

Meantime, ratings for "Forbidden Thrills" had continued to drastically plummet, especially after the global epidemic of disasters. Religious leaders deduced the worldwide calamities were a direct result of the popularity of this ubiquitous program, while scientists were frankly stumped. People believed the pundits, and "repented" by tuning out the show altogether, pretending they had never been intrigued, only duped. Nobody knew all of this was the result of an ex-headhunter using his voodoo doll as a pincushion.

Kiko and Dick were all that were left now, but they

had also tired of the intrusive media attention. They missed Estrella and the others, and felt as if they had lost their anchor, simply drifting in a lonely sea of pointless mayhem. The cats told them why she had killed herself, after killing LeRoy and Nina, who were actually Boris and Clara. They understood and accepted her decision, though they did not like it.

"She was like a mother to me," Kiko said, licking her own tears as they fell down her cheeks and onto her lips.

"She was a hot piece of ass," Dick said sadly. "I'll sure miss fucking it."

They tried to maintain a united front of formality for the sake of their public, but things were simply not the same. Dick and Kiko could not handle this grueling workload themselves, and they began skipping the sex and going directly to killing and eating the guests. Ratings began to sink, and sponsors pulled out in droves. They lost what little was left of their once loyal audience.

During the filming of a session one night, Dick and Kiko suddenly turned on the camera crew, viciously slaughtering them all. Then they turned on each other, wildly fucking before ripping each other's heads and limbs off. Though filmed live as usual, at least until the cameraman was killed, this session was rebroadcast with a great degree of hype, billed as the Series Finale, and achieved the highest ratings yet, so the show went out with a bang. The audience would soon follow suit.

THE DEEP END

The local earthquake and subsequent tsunami happened suddenly, without warning, at least by standard scientific detection, though it was part of a worldwide trend. They were accompanied by an epic thunderstorm, followed by giant fire-breathing dinosaurs rising from the depths of the ocean, wiping out everything in their collective path, the massive wall of water washing away the burning structures in the low-lying areas, including L'Hotel du Frisson, now empty of staff or guests, though full of frustrated spirits, and Café du Frisson, which was full of patrons, along with Juan and Carlos, who actually welcomed the respite from their perpetual employment. Only the cats, Pheromone and Endorphin, were spared, since they had intuitively sensed big trouble coming and headed for high, safe, dry, solid ground the day before. They did not consider any of this Divine Retribution; it was just the way the world worked. Sometimes things suddenly happened, changing one's situation, without logical reason or rational explanation. Not even The Mantis Man, who cackled with vengeful glee even as he drowned alongside his hated fellow homo sapiens, was truly to blame. He was merely a catalyst for events that would've happened anyway.

Once the earth had stopped shaking, the tides had receded and the giant fire-breathing dinosaurs had returned to their underwater caverns, the skies cleared and a beautiful rainbow beamed across the brilliantly blue firmament, perfectly clear except for some fleecy cumulus crowds, illuminating the corpse-strewn landscape below. The benevolent soul of Israel "IZ" Ka'ano'i Kamakawiwo'ole serenaded the spirits of the dead with "Over the Rainbow" as they dispersed and ascended. Angels floated blissfully through the heavens and beautiful mermaids frolicked playfully in the peaceful sea. The faceless Force of Nature, which had no specific agenda, had casually obliterated the living and the undead alike, inadvertently freeing the trapped souls of the dead, who finally moved on to their ultimate fates, scattered separately across the cosmos…

The musician suddenly opened his eyes, his head heavy with fever. It was dark, and a raging thunderstorm shook the windowpanes. In a lightning flash, he noticed a syringe and a whiskey bottle on the floor, next to his saxophone and suitcase. Another flash illuminated a bra, high-heeled shoes, and a hatchet. Trembling, he turned on the lamp, and beheld with fearful awe the nude body of a beautiful woman, whom he recognized as the hotel manager, lying unconscious on the bed beside him, the sheets soaked with blood and semen, the hideous bellhop laughing maniacally in the corner of the room.

41631491R00229

Made in the USA
Lexington, KY
21 May 2015